FOR
LOVE
&
Bourbon

KATIE JENNINGS

Sapphire Royale
publishing

Cover design by Katie Jennings

Cover design consultant, interior book design, and eBook design by Blue Harvest Creative
www.blueharvestcreative.com

Published by
Sapphire Royale Publishing

ISBN-13: 978-0692445235
ISBN-10: 0692445234

Visit the author at:
www.katieajennings.com & www.bhcauthors.com
www.facebook.com/authorkatiejennings
www.twitter.com/dryadquartet

Visit the author's website
by scanning the QR code.

ALSO BY KATIE JENNINGS

Things Lost in the Fire
So Fell the Sparrow

THE VASSER LEGACY

When Empires Fall
Rise of the Notorious
Rulers of Deception

THE DRYAD QUARTET SERIES

Breath of Air
Firefight in Darkness
A Life Earthbound
Of Water and Madness
The Dryad Quartet Special Edition

MULTI-AUTHOR COLLECTIONS

In Creeps the Night

Keep your friends close, and your bourbon closer.
~ Old Kentucky Proverb ~

Prologue

BELFAST, NORTHERN IRELAND

Fine Irish whiskey fueled his temper. That same whiskey kept him from hurling his glass into the wall, the drink too precious to waste. Even in this state of rage he maintained control, a skill he was well known for. A skill he utilized now in the face of this most disappointing news.

Ned Brannon released a slow, measured breath to relieve the tension in his shoulders before facing his oldest son.

"Killian will be free by mornin'." He lifted the whiskey to his lips and settled back in his desk chair. The office around him was orderly and sparsely decorated, with brick walls and industrial metal furniture. It suited his needs just fine. "The Gardaí have only suspicions, no proof."

Rhys Brannon clasped his hands at his back, his stance rigid and unyielding. The dim light of the single bulb above the desk cast shadows over his sharply honed, emotionless face and accented the copper in his russet hair. "We were careful. We left no witnesses."

"The car bomb in Dublin killed three guards and seven civilians. Under other circumstances I would consider that a grand success." Ned peered into his glass, considering. "But two of those seven were Americans."

A light sheen of sweat appeared on Rhys' forehead. "The goal was to hit the Garda Headquarters. Additional casualties were expected."

"Yer brother sits in custody right now because the Americans want blood." Another rush of anger, cooled before it could surface. Ned leveled his gaze with his son, his bronzed eyes unforgiving. "Some in The Irish Republican Army may disagree, but the added pressure to make arrests will weaken our ranks. They will try and scare Killian into givin' them information, which he will not do. I cannot say the same about any others they lift."

Rhys bowed his head in acknowledgment. "Either way, our message has been heard, Da. The fight continues."

Ned gave a slight nod and took another drink of whiskey. It was his family's two hundred year old recipe, the one that had made Brannon a household name. Unknown to many and certainly unproven, that same whiskey brought in money he then shared with his IRA brothers. For years the cause had been funded by Brannon Irish Whiskey—a proud product of Northern Ireland, a symbol of rebellion.

A catalyst for revolution.

"Boss?" The door opened to reveal Ned's oldest and most loyal associate, Ronan Campbell. He slipped into the room, a piece of paper clutched in his hands. He nodded to Rhys before facing Ned. "Can I have a word?"

"Aye." Ned motioned for Rhys to leave them. Once alone, he studied the man before him. Ronan's bald head caught the light, his brown eyes sunken in a gaunt face prone to scowling. Of a wiry build and nearly too tall for the room, he looked younger than his fifty-one years but every bit as shrewd.

Ned set aside his drink. "Ye will arrange to get my son out of custody." It was spoken as an order, not a question.

"He'll be out this time tomorrow," Ronan confirmed.

"Good." One eyebrow lifted as Ned surveyed his old friend. "What is it, then?"

"I found somethin' ye need to see." Ronan offered the paper he held, paused as Ned looked it over.

First came the shock, then the distinct flicker of wrath. The page crinkled under Ned's fingers, almost tearing the image of a red-haired woman smiling with a glass of whiskey in her hand. His careful control nearly shattered as he stared into the eyes of a traitor.

Forcing back the urge to rip apart the woman's face, he turned his attention to Ronan. "Where did ye get this?"

"The webpage for Lucky Fox Whiskey. It was added yesterday."

Another wave of surprise hit Ned as he swallowed this new information. "She's in Kentucky."

"It would appear so."

The woman smiled up at Ned, mocking him. His hand shook as he downed the last of his whiskey, a sneer forming on his lips. "Me cousin has been keepin' secrets from me."

"Money has been the only sign of his loyalty for years," Ronan reminded him. "His da had a traitorous heart. The son may be no different."

"Aye." Ned tossed the paper on the desk, rubbed the golden-brown stubble on his chin. "Ye know what needs to be done."

Ronan lowered his head a fraction, dark eyes blazing. Without a word, he left the room.

Turning the empty glass over in his hand, Ned glanced at the woman once more. Violence and betrayal exploded within his heart and inspired him to at last launch the tumbler at the wall.

As shards of glass dripping with the remnants of his family's whiskey fell to the floor, a cruel smile deepened the hard lines of his face. He likened himself to a bloodthirsty hound, hot on the scent of a wily fox. Before long the hunt would come to an end and he would, at last, make her pay for what she had done.

PART 01

LUCKY FOX
B O U R B O N

*I have never in my life seen a Kentuckian who didn't have
a pack of cards, and a jug of whiskey.*
~ Andrew Jackson ~

CHAPTER

One

FOX HILLS, KENTUCKY

P ull!"
 Her eyes honed in on the flash of orange as it soared through the air. Instinct and skill guided her toward the exact moment to pull the trigger.

The resulting blast kicked the shotgun into her shoulder, but she held her ground and watched with triumph as the clay pigeon exploded in a cloud of dust. With a hoot of laughter, she lowered the gun and faced her grandfather. "That's five for five. Looks like I win."

Joe Brannon cocked his chin, the unmistakable flavor of Ireland in his voice. "Now, it's not over yet, dearie. Best outta ten is what we said."

"Best out of five," Ava corrected with a wink. She blew a vivid red curl out of her face, checked her watch, and shrugged. "Oh, what the hell. We have a few minutes."

"Sure we do." Joe nudged her out of the way, his own shotgun at the ready. He fitted it against the crook of his shoulder and chest and lifted his eyes to the sky. "Pull."

Ava released the trap and sent another clay pigeon hurtling into space. Within seconds Joe fired and blew it to pieces.

He cast a wicked glance her way, the dimples in his cheeks flashing. The chilly October wind sent strands of his thick white hair dancing. "That's five to yer five."

Delighted by the challenge, she shifted into position. "We'll see about that."

After settling the score at an even tie, Ava tucked her shotgun into its pink camo case.

"You taught me to shoot so good that now you can't even beat me," she joked, her tone warmly Southern with a hint of wood-fire smoke. It suited the rest of her—her body athletically built and lean, tucked into faded jeans and cowboy boots. Her grin was as quick and devious as her grandfather's, a testament to the Irish in her blood, while her heart would always belong to the South.

Stowing his own gun away, Joe peered out at the expanse of their wooded, fifty-acre property and the scattered orange remains of their targets. "Aye, but ye've never bested me on the rifle, have ye?"

"Not yet. For now you're the master on the long-range." She hooked her arm in his and led him to the side by side four-wheeler they used to get around the grounds. "But there's still time."

They loaded the gun cases into the back of the four-wheeler and hopped inside, Ava in the driver's seat. She took off down the gravel road that led from their private shooting range to the family home and, a ways farther, to the Lucky Fox Whiskey Distillery. It was the pride and joy of their little town of Fox Hills, and Joe's legacy.

"Mama's gonna be mad we skipped lunch again," Ava mused as they drove past the sweeping ranch house with its wrap-around covered porch and cheerful yellow paint. Burgundy and orange sassafras trees surrounded the home, their lemony-scent tickling her nose.

Joe chuckled. "Yer ma will get over it. We've got more important things to do."

"Like pick the barrel for your signature 'Lucky Joe's' batch. In case you needed another reminder that you'll be turning seventy soon."

"Aye, but a happy occasion it will be. I've much to be proud of in me old age."

Reaching for his hand, she smiled. "That you do."

The road curved around a bend lined with yellow birch trees, bringing them to a massive stone-gray metal building that housed the distillery. Beside it was another smaller metal building used as the barrel house. At the top of each building hung the company logo, the silhouette of a running fox above bold, vintage lettering that read "Lucky Fox Whiskey." Surrounding the structures were lofty elms, their leaves as golden as the drink made within the walls.

Several cars were parked outside the visitor's center, which meant her one o'clock tour would be packed. Ava didn't mind, though. She had been entertaining tourists and locals alike since she had been barely legal to drink the whiskey herself. Now at twenty-seven, the ins and outs of the distillery and every aspect of the product were as much a part of her as her own lightly freckled skin.

They parked and headed into the barrel house. The three-story high steel building was quiet and nearly as chilly as it was outside. All part of the aging process, Ava thought as she rolled down the sleeves of her red and black flannel shirt and admired the rows of oak barrels. Kentucky's cold winters and warm summers were as crucial to the process of making good whiskey as the corn it began as.

The barrels were stacked three rows deep on either side of her on ceiling high, wooden racks, all properly labeled with the year and batch number burned into the wood. She caught the warm, vanilla scent of sleeping whiskey and the earthy notes of charred oak. It was a fragrance she associated with home, and of course, tradition. A few employees wandered the rows with clipboards, keeping tabs on which barrels were ready to be emptied and which ones would benefit from time's delicate hand.

"Which barrel should we be pickin', dearie?" Joe asked, though she knew he was merely testing her. He would have his favorite in mind and would be curious to see if she picked the same one.

Knowing him as she did, she looked to the top rack, scanned the barrels. "Let's see…since this will be your signature single barrel bourbon, we can't be hasty in our decision." She walked along the aged pine floor, tapping her index finger to her lower lip. "We need something with a kick to it to suit your sharp eye and sharper tongue. A smooth burn was just never your style."

He fell into step beside her, patiently listening.

"You're an immigrant who chased your dream all the way to America after starting a feud with your own family over a disagreement on how whiskey should be made, so it has to have history, character, and a hint of rebellion." She faced him, her hazel eyes afire with pride. "With your humor and lighthearted approach to life, it can't be sophisticated, but rather humble and rough around the edges just like the town you made your home."

She angled her chin, decision made. "There's a 2006 barrel up on top there. That was the first time you won Distiller of the Year *and* when you officially brought me on as your apprentice here in the distillery. It was also the year we tried increasing the percentage of rye in our recipe because you felt like spicing things up. If I've learned anything from you, that barrel up there will have the perfect amount of bite, character, and history, and you'll get a kick out of pre-senting such a bold, unapologetic bourbon as your signa-ture flavor."

Joe gave a brisk nod and glanced up at the barrel. "Aye. That I would."

"Well? Is that the one, then?"

"Sometimes I think ye know me better than I know me own self." He patted her shoulder, then pressed a kiss to her temple. Their eyes met, hazel into cornflower blue. "Some-day ye'll be making yer own signature whiskey. I expect it'll have a bite to it, as well."

She flashed him a wicked grin. "As your granddaugh-ter, no one would expect any different."

AVA WALKED up the front porch steps of her family's ranch house as the sun dipped below the rolling Kentucky hills. She kicked off her boots in the entryway, knowing her mother would scold her for dragging sawdust, dirt, and trac-es of whiskey onto the weathered oak floors. The house itself was nearly a hundred years old, and had been in the family since Joe had come over from Ireland in the 1960s.

She caught the scent of her mother's chicken dump-lings and her mouth watered. Steering her way into the oversized country kitchen, Ava spotted her mother singing along to Tanya Tucker's rich, brassy voice, swaying her hips at the kitchen sink.

Overcome with affection, Ava came up behind her and gave her a big hug. "Boo."

Sandra Brannon jumped with a startled laugh. "Oh, heavens, Ava. You know better than to scare me like that."

"If you don't want people to scare you then you should turn the music down." Ava lowered the volume on the old cassette player herself, amused. Her mother had been listening to that same album since she'd been a child. "And really, Mama, don't you think it's time you gave the '90s music a rest and stepped into the 21st century?"

Fixing one of the pins in her waves of auburn hair, Sandra chuckled. Though she'd edged over fifty years of age, she retained the unlined, youthful beauty of a happy, contented soul. It was just one of the many things Ava loved about her. "Tanya's been with me through some very tough times, honey. You don't just turn your back on that."

Ava took a seat at the kitchen island, strumming her fingers on the white-tile surface. "Whatever makes you happy, I guess. So Grandpa Joe and I picked a barrel for the Lucky Joe's batch. We're gonna taste it soon and make sure, but I think we've got a winner. I'm sure when he gets in he'll tell you all about it."

"That's great news." Sandra turned back to the sink to finish washing the produce she grew fresh in her garden. Ava watched her for a moment, enjoying the timeless ritual of her mother preparing dinner.

The front door opened and her brother Adam entered the kitchen. As her twin, he had the same auburn hair and hazel eyes, the same finely honed, sharp-edged face. He was a picture, always had been, a fact he took advantage of as often as he could. But even being the town heartbreaker wasn't enough to satisfy him. For that, Ava knew Adam turned to whiskey.

"Where've you been?" Ava asked, though she already knew. He made a habit of spending his days hanging out downtown, a slave to his own demons.

"Out." He kissed their mother on the cheek before throwing open the fridge and grabbing a carton of orange juice. Taking a swig of it, he shot his sister an annoyed look. "What?"

Ava shrugged. "Nothing."

Adam took another drink before replacing the container in the fridge. Saying nothing, he left the room. Ava watched him go, part of her wishing she knew how to help him while the sinner in her damned him to hell for his foolishness.

The door opened again and her father stepped in. He set aside his briefcase on the bench in the entryway and hung up his coat.

Donned in a dress shirt and neatly pressed slacks, Ty Brannon fit the part of the company's general manager. He had been in charge of the business end of the company for over twenty years, tackling the financials and marketing his father had no interest in. Ava thought the position suited him, as he preferred the predictable nature of numbers and figures to the bustling, high-energy environment of the distillery.

With thick, coffee brown hair and even darker eyes, he had none of his father Joe's looks and instead was a spitting image of his mother, Vivian. Ava barely remembered her, as she died when Ava had been a child, but from the countless images of her throughout the home the resemblance was clear. Ty had also inherited Vivi's firm, sober temperament and cool reserve, a trait which had brought him head-to-head with Ava and Adam on many occasions during their rebellious teenage years.

"Hi, Daddy," Ava greeted as she flipped through one of her mother's home decorating magazines.

"Hey, baby." Ty gave his wife a kiss, then sniffed at the dumplings cooking on the stove. "Smells good."

"It's your favorite." Sandra transferred her heirloom tomatoes over to the island so she could dice them. She reached over to close the magazine Ava was reading, a playful smile on her face. "Why don't you go have some fun after supper? You could use a night out. Maybe take Adam with you."

Ava snorted. "Like he needs to spend more time at the bar."

"What he needs is the guidance of his sister. You've been ignoring him lately. I can tell he misses you."

"I've been busy, Mama," Ava defended, irritated that she felt even the least bit sorry. "Unlike him, I actually work for a living."

Sandra sliced into the tomatoes, her movements swift and practiced. "Seems I saw you and Joe shooting skeet this afternoon. Adam might like to be invited next time y'all go."

Ava's mouth opened to retort, but manners had her promptly closing it. She nodded. "Yes, Mama."

Ty patted her on the shoulder. "I'm gonna go wash up. See your brother behaves tonight. He needs the influence of his older sister."

"I'm only five minutes older," she grumbled as he walked away.

"He looks up to you, Ava," Sandra reminded her, scooping tomatoes into a big salad bowl filled with romaine lettuce.

"Just because he's too damn lazy to learn the ropes at the distillery doesn't mean I have to take time out of my busy life to baby him. He's a grown man."

Sandra sighed. "You make me feel so old sometimes. Just yesterday y'all were nothing but babies."

Ava rose to set the table for dinner. "Oh, please. You're not old."

Her mother came up behind her with the wooden salad bowl. "You just wait till you have grown-up babies."

"Like that's ever gonna happen."

"Never say never, honey."

"I'm too busy. Between the daily tours, helping out at the distillery, and planning for each new batch, I'm tapped out. No time for dating." Ava pulled plates out of a cabinet, arranged them on the table. "Besides, I love my life just the way it is. There's nothing about it I'd change."

"Nothing?" Sandra asked mildly, turning to tend the dumplings on the stove.

Ava stared at her mother's back, wishing she could defend her statement with one-hundred percent certainty. The fact that she couldn't left her feeling frustrated.

Ignoring the question, she plopped down at the dining table and fixed a smile on her face. "Dinner smells lovely, Mama."

CHAPTER
Two

Though a comfortable night in with a good book and a glass of bourbon sounded preferable, Ava found herself heading downtown instead. And since part of her felt guilty, she had coaxed Adam into joining her. Better she keep an eye on him than he get into trouble on his own.

It was a five minute drive from their property to downtown Fox Hills, where the majority of the town's residents lived and worked. With less than a thousand people, it was customary that the local bar be the highlight of every Friday night. And since the blood of the town ran hot with whiskey, it was only natural that the residents' blood run hot with it too.

Adam relaxed in the passenger seat, one arm out the window and the other hogging the center console. His earlier irritation with her had passed at the prospect of a night out.

"So what're you gonna do if Beau's there tonight?" he asked, angling his head to give her a devious look. "Raise some hell?"

"You'd like that, wouldn't you?"

He shrugged. "I'd like to kick his ass, but that badge on his chest means I'd spend a night in jail and honestly, it just ain't worth it."

"*He's* not worth it," Ava corrected.

"He's still crazy about you, you know that, right?" Adam asked her, tapping his hand to the beat of the outlaw country spilling out of the radio.

Ava laughed. "We haven't dated since high school. And I only slipped up once and let him get me drunk and take advantage of the situation. Trust me, I've learned my lesson where he's concerned."

"I should kick his ass for that alone. Not to mention all the times he talks shit about us behind our backs."

"Don't let it get to you."

"Speak for yourself. You sit on that high horse of yours, but you're just as bad as me." He reached out to pinch her knee, amused when she shifted away. "You're hot-headed as all hell, you drink too much, you can't commit, and no matter how hard you try, you let other people's opinions of you get under your skin."

"I do not," she defended, though she knew he was right. "Damn it."

He chuckled as she pulled her Chevy pickup truck into a spot on the street in front of the bar, aptly titled Whiskey Bent. It was a staple in Fox Hills and had, since its inception, served every brand of Lucky Fox Whiskey to tourists and locals alike.

"Whatever. Let's both just try and behave, all right?" Though she was serious, her face broke into a smile at the knowing look he gave her. "What?"

"This is our town, Ava. Behavin's just not what we do."

Inside the bar the lights were dim and the country music was hopping. Sawdust shavings littered the concrete floor and billiards tables lined one wall beneath neon signs for Budweiser, Bud Light, and Blue Moon. In the center of the room lay a wooden dance floor already crowded with cowboy-hat-wearing locals in various degrees of intoxication. Their boots shuffled over the floor as they line-danced, never missing a step. Ava grinned, itching to join them. It was as much a tradition as the whiskey that flowed freely from the bottles lining the back of the bar.

She settled onto a barstool and waved to her childhood friend and bartender, Brandy. The petite blonde sauntered over with a dimpled grin and sassy sway of her hips.

"I was wonderin' if I'd see y'all tonight," Brandy greeted, her diamond-blue eyes shifting from Ava to Adam. Her smile deepened. "What can I get ya?"

"The usual for both of us, darlin'." Adam leaned against the wooden bar top casually, already scoping out the bar for something, or someone, to interest him.

As Brandy turned to pour them both three fingers of Lucky Fox Distiller's Choice Bourbon on ice, Ava jabbed her brother in the side. "Since you had the nerve to pester me about Beau, it's only right I get on your case about Brandy. When the hell are you gonna get over yourself and ask her out?"

Adam frowned and stared at his pristine black leather boots. "She's not my type."

"Bullshit." Ava rolled her eyes as Brandy handed them both square glasses packed with ice and rich, golden bourbon. "Thanks, honey."

"No problem." Brandy flashed another smile before whisking off to take care of other customers. Ava watched her go, shaking her head. "Maybe we're both too picky."

"Or maybe we're just better off alone." Adam took a slow sip of bourbon, set aside the glass. "Excuse me."

He wandered off to persuade a giggly brunette to dance. Ava crossed her legs and leaned back comfortably against the bar. As she sipped her drink, she observed the old familiar antics of a typical small town Friday night.

Cowboys and ranch hands, slathered in smell-good to hide the scent of sweat from the day's work, cozied up to the same bleach blonde country girls they'd known since the day they'd been born. A group of the distillery employees shot darts and played pool in the corner, blowing off steam with a pitcher of beer. Sidled up to the bar, the salty older folks cracked jokes and knocked back whiskey, reminiscing of times gone by in a town where it seemed nothing ever changed.

Most nights her grandfather would be among them, the song of Ireland in his voice mingling with the southern drawls of people he'd come to love better than his own family back on the Emerald Isle. The feud that had made him a legendary distiller was a well-known and celebrated aspect of the Brannon legacy. It was also a source of pride for Ava to know her grandfather had come out on top, despite all the odds. That was why he called his whiskey "Lucky."

"It's a mighty shame to be drinkin' alone, sweetheart."

Ava glanced over as Beau Rollins approached, all cowboy swagger in his boots and dusty jeans. Fastened over the heart of his plaid shirt was the badge he had gotten a year earlier when his sheriff father retired and passed him the torch. Beau's short crop of dark hair framed a handsome face her grandfather often likened to the Devil's, all hard lines and wickedness. Perhaps it was the bad boy look that had drawn her all those years before, though she'd learned her lesson there. Men, particularly ones who looked like Beau, were not to be trusted.

She motioned toward the crowd. "I'm not really alone, am I?"

He settled onto the barstool beside her and ordered a beer. "Hard to really be alone in this town, but if I had to locate somebody who looks lonely, I'd point at you."

With a snort, she knocked back more bourbon and shrugged. "What the hell do you want, Beau?"

"Can't I make conversation with a beautiful woman?"

Her eyes shot to his and burned. "Keep dreaming, buddy."

A sly smile contorted his mouth, revealing a flash of teeth. "Hard not to when you're lookin' as fine as you are tonight."

"And it's hard not to knock that grin off your face."

Beau chuckled. "Ouch. I always loved your fire, Ava."

"Too bad I never loved you back," she replied, bringing her whiskey to her lips. "Don't look for a revival of old times, Sheriff. It ain't gonna happen."

Undeterred, he drank his beer and scanned the bar. "You'll come around. This is a small town with few options. Won't be long before you're knockin' on my door again."

That got her going. A snide laugh bubbled from her throat as she set aside her drink and rose to her feet. She jabbed a finger in his chest, just to make a point. "You think I'd give you a second chance after the things you said about me? About my *family*?"

"Just callin' it like I see it." He brushed off her statement like a bothersome fly. "The whole damn town's in love with you, Ava. I didn't hurt your precious reputation. Stop worrying so much."

Anger flushed her face. "You called my brother a drunk and me a whore. Somehow I think that's liable to hurt me. But you don't give a damn, do you?"

A spark lit in his eyes. "Again, just callin' it like I see it, sweetheart. Besides, if I remember right it wasn't too hard to get you out of those jeans and into the back of my truck. Damn easy, actually. All you need's a few shots of that whiskey—"

She wheeled back to throw a punch only to be stopped by her brother mid-swing. Adam wrangled her into his arms, barely strong enough to hold her.

"Stop it, darlin'. Not worth it, remember?" he muttered into her ear, smoothing out the worst of her temper. Beau was on his feet, prepared to fight back if necessary. The golden badge he wore glinted in the bar lights and had Ava swearing under her breath. Damn it all to hell.

She shook Adam off her and raised her hands in a show of peace. "All right. I'm fine."

"You sure?" Adam hovered beside her, eyeing Beau with intense dislike.

"Yeah." Grabbing her drink from the bar, she turned to face the crowd that had gathered around to watch the fight brewing. She offered them a fiery grin and raised her glass in a toast. "Let's make some noise for our *generous* sheriff over here who has just graciously offered to buy y'all a round of Lucky Fox Bourbon!"

The bar erupted in whistling cheers. Ava made a point to meet Beau dead in the eye. "Enjoy picking up that tab, Sheriff."

He gaped at her and at the patrons who came by to slap him on the shoulder and thank him for an offer he hadn't even made. He'd be a fool to try and back step it now, she knew, which meant he'd be shelling out a couple hundred bucks just for messing with her. That'd teach him.

With a devilish wink, Ava hooked her arm in her brother's and led the way out to the dance floor. Her favorite song had just come on and she was ready to have some fun.

Adam gave her a quick kiss on the forehead. "Good move, darlin'. Damn good move."

"I told him I'd knock that stupid grin off his face." She laughed and stepped into the line that had formed, Adam at her side. They kicked their boots and sang along to Luke

Bryan, drinks in hand and the whiskey flowing. All on Beau's dime, of course, which made it taste even sweeter.

There in that bar with people she'd known all her life, music that spoke to her soul, and whiskey her very own hands helped create, she was on top of the world.

Nothing was missing, she told herself. Life was perfect just the way it was.

CHAPTER

Three

WASHINGTON, D.C.

Special Agent Cooper Lawson didn't make a habit of placing bets, but he'd wager an entire year's pay that the Brannon family of Kentucky was cooking up more than just whiskey. He was positive they were funding terrorism that had gotten two Americans killed in a car bombing in Dublin.

As an agent with the Terrorist Financing Operations Section of the FBI's Counterterrorism Division, that made it his business and, frankly, he had a bone to pick with anyone who dared send money overseas to sponsor terrorist activities, even if it *was* the IRA.

Across the table from him, his partner was busy sucking down two fingers of Lucky Fox Distiller's Choice, chipper as can be.

"You realize you're contributing to the problem, right?" Cooper nodded at the glass of whiskey, amused by the irony of it.

Special Agent Marco D'Amico shrugged. "What? It's good stuff. Innocent until proven guilty, my friend."

"Please. You know they're guilty. At least, we know Ty Brannon is," Cooper reminded him, taking a pull from his own bottle of Sam Adam's. They sat in the same old bar they'd always gone to, packed with FBI agents, lobbyists, and political goons. Big screen television sets lined the brick walls, set on non-stop ESPN. Cooper's gaze drifted to watch the horse race someone had turned on, mildly interested in it. "We just gotta get down there and prove it."

"All in good time. Until then, I'm going to enjoy this glass of especially fine bourbon."

Cooper chuckled and picked at the label on his beer. "If we find what I think we'll find on Brannon's computers that may be the last taste you get of Lucky Fox whiskey."

"All the more reason to enjoy it." Marco grinned. "You ever been down south?"

"Nope." Cooper settled back in his chair. "Never had a reason to. Until now."

"Whole other world, my friend." Ice tinkled as Marco lifted his glass in a toast. "Us New York boys are gonna stand out like sore thumbs."

"As if the badge wasn't bad enough." Though Cooper itched to dig out the file he had on Brannon from his briefcase, he resisted the urge. He'd pored over its contents hundreds of times already, prepping for the task of heading the team down in Louisville on the investigation. Within twenty-four hours he'd land in Kentucky and be able to confront the man behind the file. The man who he was convinced was sending money to family in Ireland to fund the IRA.

Cooper's blood ran green with Ireland himself, though a few generations separated him from the country and its notorious war with Britain. What he knew about it he'd learned since taking on the assignment. Under any other circumstance he wouldn't have given a damn, but two Americans were dead. The IRA, and most likely the Brannons, were to blame. He meant to see that they pay for the blood they'd spilled, even though they were thousands of miles away from the conflict.

He had hair the color of dusted gold, cut in trim waves and neatly combed around a long, inquisitive face. His deep, cobalt eyes were always searching, always analyzing. An inherent ability to solve complex puzzles and a bright, intelligent mind had made him a shoe-in at the FBI.

A personal reason made the decision necessary.

He'd been born in the heart of New York City, the son of a rookie cop and a homemaker. Raised on a staunch belief in truth and justice, his dream had been to follow in his father's footsteps and join the police force himself.

At least, until that fateful September day changed everything.

Avoiding the thought, he polished off his beer and set aside the bottle. A waitress promptly came by to collect it and offer another, which he refused. He turned his attention back to Marco. "What do you think Brannon's going to say when we show up?"

"If we're lucky, he'll fess up. But the odds are he'll lawyer up instead."

"I wonder if his wife and kids have any idea what he's been up to."

"If they do, we'll find that out soon enough."

"I can't imagine they don't know their own relatives are on Ireland's SDU watch list."

Marco laughed. "What? You think that shit comes up at Thanksgiving dinner? From what I hear, the American Brannons have a fifty-year-old feud with the Irish line. Most likely, Ty's the only exception to that feud."

"Feud?" Cooper reached now for the file folder in his briefcase, perusing through it for mention of the turmoil between the two sides of the Brannon family. Had he seen it somewhere?

"Yeah. The old man—Joe, I think his name is? He broke free from the Irish clan back in the '60s when they had a disagreement over the recipe for Brannon Irish Whiskey. Didn't you know any of this?"

"It wasn't written down…" Cooper scanned the contents of the folder, though he knew it wasn't included. Clearly the FBI thought that little detail not worth mentioning.

"Visit the Lucky Fox website. It's all on there," Marco said, distracted as the waitress passed by again. He ordered another glass of whiskey while Cooper thought over this new information.

A feud between the Irish and American sides of the family painted a completely different picture in his head of Ty Brannon. The man had probably hidden his money contributions to the IRA from his father, which meant the rest of the family likely had no idea about it either.

That should make for an interesting introduction, Cooper mused. What would the family say if he came right out with the allegation that Ty was accused of funding a deadly terrorist group, comprised of their own family members? Would they balk and clam up, lawyers at the ready?

Perhaps. It would be wise of them to do so. Barging in with a warrant to search a person's computer files had a tendency to put them on edge.

The IRS had Brannon on tax fraud, that much had already been established. The money shuffled overseas into a Swiss bank account had missed the tax man's hands. He'd lead with that charge, giving himself leg room to wean information out of the other members of Ty's family on what they knew about the IRA.

If he was lucky, he'd gather enough information from both Ty's computers and his relatives to put him away for good.

OUTSIDE THE windows of his tenth story apartment, it rained like hell and lightning jutted across the blackened sky.

Cooper busied himself tossing clothes into a suitcase, distracted by the James Bond movie playing on the television. He turned at the sound of gunshots, grinning at the image of Bond taking down yet another baddie.

He tossed his cell phone charger and an extra set of razors into the case, humming the Bond theme song to himself. When a commercial came on for Irish Spring soap, his mind clicked into another gear and sent him straight to his desk, where his laptop was buried until a pile of books and paperwork.

Shoving a few things to the ground in the process, he dug out his computer and carried it to his bed. Within seconds he was searching the internet for the Lucky Fox Whiskey website.

The first thing he noticed was the smiling, radiant face of a beautiful woman holding a glass of golden-colored whiskey on ice. He skipped straight to the "about us" page, eager to confirm if what Marco had told him was true.

At the top of the page was a portrait of the family, three men and one woman, a list of names below. He scanned the smiling faces, a stab of guilt hitting him as he realized they had no idea of the storm to come. His eyes trailed to the dark haired man he recognized as Ty Brannon. The guilt he felt hardened to disgust as he stared into the man's eyes, knowing he'd been likely lying to his family and betraying his country for years. He could think of nothing more despicable.

Reading on, he familiarized himself with the feud Marco had spoken of. He already knew about Brannon Irish Whiskey, the two-hundred-year-old distillery the Brannons in Ireland owned and operated. But what he hadn't realized was that Joe Brannon's Lucky Fox Whiskey was a completely separate entity. According to the website, at the ripe young age of twenty, Joe had approached his father with a daring new recipe for whiskey that he was convinced surpassed the brilliance of the one they'd used for ages. Instead of being met with gratitude, he was criticized and disowned from the family as if it were blasphemy. Not letting his family's impudence get in the way of his ambition, Joe set sail for America, the land where he'd been told dreams came true.

And come true they did. He found his way to Kentucky and, with help from a local bank, purchased an old, pre-prohibition moonshine distillery and began to ferment his own recipe for Irish whiskey. Though it took a few years to really take off, Lucky Fox Whiskey became a staple for whiskey drinkers. Inspired by Kentucky's Bourbon Trail, Joe expanded his brand to include several styles of bourbon.

The rest, after that, was history.

Cooper scrolled back up to the image of the family, his gaze falling this time to the old man at the center of the group. He had a shock of white hair, glittering blue eyes and an impish grin that reminded him of a Leprechaun.

"You must be Joe," Cooper murmured, admiring the man for his tenacity. It had taken guts to leave everything he had known and uproot to a new country and an entirely different culture without any idea if it would work out. Guts and straight up ambition.

Beside Joe stood a young woman with auburn curls of hair, her arm wrapped playfully around his shoulders.

Her smoky smile caught Cooper's attention, the curve of it both a secret and an invitation. Just who was she to Joe, and why did the laughter lines of her face intrigue him the way they did?

Ava Brannon. He read her name over and over, matching it to her face and losing himself in his own curiosity. She was close to Joe, likely his granddaughter. Was the beautiful Ava the daughter of Ty Brannon? Did she have any clue what her father was up to?

His thoughts were disrupted by the ringing of his cell phone. He fumbled around for it, finding it underneath the suitcase he had set up on the bed. Seeing his mother's name on the caller-ID brought a grin to his face.

"Hey you."

"*I didn't wake you, did I?*"

"Nope. Just packing."

"*Where are you going?*"

He fell back against the pillows of his bed, making himself comfortable. "Louisville. Got a case down there."

"*Say hi to Elvis for me.*"

"That's Memphis, Mom."

"*Oh. Well, same area, right?*"

Laughing, he brushed back his hair and sighed. "Sure. How are you?"

"*Just fine. Robert's surprised me with a trip to Hawaii. Can you imagine it? Me, on the white-sand beaches of paradise.*"

"That's great." Cooper glanced at his watch, noted it was nearly ten o'clock. "I'm glad he's taking good care of you. I worry sometimes. With me in D.C., I—"

"*You don't need to worry about me, Cooper. If anything I worry about you, all alone in that tiny little apartment.*"

"I'm thirty years old," he reminded her. "Cut the cord already."

"*A mother never stops worrying.*"

"Well, you should." He muted the television, his eyes fixated on Bond as he silently went about seducing the vixen heroine. "So everything else okay?"

"*I finally went to the memorial at Ground Zero today. It's only taken a decade for me to get the courage to go.*"

Cooper tensed, a jolt hitting his heart. "Did you find his name?"

"*I did.*" She paused, as if searching for the right words to say. "*You should go, baby. Get closure.*"

"It's closed. I'm good." He tried to wrangle the knot from his throat, despising himself for it. "I promise."

"*Your father was a hero. He'd be very proud of you.*"

"I know." Unsettled, he closed his eyes. "I miss him."

"*So do I.*" She sighed, the sound weighted with a grief no manner of time could ever heal. "*Keep fighting the good fight, Cooper. Keep us all safe.*"

"I will." He said goodbye and hung up the phone, the heartache lingering. Thoughts of his father—the tall, proud policeman dedicated to serving others—flashed through his mind and brought a heaviness to his chest. His old man had been one of the few to dive into the first tower after the plane hit, seeking to save anyone who could be saved. Little did he know the tower was destined to collapse upon him, burying him under steel and ash, never to be seen again. Life, gone in the blink of eye.

That was the day Cooper decided being a cop was no longer for him. He wasn't going to serve and protect the public like his old man. No, he had a bigger mission in mind. He wanted to join the forces that brought terrorist organizations to their knees.

He thought back to the day he had graduated college and informed his mother he was joining the FBI. Surprise had been her initial reaction, but with it came a glow of pride. He sought vengeance against those who had taken his father from him, and as much of a pacifist as his mother was, she couldn't deny him that right.

Now, years later, he was finally in a position to do some good. The death of two Americans at the hands of Ned Brannon and the IRA was exactly the kind of case he'd been hoping for.

Soon, he'd help take down one of the biggest arms of the Irish Republican Army, and hopefully earn himself a promotion to the branch that targeted those who wrought havoc on September 11th, 2001.

CHAPTER

Four

Her favorite thing about early mornings was the fog that cloaked the countryside. It crept in among the trees and cooled the skin of her face as she jogged, her beagle Remy skipping ahead of her. He busily sniffed the ground, always on the hunt for some elusive prey.

Ava huffed out a cloud of breath and kept moving, her body a finely tuned machine well accustomed to the strain of a long morning run. It gave her time to clear her head and plan for the day while the rest of the town was barely waking up.

Life in Fox Hills was as reliably predictable as the sunrise. There was comfort in that. She knew without a flicker of a doubt that old man Thornton would be there to open up the pharmacy his family had owned for three generations. Miss Joy would awake bright and early to bake apple pie at the diner on Main Street. The employees at the distillery would arrive on time at eight o'clock, metal lunch pails in hand and wearing sleepy smiles. Children would shuffle off to the schoolhouse while pickup trucks loaded with hay would rattle through the streets. Solid country gold would be found on nearly every radio station and ice would melt into whiskey in glasses all across town.

Every day was the same, every week the same after that. Months and years had passed by, leaving her edging toward thirty and wondering where the hell the time had gone. It seemed like just yesterday she'd been a child eagerly watching her grandfather slip a thief into an oak barrel to sample its contents for that perfect balance of spice and natural character. That child had grown into a woman for which whiskey wasn't just a profitable enterprise, but a fundamental way of life.

Not that she wasn't happy, she assured herself. Her life was filled with blessings. She had her grandfather, her parents, her brother—frustrating as he could be sometimes—and the whiskey legacy that would be hers to pass on someday.

Someday. Her chest tightened at the thought, not liking to think that far ahead. Better to stay focused on the present, on the real, and not get lost in the what-ifs of the future.

Remy caught the scent of something in the trees and deserted her, lost in the hunt. She whistled to him, but it was useless. Once the dog was on the move, it was impossible to reign him in. She kept running, knowing he'd catch back up with her once his curiosity was satisfied.

As she hopped onto the gravel road to head home, in the distance she spotted her father leaving the house. Briefcase in hand, he slipped into his gleaming black Cadillac sedan, the one luxury he allowed himself from the wealth Lucky Fox provided.

She picked up speed, hoping to catch him, but he pulled away without seeing her. Out of breath, she came to a stop and rested her hands on her knees. Remy trotted up beside her, licking her arm in an affectionate kiss.

Rubbing his fur, she stared after her father's car as it disappeared into the fog. It was unlike him to leave so early. Most mornings he met with her and her grandfather to talk business before they went about their individual duties. She wondered if her run had gone longer than expected, only to glance down at her watch and see she was right on time.

Strange, she thought as she straightened and made her way into the house. Was there something important happening at the office that she'd forgotten about?

Shrugging it off, she went in to shower and prepare for the day.

THE MIDDAY flight to Louisville went quicker than he'd expected. He hoped their stay would be just as brief.

If all went as planned, Cooper hoped he would be digging into Ty Brannon's computer files by morning, knee deep in evidence gold. Then they would make their case and put a stopper in Ned Brannon's American cash flow once and for all.

As for the money Ned funneled into the IRA from his own whiskey distillery, Cooper would leave that to the Irish to sort out. Considering their inability to do so thus far, he had a feeling Ned was skilled at covering his tracks.

His cousin Ty, however, wasn't nearly as clever.

Cooper eyed the Kentucky countryside out the window. Marco drove, poorly singing along to some uppity pop song a grown man had no business knowing the words to. Since it was Marco, who had been his best friend since the academy, Cooper didn't judge. Hell, even he had to admit the song was pretty catchy.

"Hey, look. Horses." Cooper sat up in his seat and slipped off his sunglasses. All around them were emerald green fields fenced in by low stone walls. A small herd of russet brown horses, heads bent and coats shining, picked away at the grass.

Marco nodded, taking a break from his song. "Yes, Cooper. Hor-ses." He elongated the word into syllables, his charming Italian face split in a mocking grin. "They like hay and running around and stand up when they poop."

Cooper feigned a look of horror. "What *monsters.*"

"No worse than the sewer rats back home."

"Hey now, sewer rats are just misunderstood," Cooper defended, changing the radio station. Country music poured out of the speakers over Marco's yelp of protest. "There, that's better."

"Since when do you like country?"

"When in Rome, my friend. When in Rome." Cooper looked out the window again, tapping his hands on his knees in time to the rockin' country beat. It wasn't half bad, he decided. A bit twangy for his taste, but then again not everyone can sound like Ozzy.

"Thank God I went against your suggestion and booked us a hotel in town instead of in Louisville. This is the longest thirty minutes of my life," Marco groaned, throwing his head back against the seat in protest. "How are we *still* not there?"

"Isn't that the sign?" Cooper pointed at a large, wooden billboard that read:

Welcome to Fox Hills! Where Lucky Fox Whiskey Calls Home.

Painted beside the words was a grinning orange fox holding a four leaf clover. It was meant to be amusing, but Cooper only felt annoyed by it.

"Finally." Marco shifted and dug out a pack of gum from the center console. He offered one to Cooper, who refused, then popped a piece into his mouth. "Whole lotta nothing out here, huh?"

"Yeah." They began to see barns and small, country homes scattered along the grassy hills, accompanied by more horses and the occasional cow. Soon the houses gave way to storefronts and cross traffic, leading him to believe this to be the center of town. Marco slowed down to the posted speed limit, a crawling fifteen miles per hour, and cruised down Main Street.

It was a quaint little place, Cooper decided as he admired the hodgepodge of buildings and tree-lined streets. It was an odd mix of weathered brick and colorfully painted stucco with old-fashioned signage he figured must have been there since the 1950s. Glass windows shined and the sidewalks were dutifully swept, maintaining the image of a country tourist town. With the trees in full autumn splendor, it was picturesque and charming.

Everywhere he looked there were references to Lucky Fox Whiskey and its famous distillery, the town's pride and joy. The bakery advertised bourbon drizzled cupcakes and candy. The local honky-tonk bar boasted the full line of Lucky Fox whiskies. Even the pharmacy had a sign that read, "Got a Lucky Fox Hangover? Relief Inside!"

"They sure are gaga about their whiskey," Cooper murmured, unsure if he was amused by it or disturbed. He knew there wasn't much to do in small towns, but to commit an entire way of life to a distillery seemed like overkill. The Brannons might as well have been royalty for all the adoration of the townspeople. Would they feel the same after he exposed the family's dirty secrets?

"I like it." Marco rolled into the tiny parking lot behind the Fox Hills Inn and parked. "It's got character."

"You just like it because you like whiskey, which honestly makes you a bit biased." Cooper grabbed his briefcase and slipped from the car. Marco popped open the trunk.

"I'm telling you man, you gotta try it. Beer'll never taste the same."

"Why would I want to ruin my favorite drink?" Cooper joked, shooting his partner a wry grin.

"Because there's more to life than the same old shit. Broaden your horizons."

"I like my same old shit."

Suitcases in hand, they walked around to the front of the brick building with its scarlet red awning and welcoming glass entryway. Marco held open the door, looking smug.

"No, you don't. We both know you're dying to find out what all the fuss is about. You wanna know why this entire hick town is bonkers over a bunch of distilled corn."

Seeing his partner's point, Cooper shrugged. "Maybe. Then again, that same distilled corn is helping finance a terrorist organization. It'd be hypocritical of me to enjoy it too much."

"Uh huh. Stop being such a saint." Marco followed him into the lobby, shaking his head. "Talk to me again once you've given in and tasted it."

Cooper grinned. "What? And give up my sainthood?"

SHE WOULD'VE missed lunch again if Adam hadn't shown up at the distillery, take-out bag in hand.

"Spare a minute?"

Ava sniffed the air. He'd brought her favorite—pastrami sandwich on rye. "For a man with food, I've got all the time in the world."

She accepted the bag and motioned for him to follow her into the small, cluttered office she mostly used for storage. Clearing off one of the two guest chairs for him, she set the bag down on top of a stack of paperwork and sat behind the desk.

"Grandpa around? I got him one, too," Adam told her, digging out the sandwiches and handing her one wrapped in foil.

"He's off somewhere." Ava's brows lifted. "Look at you, Mr. Nice Guy. What's the occasion?"

"Nothing. Just wanted to drop by and see how y'all are doing."

She snorted. "Uh huh. You don't do something this charitable unless you want something."

Temper sparked in his eyes. "That's not true."

Through a bite of pastrami, she smiled. "Sure it is. But I appreciate the offer, anyway."

He opened up his own sandwich, a scowl tightening his face. "If you must know, I'm avoiding Brandy."

"What'd you do this time?"

His shoulders rose in a half-hearted shrug. "Nothing I should be sorry for."

Concern for her friend warred with amusement at seeing her brother so irritable. "I'll be the judge of that. What happened?"

"The girl I was hittin' on the other night at the bar, the brunette? Well, that was Brandy's cousin. She was visiting from out of town."

Ava couldn't help but laugh. "Oh, good job, Casanova."

"I know." He frowned, and she could see from his guilty look that he felt worse about it than he let on. "But hell, how was I supposed to know? And honestly, why should Brandy care? We're just friends."

"You know she's always wanted more than that from you," Ava reminded him.

"Yeah, well, it takes two."

Ava pursed her lips, hackles rising in defense of her friend. She hated being in the middle, but this time he was wrong and she had no qualms letting him know it. "You know what your problem is?"

He gave her a steely look. "What?"

Setting aside her sandwich, she sat back in her chair and crossed her arms. "You tell the world—and most importantly you tell yourself—that you don't give a shit about Brandy. But then you go out of your way to avoid her when she's pissed at you because underneath it all, you feel bad. If you really didn't care, you would have no problem setting foot in that bar and flirting with the rest of Brandy's cousins if they decided to show up."

He avoided her eyes. "I didn't know the girl was her cousin—"

"Exactly. You admit that if you did know, you wouldn't have done what you did." Ava threw up her hands, exasperated. "Adam, when are you going to get it through that thick skull of yours that you're being a jackass?"

He sucked on his teeth and shook his head. Bolts of anger sparked from him as he rose to his feet. "Right. I'm the jackass. I ain't ever led her on, Ava. Never. If Brandy wants to assume there's something more between us, then that's her problem."

"Then be honest with me, right here, right now. Why don't you like her?"

A flicker of something akin to pain flashed in his eyes, but was quickly buried. "I don't have to explain it to you, or to anybody. Tell grandpa I said hello."

He tore out of the room, leaving the door wide open. She chewed on her lip, annoyed at both herself and at him for being so pigheaded.

Joe popped his head into the office. "Was that Adam I just saw leavin'?"

She sighed, held up his sandwich. "Yeah. He brought you this."

He came into the room and accepted the roast beef on sourdough. "Ah, the boy knows what I like. What's he doin' takin' off without sayin' hello?"

"I pissed him off." She motioned for him to sit down. "He's very frustrating."

Joe chuckled as he lowered into the same chair Adam had occupied moments earlier. "Aye, siblings often are. What'd he do this time?"

"Hurt Brandy's feelings. But then, what else is new?"

Considering, Joe took a bite of his sandwich, chewed. "She's a sweet girl. He'll open those eyes of his someday."

"I hope for her sake she's happily married with five kids by the time that happens. She can do better."

"She keeps our boy in check. She's good for him."

"Yeah, but clearly he's not good for her," Ava grumbled, rubbing her face with her hands. "How the hell am I supposed to sit here and simultaneously defend my best friend and my brother? I just can't do it."

"Then don't." He grinned, wiping a smear of mustard off his chin. "This is just one of those things that work themselves out in time, dearie. No reason to get all up in a fuss about it."

A small smile crept over her lips. She stood and kissed his forehead. "All right. I gotta go get ready for the next tour. Enjoy that sandwich. Adam probably won't be by again for a while."

"He never strays too far," Joe mused. "It's hard to resist the pull of family. No matter how hard the boy tries."

CHAPTER

Five

With the raid planned for the following day, Cooper was left with the afternoon to explore. His curiosity took him to the streets of Fox Hills, hands buried in the pockets of his slacks and the hazy autumn sun teasing the gold out of his hair. He smiled at the people he passed on the sidewalk, noting the tourist season was in full swing.

The town buzzed with the discussion of whiskey. From the making of it to the drinking of it, everywhere he went someone was on the topic. From snatches of conversation, he discovered Fox Hills to be along the famous Kentucky Bourbon Trail, a long line of age-old distilleries known for the crafting of world-renowned whiskey. Something about limestone in the water and a lack of iron in the soil made the area ideal. Interest piqued, he vowed to look into it the second he got back to his hotel.

Until then, he was content to simply wander. Marco had latched himself onto the television to watch the Giants game, but he didn't mind being alone. It gave him time to observe and process this little speck on the map before diving into the investigation that had brought him there.

Before he realized where he was, he stopped before a sign that pointed up a gravel road and read, *Lucky Fox Whiskey Distillery—Tours and Tastings*. He stared at it for a moment, weighing his curiosity against protocol. What harm would it cause to take a peek inside the distillery? he wondered, eyeing the oversized metal building up the road. The soft glow of the sun gave it a luminescent quality, while the surrounding wild grass danced in the breeze.

Something about it pulled on him. He couldn't say what it was—the intrigue of the case he was on, the eagerness to learn more about the Brannons, or maybe the faint scent of oak on the brisk Fall air—but before he could tell himself no, his feet began to move.

He bent his head and hiked up the road, smiling at cars as they drove to and from. Checking his watch, he noted it was nearly four o'clock. If he was lucky, they'd have a late afternoon tour.

Eagerness filled him as he approached the building, admiring the running fox logo at the top that he remembered from the company's website. It was clever, he thought. The fox on the run from its own past, out to make its fortune in a brave new world. Joe Brannon had spawned his own little empire in Fox Hills. An empire that was slowly but surely being sent away to the very same people Joe had run from.

Time would tell if Joe had any idea what his son was up to. Cooper's gut told him he didn't, which made the decision to check out the distillery all the more acceptable in his mind. This was Joe's territory. Whatever mess Ty was wrapped up in didn't change that fact.

A pretty brunette greeted him as he entered the building, all dimples and Southern charm. "Welcome to Lucky Fox! What brings you here today?"

Cooper returned her smile before glancing around at the high-ceilinged room. It was as warm and inviting as a log cabin, with an oversized stone fireplace against one wall framed by scarlet leather armchairs that invited one to sink into them and enjoy a drink. A long tasting bar lined the wall straight ahead on the left, where even now a bartender was busy pouring samples for a group of tittering guests. A gift shop filled with Lucky Fox paraphernalia was on the right, packed with everything from shot glasses to fox stuffed animals to post cards.

Directly ahead of him were two handcrafted iron doors with a sign above that said the room beyond was the distillery.

He nodded to the doors. "There a tour coming up soon?"

"You're in luck! Our last tour for the day is at four o'clock. Is this your first time here?"

"Yep." He gave her a sheepish smile. "I'm in town on business. Thought I'd pop by and see what all the fuss was about."

"Wonderful. Here." She whipped out a clipboard and a pen, made a notation and then handed him a business card sized ticket. "We offer three different tours, but your first is complimentary. Just hand this over at the double doors there and enjoy."

"Hey, thanks." He accepted the ticket and walked around, mentally taking notes. It wasn't nearly as sophisticated as he had expected, but instead homely and inviting. The employees were bubbly and sincere, the guests relaxed and cheerful. Without realizing it, he soon forgot the reason for his visit and instead began to enjoy himself.

At four o'clock, the double doors swung open and a balding, middle-aged man called for the tour guests to gather around. Cooper shuffled forward along with a dozen other people, all eager for a look inside the distillery. With his height, Cooper towered above most of them and took advantage of the view to peek beyond the doors. He caught a flash of red, gone before he could decipher its origin.

The man led the group through the doors, welcoming them into a room with high stone walls and three enormous copper stills. As he began a brief introduction, a woman appeared at his side. The sight of her caught Cooper off guard as recognition hit him.

Ava Brannon. Her name came to him as swiftly as if he'd been punched in the gut. And really, the sight of her was a blow to the senses all in itself.

She was taller than he'd expected, with a cascade of vibrant red hair that spilled over her shoulders. The jeans she wore were skintight and faded, paired with a denim shirt and scuffed cowboy boots. Beside her, he felt ridiculously overdressed in his business suit and tie. The fact that she looked so comfortable in her own skin made him feel itchy in his.

"Welcome to Lucky Fox Whiskey, y'all." Ava beamed, fixing her hands on her hips. "My name is Ava Brannon, and I am the granddaughter of our master distiller, Lucky Joe. I'll be your guide today. Feel free to ask any questions you have while we go. This ain't one of those high-brow, keep-your-mouth-shut tours. We invite you to enjoy your stay here as if you're one of the family. Because today, you are."

The group buzzed with anticipation, but Cooper couldn't focus. He couldn't stop staring at the Lucky Fox heiress with her smoky southern voice and electric smile.

When they locked eyes, he saw a spark there that might as well of set his insides on fire.

AVA'S MOUTH curved to one side, a natural reaction to the sight before her. Just where did that tall, cool drink of water come from? she asked herself. It wasn't often some golden haired Adonis strolled into one of her tours, looking delightfully nerdy in a tailored business suit. When he adjusted his tie, clearly uneasy, she had to bite back a laugh and refocus her attention on the group.

"Let's begin with a little bit of history. Grandpa Joe may not have been born in Kentucky, but he sure fell in love with it the second he arrived here from Ireland back in 1961. Whiskey is in his blood, you see, as the Brannons have been making Irish Whiskey in Ireland going back two hundred years. But Joe had a vision the rest of the family couldn't see. While the Brannons had always created pure pot still whiskey, a blend of both malted and unmalted barley distilled in a pot still, Joe knew that by adding a blend of grain whiskey it would cut the aging time by a third *and* improve the flavor profile. The blend would create a softer, brighter whiskey less harsh on the tongue and more palatable to the increasing market of whiskey drinkers. His father and brother, of course, disagreed. So Joe said boo to tradition, packed his bags, and headed west to America. Whiskey recipe in hand, he landed in New York and asked anyone who would listen where he could go to make whiskey. As fate would have it, he stumbled upon a beautiful young nurse named Vivian "Vivi" Wallace at a local Irish pub, and learned his destiny lay several hundred miles to the south in her hometown of Fox Hills, Kentucky.

"Ever the charmer, Joe convinced Vivi to take him home to Fox Hills with her, and she did. Within a month they were married, and within two he'd talked the Fox Hills Savings and Loan into giving him money to buy this very facility you see here today. Now, at the time it wasn't nearly as grand. But you can imagine a hardworking, fearless Irish immigrant, bent on proving his own family wrong and making whiskey the way he knew it should be made."

She paused as an older woman in front raised her hand. "Yes?"

"How'd he get into making bourbon? Is it completely different?"

"Ah, yes. All bourbon is whiskey but not all whiskey is bourbon. Bourbon has its own specific rules to follow that separate it from Irish and even Tennessee whiskey, which we'll get into later. Joe discovered bourbon the minute he set foot in Kentucky. It was given to him by a bartender who refused to serve anything else, so Joe gave it a try. From that moment on he was hooked, and couldn't resist putting an Irish spin on it when it came time to create his own batch."

Ava motioned behind her to the trio of copper stills lining the wall. Elongated with a bulbous base, each still connected to the wall where pipes ran between them and down into a tasting chamber. Signs near the gleaming copper warned not to touch the hot metal.

"We are one of only two bourbon distilleries in America to do things with a European flair. That means we triple distill our bourbon in copper pot stills, just like how single malt Irish whiskey is made. The boil ball at the bottom lets the vapors expand and contract, then pushes them up through the gooseneck. The gooseneck slows the vapors down, causing some to slide down the copper, a crucial part of the process. We then smell and taste it to determine when to forward it on to the next still. After all three stills it's ready to go into the barrel. But of course, before it's ready to be distilled, all whiskey starts with a few classic ingredients."

She walked over to a display of large glass jars, each filled with a different type of grain in varying quantities.

Resting her hands on the three-quarter-full jar of corn kernels, she smiled. "You asked what sets bourbon apart from other whiskies. Bourbon—by law, in fact—must be made with at *least* fifty-one percent corn. The remaining ingredients vary from distillery to distillery. Most use a combination of corn, rye, and malted barley. Here at Lucky Fox, our classic bourbon is comprised of seventy-two percent corn, eighteen percent rye, and ten percent malted barley. To convert starches into sugar, you must have at least ten percent barley in the mix. Otherwise the magic just won't happen, folks."

A few people chuckled as she lifted her gaze to the handsome stranger in the back once more. He was watching her attentively, looking very much like a kid enthralled by a flashy science experiment. Seeing the interest in him flattered her, especially since she noted some of the other guests were looking a tad bored.

Shifting gears, she motioned to another set of iron doors against the back wall. "Shall we move on?"

Taking the tour through the bustling distillery, she showed them where the corn mash was blended with yeast in giant churning vats and prepared for distillation. While listening to more questions, she caught the eye of Mr. Science Nerd.

He acknowledged her with a nod and a subtle smile, one that lit a flame within her that had for so long been extinguished.

THE TOUR ended back inside the visitor's center, where guests were invited to taste the whiskies they'd watched be crafted in the distillery. While some crowded around the tasting bar and others darted off to the gift shop, Cooper made his way to a smaller bar counter be-side the distillery doors, where Ava was busy completing the sale of a bottle of Lucky Fox 101 Bourbon. She thanked the middle-aged man who purchased it, her laughter more genuine than anything Cooper had ever heard. The open, honest way she moved and spoke captivated him.

Once the man was gone, Cooper sidled up to the bar and fixed on a casual grin. "For a guy who's never tried whiskey before, where would an expert like yourself sug-gest I start?"

Ava feigned a look of shock. "Never tried whiskey be-fore? God-almighty."

"Don't take this the wrong way," he began, resting his elbow on the bar. He leaned in conspiratorially and low-ered his voice. "But I'm really more of a beer guy."

"Well, we'll just have to change that." Ava winked and grabbed a bottle of Lucky Fox Honey from under the bar top. She placed it in front of him. "Now, before you go all, 'that's a girlie bourbon' on me, hear me out."

Cooper laughed. "All right."

She tilted the bottle back so he could read the label. "Our Lucky Fox Honey is a bourbon-based liqueur. It's only 70 proof, so it's easier on the palate than the straight bour-bons. For someone who's never tried the hard stuff before, this is a good way to get the flavors of bourbon softened by notes of honey, caramel, and a splash of citrus."

Uncorking the bottle, she poured a small amount into a glencairn glass and handed it to him. Both humor and challenge filled her eyes. "You man enough to try it?"

Cooper lifted the bell-shaped glass to his nose, breath-ing in the unmistakable aroma of sweet honey. Intrigued, he took a small sip. His taste buds were immediately assault-ed by a rich, smooth explosion of honey married with the spice of something oaky and earthy. Before he had a chance to explore all the flavors, he swallowed and coughed.

Ava's face lit with a delighted grin. "Not so girlie, is it Slick?"

He laughed again. "No, not really. Not what I expected, either."

"You get used to the burn." She tilted her head to the side, admiring him. Most men would have been embarrassed as hell to admit they knew nothing about whiskey. He seemed more interested in learning than pretending. "If you're feeling up to it, I can give you something with a bit more kick to it. I promise it won't kill you."

Drinking the rest of the honey bourbon sample, Cooper nodded. He set his glass down in front of her. "Hit me, bartender. Just not too hard. I'm a sensitive soul."

She threw back her head and laughed, big and bright, and had his insides twisting up again. "All right, then. This'll be good for you."

She presented a bottle of their Distiller's Choice, the prime bourbon Cooper had seen Marco drinking back in D.C. He watched her pour an ample amount into his glass, then nudge it across the counter to him.

Without hesitating, he nosed it, breathing in the beautiful bouquet of wildflowers and toasted vanilla. "Wow," he murmured, taken aback by it. "How do they get it to smell like that?"

"It's all in the charred oak barrel," Ava explained, leaning closer to him across the counter. Her smile widened, bringing out a sexy little dimple in her right cheek. "It's what makes bourbon unique. Come back tomorrow for the barrel house tour and I'll give you a little lesson."

He could smell the spiced apple scent of her perfume, could see the flecks of gold in those hazel eyes of hers, and found himself easing away. How had he gotten so close in the first place?

"Maybe I will," he replied, sipping the bourbon. His focus was elsewhere and had him downing it without really tasting it. "It's good."

One of her eyebrows arched. "Good?"

He set the glass down, gave a brisk nod. "Stronger than the honey, I'll give you that. Definitely got the burn, but the vanilla is in there somewhere too. I liked it."

She straightened, corked the bottle of Distiller's Choice. "It's one of our best."

"I can see why."

Ava paused and considered him. He looked like a kid caught with his hand in the cookie jar. A rapid shift from the carefree charmer he had been when he first walked up. Maybe he was married. "Anything else you'd like to taste?"

Cooper cleared his throat and ran a hand through his hair. "I'll take a bottle of the 101."

She managed a surprised laugh. "You sure you can handle it?"

"Yeah." He dug into his coat pocket for his wallet, felt his badge. Guilt raced through him knowing he had entered into a conversation with her under false pretenses. Then again, he *was* genuinely interested in what Lucky Fox had to offer, wasn't he? It was perfectly innocent.

But then she cocked that chin and looked at him with suspicious eyes that told him she was onto him.

Christ. She may actually kill him when she found out. He might not make it back to D.C. alive. Marco would have to cart his charred body back in a duffle bag, present it to his sobbing mother. It had definitely been a mistake to come.

Then again, he *was* enjoying himself. That had to be worth something, right?

Ava slipped a bottle of the 101 bourbon into a gift bag and told him the total. He started to hand her his credit card, only to backtrack and give her cash instead. Better to not leave a paper trail.

She rang up the sale and offered him a pleasant smile. "Thanks for visiting us, Slick. I hope you enjoy that 101."

Their eyes met as he grabbed the bag. "If I don't, I know who to complain to."

Her grin turned wicked. "I'll just tell you to man up and put it on ice."

He let out a sound caught between a laugh and a groan. "Good to know. Nice to meet you, Ava."

She stared after him as he walked away, resting her chin in her hand. Her grandfather came up beside her, rested a hand on her shoulder. "Time to get home, dearie."

"Yeah. Okay." She took a deep breath and attempted a smile for him. "I just sold a bottle of 101 to a guy who'd never tried whiskey before today."

"Oh, my." Joe chuckled. "That's a right cruel thing to do."

"He'll be able to handle it," she decided. "In fact, he may even love it."

"Some men aren't afraid of a little burn."

PART **0 2**

LUCKY FOX 101
STRAIGHT KENTUCKY BOURBON

How well I remember my first encounter with The Devil's Brew.
I happened to stumble across a case of bourbon—and went
right on stumbling for several days thereafter.
~ W.C. Fields ~

CHAPTER

Six

The Lucky Fox office in downtown Fox Hills was nestled in a quaint, two-story brick building between a hair salon and the local deli. Cooper savored the scent of cold cuts and freshly baked bread as they walked past to their destination.

Marco held open the door. "After you, oh-saintliness."

Cooper stifled a yawn. "Damn right."

"Didn't sleep well last night?"

He thought of the bottle of Lucky Fox 101 sitting on the dresser in his hotel room. Most of the night he had stared at it, unable to stop thinking of the woman who had sold it to him. He couldn't bring himself to taste it just yet, not while knowing his investigation would soon turn the Brannons' world upside down.

"You know how it is. Stiff bed," Cooper replied easily. He ducked past his partner into the Lucky Fox office.

The waiting area held a traditional oak receptionist's desk, leather arm chairs, and a hunter green sofa. Paintings of the Kentucky landscape and warm, neutral tones gave the space a cozily inviting look. Not at all what Cooper would have expected the corporate office of a multi-million dollar company to look like, but then again, this wasn't some New York City high rise.

This was small town Kentucky.

The white-haired receptionist glanced up as they entered, her cheerful smile faltering. Behind gold, wire-rimmed glasses, confusion filled her eyes. "Can I help you?"

Marco whipped out his badge. "Agent D'Amico and Agent Lawson with the FBI. We're here to see Ty Brannon."

The woman eyed his badge with surprise. "Oh, my. Yes, one moment, please."

She ducked down a hallway into an adjoining office, speaking in a hushed whisper to the person inside. Moments later, Ty Brannon appeared, clad in a trim business suit with his dark hair neatly combed. Cooper studied him, getting the impression the man had expected them.

"Come in, please." He ushered them into his office and closed the door.

Cooper turned to him. "Mr. Brannon, we—"

"I know. The tax thing, right?" Ty offered a tight smile as he settled behind his desk. The room had similar oak and leather furniture as the front, with the family portrait that Cooper recognized from the Lucky Fox website hanging on the wall behind Ty's desk. His eyes hovered over Ava's face before he reverted his attention back to Ty and sat down. "I assure you, I'm cooperating fully with the IRS and the issue has been handled. I don't know why they sent you."

"We have a warrant to seize your computers," Marco began, handing Ty the paperwork. "The details are enclosed."

Ty examined the pages, his face draining of color. "What do you need my computers for?"

"Financial records, proof of money transfers and communications with your cousin, Ned Brannon," Cooper supplied. He waited until Ty's gaze met his before he continued. "Are you aware that Ned is on Ireland's SDU watch list for suspected terrorist activities with the Irish Republican Army?"

"What? That's ridiculous," Ty replied, setting aside the warrant. He folded his hands, likely to keep them from shaking. "I know nothing about the IRA. If he's involved somehow, I have no part in it."

"But you send him money." Marco crossed his legs, relaxed. "Under FATCA we were able to uncover your overseas Swiss account. The same account withdrawals have been made from consistently for over twenty years from a bank in Dublin."

Ty wet his lips. "Look, I'm aware some of the money may have slipped through without taxes being paid. I'm willing to pay those penalties—I've already spoken with an IRS attorney who's made the arrangements. But I don't know anything about withdrawals or about Ned's business."

"Why put the money in a numbered Swiss account, then?" Cooper asked. "Unless you wanted to hide its purpose?"

"Why does anyone use Swiss accounts? That doesn't make me an instant criminal." Ty closed his eyes and rubbed his forehead. "Look, you have your warrant. I can't stop you. But I won't answer any more questions without my lawyer present."

"That's your right." Marco rose, tucked his hands into the pockets of his slacks. "The team from the Louisville field office should be here any minute. They'll be processing the files on all the computers in this office, and any you have at home, as well."

"I just have a laptop at home. Should I go—"

"I'll get it," Cooper cut in, facing Marco. "You hang out here, wait for the team. I won't be long."

"Agent," Ty called out before Cooper could leave. Concern deepened the lines of his tired face, giving him a vulnerability that Cooper steeled himself against. "When you see my family, don't tell them anything more than they need to know. I don't need my reputation slandered prematurely."

Cooper nodded. "You'll need to close down the office for the time being. The team will set up base here to go through everything. We'll be as discreet as possible, but I can't guarantee people won't talk. You may want to consider telling your family the truth."

Ty's face reddened. "They're my family. I'll decide how and when to tell them."

Cooper left the office, a copy of the warrant in his coat pocket. Hopping in the department issued black sedan, he whipped out onto the street and headed for the Lucky Fox Distillery.

"THERE ARE eight hundred and twelve barrels in this building. That amounts to just over forty three *thousand* gallons of whiskey." Ava enjoyed the surprised faces of her tour guests as they gazed around in awe at the barrel house. "Fun fact, there are actually more barrels of bourbon in Kentucky than there are people. In case you couldn't tell, we really enjoy our whiskey.

"That beautiful aroma you smell is what we in the business like to call the 'Angel's Share.' It's the small amount of water and whiskey that seeps through the barrels as they breathe." She walked over to a barrel resting on the closest rack and pointed to a sap-like substance crusted around a crack in the wood. "Sometimes it's even visible, like this, on the outside of the barrel. We call this barrel candy, and yes, you can eat it. It tastes a bit like caramel, believe it or not."

A few visitors snapped off pictures. "Another thing you'll notice is that it's pretty darn chilly in here. Kentucky's cold winters and warm, humid summers actually help with the aging of the whiskey. As the temperature rises and falls, the barrels expand and contract, allowing the whiskey to seep into the wood and pull out the flavors."

Her eyes shot to the doors of the barrel house as a man entered. It threw her momentarily off balance to see it was the whiskey novice from the day before, looking just as slick in his suit and tie and windswept blond hair. An easy smile played over his lips as he strolled toward the group, his hands tucked into his pockets.

She returned the smile before switching her attention back to the tour guests, not willing to give him more acknowledgment than that. "Y'all want to see the inside of one of the barrels?"

In the center of the room was a square table with a halved barrel propped up on top of it, displaying the charred interior. She patted it with a grin. "I said before how the true magic of bourbon is in the barrel. By law, bourbon must be aged in charred, new white oak barrels for a minimum of two years. We age most of ours anywhere from five to eight years.

"First we toast the inside of the barrel with radiant heat, no flame, for about twenty minutes to cook the sugars and bring out the caramel and vanilla flavors that are in the wood to begin with. Then we turn up the heat for twenty seconds and char the wood, just enough to burn off a few layers without ruining the toasting. This charring is what gives bourbon its rich, golden color. No other flavorings can be added—what you taste is all natural. In fact, these bourbon barrels have so much flavor that we even re-use them to age our Irish whiskey."

"So what was the Irish whiskey aged in originally?" the mystery man in the suit asked from the back of the group.

"You said Joe got into bourbon making later, so I can't imagine he had bourbon barrels lying around."

Ava angled her head, impressed by his memory. "Sherry barrels. That's what the Brannons have always done. But Joe discovered that the bourbon barrels actually add a unique flavor to the whiskey that rivaled what his forefathers produced."

She fielded a few more questions, then set the group loose to explore the barrel house or head back to the visitor's center for a tasting.

Cooper watched her shake hands with a few of the guests, biding his time to get her alone. His gut twisted when she turned to face him, as if knowing he wanted to speak to her.

"I see you're alive and well. I take it the 101 didn't hurt too bad?" she teased, resting a hand on her hip.

"I didn't have the chance to try it yet, actually," he admitted.

"Oh. That's a shame." She motioned around the barrel house. "So, what do you think?"

Cooper stared up at the sky-high racks of barrels and breathed in the earthy sweet scent of the air. "It's pretty cool."

She laughed. "It's more than just 'cool.' It's a time-honored tradition. There're barrels here that won't be ready for nearly a decade. Can you even *imagine* life that far ahead? We have to. If we don't, then we run out of whiskey and our company fails. That's why this room is so important. The future sleeps here."

His eyes caught hers and held. The passion he saw there—for her family's company, for the product they created—brought on a wave of guilt knowing he was seconds away from damaging it. Maybe not permanently, perhaps barely at all. But there was no denying it would sting her pride.

She glanced down at her watch. "You missed the first part of the tour, but I have a few minutes to spare if you'd like me to give you that little lesson we talked about yesterday."

"I'm afraid my business here is not entirely personal." He reached for the warrant in his coat pocket, brought his badge out with it. She eyed both curiously, her smile fading as he flipped open his badge and showed it to her. "I'm with the FBI."

Ava's lips parted in surprise as she grabbed his badge and studied it. "Is this a joke?" He was smiling in his picture, but there was no trace of it on his face now. Only a hint of regret behind a mask of steely resolve. The contrast startled her.

"No, it's not."

"So why are you here..." She read the name on his badge and sneered. "Agent Cooper Lawson? We haven't done anything wrong." She shoved his badge back at him, hackles rising in defense. "You tricked me. Came in here, all curious and flirtatious. What were you doing? Scoping out the place?"

Since he couldn't deny it, he pocketed his badge and handed her the warrant instead. "I have a warrant to confiscate Ty Brannon's personal laptop. I'll need you to take me to it."

Dread dropped heavy in her stomach as she scoured the warrant. It said nothing of the charges, only what the FBI was allowed to confiscate and what they could look for.

Financial transactions from the company. Personal bank records. Email correspondence.

Good Lord. What was her father involved in?

She started to rip into Cooper, only to notice a few of the tour guests and two of her employees frozen in place, gawking at her. She cursed under her breath, struggling to quell her temper. No matter how much she wanted to, she couldn't refuse a warrant and she sure as hell wouldn't cause a scene. Until she figured out what was going on, she had to keep up appearances.

Bringing her eyes back to his, she lifted her chin with a tight-lipped smile. "All right, Agent Lawson. Follow me."

She folded up the warrant and nodded reassuringly to her employees as she passed, knowing they would be hopping on the gossip wagon the second she left. An FBI agent didn't just trot into Fox Hills every day, flashing his badge and presenting warrants. It would be the talk of the town by sunset, guaranteed.

Grumbling obscenities under her breath, she took Cooper to the four-wheeler parked out back. She hopped inside and scowled at him.

"Get in. I'll take you up to the house."

He hesitated, eyeing the four-wheeler doubtfully. "Why don't I just follow you in my car?"

She rolled her eyes. "What do you think I'm gonna do? Take you out back and shoot you?"

His mouth twitched. "I wouldn't put it past you."

"Oh, that's real nice, funny guy. You may not be welcome here, but my mama still raised me with some damn manners." Her temper came roaring back, and along with it came the worry and the fear. Pride wouldn't allow her to display any of it, though it simmered just under the surface. "Just get in. I don't have all day."

He did as he was told, though he sat on the edge of the seat as far from her as possible. He gripped the bar that supported the vehicle's roof, silently wondering how fast it could go and if she'd push it to the limit just to punish him. He wouldn't put that past her, either.

They pulled onto the tree-lined gravel road that led away from the distillery. Sunlight broke through the canopy of leaves overhead, bits of blue sky visible through all the shivering gold.

"The house is just a ways up here," Ava informed him. "My mother will likely be home. You are not allowed to speak to her. We go in together, get the laptop, and then I drive you back to your car. No snooping around and no questions without our lawyer."

Cooper bowed his head. "Understood."

For a while they drove in silence. He took in the sights around him, charmed by the countryside. He could see the appeal of it; the miles of open grassland and pockets of forest, the ground sloping in gentle hills. There was a reason people escaped the city for the sanctuary of dusty back roads and cozy little towns, though he knew the monotony of it would drive him mad.

Then again, the woman beside him was anything but boring. He sincerely regretted that he may have lost the opportunity to get to know her better.

"So, you grew up here?"

"I said no questions," she growled, clenching her jaw. When he said nothing else, her temper deflated. She brushed strands of hair from her face, annoyed with herself for feeling the need to be polite. "Yes. I was born on this very property."

When he gave her a surprised look, she frowned. "What?"

"Next thing you'll tell me is they gave you whiskey instead of milk as a kid."

Sarcasm and humor softened the tension in her shoulders. "That's right. Can't be initiated into the family until you can polish off an entire bottle of bourbon in an hour. Gotta train for years, so we start young."

Seeing his expression wrought with confused horror gave her an immense rush of pleasure. "I'm just kidding, Slick. Don't get your panties in a knot."

He let out a half-laugh. "Right. I'm not usually so gullible."

"Neither am I." She turned her eyes back to the road. "Still got nice and fooled by you, though."

"Look, I wasn't trying to—"

"You don't need to explain yourself. I don't want to hear it, anyway."

They came around a bend that opened up to a sprawling ranch house nestled on a quiet corner of the property dotted with trees. Ava parked in front of it and cut the engine.

"Remember what I said." She hopped out and sauntered up the front steps of the house, leaving him to trail behind.

He followed her in, overtaken by the smell of freshly baked apple pie and cinnamon. He breathed it in, his mouth watering. "Now *that's* what home should smell like."

Unable to help it, Ava filled with pride. "I agree."

They cut through the cozily furnished living room with its rustic leather sofas and brick fireplace, heading for a room at the end of a long hallway. Cooper's eyes caught the family portraits lining the hall, seeing glimpses of Ava as a child, attached at the hip to a young boy whose face mirrored her own.

He recalled seeing the man in the portrait hanging in Ty's office, but hadn't given him much thought until now. "You have a brother?"

Ava pursed her lips and faced him as she stopped before her father's office. "You just can't help it, can you? You have to know the how and the why of everything. It's infuriating."

He shrugged. "I'm just curious."

"Yeah, well part of our arrangement was that you'd check that curiosity at the door." She swept into the office, prompting him to follow. There was a laptop resting on the antique walnut desk that she hastily stuffed into a sleek black case and handed to him. "There you go. Now get the hell out."

He slung the laptop case over his shoulder and glanced around the office. It had a lovely view of the garden outside, where he could see a woman wearing a wide-brimmed straw hat busily tending rose bushes.

He started to ask if that was her mother, then bit his tongue. The woman was her spitting image, anyway. Though softer, more elegant in the way she moved that contrasted with Ava's intensity.

As Ty Brannon's wife, would the woman know of his connection to the IRA? Or was she just as clueless as he was willing to bet Ava and her grandfather were?

Returning his attention to Ava, he nodded. "Thanks. I'll be in touch if I need anything else."

"I'm sure you will." She ushered him out of the room and shut the door, then forced him back out of the house. Once they were seated in the four-wheeler, she let out a huff of breath and met his eyes. "Why can't you tell me what this is all about? Seems a bit unfair, don't you think? I just have to let you into my home and hand over my property without a clue what you're after."

He cradled the case in his lap and studied her. "The warrant details what we're looking for."

"No, it says what you'll be looking *at*, but not what *for*." Frustrated, she started the engine and headed back to the distillery. "Is my father in some kind of trouble?"

"Some kind, yeah." He tried to keep his voice light but the truth made it difficult. "My partner's downtown meeting with him right now. The office will need to be closed temporarily while we investigate."

A sick feeling came over her. "How long?"

"However long it takes for us to find what we're looking for."

"And if you don't?"

His fingers tightened over the laptop case. "Then he's an innocent man and we'll get out of your hair."

A sardonic laugh slipped out of her. "But not before turning our lives upside down."

He said nothing as he looked away, reminding himself of the reason for the investigation in the first place. There was blood on Ty Brannon's hands, he was sure of it. And if exposing the truth made him the bad guy in Ava's eyes, then so be it.

In the end, all that mattered was getting justice.

CHAPTER

Seven

Adam brought the glass of bourbon to his lips, savored the taste. His eyes caught Brandy's as she slipped out of the back room, having just clocked in for the night. The flush that brightened her cheeks and the downturn of her lips brought on an unwelcome rush of guilt.

Though she looked like she'd prefer to run the other way, out of duty she went straight to him. "Can I get you anything?"

He set his glass down on the bar, jostled the ice around absently. His eyes remained locked on hers. "You still upset with me?"

She shifted her weight, eyed the other bartender who was busy tending a cluster of tourists fresh from the Lucky Fox distillery. "No. Why would I be mad?"

"You know why." Irritation flooded him as he knocked back the last of his drink and motioned with the glass for another.

Brandy turned to grab the bottle, buying herself a moment's time to collect herself. When she faced him again, she was smiling. "Rebecca said she had fun with you the other night. She was sorry to have to leave so soon."

"I don't give a shit about your damn cousin, okay? I was just having a good time. It didn't mean anything."

She stiffened and poured him two fingers of bourbon. "That's nice. It didn't mean anything to me, either."

"Then why are you actin' like you're pissed at me?" he demanded, his upper lip curling with disgust at both himself and her. "I swear, everything I do seems to rile somebody up. Between you and my sister I just can't catch a goddamn break."

Brandy softened, sympathy in her eyes. "Well, I'm not angry with you. So don't worry."

It only bothered him more that she could cave so easily. Could forgive, forget. He'd never known how to pull off such a trick and knew he sure as hell didn't deserve her complacency. "Brandy, for once could you just grow a spine and yell at me, throw something, anything? All this passive-aggressive bullshit is driving me insane."

Her lips parted with insult and surprise at his outburst. Her hands shook as she wiped them on her apron. "Either I'm too mad or I'm not mad enough, Adam. A girl can't see straight when you're shiftin' moods like this. Excuse me."

She left to greet a few newcomers at the bar, employees from the distillery. Adam frowned at his drink and closed his eyes, trying to clear the image of her distressed face from his mind. He hadn't meant to hurt her feelings, though yet again his temper had walked off with his tongue.

Gulping down his bourbon, he felt someone sit beside him. When he lifted his head, he saw Beau, looking smug.

"Well, Brannon, sounds like you got yourself a big problem."

Adam didn't want to take the bait, but couldn't help himself. "Oh yeah? What's that?"

"Word is the FBI was flashin' warrants around at the distillery and the downtown office today. I'll be meetin' with them tomorrow to find out what's goin' on, but the whole town's a-buzzin'."

Adam's brow furrowed as he faced Beau. "What the hell are you talking about?"

A slimy, delighted grin formed over Beau's lips. "Current theory is the old man's being deported back to Ireland for cookin' the books. Know anything about that?"

It took all he had not to laugh. He waved off Beau's claims carelessly. "Why don't you go gossip with the old biddies at the hair salon and leave me the hell alone?"

"It ain't gossip, son." Beau shifted in his seat, whistled the distillery employees over. They approached, eyes alight with excitement. "Boys, tell Brannon here what y'all told me."

Adam lifted his gaze, a feeling of panic rising up within him as the employees related what they had witnessed in the barrel house between Ava and the man bearing an FBI badge and a warrant.

"Christ," he muttered, catching Brandy's eye as she hurried over.

"Everything all right?" she asked, resisting the urge to comfort him. He was white as a sheet.

He nodded, not even realizing he was doing it. It felt like his head floated above his body. "Yeah, darlin'. Excuse me."

Resisting the desire to punch Beau in the face simply for being there, he fled the bar and went straight home.

WHEN THE front door opened, Ava pounced. Seeing it was only Adam had her cursing aloud.

He rounded on her. "What is this shit I hear about the FBI?"

"I don't know," Ava fired back, hands clenched into fists at her sides. "Daddy won't answer his cell. I called the office but he's not there. I don't know what's happened to him."

"He's probably just taking some time to cool off," Sandra suggested, her face lined with worry despite the smile she offered up. She sat on the sofa, her hand locked in Joe's. "When he gets home, I'm sure y'all will get the answers you need."

"I better." Festering with anger, Ava paced the living room.

Adam leaned against the wall, arms crossed. "The whole town's talking about this."

"You think I don't know that?" Ava snapped.

His eyes narrowed. "I had to hear it from Beau. Would've been nice of you to give me a head's up."

"And tell you what? I don't have a clue what they're after." Ava tossed up her hands in defeat. "He wouldn't tell me anything."

"The FBI agent?"

"Yeah." She stopped pacing and took a deep breath, held it, released. A scowl tightened her face at the memory. "Agent Cooper Lawson. Bastard came into the distillery for a tour yesterday, acting like some normal guy. Then he comes back today and flashes his badge in my face with a goddamn warrant."

"So we have no idea what the charges are?"

"None." Feeling her energy waning, she sat down beside her mother and sighed. "And we won't know until Daddy gets home."

On edge, Adam walked to the kitchen, poured a glass of whiskey. He brought it and the bottle to the living room and sat down across from his family. After taking a sip, he passed the glass to Ava.

She accepted it, meeting his eyes. "Sorry you had to find out from Beau. It slipped my mind."

His head dipped in a nod. "I get it. I can be easy to forget."

Ignoring his statement, she drank the last of the whiskey, then refilled it and handed it to her grandfather.

"Thank you, dearie." Joe held it in his hands, giving her a cheery grin. "We'll get this straightened out. Don't you worry."

"How can you be so calm?" she managed. She looked to her mother. "Both of you. You make me feel like I'm overreacting."

Sandra patted her knee. Before she could speak, the front door opened.

Ava's eyes shot to the entryway. Her father came in, set his briefcase down like normal, and removed his coat.

All the words she wanted to say seemed stuck in her throat as she stared at him, going about his routine like nothing was wrong. It took Adam saying something for her to snap out of it and jump to her feet.

"What's going on, Dad?" Adam asked, storming up to their father as he entered the room.

Ava was at his side in an instant. "The FBI? What do they want?"

Ty let out a slow exhale, his eyes tired as he faced his children. He attempted a reassuring smile. "It's just a routine thing. Nothing to worry about."

"Routine? How so?" Ava demanded, wanting nothing more than to wrestle the truth from him. Already it felt like pulling teeth.

"The IRS is concerned I may not have paid taxes on a bit of money. I've already spoken with the attorney and we're in the process of gettin' this cleared up."

"So why is the FBI searching your computers?" Ava frowned.

"They're just looking into the financials of the company to verify where the money went and if there's any other money that went unclaimed on the tax return."

Though she wanted to be reassured by her father's words, Ava couldn't let go of the dread she felt. And though she was certainly no expert, she found it implausible that the FBI would bother with something as mundane as tax evasion. "This is all just about taxes, then? Nothing more?"

"Nothing more." Ty rubbed her back, then faced his son. "I promise."

Adam let out a rush of breath, relieved. "Well, that's good, then."

Sandra smiled and rose to her feet. "See? I told you kids it'd be just fine."

Joe also stood and went to his son, slapping him on the back. "Damn tax man can never take enough, can he?" he joked with a wink.

Ty's gaze drifted to Ava's, and she knew he could tell she wasn't satisfied by his explanation. He pulled her in close for a hug, and she tried to let his presence comfort her.

"Don't worry, baby. Everything will continue on just like normal."

She wanted to remind him that the whole town was already in a gossipy frenzy over the news. In the end, it wouldn't help.

Instead, she'd check in on their little FBI friends in the morning and make sure everything was as it seemed.

THE FIRST thing Cooper did upon returning to his hotel room for the night was open the bottle of 101. He didn't even give it a second thought—he simply twisted off the top and poured himself a shot. He lifted the glass, sniffed, then swallowed.

Ready for the burn, eager for it, he sucked in a breath and let the whiskey warm his insides. It sank into his bloodstream with a hot kick that sent a shiver down his spine.

Feeling marginally better, he lowered himself into the desk chair. He stared at the whiskey, tilting the glass to admire the color of it in the light. It was a vivid, rich gold, much darker than the Honey or Distiller's Choice he'd tried the day before. The 101 was heavier in every sense of the word. And at that moment, he was pleased with his choice. Beer, as much as he loved it, just wouldn't do the trick. Something stronger was needed after the day he'd had.

They hadn't found anything usable on Ty's computers. Not yet, anyway, he reminded himself. Regardless, he thought they'd be swimming in evidence after the first sweep. Instead they were coming up empty and it frustrated the hell out of him.

The Swiss account alone was proof that Ty was hiding something. It was the very piece of evidence that had brought them down to Kentucky in the first place. If they were unable to prove Ty knew the money was being withdrawn by someone in Dublin, most likely Ned Brannon, then the entire case may fall apart. They needed something more substantial to tie him to the Irish side of the family, something like emails detailing dollar amounts or phone calls timed conveniently with the withdrawals.

Cooper knew he had to have faith in his team to find it, whatever it was.

In the next room over, he could hear the faint sound of the football game Marco was watching. Because it reminded him of home, he settled back in his chair and began to relax.

He'd come a long way from the lively streets of D.C. He wasn't going to let anything get in the way of finding the truth. Not even whatever twisted form of guilt he felt for involving Ava the way he did.

Impartiality in a case usually came naturally to him. Never before had he felt the need to protect someone he didn't even know, had no connection to. She was just another case file, an unfortunate bystander in the storm her own father created. Whatever happened to her or the Lucky Fox Distillery was none of his business. All he was allowed to care about was proving Ty Brannon's guilt.

And it needed to stay that way.

He stood and went to the window, pulling aside the drapes. From his view on the third floor he could see much of downtown Fox Hills as everything shut down for the evening. In the wash of moonlight and street lamps, he watched people drift in and out of the local bar across the street.

That was when he saw her. Face lit with laughter, Ava exited the bar and waved goodbye to whoever was inside. Though he couldn't hear her, he imagined her voice in his head, that husky lilt such a warm contrast to the sharpness of her tongue. Keys in hand, she made her way to a blue pickup truck parked on the street.

Her gaze drifted upward, landed on his. He tensed, then lifted his glass of bourbon in a silent toast to her.

The smile she wore faded. She stared at him for a long moment, then climbed into her truck and drove away.

CHAPTER

Eight

She did her best to run damage control. Though it took all her energy to put on a radiant smile and act like nothing was wrong, she felt she pulled it off. The townspeople had their answers, and her employees were confident the issue was being handled.

A little bit of unpaid taxes. Completely accidental, of course. Leave it to the government to overreact and send the FBI knocking to confiscate computers over an innocent little accounting error. Nothing more than a routine search, she'd assured them. The company was doing just fine and soon everything would get back to normal.

It had sounded so good that she almost believed it herself.

Ava didn't want to doubt her father. The rest of the family seemed content with his explanation, so why wasn't she?

Something in her father's eyes had changed, she realized. There was a sense of apprehension in them now that never existed before. The cause of it could have been stress, but what if it was something more?

Shaking off the thought, she parked in front of the Lucky Fox office downtown and cut the engine. In front of her was a white van with the FBI logo and the phrase "Computer Analysis and Response Team."

Irritation rushed over her at knowing tourists and locals alike would witness the FBI's presence at her family's place of business. Nothing she could do about that, she reminded herself. Nothing except save face publicly and hope the storm blew over quickly.

Taking a deep breath, she hopped from the truck. Though she had a key, she decided to knock instead. She wasn't sure what to expect with the FBI rummaging around inside, but planned to weasel her way in to snag some paperwork and get answers.

A dark-haired man in his early thirties with an unlit cigar hanging from his mouth answered, looking like an Italian mobster straight out of *Goodfellas*, suit and all.

Marco grinned and gave a brisk nod, speaking around the cigar. "Can I help you?"

Ava eyed the cigar with a spark of outrage. "Are you smoking in my office?"

"What, this?" He pulled the cigar from his mouth and stared at it, then at her. "It's just for show. You must be Ava." He extended his free hand. "I'm Agent D'Amico. But you can call me Marco."

She accepted the handshake, brows raised. "How do you know who I am?"

"Your picture's on the wall inside." He stepped backward, invited her in. "I love Lucky Fox bourbon, by the way. Big fan."

"Is that right?" She spotted two more agents in the reception area, one working on the secretary's computer and another seated on the floor, organizing stacks of paperwork into piles. Rock music played from a portable radio they'd brought in, and the middle-aged black man at the computer bobbed his head in time with the beat. The agent on the floor—a leggy blonde smacking on a piece of gum—gave her a passing, disinterested glance when she entered.

Ava faced Marco. "For someone who claims to love our product you're sure going out of your way to see we stop producing it."

He held up his hands in defense. "Hey, now. I don't make the calls. I'm just a minion sent to take care of business. It's not personal."

"Not personal to you," Ava replied, resting her hands on her hips. "It's not your company under investigation for tax fraud."

Marco's mouth opened, then promptly shut again. She recognized biting one's tongue when she saw it. Before she could press him on what he was about to say, a voice called out from her father's office.

"Marco, where's that cold cut sandwich you promised me? I'm going to starve in here."

Ava shot Marco a knowing look, then walked down the hallway. She came upon the door to her father's office and leaned casually against the frame.

"Hey, Slick."

Cooper tore his eyes from the screen of Ty's laptop, blinking at her from behind rectangular black framed glasses. "Oh, hey. You're not my sandwich."

"I'm afraid not." She crossed her arms, nodded at the computer. "Find what you're looking for yet?"

"Not yet." He came to his senses and quickly closed the laptop, overturned some of the paperwork sitting on the desk. "How'd you get in here?"

"Your buddy Marco let me in." She tried to catch what was written on the papers he was hiding, but he was too quick. "Is this not allowed?"

"Probably not." He removed his glasses and rounded the desk with a friendly grin. He placed a hand on her shoulder to urge her from the room and back into the reception area. "But since you're here, is there something I can help you with?"

"I just need some of the payroll paperwork." She started for the receptionist's desk, only to have him step in front of her, blocking the way. The agent sitting there eyed her suspiciously before returning to his work.

Cooper chuckled. "Not so fast. While the investigation is going on I can't give you free reign of the office at the risk of you tampering with evidence."

Frustration filled her at the patient look in his eyes, like he was kindly scolding a naughty child. "I need that paperwork or else I can't pay my employees."

"Gotcha. Tell me where it is and I'll get it for you."

She let out a huff of breath and pointed at the top drawer of the receptionist's desk. "It'll probably be with Dolly's stuff."

"Right." Cooper yanked open the drawer, pulled out some paperwork. "This it?"

"Yeah. Thanks." Ava accepted the documents, tucked them under her arm. She watched him carefully, wondering how to go about getting information from him. Since it'd worked before, she settled on being flirtatious. She angled her face up to his and gave him a slow, sugary smile. "So, Agent Lawson, how're you liking Fox Hills so far?"

Over her shoulder, Cooper saw Marco's eyebrows shoot up.

Clearing his throat, Cooper settled on the edge of the desk. "It's good. Nice little town. Friendly people."

"Except that sheriff guy. What's his name?" Marco cut in, snapping his fingers. "Brad. Billy..."

"Beau," Ava supplied with a snort of laughter. "Why am I not surprised he came sniffin' around here?"

"Strutting around is more what he did," Marco recalled. "Came in acting like he was one of us, like he had some right to know what's going on just because he wears a badge. I told him if he wanted to help out he could start by getting me a sandwich from next door."

"He didn't like that," Cooper mused. His eyes met Ava's. "Beat his chest a bit and made a few empty threats, but we got him out of here."

Ava grinned. "Good for you. Here I thought I was the only one brave enough to put him in his place."

"What's he gonna do? Call the cops?" Marco joked, biting down on his cigar.

"So what did you tell him about the investigation?" Ava asked.

Cooper and Marco exchanged looks. Cooper spoke first. "Not much."

"Just the tax fraud stuff and the...what was it again?"

"Nice try." Cooper got to his feet, gave her shoulder a friendly pat. "Look, I know you want answers. You won't find them here."

Ava frowned as he started to lead her out of the office. "So what am I supposed to do, then? Just sit around and wait for you to finish whatever the hell it is you're doing?"

"What you should do is go about your life like normal and forget we're even here," Cooper advised, opening the door for her. His face was serious now as they locked eyes. He reached into his coat pocket and handed her his business card. "If you need anything else, just give me a call. My cell's on there."

She wanted to crumble up his card and throw it back in his face, but withheld the urge and pocketed it instead. "Fine. Goodbye, Agent Lawson."

Keeping her temper painfully in check, she stepped out into the midday sun only to watch it disappear behind a cluster of storm clouds. Thunder rumbled somewhere in the distance and had the hairs standing up on the back of her neck.

Great, she thought. She was no closer to getting answers than when she'd shown up.

On the bright side, at least she could spread the word around town that Beau had gotten his ass handed to him by the Feds.

COOPER WATCHED out the window as she drove away.

"So I guess her old man decided not to tell her," Marco said, twirling his cigar around in his fingers.

"Guess not." Cooper stuffed his hands into his pockets, then spotted the clouds rolling in. "Might get a storm tonight."

A sly grin played over Marco's face. "She's a spitfire, isn't she?"

"Who?"

"That Ava chick."

Cooper gave a half-hearted shrug and headed for Ty's office, not wanting to discuss it. "She's okay."

"She's more than okay. That's a woman who's fine and damn well knows it, too."

Sitting behind the desk, Cooper tapped back into the laptop. Marco followed him into the room, prowling around the office with the cigar tucked between his teeth.

"Her family is indirectly responsible for the deaths of two Americans," Cooper reminded him, slipping on his glasses. His system was on overdrive from having her there, invading his space. He swore he could still smell her, spiced apples and rich vanilla. "And we still don't know for sure that she's not involved."

Marco waved off the thought. "Please. If she knew she wouldn't be trying to get answers out of us. She's clueless."

"Or she's playing dumb so we'll trust her enough to let something slip." He dug back into Ty's emails, scouring for any correspondence from Ned.

"Well, she won't get anything outta me. I can't say the same for you." Pulling the cigar from his mouth, Marco inspected it. "I saw that look in your eyes when she turned up the heat. You like her."

Cooper snorted. "I do not."

"And I spotted that bottle of 101 in your room. I damn well know you don't like the stuff. You want to impress her."

A deleted email from two days earlier caught Cooper's attention. He opened it, read the brief but troubling message, and frowned. "Hey, come look at this."

"What?" Marco skirted around the desk and leaned over Cooper's shoulder. His brows furrowed as he read aloud. "'I know she's with you.' What's that about?"

"No idea." Cooper rested his chin in his hand, tapping his fingers against his cheek. "It's not from one of Ned's known email addresses or his sons', but I can trace where it came from."

"Could be completely unrelated." Marco straightened and folded his arms. "We're looking for money requests and mentions of the IRA. I don't think this fits."

Cooper pulled up the IP address, ran a search on it. "It came from an ISP in Ireland. This might fit more than you think."

"Ned's been careful to cover his tracks before. Why let this one slip through?"

"Not sure. Doesn't look like Ty responded to it, though." Cooper did a search of the address in Ty's emails, came up empty. "He's never received anything from this email before. Think he knew who it was from?"

"Maybe. He went to some effort to hide the email. If he didn't know what it was about, why bother?"

"True." Adjusting his glasses, Cooper glanced up at his partner. "I wonder who our mysterious 'she' is."

"Might not be a person at all. Could be a code for something."

"Or a threat." The thought left Cooper's mouth subconsciously, surprising him. His eyes glazed over as he ran with it, his pulse kicking up. "What if Ned knows we're investigating his cousin? He might have tried to access the Swiss account only to find it's locked up. So he creates a new email account, gets this message over to Ty as a way to acknowledge that their business arrangement is over."

"I guess. But that's pretty obvious, isn't it? Ned knows the shit he kicked up by killing those two Americans. Surely he expected this."

"Or maybe he expected Ty to handle it better. It's only a matter of time before we have concrete proof that Ty knew the money he was depositing into the Swiss account was going to fund the IRA. We'll be able to shut him down and Ned's income stream will dry up. He's got to be pissed. This is his threat telling Ty he knows the FBI is here and to figure it out."

Marco nodded. "Only Ty has no idea what to do. All he cares about at this point is protecting his wife and kids from the backlash."

Cooper let out a rush of breath. "I don't think he'll be able to. Ned'll do whatever it takes to keep that money coming in. He may try and make another contact within the family, start fresh after Ty's arrested. We need to screen the family, see if any of them have allegiance to the Irish side."

"That might be tough to do without revealing what we're looking for," Marco pointed out.

Cooper sat back in the chair and rapped his hands on the armrests. "Depends on how we do it. If I were Ned, I'd go after the young, impressionable ones."

"Ava and her brother."

"Yeah. Though Joe's the only one we know for sure has been to Ireland. Feud or not, we don't know how his allegiances fall in regards to the IRA."

Marco sat on the edge of the desk, tucked the unlit cigar into his jacket pocket. "Let's try something. Reply to that email, let's see if we get a bite back."

"It'll have to be a vague response, since we don't know for sure what the email is about," Cooper began, clicking into the computer. He brought the email back on screen from Ty's account and hit reply. His hands hovered over the keys as he considered what to say. "Maybe, 'What do you want me to do about it?'"

"That works. Try that."

Cooper typed out the message, read it over a few times, then hit send. He sat back and folded his hands behind his head, releasing a steadying breath. "All right. We'll see if we get anything back."

Marco got to his feet. "Give it a day or two. If we get nothing, we'll start bugging the family about the Irish connection."

"Sounds like a plan."

CHAPTER

Nine

As the last guest of the day shuffled out of the visitor's center, Ava closed the door and leaned against it gratefully. A tour bus of winos from California had swept in an hour before closing, their final stop for the day on the Bourbon Trail. Her staff had been accommodating as usual, but Lord had the group tried her patience.

She'd had to explain more than once that winemaking and whiskey distilling were two completely different animals. Other than some types of wine being aged in a barrel, they didn't have much in common. Especially the taste profile, which a few of the fragile flowers had found a bit too "brutal." They'd tossed perfectly good whiskey in the throwaway pot and fanned their faces in morbid horror.

What else could be expected from people whose taste buds were as refined as a cheap Moscato? she asked herself. They wouldn't know a good whiskey if it bit them in the ass.

After waving goodnight to the last of the employees, she went to the tasting bar to clean up a few of the left-over glasses. Humming an old Hank Williams song, she washed and dried the glencairns and didn't notice her brother come in.

"You're here late," Adam said, strolling toward her with his hands tucked into the pockets of his jeans. His mouth spread in a lazy grin, one she recognized as being laced with liquor.

"Had a tour group come through last minute." She placed the clean glasses back on the shelf, then faced him. "What are you doing here?"

He let out a dry laugh. "Why does my presence around here bother you so much? This company's mine as much as it is yours."

"Think again," Ava replied, resting her hands on the bar. "When you don't put any effort in, don't expect to reap any of the rewards. All you're good at is drinking our whiskey, not making it or selling it."

Anger had his brows pinching together as heat flushed his face. "Is that what you really think? That I'm useless?"

Her own temper had words pouring thoughtlessly out her mouth. "What were you doing all day while I was here working? Oh, that's right. You were drinking. Just like you always do. I gave up expecting anything useful out of you a long time ago."

She saw a flicker of pain in his eyes and knew she'd hurt him. Almost instantly it was gone, replaced by indignation. "This is my family, too. I deserve a place at the table. Stop shutting me out and then getting mad at me for keeping my distance."

"How do I shut you—"

"I was the last to find out about the FBI investigating Dad," he argued, approaching the bar cagily. "You didn't see fit to tell me you went to the office two days ago to get answers from those agents. I have to learn all this shit second-hand, usually from Beau, which pisses me off in itself."

"I don't know anything more than you do—" Ava began, only to be cut off by him.

"With the way you and Dad have been acting lately, it's clear y'all are keeping secrets from me. You think I'm too stupid to see it?"

Ava's brows rose. "What the hell are you talking about?"

"You're off having private little meetings with the FBI, and Dad's been shut up in his office for two days and has barely said a word to anybody."

"First off, I'm not having 'private' meetings with the FBI. I went over there to get some paperwork. That's it. And of course Dad's in his office all day. He's having to run the company from home while the main office is shut down."

Adam started to reply, only to turn at the sound of the door opening. Cooper stepped in, donned in a thick black coat against the icy wind. He stared at the two of them, realizing he'd interrupted something. The tension in the room was only perpetuated by the sparks flying off the both of them. He was surprised he couldn't hear it crackling in the air.

"Sorry to bother you…I can come back later if you're busy." He met Ava's gaze, watching her take in deep breaths to soothe her temper.

"No. It's okay, Agent Lawson. Come in." She waved him over as her brother erupted with cynical laughter.

"Not meeting with the FBI, huh?" Adam scoffed. "You really are an awful liar, Ava."

She bristled, but ignored his comment and turned to Cooper in a businesslike manner. "What can I help you with?"

Instead of answering her, he extended his hand to Adam. "I don't believe we've met. I'm Agent Cooper Lawson. I'm heading the team that's investigating your father."

Adam sneered down at the offered hand, but manners had him accepting it. "I'd say I'm pleased to meet you, but under the circumstances, I'm not."

Cooper's mouth twitched. "I get that." He could smell the hint of whiskey on the man's breath, likely fueling the hostility that raged just under the surface. His resemblance to Ava was there in the angular curve of his jaw and the fire in his hazel eyes. He carried himself similarly, too. Like a man too arrogant to know his limitations. "We should be out of your hair soon."

"You better be." Adam angled his head to level his gaze with Cooper's, who was taller by half a foot. "You've caused enough trouble for our family as it is."

Without looking back at Ava, he stormed out of the building. The door swung shut behind him, and Ava stared at it for a moment before releasing a heavy breath.

"He's right, you know," she murmured, resting her elbows on the bar and staring up at Cooper. A tired smile softened her features. "You've really put a wrench in things, Slick."

He approached the bar, settled onto one of the stools. "Just doing my job."

She snorted. "What a noble job, too. Digging through innocent people's stuff to find proof of wrongdoing. How in the world do you sleep at night?"

He only grinned. "Like a baby."

"Mmm. So, you try that 101 yet?"

"Actually, I did."

Ava's eyebrows rose. "If you say it was just 'pretty good' I may have to punch you. And if you say it was 'brutal' like my last tour group, then I'll really have to kick your ass."

He laughed. "I enjoyed it. I toasted you with it the other night, remember?"

"I do." She tilted her head, considering him. "I was busy trying to ease everybody's worries about you. Not an easy task. This town relies on Lucky Fox. If the company's in trouble, people deserve to know. I hope you didn't force me to lie to them."

Keeping his expression carefully blank, he pointed behind her to a shelf holding several bottles of Lucky Fox Irish Whiskey. "I'd like to try that one, if you don't mind."

She followed his gaze, selected one of the bottles. "Well, we're technically closed, but I guess I can make an exception. And since it's been a rough day, I'll join you." Bringing out two fresh glencairns, she poured a generous amount of Irish whiskey into each. She handed him one and lifted her own. "*Lig an fuisce a thabhairt dom ar shiúl.*"

"What does that mean?" Cooper asked, tapping his glass to hers.

A devious grin brightened her face. "It's Celtic for 'Let the whiskey take me away.' It's tradition to toast a glass of Lucky Fox Irish Whiskey that way."

"I see." He breathed in the scent of the drink, then sampled it. It was refreshingly light and floral compared to their selections of bourbon, with a smooth spice that caught him off guard. "Wow, that's good."

She sipped her own, pleased he enjoyed it. "There's a reason our whiskey outsells the Brannon line two-to-one."

"To be fair, I haven't tried theirs. But I'll take your word that this is better."

"The original Brannon recipe has its beauty, of course," she explained, examining her glass in the light. She brought it to her lips again, savored the spicy, flowery aroma and drank. Her eyes fluttered closed as a contented smile warmed her face. "But it just doesn't compare to this. The vanilla in the bourbon barrels perfectly balances with the nutty spice of the barley. And that finish...smoke and honey. There's nothing like it."

Cooper found himself leaning closer, entranced by the scent of her and of the whiskey that coated his mouth. When she reopened her eyes and met his, he watched an awareness come into them. A kind of searching curiosity, joined by a glimmer of desire. It took all he had to remember how to breathe.

Her mouth curved to one side as she went to refill his glass. "More Irish, Slick?"

He nodded, taking a breath to refocus. There was a reason for his visit, and it had nothing to do with enjoying her company. They hadn't gotten a response back on the email they had sent a few days earlier, which meant the next step was to question the family. Though he couldn't deny he found her incredibly distracting. She was dynamic and explosive, smoothed with a hint of mind-blowing sex appeal. How she managed to look so comfortable and yet sizzle like a firecracker was beyond him.

"You ever been to Ireland? Met that side of the family?" he asked, hoping his voice didn't crack. He cleared his throat anyway and fixed on a casual smile.

"I have not," she replied easily, refilling her own glass as well. She let out a relaxed sigh and rested her forearms on the bar, toying with the glencairn in her hands. "They don't like us and we don't like them."

"The feud's a big deal then, huh?"

She nodded. "My grandpa's brother passed away a few years ago. He only found out about it when it was reported in this whiskey industry magazine he reads. His own brother was sick with cancer for five years, and the family didn't even bother to let him know." She raised her eyes to his, her humor gone. "You know what my grandpa said when he read the article?"

"What?"

"Good riddance." Disapproval hardened her face as she knocked back the last of her drink. "He never let go of the hate. God, I hope I'm not like that with Adam."

Cooper set his glass down, turned it in his hand as he processed her sudden change of mood. "Do you two not get along?"

"He frustrates me, is all," she admitted, shaking her head. "He's been given everything in the world and yet he still pisses it away on women and booze."

"But you think he's better than that?"

"Of course I do. He's my brother." Embarrassed by the tear that slipped from her eye, she brushed it away and tried to laugh. "Stupid bastard won't let me help him. Hence why he frustrates me."

Cooper smiled and reached for her hand. She stared down at it, her breath caught in her throat. When he spoke, his voice was kind, patient. Understanding. "I don't know him, but I get the impression he wants your approval. He needs to know you're on his side and that you don't think you're better than him."

"Well, I am at some things…" she began, though she felt childish for saying it. "I contribute to the family business. He goes out and drinks himself to death."

"It's not my business, but maybe you should have a heart-to-heart with him, remind him that you need him around," Cooper began. In his head, all he could think of was how easily Adam could be persuaded by Ned to fill Ty's shoes, if the need arose. He needed to do all he could to ensure that didn't happen. Squeezing her hand, he released it and got to his feet. "I should go. Want me to walk you out?"

A little bit dazed, she looked at him, still feeling the warmth from his hand tingling over her skin. "No. I'll be fine. I still have a bit to do before I leave, anyway."

He nodded, adjusted his coat. "All right. Thanks for the drink."

"Thanks for the conversation." In the soft light, the cobalt of his eyes seemed darker, deeper. Mysterious and undeniably protected. The urge to know what made him tick had her speaking freely. "Next time you'll have to tell me all your secrets. It's only fair, you know."

With a playful grin, he raised his hand in a salute. "It's a date."

He turned and left, whistling to himself. Once the door closed behind him, she let her head fall forward and shut her eyes, damning herself for a fool.

She'd always been a sucker for friendly blue eyes. But this particularly nice pair belonged to, of all things, a federal agent. An agent whose motive was to investigate her father.

She couldn't let herself get carried away where he was concerned, no matter how appealing that goofy grin of his was. Or how nice it was that he actually *listened* when she spoke. He looked her in the eye as an equal. As a person. And though he had no reason to be, he was kind to her. Kind in a way so few people were, with pure honesty.

With a frustrated groan, she poured herself another shot of whiskey and downed it. She'd be ridiculously stupid if she thought anymore about him, she decided. And even more stupid if she let him get her tipsy and talking again, revealing family business he had no right to know.

That was just a recipe for disaster.

ADAM DROVE down Main Street, a half empty bottle of whiskey beside him on the passenger seat. He considered going to the bar, but felt more like being alone. Rolling down the window, he let the night air pour over his face and caress his hair. Yes, alone was better.

On the radio, Johnny Cash's deep, throaty voice belted out the *Folsom Prison Blues*. Adam sang along, tapping his hand on the door frame of his truck.

He leaned over to grab the whiskey, only to slam on the brakes as a stray cat bounded across the road. The bottle shot forward and bounced onto the floor of his truck, out of reach. He cursed under his breath, then spotted a flash of red and blue lights in his rearview mirror.

"Oh, great," he grunted, stashing the bottle underneath the seat. He drifted his truck to the side of the road, flipped off the radio. When he saw it was Beau, he broke out laughing.

Beau came up to the driver's side window, aimed a flashlight in his eyes. "What's so funny, Brannon?"

Adam shook his head, gasping in between laughs. "I just can't get over my shit luck."

"You been drinkin'?"

"According to Ava, I never *stop* drinking," he replied, his humor fading under the heavier weight of bitterness.

"Damn it, Adam, you need to stop this," Beau demanded, his voice clipped with frustrated anger. "I can't have you driving around drunk all the time. You're liable to kill somebody."

"I'm not drunk," Adam retorted, though he tried to focus intently on Beau's flashlight. "What're you doin' carrying around two flashlights like that, Beau?"

"All right. That's it. I'm takin' you in." Beau opened the door of the truck and yanked Adam out by the collar of his white T-shirt. He turned him around to face the vehicle and pinned him against it, digging out his handcuffs as Adam burst into another laughing fit.

Across the street, Brandy saw what was happening and rushed over. "Beau! Beau, wait. Please. Don't arrest him."

"Why not?" When Adam struggled, Beau slammed him roughly against the truck. "Stop moving."

Brandy fumbled for something to say, some sort of excuse. She settled on reason. "Please. Let me take him home so he can sober up. You know he doesn't mean to hurt anybody. He just gets a little carried away."

"If I let him get away with this, it's my ass on the line," Beau told her angrily. "I won't have him thinking he can drive drunk all he wants just because of who his family is."

"He won't anymore. I'll talk to Ava, we'll get him help," Brandy pleaded, already reaching for Adam. She saw his lip was bleeding from when Beau had shoved him into the truck and winced with her own brand of anger. "Damn it, Beau. He's bleeding."

"He's fine." Beau retreated, putting away his handcuffs.

Brandy turned Adam around, inspecting him. Her fingertips fluttered over his face, gentle and soothing. "It's okay, baby."

Adam let out another laugh and spat blood at Beau's feet. "C'mon, Beau. Let's fight. I ain't done yet."

When Beau clenched his fists, Brandy thought for sure he'd take the bait. Instead, he stalked back to his patrol car. He called out to her before slipping inside. "He's your problem now, honey. See to it he stays sober behind the wheel."

Once he was gone, Brandy let out a relieved breath and faced Adam. She wiped away the blood on his lip with her sleeve. "C'mon. Walk with me to my place. You can sober up there."

Adam blinked, focusing on her. She looked so worried for him. "You don't have to protect me, Brandy. I can look out for myself."

"I just saved your stupid ass from getting arrested," she reminded him, wrapping her arm around his waist to help him walk straight. "Without me, you'd be spending the night in the drunk tank."

"Instead I get to spend it with you." He pressed a kiss to the top of her head. "Seems my luck's improving."

She bit her tongue and led the way to her apartment, which was above the local pharmacy. The flight of stairs was tricky, but they navigated into her place and she lowered him onto the hand-me-down plaid sofa she'd gotten from her grandparents.

"There. Now hang tight while I get you some water." She disappeared into her tiny kitchen, leaving him to stare around her apartment. He'd been there before, but not in a long time. Everything was in shades of blue with a quaint country flair, softly feminine and homely. Just like Brandy, he mused, breathing in the scent of her favorite French vanilla candles. Quietly lovely, reliable Brandy.

His heart ached at the thought, bringing a frown to his face as she swept back in, a tall glass of ice water in her hands. She paused, meeting his eyes.

"You feelin' okay?" she asked.

"Yeah," he exhaled, trying to ward off the feelings. He accepted the glass from her and drank greedily, barely noticing as she sat on the sofa beside him. When he was finished, he set the glass down on the coffee table, amused when she swiftly tucked a coaster beneath it.

She looked at him sheepishly, her hands winding together in her lap. "Sorry. Force of habit."

"That's okay." He turned away, rested his elbows on his knees. "Thanks for helping me out. You didn't have to."

"What are friends for?"

He nodded, staring down at his hands. He could hear her softly breathing, surprised by how much it comforted him. She was always there. And he was always making excuses not to take what she offered.

Tilting his head, he watched her closely for a moment. She looked away, uneasy under his stare. Seeing it had him wanting nothing more than to comfort her the way she always did for him. "You okay, darlin'?"

"Yeah." She offered him a reassuring smile, though it trembled around the edges. When he reached for her, cupped his hands around her face, her eyes widened. "Adam, what—"

"Don't think," he urged, taking her mouth in his. Though he could still taste the whiskey that had gotten him into this mess, the flavor of her kiss overpowered it. He delved deeper, his hands drawing back into her length of blonde hair and fisting there, desperate and eager. When she moaned, low within her throat, he felt a bolt of satisfaction course through him. He could feel her giving in, and his own response to it came as naturally as breathing.

Her heart ached and bucked, tormented by the thrill of what she'd wanted for so long. Her fingers clenched over his T-shirt, the familiar blend of whiskey and his cologne filling her senses. The feel of his body pressing her into the sofa sent her mind spinning with need, utterly lost in it. But she knew, Lord, deep down she knew he didn't mean any of it.

And that was what hurt the most.

"Please, stop," she begged, pulling away from him. She straightened her blouse where his hands had lifted it, feeling more than a fool. Tears welled in her eyes as she got to her feet, needing to put distance between them. "I can't do this, Adam. I just can't. I'm so sorry."

He struggled to get his breath, confused by her refusal. When he saw the agony in her eyes, he hated himself for causing it. "Don't be sorry, Brandy."

She hugged herself, unable to look at him. "You can stay as long as you need. I'm going to bed. Goodnight."

Disappearing into her bedroom, she made the painful decision of locking her door. It was more to keep herself from rushing back to him than it was to keep him out.

When she heard her front door slam shut, she allowed the first tears to fall down her cheeks.

CHAPTER
Ten

After a restless night's sleep, it took all of Ava's willpower to slip on her running shoes and sweatshirt and head out into the brisk morning air.

She was too dedicated to her routine to skip a day, no matter how sluggish she felt. Forcing her numb legs to move, she jogged out of the house and along the gravel driveway, ear buds blasting out some peppy Carrie Underwood tune to shock her brain awake.

Soon her body began to heat, pumping blood to her limbs and quickening her breath. The sun broke through the foggy haze, casting an orange glow over the fields.

A popping sound caught her attention, had her tearing out the ear buds to see if it was just a glitch in the music. She stopped running, listened.

When she heard it again, she recognized the sound. Gunshots. Her gaze locked on the shooting range that was only a hundred yards or so away, and saw someone taking aim at the targets. More popping sounds shattered the quiet morning air as whoever it was slammed lead into bales of hay.

She took off at a run again, wondering who it was. As she approached, she recognized her father's crop of brown hair and dusty green jacket.

"Mornin'!" she called out, smiling now as she came up behind him. He glanced over his shoulder, lowering the pistol he'd aimed downrange. He popped out the bright yellow earplugs he wore and placed the gun on the wooden table in front of him.

"Mornin'." Ty's mouth lifted in a smile, though she saw the strain behind it. He looked like he hadn't slept, either.

She nodded at the case of .22 ammo resting on the table. "Blowing off some steam?"

"Something like that," Ty replied, stuffing his gloved hands into his coat pockets. His breath streamed out in a white cloud. "Just had a lot on my mind."

"We all have." Sympathetic, she went to him for a hug, pleased when he held her close. "I feel like we've barely spent any time together. Even with you being at home now, I hardly ever see you."

"It's been an adjustment bringing the business home," he admitted, kissing the top of her head before she pulled away. He gave her chin a light tap, his face softening. "How've you been holding up?"

"Oh, fine." She brushed off his concern, though she wanted nothing more than to share her doubts with him. Her suspicion that he was keeping something from her. "Brandy called me last night, said Beau nearly arrested Adam for drunk driving. Thankfully, she talked him out of it, only on the condition that I keep a closer eye on him."

Ty sighed, shaking his head. "When will that boy learn?"

"I'm afraid until he does something he can't take back, like hurting somebody, he won't," Ava told him, both angry and miserable at the thought. "I don't know how else to get through to him. I can't just lock him up in his room day and night."

"You'll figure something out." Ty patted her on the shoulder and turned away. He began loading more rounds into the magazine of his pistol. "If anything were to happen to me or your mother, I'd need you to take care of Adam. You were always so much stronger than him."

Ava's brow tightened as she came up beside him. "You say that so ominously. Is everything all right?"

"Everything's fine, baby." Ty popped the magazine back into the pistol, racked the slide. He stared at it for a long moment, as if searching for the right words to say. When he spoke, she picked up on a notable sadness in his tone. "You know I'm proud of you, don't you?" he asked, angling his head to meet her eyes. "You've grown into such an incredible woman, Ava. And I love you very much."

A jolt of panic shot through her, unsettled by the words he so rarely said. "I love you too, Daddy. Are you sure nothing's wrong?"

"Yes." He looked down range as the sun crested over the trees. "I've raised you to trust in family, no matter what. But I need you to promise me something."

"Anything." She rested her hand on his shoulder, seeking to comfort them both. He was scaring the hell out of her. "What is it?"

His dark eyes unfocused, as if he were lost in some old memory. "Never try and contact your relatives in Ireland. As far as you're concerned, they don't exist."

Thrown off by his request, she urged him to look at her. "What are you talking about? Have you even met them before?"

"No." He gave her a small smile, then tucked his ear plugs back in. "Just promise me, okay? I'll see you back at the house."

Her lips parted with confusion as he angled away from her, holding the pistol in his hand. He fired at the target, a swift succession of pops that, given the hardened lines of his face, seemed driven by rage. By hate.

For the first time in her life, she looked at her father like he was a stranger. She backed away from him, a million questions racing through her mind. Not knowing what else to do, she took off at a sprint, her speed that of someone running for their life.

COOPER KICKED back in Ty's desk chair, cell phone to his ear. He rubbed his temple, hating to have accomplished so little since arriving in Fox Hills. Not only was it a blow to his pride, it was also a misstep for his career. If he couldn't put all the pieces together, he may never get that promotion that would bring him one step closer to hunting the real threat to U.S. national security.

"We're just not finding much of anything," he explained to his boss, staring at Ty's desktop wallpaper in frustration. It was a recent picture of Ty and his wife, smiling together at what looked like Niagara Falls. "We have on record all the deposits to the Swiss account, found where he filed the transactions in his financials to avoid paying taxes, but it ends there. I can't find evidence proving he gave Ned the account number or the access code to withdraw the money. We're still checking the phone records, but that'll take days. Maybe weeks."

"*What about that email you found? The one about 'knowing she's with you'?*" Assistant Director Ron Horvath asked, the distinct sound of Jersey in his gruff voice. Cooper heard him slurping his treasured cup of coffee, likely his third that day. And, Cooper thought as he checked his watch, it was barely past ten o'clock in the morning.

"We never got a reply back, so I assume if it was from Ned, he's deleted the account or knows we're on to him." Cooper tapped his fingertips on the desk, irritated by the thought. "It was a long shot, anyway."

"Any idea on who the email could be referring to?"

"Nope. Guess we won't find out, either. I figured it was referring to us being here."

"It's possible. I assume Ty Brannon isn't talking?"

"Yeah, he lawyered up the first day. The team's still going through all the paperwork here in the office. We found a box of stuff that dates back twenty years or more, so we're hoping there'll be something useful inside."

"Good." Horvath cleared his throat and fell into a coughing fit, a side effect of thirty years as a smoker. Cooper waited patiently for him to get his breath, picturing the old man in his trademark brown suit, a thin sheen of sweat on his balding head. He'd be digging out a piece of Nicorette gum at that very moment, popping it into his mouth despite how much he hated the stuff. *"Keep searching. And make sure you keep an eye on Brannon."*

"Will do." Cooper said goodbye and hung up the phone, tossing it aside on the desk. He looked up as Marco entered.

"Hey, man. You know that box of old paperwork we found under a ton of crap in the back office?"

"Yeah, what about it?"

Marco's face split in a mile-wide grin. "You gotta come see this."

Cooper jumped to his feet and followed his partner into the reception area, where the blonde agent named

Tracy was busy staring intently at what looked like an old plane ticket.

She handed it to Cooper. "It's a Delta Airlines ticket to Belfast, dated March 1985. It was stuffed inside this old accounting journal." Holding up the black leather journal with its yellowing pages, she gave them a smug smile. "I think you owe me one, boys."

"Damn right we do." Cooper pored over the ticket, astonished by the find. "We'll have to cross reference this with Delta's records, but I'd say this proves Ty Brannon went on a trip to Ireland."

"And just what do you think he did while he visited?" Marco pressed, wiggling his brows.

Cooper glanced up at his partner, a spark of victory shooting through him. "He joined the IRA."

AVA STOOD before the 2006 barrel she and her grandfather had selected, her mind on other things. He removed the bung from the barrel and slipped the copper whiskey thief inside to collect a sample to taste. When he handed her a glencairn filled with the precious liquid and a dash of fresh water to bring out the aromas, he had to whistle to get her attention.

"Ye in there, dearie?" Joe teased.

She blinked, then accepted the glass he offered. "Sorry. Just distracted."

"Well, today's no day for distractions. Give her a taste, see what you think."

Ava smiled and held the bourbon up to the light, noted the rich amber color and approved of its clarity. She let out a breath and closed her eyes before lifting the glass to her nose. Breathing in slowly, she picked up on the oaked vanilla and warm caramel notes first. Taking another breath, she tried again and this time focused on the fruit accents, a subtle cherry with a dash of spiced apple.

Pleased, she lowered it to her lips and savored a small taste of it. As expected, it was honey sweet on the tip of her tongue, dry at the back, with a fiery bite to it that tingled along the sides of her tongue.

She swallowed, then opened her eyes and beamed. "It's perfect. Absolutely perfect."

Joe sipped the bourbon himself, looking equally as thrilled. "Couldn't agree more. A fine selection for Lucky Joe's."

Emotion overtook her as she stared at him, wondering if she dare ask him about what her father had said earlier that morning on the range. Would he have insight into what her father meant when he said she should avoid the Irish side of the family at all costs? Or would he just brush it off, as he did most things he didn't want to worry about?

Knowing he'd choose the latter had her biting her tongue. It was no easy task, but any mention of Ireland was always a touchy subject with Joe. This would certainly be no different.

She only had one other option. If her hunch was correct, then her father *was* keeping a secret from her, something that likely involved their Irish relatives. If anyone would know the truth, it'd probably be the FBI.

Checking her watch, she saw it was nearly three o'clock. She handed her grandfather back the glass. "I need to run an errand in town. I'll be back before my four o'clock tour."

Joe nodded, lifting the empty glass in a toast. "Ye did good, dearie."

"*We* did good," she corrected, blowing him a kiss before racing out of the barrel house.

Minutes later, she pulled up in front of the Lucky Fox office. She wasted no time barging up to the door and giving it a fierce knock.

Marco answered, a Bud Light in his hand and a stupidly huge grin on his face. "Hey! What's up, dollface?"

Ava arched an eyebrow. "First you're smoking cigars, now you're drinking? Do you even work or are you just here to use my office as your party house?"

"Both?" Marco answered, looking sheepish. "One sec, 'kay?"

He eased the door closed and muttered something to the people inside. She heard papers rustling and through the crack in the door saw documents being turned over and covered.

She sighed. "I promise not to snoop around. I just need to talk to you about something. It's about Ireland."

The door flew back open and Marco gaped at her. "Come again?"

She frowned. "It's about Ireland?"

"Oh, boy." He grabbed her hand and dragged her inside, shutting the door promptly behind her. Within seconds she was in her father's office, where Cooper was just ending a phone call. His own beer was wet with condensation on her father's desk.

Cooper glanced up at her, an instinctual smile lighting his face. "Hey, you. Everything okay?"

She only shook her head, easing down into one of the chairs across from him. "I need to ask y'all something. And I need you to be one hundred percent honest with me. Can you do that?"

Cooper sat forward, resting his elbows on the desk. That sincerity was in his eyes again and had her stomach clenching in knots. "I'd never lie to you, Ava. I may not be able to answer all your questions, but I won't tell you a lie."

Though it bothered her to feel tears spring into her eyes, she made no effort to wipe them away. "What's going on with my family in Ireland? My father warned me this morning not to contact them. I need to know why. Are they dangerous?"

She saw the flicker of acknowledgment pass over his face and knew in that instant she'd hit the mark. He glanced up at Marco and the two exchanged a knowing look.

When he faced her again, she found she was holding her breath.

"I gave you my card the other day. Did you look at it?" he asked.

The question caught her off guard. She shook her head, then remembered she'd stuffed it into her coat pocket. She lifted it out, held it up. "No. I still have it, though. Why? Does it matter?"

His face revealed nothing. "Read what it says under my name."

Feeling her patience wearing thin, she looked at the card and read aloud. "Cooper Lawson, Special Agent. Counter-terrorism Division." She paused, reading the last two words over a second, then a third time. Her eyes narrowed even as her stomach did a little flip. "I don't understand."

"In hindsight, it was pretty careless of me to give you that card before you knew the whole story. Then you might've realized that we're not just here looking into your dad's taxes." He managed a dry smile. "I'm a little hurt you didn't fawn over the card at night, thinking of me. But that's neither here nor there."

She grimaced, a spark of heat lighting in her eyes. "What's really going on, Slick? What has my father gotten himself into?"

Cooper released a slow exhale, resigned that it was time to come clean. "We have reason to believe he's been funneling money to his cousin, Ned Brannon, who is a known ringleader for the terrorist group, the Irish Republican Army."

"Also known as the IRA," Marco supplied, his earlier humor gone. Only pity and a quiet seriousness remained in its place. "Some of the money your father transferred out of the country had unpaid taxes on it, which was what threw up the first red flag. The second came when they passed FATCA, which exposed the identities of all foreign bank account holders. We found out Ty had an account with a Swiss bank, and learned there have been withdrawals taking place for several years from the bank's location in Dublin, totaling over one million dollars."

Ava processed the information numbly, unable to make sense of it. Anger bubbled up inside of her, a quick gut reaction in the defense of her father. "This is bullshit. He wouldn't do that. How could he move all that money around with none of us noticing?"

"You tell us," Cooper replied, sorry to see the flare of panic and disbelief blending with her fury. "From what we gathered, Ty manages all of the financials for the company and has for many years now. Do you pay attention to the profits and where they go?"

"No," she admitted, frustrated with herself. "But he's never mentioned the IRA before and he explicitly told me this morning that he doesn't know any of the family in Ireland."

"He's lying," Cooper said simply. He nodded to Marco, who disappeared into the reception area for a moment. When he returned, he handed Ava a clear evidence bag with a ticket stub in it.

She read the faded text on the old plane ticket, her heart pounding in her ears. "This doesn't prove anything," she managed, thrusting it back at Marco.

"It proves he's been to Ireland."

Her hands were shaking as she ran them through her hair. "I don't believe this. I can't."

"It's a lot to take in." Cooper watched her carefully, saw the acceptance begin to soften her face. Her eyes were glassy and unseeing as she came to terms with the truth.

"I need to talk to him," she murmured, already rising to her feet.

Marco caught her, lowered her back down. "Not so fast."

She frowned up at him. "What? Don't tell me I'm not allowed to say anything."

"He didn't want you to know. I believe he has his reasons for that, and if the warning he gave you this morning is any indication, he's fearing retaliation from Ned," Cooper explained. "For your own safety, this conversation cannot leave this room."

"Retaliation?" Her brows shot up. "What is this, Gangland?"

"The IRA is a dangerous group. The only reason we're here now is because they claimed credit for a car bombing in Dublin a couple of weeks ago that killed seven innocent people, two of them Americans."

"Sweet Jesus," she breathed, covering her mouth with her hand. She closed her eyes, her heart aching at the thought. "There's no way my father was okay with the slaughter of innocents. I won't believe that."

"Maybe not. But his money still financed the operation."

One of the agents from the other room called for Marco. He ducked out, closing the door behind him.

Cooper leveled his gaze with hers and attempted a smile. Though he didn't believe what he was about to say, he knew it would comfort her. "Look, I know this all sounds scary, but here's the thing—when we spoke to your dad, he claimed he had no idea the money was being withdrawn from the account in Dublin. It's entirely possible he's innocent and Ned simply found a way to hack into his account and steal the funds. If Ty didn't pay much attention to the account, he might have never noticed. And when he visited Belfast, it's possible he went to meet the family but it doesn't concretely prove anything more than that."

"He could be innocent," she repeated, a shimmer of hope and relief washing over her. "Yes, that's probably all this is. A misunderstanding."

"And if it is, then we'll find out." He stood up and knelt beside her chair, taking her hand in his. She stared into his eyes, letting the calm she saw there soothe the worst of her worries. "For now, I need you to keep all of this to yourself. If anyone asks, you don't know anything new. And I promise you, the second I find out more you will be the first to know."

With her free hand she wiped away a tear that fell, not ashamed of it. Somehow she knew he didn't judge her weakness, not in the face of all she had just learned. "All right. I'll keep your secret."

"Great." He started to rise, only to have her pull him back down. Her eyes shimmered with unshed tears, but the fire was back in them. It relieved him to see her smile, warm and a little bit wicked.

"I should hate you right now, but somehow I don't," she mused. "How do you do that? Convince me you're not the bad guy as you investigate my family for funding terrorism?"

"I'm just out for the truth."

She snorted. "Please. I'm sure there's something in it for you, too. You probably take home a handsome paycheck and drive a nice car and live in some big, fancy apartment..."

He only smiled. "I have my motivations, yes. And they don't involve things money can buy." He helped her to her feet, then eased away from her. He'd been getting entirely too comfortable in her presence. "I'll be in touch."

She pondered his words, the mystery of him growing ever bigger. "I'll see you around, Slick."

She headed back to the distillery, the information she'd learned tucked safely at the back of her mind.

CHAPTER

Eleven

Standing beside the window in the reception area of the Lucky Fox office, Cooper watched the scene outside unfold with mild curiosity. The wind was up, freeing burgundy and orange leaves from the trees. They tumbled to the sidewalks, only to cartwheel across the concrete at the whim of the breeze.

The workday was over, meaning what passed as rush hour in Fox Hills was busy crowding the streets. A scattering of cars cruised slowly down Main Street, those inside waving hello to neighbors and friends as they went. Locals and tourists alike strolled down the sidewalks, dashing into the market for the night's dinner or the bar for a Happy Hour drink. Some had young children, bundled up in scarves and coats. He couldn't hear them, but he imagined their laughter and carefree banter as the families joined together after a long day of school and work.

In D.C., he'd spent very little time observing those around him. The city moved too fast, just like he did when he was in it. Everything was about the destination and not the journey to get there. His job demanded his full attention, leaving little time for enjoying anything else.

But here, in this pleasant little Southern town, he found himself taking time to breathe. Time to really stop and think.

And all that thinking was getting him in trouble.

Ava remained a distraction any smart man in his position would try his damnedest to forget. He was getting too close. Letting himself step into her life as more than just a federal agent. They were becoming something of friends. Confiding in each other, sharing moments of brutal honesty. More so on her part than his, as his walls remained as fortified as ever. But knowing she trusted him enough to show that vulnerability…it was humbling.

Humbling and career-ending, if he wasn't careful.

He couldn't stay away from her, he knew that much. He was too invested, both in bringing her father to justice and in giving her the truth. She deserved to have proof of what her father was capable of, no matter how painful it was.

Though she was still holding on to the hope that her father was innocent. He'd given her that to help ease the burden, but in time she would see the reality of it. The pieces were coming together. They just needed a bit more time.

Behind him, the agents were slipping into their coats, ready to call it a day. Marco came up and placed a hand on his shoulder.

"Hey, isn't that old man Joe?" Marco asked, pointing out the window. Across the street, Joe Brannon walked cheerfully into the pharmacy, exchanging a cheek kiss with a pretty, petite blonde who was just leaving the building.

Cooper made the decision instantly. "Let's go talk to him."

"Right on." Marco clapped his hands and was halfway out the door before Cooper could even grab his coat.

They dodged a few cars on their way to the pharmacy, earning curious looks from the locals. Cooper's eyes swept the room as they entered. He spotted Joe chatting up the white-cloaked pharmacist at the wide wooden counter.

The pharmacist saw them first, his smile fading. He was an aged, rounded man with salt and pepper hair and warm brown eyes that went from polite to disapproving in an instant.

Cooper slipped on a grin anyway, keeping the mood light. "Joe Brannon?"

Joe twisted around to face them, took stock. He nodded. "Aye. Who's askin'?"

"Special Agent Cooper Lawson with the Federal Bureau of Investigation," Cooper began, flashing his badge. He tilted his head to Marco. "This is Special Agent Marco D'Amico. We're in town investigating your son."

Joe puffed up his chest, though his cheery smile remained. "I was wonderin' when ye would be comin' to see me." He glanced over his shoulder at the pharmacist, chuckled. "Can ye believe this nonsense, Gary? Ty's no tax cheat. Typical waste of tax dollars if ye ask me."

The pharmacist crossed his arms, eyed Cooper and Marco. "Ty Brannon is an upstanding member of our community, fellas. I know it don't seem like much, but we in Fox Hills love our whiskey, and we love our Lucky Fox. You come after one of ours, expect a bit of resistance." He paused, his teeth flashing in a bold smile. "Polite, of course."

Cooper bowed his head, acknowledging the warning for what it was—protective, instinctive. And in the man's eyes, necessary.

"Understood." Cooper motioned for the exit. "Mind if we talk in private, Joe?"

"Whatever ye got to say, ye can say in front of everybody," Joe replied easily, cocking his chin. The movement was so very like his granddaughter that Cooper nearly laughed.

"This is really something better discussed in private."

The pharmacist nodded. "It's okay, Joe. Go on ahead. I'll just get your prescription filled."

Joe's mouth twisted in an irritated pout, but he slapped the counter and started for the door. "All right, boyo. This way."

Cooper and Marco followed him out of the pharmacy and to a wooden bench outside the building. Joe took a seat and dug into his pocket for a pack of chew. He popped a chunk into his mouth.

"I'm all yers."

Amused despite everything, Cooper knelt down to level his gaze with the old man's. "Are you in contact with the Brannons in Ireland? Specifically your nephew, Ned Brannon?"

Joe turned his head and spit, a scowl tightening his face. "No. Dead to me, they are."

"When was the last time you spoke with Ned?"

"The lad was nothin' but a child when I left Ireland. Ain't spoken with him since."

Cooper shifted his weight, exchanged a brief look with Marco. When he turned back to Joe, he decided to up the ante with a loaded question. "Do you know what the Irish Republican Army is?"

He wasn't disappointed by Joe's reaction. The man flushed a violent shade of red, fire in his eyes. "Ain't no Irishman hasn't heard of the IRA, boyo. Let's get this clear, I left all that shite behind the second I left that godforsaken country. I'm an American, plain and simple. I have no allegiance to the IRA or to Ireland."

"I figured as much," Cooper conceded, rising to his feet. He adjusted his coat against the chilly wind. "I think we got what we needed. Have a good night, Mr. Brannon."

He and Marco headed back across the street, leaving Joe stewing on the bench. Cooper imagined the old man spitting his tobacco, cursing their names.

"You think he's telling the truth?" Marco asked the second they were back inside the office, away from prying eyes and ears.

Cooper nodded. "Yeah. I do. From what I know about the guy, he's dead serious about this feud. It wouldn't surprise me if he has no idea what his son is up to. If he did, he'd probably blow a gasket."

Marco laughed. "I wouldn't want to be on the receiving end of that guy's temper. That small glimpse of it was good enough for me."

Cooper glanced out the window, saw Joe was gone. "Tempers run hot in that family, that's for sure."

"All except Ty, surprisingly," Marco mused. "The one who actually has a reason to flip out on us is the most calm. The most controlled."

Cooper shut the blinds, faced his partner. "He's leading a double life. Of course he's controlled. It comes with the territory."

AVA ACCEPTED the glass of bourbon from Brandy, catching her friend's eyes across the bar. "Thank you again for taking care of Adam last night. I don't know what I'd do without you."

Brandy mustered up a smile. Though her heart ached, she refused to let it show. "It was nothing, honey. I was happy to help."

"I don't know what gets into him sometimes." Ava took a generous sip of her drink. Even the premiere flavor of their Distiller's Choice couldn't quell her urge to scream. She rubbed her forehead, feeling a headache coming on. "With everything else going on, the last thing I need to worry about is Adam getting into trouble."

"He's gonna be just fine, Ava," Brandy assured her. "He means well. The stress just gets to him."

Ava cast a knowing look at her friend. "I forgot. I'm talking to my brother's serial apologist."

Brandy's face fell. She wiped off the counter, avoiding Ava's eyes. Guilt swam over Ava as she took her friend's hand in hers. "I'm sorry, that was rude. You know how I get when I'm ornery."

"What, am I your apologist, too?" Brandy asked, though there was a hint of humor in her voice.

Ava grinned, relieved her friend was so forgiving. God knew she didn't deserve it half the time. "Hey, if Adam gets a cheerleader, I sure as hell want one."

"You certainly need one these days, sweetheart," Beau said as he sidled up beside her. He nodded to Brandy, who pulled a Bud Light from the cooler and popped off the top for him. Before he raised the bottle to his lips, he grinned. "Word is those agents were talkin' to old man Joe a couple hours ago. According to Gary, they meant business. And when ol' Joe came back from his little talk with them, he was spittin' mad. Whatever they said ticked him off bad."

Though his words had a heavy ball of dread dropping in her stomach, Ava only lifted a brow and returned his sickly sweet smile. "What I heard is those agents kicked you out on your ass when you went nosing around the office. Tell me, Beau, how does it feel to be knocked down a peg?"

A flush of rage and embarrassment colored his cheeks. He took a long pull from his beer before acknowledging her.

"Sounds to me like you're gettin' real friendly with those boys, Ava. Makes a man mighty suspicious when it's *your* family they're investigating."

"What should I do? Tear up the warrant in their faces and tell them to fuck off?" Ava remarked with a cynical laugh. "That'd go over real well."

"They've been here for a week. If it's just tax fraud they're lookin' for, why's it takin' so long?" Beau asked, his voice carrying over the music belting out of the jukebox. Several people glanced over, eager to hear her answer to the question.

Ava struggled to maintain her carefree grin, noticing she had an audience. The foreman from the distillery, a portly man named Ed Barrow, edged closer to her. When he caught her attention, he tipped his ball cap politely.

"We were all just fixin' to ask you that question, Ava. What's going on?" Ed clutched his beer tighter in his hand, his face lined with worry. He had known her since she was a child and had never once looked at her the way he was now. With doubt. Distrust. The cluster of employees hovering behind him looked just as concerned. Seeing it shot an arrow of sympathy and regret into her heart.

"It's like I said before, Ed. There was an accounting error and some taxes weren't paid. That's all." She made a point to look each employee in the eye, ensuring they all heard her. Whether or not they believed was another story.

"Seems strange, don't you think? The FBI coming out here to check on a bit of unpaid taxes?" Beau said, earning a few nods of agreement from the others.

Ava felt the first bolt of panic hit her, and the only defense she could muster was anger. Beau was cornering her into a tight spot, one she knew she'd have trouble digging out of. The truth, unfortunately, was not on her side. And damn him, he knew it.

"Why don't you just mind your own business, Beau?" She jumped to her feet, got in his face. She reigned in the desire to slug him, though her vision hazed red with it. "I've said my peace, explained what's going on. Why can't you leave it at that?"

"Because things just ain't figurin' right, sweetheart." Beau motioned to the others. "You think anyone here really believes you ain't hidin' something?"

Her mouth opened and closed as she fought for a comeback. She'd never been a great liar, and now when it really mattered that she reassure her employees, she was falling flat on her face.

In an instant, her grandfather was at her side, wrapping an arm protectively over her shoulders. His grin was bold and more than a little sharp around the edges. She'd never been so grateful for his presence in her entire life.

"Here now, let's get a round of Irish for the lot of ye," he declared, gesturing to Brandy. He edged Beau out of the way, and, though shorter than most of the men in the bar, commanded the room's attention with ease. "There's nothing for anybody to worry themselves over. Lucky Fox is goin' strong as ever. This business with the Feds is just that, a business matter that's bein' taken care of." Moments later, Brandy handed him a tray of shot glasses filled with whiskey. He took one, passed the tray around. Lifting his glass in the air, he flashed another fiery grin. "Now, I don't want to hear another word about it. *Sláinte!*"

To Ava's surprise, the group followed her grandfather and toasted, a mixture of relief and joy on their faces. She raised her own glass, though her hand shook once as she downed the liquid inside.

That had been close. Much, much too close.

AN HOUR later, she sat with her grandfather at the kitchen table. He poured them both a generous glass of whiskey, not bothering with ice. The golden light above cast shadows over his face, bringing out the lines of a barely restrained temper.

Since leaving the bar, he hadn't said a word to her. The jovial persona he had portrayed for the crowd was gone, as though he'd torched it the second he no longer needed to pretend. With her, he could be honest. And seeing the storm brewing within him, just itching to strike out, alarmed her in ways she never thought possible.

She watched him warily as he tossed back his glass, looking like a man trying desperately to calm down. The last time she'd seen him drink like that was when a good friend of his had passed away unexpectedly, some five years earlier. Then it had been the shock of mortality that had driven him to the bottle. This time she knew it was for a very different reason.

Because it was easier—and safer—she decided to pursue a roundabout route to get to what she wanted to know.

"I wish I could take a baseball bat to Beau's smug face," she said, taking a big gulp of whiskey. She swallowed it eagerly, then breathed out a relieved exhale. Her lips curved, though there wasn't much humor in it. "If only it wasn't against the law to hit the sheriff."

Joe snickered coldly, draining the last of his glass. He refilled it, not missing a beat. "The lad's a bigger whore for gossip than Miss Dolly at the hair salon on a Tuesday afternoon."

"He's more than just a gossip. He likes to instigate trouble. You'd think being made sheriff would've matured him a bit, but he's just the same old rowdy bad boy he's always been."

Joe toyed with his glass. "I'll never understand what ye saw in him."

Ava shrugged. "I was young. I saw this good looking boy with a pickup truck and the Devil in his eye and thought it'd be fun. And it was, for a while. Until the darker side of his nature clashed with the fire in mine, and the blast nearly killed us both."

"Sometimes what we think we want is the furthest thing from what we need, dearie," Joe told her. The thought seemed to quell some of his anger, at least for now. His voice became softer, reminiscent of an easier life, long past. "But when we find what we need, there's nothing better."

His words hit a chord with her. Beau was certainly the type of guy she'd always thought she wanted. Untamed, unpredictable. A wild card with an arrogant streak to keep her on her toes. She had always secretly thrilled in the tumultuous relationships—the Rhetts and Scarletts, the Heathcliffs and Cathys. What she had failed to realize for so long was that they always went down in flames, leaving nothing but ashes behind.

Cooper Lawson was a different breed of man. She'd recognized that from the second she laid eyes on him. She knew better than to hold out hope for a future there, but would be lying to herself if she pretended for one second that she didn't feel a connection. A desire that outshone all practicality, all reason. A need that would surely get her in trouble before this mess was over with.

Lifting her drink to her lips, she eyed her grandfather over the rim. "So was Beau lying when he said those agents spoke with you today?"

A scowl hardened Joe's face. "Aye, they had a talk with me."

She could sense that he was still sore from the conversation. Though it was a gamble, she had a hunch she knew why. "They asked you about the IRA. About Ned."

He polished off his whiskey. He poured yet another before responding. "Told them I couldn't give a rat's ass about either."

Ava's heart clenched. Despite her promise to Cooper not to say anything, she couldn't hold back. Not from her grandfather. "Did they also tell you that they think Daddy's been sending money to Ned for the IRA?"

Surprise flashed in his eyes. His hand shook as he drank. "No. I won't believe it."

"They don't have much proof, just theories right now." She paused, deciding to lay it all on the table. "They found a plane ticket to Belfast from thirty years ago. Did he go to Ireland?"

Joe lowered his head, cursing under his breath. For a moment he said nothing, and her heart sank with each second that ticked by. "He was eighteen. Wanted to find out for himself if there was any truth to all I'd told him about the family, the feud. I didn't even know he'd gone until he was halfway across the sea."

"He just up and left without a word?" Ava asked, astonished to hear of her prim, structured father being so spontaneous. "Did you think he'd come back?"

"Oh, I knew he would." Joe bristled, eyes blazing. He wagged his glass at her, the whiskey inside sloshing around. "I knew he'd go and see the truth. Bunch of radicals, they are. No-good, bloodthirsty heathens."

"So you knew," Ava realized, stunned. "You knew they were involved in the IRA."

"Aye." His temper sizzled, regret seeping in to douse it. His white brows knit together as his gaze met hers. "Me own brother Jack was the first to fall in line with the rebellion. Most of us agreed with the idea of it, of course. But it was the violence I couldn't condone. I left long before the worst of it, the time they called The Troubles, but occasionally I'd hear rumors of what Jack and his sons were up to. Turned the family business into a cash cow for war money. Stayed under the radar just enough to not get arrested, but anyone with eyes could see the truth."

"But you had no reason to believe Daddy was involved?"

"We didn't discuss it. He spent a few weeks there, came home. We never spoke of it again. I didn't want to know what he'd seen and done, and he didn't want to tell me."

She nodded and sat back in her chair. "He could still be innocent. I have to hold onto that."

Joe reached for her hand, gave it a reassuring squeeze. "Yer da is a good man, dearie. If Lucky Fox money did find its way to Ireland, it was likely Ned who stole it."

She let his words give her some measure of relief. "Lord, I hope you're right."

PART 03

LUCKY FOX
Honey

I wish to live to 150 years old, but the day I die,
I wish it to be with a cigarette in one hand and
a glass of whiskey in the other.
~ Ava Gardner ~

CHAPTER

Twelve

Guilt he didn't understand kept him away from Brandy. A few days had passed, and still it lingered. Stuck like a knife in his back, a pain that ran helplessly deep.

In all his young, self-centered life, Adam had never known an ache so distracting.

The truth was, he didn't know what to say to her. What happened between them had been a mistake—an unfortunate byproduct of whiskey and bitterness and a lurking desire he'd been unaware of until that moment. Until he'd felt the warmth of her skin beneath his hands, tasted the honey of her lips. Brandy, like her namesake, was a sweet and generous drink to be savored in slow, tender sips by the heat of a smoldering fire.

In his haste, he'd neglected that fact and tried to take her coldly, thoughtlessly. And in truth, cruelly. Knowing it brought out a hatred for himself he'd never thought he could feel. But there it was, staring him in the eye like a monster in his own image, ready to bring him to his knees.

She deserved an apology. If it wasn't for his pride, he would've offered her one the instant she'd broken the kiss with those tears in her eyes. All that hurt mixed with the flush of passion he'd given her cheeks.

In that moment, he had understood her. Had seen the way his careless hands had curled around her heart and strangled the love out of it, thirsty for the taste but not for the package it came in. How could he have been so blind to it before?

He'd never wanted to see it, he admitted to himself. It had been easier to assume she'd always be there, the faithful friend he didn't deserve. Somewhere along the way, she'd gone and fallen in love with him. And he'd done all he could to convince her to change her mind.

Out of fear, he acknowledged. Out of the damnedest, stupidest fear of losing some part of himself that wasn't worth having. Giving himself to another person was not a task he approached lightly. He wanted no part of the tangled torment of falling in love.

And so he would push her away, like he'd always done. Because he was a coward.

He walked into the bar, knowing she would be going on her lunch break. When he saw her chatting with a patron and refilling the man's whiskey, he felt that knife in his back twist. She'd pulled back her hair into a neat tail, like she often did, leaving strands of her bangs loose to frame her face. The smile she offered her customer drove that knife a little bit deeper.

God, she was beautiful. Why had he never noticed before?

When they locked eyes across the room, he saw that smile fade. She untied her apron as he approached and avoided looking at him again.

He came up beside her anyway, leaning against the edge of the bar. "I'm here to treat you to lunch."

Brandy took her time folding her apron. "That's very nice of you, Adam. But I brought something to eat."

"So save it for tomorrow. Come out with me today." He wanted to reach for her, to drag her from the bar if that's what it took, but pocketed his hands instead. "We need to talk."

"We do?" She looked up at him now, brushing bangs out of her eyes. "About what?"

"You know what." He glanced around, noting a few locals listening in nearby. Irritated, he leaned in closer and lowered his voice. "Please. Don't make me beg, darlin'."

She let out a slow, measured breath. Without a word, she set aside her apron, grabbed her purse and coat from a drawer under the bar, then looked up at him expectantly.

Adam's mouth quirked in a smile, pleased to get his way. "Good. C'mon."

They walked a block down to a sweet little café his mother used to take him and Ava to when they were kids. Inside was clustered with the local crowd, joined by a sprinkling of tourists all crammed into the dining area with its sunny yellow walls and lace curtains. Everyone looked up when they walked in, but he was used to that. He led her to a booth in the back corner, helped her out of her coat.

"Thanks," she settled onto the bench seat, chewing nervously on her lip. She hid her hands in her lap, not wanting him to see them shaking. After days of not knowing where he'd gone to or if they would ever reconcile, seeing him now was like being doused with a bucket of ice water. An unwelcome shock to the system.

He ordered them both some coffee to start while she fixed her eyes on the plastic menu in front of her, not really seeing the words. She couldn't muster up an appetite, anyway.

Adam folded his hands over the table. He stared at her intently, though she still refused to raise her eyes.

"I don't want this to come between us, Brandy. We both know it was a mistake."

A lump formed in her throat, blocking the words she wished she was brave enough to say. Instead she nodded, secretly collecting the pieces of her broken heart.

He ran a hand over his face. "I was drunk, and—"

"It's okay, I understand," she managed, attempting a smile. She was fully aware it trembled and despised herself for it. "There's no hard feelings, Adam. Nothing between us has to change."

But it already has, he realized with a sinking feeling. Lord, it already has.

"I kissed you because—" He stopped when the waitress dropped off their coffee along with a bowl filled with tiny half-n-half cartons. He waved her off, needing to finish his thought. "I kissed you because it felt right, okay? Even though it was a mistake. We're friends—we've always been friends. I don't want to lose that just because we want to fool around."

"Fool around," she repeated, the words sounding vague and meaningless coming from her lips. Before he could think of a way to rephrase it, she spoke again. "I made it clear I don't want to…fool around…with you. If you thought I did or that I wanted something more, I'm sorry. I don't."

It surprised him to feel hurt by her statement. "Really?"

She took her time doctoring her coffee with sugar and cream, stirring it with her spoon. "Really. I care about you, Adam. And I want you to be happy. That's where it ends."

The lie ate away at her, but she sipped her coffee and ignored it all the same.

Adam considered her words, unsure how they differed from what he'd expected her to say. What he'd *hoped* she would say. Surely this was the easier path, wasn't it? She claimed there were no hard feelings and was giving him the out he'd been searching for.

So then why did he feel so goddamn empty inside?

"We've known each other since we were kids. I'd always thought you had a crush on me. I thought I took advantage of that," he admitted, clutching his coffee mug tightly in his hands. The burning heat seared his skin but he didn't care. "I guess I'm happy to hear that's not the case."

"We ain't kids anymore, honey," she reminded him, her lips curving.

"Sometimes I don't feel like much of an adult, either. I guess it shows."

"Your family's going through a rough spot right now." She set down her mug, her eyes softening. "Once it's over, things will get back to normal."

"Will they?" he asked, knowing she didn't have an answer. He frowned, feeling that bitterness swell inside of him again. "Ava's keeping secrets from me. They all are. They think I can't handle the truth of what's goin' on."

"I thought it was just a tax thing?"

"C'mon, you really think the Feds would bother if it was only that?" Adam retorted, letting the resentment that always simmered just beneath the surface consume him. "There's something else going on. I can feel it."

"Why don't you ask Ava? I'm sure she'll tell you," Brandy suggested, taking another sip of coffee.

She nearly dropped her mug when he slammed his fist down upon the table. "I tried that. She lied right to my goddamn face, then lied to the entire town."

"How do you know she's lying?"

He leveled his gaze with hers. "If anyone knows my twin sister, it's me. She's hiding something."

Brandy pursed her lips, hating to have her loyalty split between them. "I don't know how to make this better, Adam. I'm sorry. I have to get back."

She slid from the seat and pressed a quick kiss to his forehead. "Thank you for the coffee. I'll see you around."

He stared after her as she walked away, his breath caught in his throat. He could still feel the warmth of her lips on his skin, and all it did was torment him further.

AVA HAD to hand it to her grandfather. When he spoke, people listened. And not only did they listen, they trusted every word he said. It came from being one of the town's oldest and most beloved members. It also came from being the kind of man not known for talking bullshit.

She wondered if, once the investigation came to a close, the people of Fox Hills would ever come to understand that he had lied to them. Given them assurances he had no business giving. So much of this was out of his control, but he'd stood taller than his five-foot-seven frame and lambasted anyone who dare challenge his assertion that all was well with Lucky Fox Whiskey.

He'd done what she had been unable to do. In her youth and inexperience, she had gotten flustered and let her temper fly. She had let Beau get under her skin, when she should have stood firm and not given credence to his accusations.

Thanks to her grandfather, the gossip had died down and their employees seemed content. The local press had been courteous enough as a favor to her grandfather to not publish anything about the FBI's presence in Fox Hills, which meant the nationwide media wasn't covering the topic either. So far, despite all her fears, Lucky Fox seemed to be weathering the storm quite nicely.

The same couldn't be said for her family. It had been nearly a week since she'd learned that her father had lied to her. He could have had completely innocent, noble intentions, but a lie was a lie and he was her father of all people. They had been thick as thieves her entire life. She had gone to him for everything. For him to not trust her with the truth stung almost as badly as the doubt she held over his innocence.

Despite his promise to do so, she hadn't heard any news from Cooper. She had seen him nosing around town, usually with that partner of his, but he hadn't said a word to her about the case. Just what they were waiting for, she wasn't sure.

Any attempts to question him about it were met with non-answers and quick brush-offs, leaving her frustrated and angry. After every conversation, she'd storm off only to run into him again the next day, a habit that was only irritating her more.

It was obvious that he was going out of his way to see her, whether it be at the distillery or in town when she ran errands. She was starting to notice the looks they were getting, and knew their little "friendship" or whatever the hell it was had sparked a barrel full of rumors. It would be in her best interest, and in the best interest of her family, if she stop socializing with him altogether.

But, damn it, she liked it. She liked him. And it grated on her nerves whenever she felt that little flutter in her belly just at the sight of him. He had no right making her feel that way. It was asinine, juvenile. Pathetic.

Then he'd smile that boyish grin and none of that seemed to matter.

She rolled up to the bar and, because it felt appropriate, banged her forehead a few times against the steering wheel in an attempt to knock some sense into herself. It didn't work, and instead left her with a mild headache. With a groan, she hopped from the truck and headed inside, wanting nothing more than a drink and to dance off some of this restless energy.

The familiar sights and sounds within the bar brought some measure of comfort. Alan Jackson crooned out of the radio about a muddy river in Georgia, putting a bounce in her step. She smiled as she waved to her grandfather and his friends, the group of them huddled around a table playing cards and tossing back whiskey. Laughter blended with the music, wove in-between snippets of conversation she caught as she leaned up against the bar. To her relief, no one seemed to be talking about Lucky Fox or the FBI.

She flagged down Brandy, feeling better already. "Gimme a beer tonight. You know what I like."

"Comin' right up." Brandy winked and dug into the cooler. She removed the cap on a bottle of Kentucky Ale and handed it to Ava.

"Thanks." Ava took a long, eager sip, then set the bottle down. "Lord, it's been a long week."

"Tell me about it," Brandy sympathized, tossing a coaster under Ava's beer. "Why don't you go dance?"

"I might." Ava turned, watching the group already getting rowdy on the dance floor. She tapped her foot in time with the beat, eager to join them. Instead she faced Brandy again, sensing her friend's melancholy mood. "Is everything all right, honey?"

Brandy tensed, then smiled and tucked a few stray strands of hair behind her ear. "Of course. Just tired, is all."

"Hmm." Ava continued to watch her, not believing one bit of it. "You seen Adam?"

Brandy pointed to the old jukebox. "He's over there. With your mama."

"Mama's here?" Ava twisted around, craning her neck to see. She spotted Adam with her mother, the two of them searching the jukebox for the next song. Her brother grinned while their mother laughed, and seeing it brought a twinge of joy to her heart. "Well, I'll be damned."

"She said her book club let out early, so she met up with Adam and he talked her into going dancing," Brandy explained. "Ain't that sweet of him?"

"Yeah. Yeah, it is." Ava started to go to them, only to freeze as Cooper and Marco entered the bar. All at once her defenses rose and her heart leapt into her throat. Cooper spotted her almost immediately and navigated the crowd to reach her.

"Hey," he greeted, his voice raised over the music. For the first time since he'd come to town, he was dressed in something other than his usual business suit. Instead he wore nicely fitted jeans paired with a white button up shirt and a charcoal gray sport coat.

"Hi, Slick." She angled her chin, hoping she didn't look as pleased to see him as she felt.

"Funny running into you here. This is our first time inside. Thought we'd see what all the fuss was about." He motioned to Marco, who went straight to the bar the second he spotted Brandy.

"Why, hello there." Marco delivered his most charming grin as he rested an elbow on the bar. He gave a quick, suggestive nod. "How you doin'?"

Brandy snorted out a laugh, unable to help herself. Ever the professional, she slapped a coaster down on the bar and offered him a smile. "Just fine, city boy. What can I get ya?"

"Your number, for starters."

Ava rolled her eyes. "Oh, geez. C'mon, Don Juan, time to move along now." She pulled him away from the bar.

Cooper faced Brandy, amused as Ava and Marco began to bicker. He held out his hand politely. "I'm Agent Cooper Lawson. That handsome devil over there is my partner, Agent Marco D'Amico."

Brandy accepted the handshake, eyes wide. "Oh. You're with the FBI."

"Yeah." He shifted as Marco squeezed in beside him, having freed himself of Ava. "You'll have to excuse my partner. He left his manners back in D.C."

"Hey now, she's not insulted," Marco shot back. He looked to Brandy. "Are you?"

"Not at all."

"Good. I kept telling Coop we had to come by this place."

Ava reached around him for her beer, accidentally brushing up against Cooper as she did so. She caught his eye as she retreated, pleased he'd noticed. "Whiskey Bent's the best place in town. They serve our full line of whiskeys."

"Oh, goodie." Marco rubbed his hands together and nodded to Brandy. "Get me two fingers of Lucky Fox Distiller's Choice, neat."

While Brandy served Marco his whiskey, Cooper ordered a beer and turned to Ava. "I have an update for you."

She brought the bottle to her lips, trying to hide the flicker of dread she felt. "Oh, yeah?"

"Yeah." He placed his hand on her lower back to steer her to a more private area of the bar. Once there he put as much distance between them as possible.

"Well, what is it?"

"Delta finally got back to us about that plane ticket. They confirmed your father was on that flight, and also found the return flight he booked for three weeks later."

She let go of the breath she was holding, relieved it was only that. "Okay. Well, I knew that already. Did you get anything else?"

His eyes narrowed, but he didn't press her on how she knew. "Not yet. We're still going through his records."

"All right." Out of the corner of her eye she spotted Adam making a beeline for the bar. Her mother was nearby, staring after him with concern. One look back at Brandy and she knew exactly what was about to go down. "Oh, shit."

"What?" Cooper asked.

She practically threw her beer at him. "Hold this."

In two seconds flat she was at the bar, wrestling Adam back from slugging Marco in the face. "Stop it! Not here."

Adam panted, red in the face as he glared at Marco, who had jumped to his feet, ready to defend himself. "He's harassin' her. Damn it, let me go."

"Not until you promise me you'll be civil. Christ, Adam, you're making a scene. Remember what you told me when I wanted to beat the shit outta Beau?"

He gritted his teeth and stopped struggling. "Not worth it."

"Exactly. He's a federal fucking agent. Knock it off." Ava released him, blowing strands of hair from her face.

Adam's fists clenched, but he made no move to strike as he squared off with Marco. "I don't know who you think you are, buddy, but she's off limits."

Brandy's eyebrows rose. Marco simply held up his hands in a peace offering. "Sorry, man. I didn't realize she was taken."

"She's not," both Brandy and Ava spoke at once, earning a fiery look from Adam and an amused one from Cooper.

Brandy excused herself and went to tend customers at the other end of the bar. Ava rested her hands on her hips and shook her head at Adam. "You're such a jackass, you know that?"

Adam scowled, but said nothing.

"What's goin' on over here?" Sandra asked as she approached, placing a hand on her son's shoulder. She turned to Ava, who shrugged.

"It's done, Mama. Nothing to worry about." She kissed her mother's cheek, then motioned to Cooper and Marco. "This is Agent Cooper Lawson and his partner, Agent Marco D'Amico."

"Oh, my." Sandra smiled politely, not missing a beat. "Well, it's a pleasure to meet y'all at last. My husband has told me all about you."

Cooper accepted the hand she offered, charmed by her sunny smile. "Thank you, Mrs. Brannon. I hope we haven't been too much of an inconvenience to you."

"Not at all. I love having my Ty at home with me," Sandra told him. "But I do hope you're nearly wrapped up with what y'all are doing. We have a business to run."

"I know, ma'am. Not much longer," Cooper assured her. He handed Ava back her beer. "I think you left this with me."

"Thanks, Slick." Ava downed the last of it and set the bottle on the bar. "All right. Enough of this bickering and seriousness. I wanna dance. C'mon, Mama."

She started to drag her mother out onto the floor, only to have her resist. "Hold on, now. I'd like to get a drink in me first. Why don't you see if one of these nice agents would like to dance?"

Adam scoffed and Marco looked expectantly at Cooper, who held up his hands. "Oh, no."

Ava's teeth flashed in a grin. Impulse trumped reason as she decided she'd love nothing more than to watch him make a fool of himself. "Oh, yes. It's time for you to get the real Southern experience, Yankee. Let's go."

She grabbed his hand and pulled him with her onto the dance floor, giggling as he nearly tripped over his own feet. He fell into line beside her as the next song geared up and the group around them buzzed with anticipation.

Ava's eyes glittered as she looked up at him. "You ready for this?"

"Not at all," he admitted with a sheepish smile. "But I'm willing to learn."

"Good." She winked, the image setting his blood on fire. "I'm an excellent teacher."

The staccato beat of Luke Bryan's "That's My Kind Of Night" pumped out of the speakers and the crowd erupted with cheers. Ava joined them and instinctively picked up on the beat, kicking her heels with her hands on her hips.

She shuffled to the left, winding her right foot behind her other leg. Cooper followed her, stumbling to try and mimic the steps. He kept getting mixed up, kicking with his left foot when he was supposed to scuff with the right, doing a full spin when everyone else did a half. Then before he could nail down one of the moves, the crowd would do some crazy stomp, clap, and twirl and be light years ahead of him. He'd never been so confused in all his life—which was embarrassing because it *looked* unbelievably simple.

When Ava glanced over her shoulder and saw him staring down at his shoes in defeat, she burst out laughing.

"C'mon, Slick. Watch me now." She hooked her arm in his and led him through it, showing him each move. He started to recognize the beat and the chorus and what moves corresponded with what lines in the song, and soon it began to make some sense. He moved with her, having way more fun than he expected.

Finally getting the hang of it, he smiled down at her, realizing that his arm had somehow encircled her waist. He could feel her body tight against his own, vibrating with that incredible energy he'd come to know her for.

She looked at him as the song came to a close, her smile brighter than the sun. His brain told him to back away, to retreat from the flame that burned hot in her eyes. The rest of his body didn't answer. Instead he felt himself drawing closer, craving that heat.

Ava froze, her face a breath away from his. It clicked in her head then what he intended to do. At first she didn't know what to make of it. Then she decided to hell with it and angled her mouth toward his until their lips all but touched.

"This should be interesting," she murmured. She insisted on keeping her eyes open and on his, wondering if he'd go through with it or not. It became something of a test in her mind, a challenge to gauge just how far he was willing to go.

He came to his senses and pulled away, unsure how he had even let himself get into that position. Christ, what was he doing?

"Ava…" he began, easing back from her so they were no longer touching. The music started up again and the dancing continued, though they remained standing stationary on the sidelines, reeling from what they'd nearly done.

"Forget it, Slick. Bad idea anyway, right?" She waved it off like it didn't matter, but her insides were churning all the same.

He managed a smile. "Right."

"I need another drink." She took off, leaving him standing on the dance floor feeling like a complete fool.

CHAPTER

Thirteen

Her first thoughts upon waking were of her father. She let the confirmation of his lie to her simmer low in her gut, unable to shake the feelings of distrust. Did she even know the man? Or was he living some double life involving their family in Ireland and the IRA?

In her heart she believed him to be innocent, or at the very least the object of a great misunderstanding. But her mind refused to let the nagging feelings of doubt go. The FBI believed him to be guilty of funding terrorism or they wouldn't be there investigating him. None of Cooper's assurances could shake that fact.

So did that make it true? Had he spent the better part of her life hiding this from her? And if so, what would happen to him once the FBI had proof?

What would happen to Lucky Fox?

Tears sprang into her eyes at the thought, spawned by both fear and anger. How dare he jeopardize everything they had? And for what? For a cause in a faraway land they had no business fighting for?

None of it made any sense. Which was why her heart still tugged at the love she had for him, no matter what the evidence suggested. She loved him, and if he was innocent, then she'd fight to the death to prove it.

The key word being, *if*.

Rolling out of bed, she tugged on her fuzzy white robe and made her way into the kitchen. Despite it being Saturday, her mother was up bright and early preparing breakfast. Ava breathed in the scent of freshly brewed coffee and biscuits baking in the oven, her stomach growling in anticipation. From his bed by the fireplace, Remy perked up with a doggy grin.

Sandra turned and spotted her. "Morning, sunshine. Coffee?"

"Please." Ava nodded before collapsing into one of the bar stools at the island. Remy danced up to her, licking her hand affectionately.

Her mother poured a cup and brought it to her, knowing she liked it black. "Looks like you had fun last night."

Because her thoughts immediately drifted to Cooper, Ava frowned. "Yeah. It was okay."

"Those agents were nice. Given the circumstances, of course."

"Mmm." Ava sipped her coffee, not caring that it burned her tongue. Her eyes closed as she savored the hit of caffeine.

"That tall one is quite handsome."

The twinge of frustrated longing Ava felt only soured her mood further. "He's a pain the ass is what he is. Everything was going great before he showed up."

"Now honey, he's just doin' his job," Sandra chided her, turning as the timer rang announcing the biscuits were ready. She removed them from the oven and placed them on a rack to cool. "Soon the truth will be out and everything will be just fine. You'll see."

Unnerved by her mother's words, Ava's fingers tightened over her coffee mug. As far as she knew, her mother had no knowledge of the IRA or Ty's supposed connection to it. "You say that like you know what they're looking for."

Sandra lifted a shoulder casually, stirring the gravy cooking on the stove. "I know your father is an honorable man. Whatever it is they believe he's done regarding those back due taxes or what have you will get cleared up in time. Have faith, Ava."

"I'm trying," Ava admitted, her breath caught in her throat. She attempted to swallow it down with another sip of coffee, wishing to God she was as oblivious as her mother. Then again, she'd sought the truth, hadn't she? It wasn't in her nature to let things lie.

A flash of sunlight reflecting off of metal bounced across the ceiling. Sandra looked outside the kitchen window as Remy let out a throaty yowl and scampered to the door. "Looks like we may have some guests for breakfast."

"What? Who?" Ava jumped up and went to the window, spotting the black sedan outside. When Cooper and Marco stepped out into the morning light, her chest tightened uncomfortably. "Shit. What do they want now?"

Before her mother could make it to the front door, Ava flung it open and faced the two agents who stood on her front porch. Remy hovered beside her, a cheerful bark erupting out of him.

Marco immediately knelt down to greet the dog, a big grin on his face. "Hey, buddy!"

Ava folded her arms and leaned against the door frame, one eyebrow lifting as she leveled her gaze with Cooper's. "Mornin'."

Cooper froze, taken aback by the sight of her clad in a big fluffy robe that slipped sexily off one of her shoulders, revealing the thin strap of nightgown beneath. Her waves of red hair were in disarray, a look that should have made her less appealing but instead had him itching to run his fingers through it.

He cleared his throat. "Morning. We need to speak with your dad."

Ava's eyes shifted from Cooper to Marco, then back again. "Why?"

"You know why." Sympathy flashed over Cooper's face and only pissed her off more.

She straightened, wishing she had the ability to slam the door shut in their faces. Since she knew that would only cause problems—and likely upset her mother—she backed up to welcome them inside.

"I'll let him know you're here."

They followed her into the kitchen, Remy trotting alongside them. Sandra greeted them with a bright smile. "Would you boys like some coffee?"

"Yes, ma'am." Marco gave a grateful nod while Cooper watched Ava walk through the living room and down the hallway. He noticed her mother staring at him and felt a flush creep up his neck, thankful when she only offered him a knowing smile before grabbing their coffee.

Ava knocked on the door to her father's office, resting her hand over the painted wood. When he called her in, she opened it slowly and leaned inside.

Seeing him standing at the window with his back to her had her hesitating. He looked very much like a man with the weight of the world on his shoulders. Perhaps he was.

"The FBI guys are here to talk to you."

Ty nodded, but didn't turn. "Bring them back."

Ava chewed on her lower lip, wanting nothing more than to confront him about his lies then and there. Fear over what he'd say to her—fear that he'd only lie again—prevented the question from leaving her lips.

"Is everything okay, Daddy?"

He still didn't turn. "Everything's just fine, baby."

"I can send them away if you want. You should really call your lawyer before you speak to them, anyway."

Ty sighed, bowing his head. She saw his hands tighten into fists at his back, then release. "Please don't interfere, Ava. This does not involve you."

"Of course it does, how can you say that?" she demanded, offended by his statement. "I'm the one having to go around town making excuses for you. If you would just tell me what's going on, I—"

He tilted his head toward her, his expression hard as stone. "Just bring them in."

Her mouth snapped shut as angry tears filled her eyes. He was looking at her the way he used to when she'd argue with him as a teenager—all stern disapproval and icy resolve. What she had done to deserve such treatment now was beyond her.

"Fine." She whirled around, eager to get away from him before she said something she would regret. Marching back into the kitchen, she nodded to Cooper and Marco. "He'll see you now."

Before they could reply she disappeared into her own room, desperate for a hot shower.

COOPER LED the way into Ty's office, Marco shutting the door behind them. They faced the man with tension sparking in the air.

"Please, sit." Ty gestured to the two chairs in front of his desk as he sat behind it.

They followed his lead, but didn't relax. This wasn't going to be an easy conversation, Cooper knew. But it was a necessary one.

"Well?" Ty asked, leaning back in his seat. Impatience hardened his features and drew frown lines around his mouth. "What do y'all need now?"

Cooper reached into his coat pocket and pulled out a photocopy of the ticket stub they had found. He placed it on the desk and slid it toward Ty. "Do you recognize this?"

Ty glanced at the paper briefly, nodded. "Yes."

"So you acknowledge that you went to Belfast in 1984 and met your cousin, Ned Brannon?"

With a long exhale, Ty tossed up his hands. "Okay. Yes, I did. I was eighteen, wanted to meet the people my father claimed to hate so much. Turns out they were just as crazy as he'd always said they were."

"Then why'd you spend three full weeks out there?" Marco asked. "And before you deny it, Delta confirmed the date of your return flight to the States."

"What difference does it make how long I spent in Ireland? I toured the area, met most of the family, saw the sights."

"You make it out to Dublin?" Cooper's eyes met Ty's, cobalt into near black. He noted the flicker of anger and recognition that passed in the other man's gaze, meaning he'd hit the mark.

"If you're thinking I went in to set up the Swiss account, you're wrong. I didn't open it till years later. Surely you know that already."

"Right. But Ned could've showed you the bank, given you instructions for the future on how to get him the money without anyone noticing. Wire transfers leave a paper trail. With the Swiss account all Ned would need was the account number and the code and no one would ever be the wiser."

Ty's face flushed. For a long moment, he said nothing. When he spoke again, his voice was cold. Ice cold. "Seems you boys have it all figured out, don't you? Why don't you just arrest me then?"

Cooper shook his head. "Most of this is circumstantial, Mr. Brannon. But I guarantee we'll find the proof we need. It may take days, weeks, maybe even months. Do you really want us disrupting the lives of your family members for that long? You can save them all a lot of trouble if you simply cooperate."

"Cooperate." Ty drew out the word, dark amusement flavoring his voice. "Gentlemen, I've been doing nothing *but* cooperatin' with the FBI. I've let you into my home, let you tear apart my place of business, interrogate my family. How much more am I supposed to give?"

Marco's brows rose. "How about the truth, Ty."

Ty snickered and spun his chair to the side so he could look out the window. "I can't wait for y'all to realize just how fruitless this little investigation of yours is."

Cooper exchanged a confused look with Marco, who only shrugged. Realizing they had hit a dead end, Cooper tucked the copy of the ticket stub back into his pocket and rose to his feet.

"Suit yourself, Mr. Brannon." Before they left, he turned once more to Ty. He wasn't sure what made him think of it, but instinct had him asking the question. "You received an email several days ago from an ISP in Ireland. It said, 'I know she's with you.' Any idea what that's about?"

Ty tensed, but refused to meet his gaze. "No."

"Was it from Ned?"

"Y'all are the FBI. Shouldn't you be able to figure that out?"

Cooper caught the sarcasm in the man's tone. It only made him more certain that Ty was lying.

"We'll be in touch." They exited the office, not any closer to finding the truth than when they had arrived.

"Can you believe that guy?" Marco murmured, jerking his head back toward the office as they headed down the hall.

"I can't get a good read on him," Cooper admitted. "This is the rudest he's been to us, but he seemed more annoyed than afraid. If he was guilty and we were getting close to proving it, wouldn't you think he'd be shaking in his boots?"

"Maybe he's a better liar than we thought."

"Or maybe he knows something we don't. Something that changes everything."

On their way to the kitchen, Ava suddenly appeared from one of the bedrooms, freshly showered with her hair towel-dried and damp. There was a warm flush to her cheeks that only brightened upon running into them.

"Oh. You're still here," she grumbled, crossing her arms over the plaid shirt she'd thrown on. She'd paired it with faded jeans and boots, looking ready to head down to the distillery and get to work.

Cooper nodded. "We're on our way out."

"Good." She shifted her weight, her eyes darting between the two of them. "Did you get what you need from my father?"

"No," Cooper replied honestly. He rubbed the back of his neck. "Not really."

Her mouth twisted in a sneer. "He's in a bad mood today. Glad to see I'm not the only one who got the brush off from him."

Marco chuckled. "If that's what you want to call it." His gaze shot to the kitchen, where Sandra was spooning a ladleful of gravy over a steaming biscuit. "Oh, man."

Ava saw what he was fawning over and rolled her eyes. "We're not doing this. You're leaving."

"But…food." Marco pouted, already edging away from Ava to try his luck with Sandra. It only took a hopeful grin for her to serve him, ever the gracious hostess.

That left Ava and Cooper standing in the living room, awkward and uneasy. She glanced up at him, motioning for the kitchen. "You might as well go have some too. Looks like you're staying."

"I already ate. But thanks," he told her, stuffing his hands in his pockets for lack of something better to do with them.

She nodded. "All right, suit yourself. I gotta get to work."

"Ava, honey, why don't you and Agent Lawson have some breakfast before it gets cold?" Sandra offered, setting plates full of scrambled eggs, biscuits, bacon, and country potatoes on the dining table.

Ava sighed. "I'd love to, Mama. But I really should get to the distillery."

"It's Saturday. You don't have a tour till this afternoon," Sandra reminded her, refilling Marco's coffee mug.

Marco scooped up a bite of biscuit slathered in gravy and groaned. "Oh. Oh, Coop. Come try this. Seriously."

Cooper's mouth twitched. "I'm good."

"Well, if y'all aren't hungry, why don't you show Agent Lawson around?" Sandra said to Ava, a sweet smile on her face.

Ava grimaced. "Why?"

"Manners, Ava."

Ava bristled, realizing exactly what her mother was doing. Damn it, it was hard enough trying to keep herself in check when it came to Cooper without her mother's interference. Why she was forcing the matter puzzled her. If anything, getting closer to Cooper Lawson would only lead to disaster. She was sure of it.

Then again, if she had a few moments alone with him she could probably goad him into telling her what he had discussed with her father. If there was any new information, she wasn't going to find out about it with her mother in the room.

"Okay, Slick. C'mon." She started for the front door, leaving him to follow.

"Where are we going?" he asked, catching Marco's eye as he passed. His partner had a stupid grin on his face that he knew had nothing to do with the breakfast he was devouring.

"Around." Ava stepped out into the light of morning, enjoying the crisp chill to the air that tickled her face. She breathed in the scent of sassafras and morning dew, grateful to be out of the house.

Cooper closed the door and came up beside her, keeping a careful distance. "You okay? You seem upset."

"Yeah, I am upset," she said flatly, turning her face up to his. "But you're gonna help me fix that. Let's go."

"I am?" He watched her hop down the front porch steps and head for the four-wheeler. She slipped in behind the wheel and waved for him to join her.

"Hurry up. I ain't got all day."

Eyebrows raised, he joined her and once again gripped the side bar, still unused to riding around in something so exposed.

She pulled out onto the gravel road and headed for the loop that traced the edges of her family's property. She didn't have a specific destination in mind. Only a goal.

For a few minutes, they rode in silence. He stared out at the beauty of the countryside, while she worked over what she wanted to say. She had to come clean about how she felt. She had to put her foot down to make sure it didn't get out of hand. And she damn well had to find out what her father had said to him.

"Last night was stupid," she blurted out, her heart choosing to begin there. It was both harder and easier than the topic of her father. At least this she could control.

"How so?"

Her eyes shot to his, burned. "You almost kissed me. What the hell were you thinking?"

"I did?" he asked, an easygoing amusement in his voice. Inside, his heart rioted. "You dragged me onto the dance floor and we got a bit close, but I had no other intentions, Ava."

"Bullshit." Her temper flared now, hot and frustrated. She had to watch the road, both out of necessity and to gather her wits. "You leaned in, and God help me, I encouraged it. Don't they have codes of conduct at the FBI? Or do you just not care if you break the rules?"

His smile faded, troubled by her words. "Nothing—and nobody—is worth jeopardizing my job."

"Funny, because you and Marco don't seem to take any of this too seriously," she fired back. She threw up her hands, exasperated with herself. "See? Y'all have me calling you by your first names now, too. This is ridiculous. I don't know what the hell has gotten into either of us."

But she did know. And she hated herself for it.

"Look, I don't know what you think the FBI is like in real life, but we're just people," Cooper reminded her. "We're not mindless drones. We can be nice, we can help people, we can laugh. I'm sorry if I gave you the impression that there was more to it than that."

"Oh." She let out a sharp laugh and shook her head. "So this is *my* fault now."

"I didn't say that."

"Sure you did. You're saying I'm delusional for feeling this way when you look at me the way you do and hold my hand and nearly kiss me on the dance floor in front of all those people? So what does all that mean, then, if you don't want me?"

His mouth fell open, no words coming to his mind. Frankly, he was speechless. Not want her? Christ, he'd spent the better part of his time in Fox Hills trying *not* to want her. And so far, he'd failed miserably.

She glanced over at him, her pride preventing her from backing down. No matter how much his response might hurt, she needed to hear it. "Well?"

A stony resolve came over his face. "Pull over."

She snorted. "What? You want out?"

"I want you to pull over."

"What happens if I don't?" she challenged, a spark lighting in her eyes. "Big, important FBI agent. You gonna point that Glock at me?"

"Not unless you give me a reason to."

The intense look he gave her sent off all kinds of mixed signals in her brain. Part of her was delighted, the other part just a little fearful. One of her eyebrows slid up. "You mean ignoring a direct order isn't reason enough?"

"Nope. But I'll ask again, nicer this time. Please pull over."

"Fine." She stepped on the brake and eased the four wheeler to a stop. Before she could say anything, he had hopped out of the vehicle and rounded to her side. She looked up at him. "What's going on?"

"Get out."

"Why?"

"Please."

"Oh, well, in that case..." she sneered, climbing out and to her feet. She squared off with him, hands on her hips. "Now what?"

"Don't speak, just listen." He took a deep breath, needing to collect his thoughts. His sanity. The electricity jumping off of her had his head spinning, making it hard to think. "I should've never gone to the distillery that day and spoken to you under false pretenses. That was my first mistake. I also should've been less of a friend to you and more of a federal agent. That was my second mistake. But I can't take those two things back now. All I can do is try and make up for them."

"How?" He looked impossibly calm and resolute, a sharp contrast to her own raging storm.

"By clarifying an important detail." A small, edgy smile teased his lips. "Plus, I'm just dying to know if it's as good as I think it'll be."

He cupped the back of her neck and dragged her mouth to his, the kiss unapologetic and searching. Drowning in the taste of her, in that hot lick of fire, he pulled her in until their bodies molded together and he could make out every curve.

She ignited against him, like a freshly lit firecracker that had just been itching for a reason to burn. He changed the angle of the kiss, needing to satisfy this desire to know every inch of her. He wasn't disappointed. She was every bit the firestorm he had been hoping for.

Though she had anticipated the kiss, even welcomed it in some dark, twisted part of her brain, nothing could have prepared her for the reality of it. He was a world of contradictions. Powerful, yet smoothed by tenderness. Coolly aware, yet driven by a heat she had never expected. And worst of all, he was at the same time so very right for her, and so very wrong.

Because she knew it would torture him, she eased back, nipping his lower lip as she did so. Her eyes slowly opened and met his, pleased to see he was just as unsettled as she.

"Should I repeat myself and say that this is a huge mistake?" she asked, her voice a husky murmur. Her hands were clenched around the lapels of his suit jacket, holding him in place. If she let go, she would have to relinquish the warmth he offered. The comfort. She didn't have the strength to part with it yet.

He exhaled, struggling to clear the fog from his brain. "I think we're past that realization."

"So what happens now?"

"I don't know." He brushed aside strands of copper hair that had fallen over her forehead, his hand lingering just below her jawline. "This doesn't change anything. I still have a job to do."

"And I still have a family to defend." She stepped back now, hugging her torso in an attempt to ward off the cold. She shook her head, her gaze unseeing as she processed everything. A cynical half-laugh bubbled out of her. "I swear, I have the worst taste in men. There must be something wrong with me."

"Gee, thanks," Cooper replied, though he was smiling now. When she looked up at him, he shrugged. "If circumstances were different, I think we'd be a pretty good fit."

The first arrow of regret hit her, right in the heart. "Yeah. I think we would. But things aren't different. And they won't ever be."

He nodded, having nothing else to say.

"Let's get back. Mama will be worried about us." Ava turned and settled into the four-wheeler, hiding her shaking hands from him.

When he sat beside her, she spoke again. "Now that that's over with, what did my father say to you?"

"He admitted to going to Ireland and seeing Ned. He also admitted to visiting Dublin. We think Ned instructed him on how to open the Swiss account."

"Damn." Ava sighed. "And here I was, praying he'd only told me one lie."

They pulled up to the house and parked. Ava hesitated, her eyes scanning the man beside her. Cooper offered her a smile, but even with his careful mask she could see he was torn between what *felt* right and what *was* right.

"It's probably best if we put some distance between us," she told him, trying to be reasonable, to make the mature choice. "As much as I enjoyed what just happened, we both know it's a bad idea."

"I agree." He avoided her gaze, focusing straight ahead. "When this is all over with, I hope there won't be any ill will between you and me."

She frowned. "I guess that all depends on how this investigation plays out, Slick. If I lose everything I have, don't expect me to forgive and forget. In the end, this comes between us whether we want it to or not."

Before he could respond, Marco emerged from the house, patting his stomach happily. "There you guys are. Ready to hit the road, Coop?"

Cooper unfolded himself from the four-wheeler. "Sure." He glanced over his shoulder at Ava, his face revealing nothing but polite interest. Any hint of the man who had just swept her into a heated kiss was gone, replaced by the federal agent with the kind blue eyes. "Thanks for the ride."

"Don't mention it." She rested her arm on the steering wheel, trying to look unaffected by what was happening. Remorse was tearing her heart to pieces, and seeing him looking so nonchalant only made it worse.

Cooper followed Marco to their black sedan, trying his best not to look at her. His partner started the car, mouth still spread in an idiotic grin.

"So, what'd you and the lovely Miss Ava talk about on your little drive?" Marco pried as they headed back to the Lucky Fox office.

"To be honest, there wasn't much talking involved." Cooper stared out the window and sighed. "This is going to cost me my career, I just know it. And you don't even care. In fact, you're encouraging it. Some friend you are."

Marco waved off the comment. "What, you think you're the first agent to have the hots for someone involved in a case? It's not like we're investigating *her*, anyway. Once we wrap up here, you'll be free to pursue her all you want."

"I shouldn't be pursuing her regardless. We don't even live in the same state," Cooper reminded him, shaking his head with a half-laugh. "But damn, she complicates things."

"Beautiful women often do, pal."

They drove in silence for a while, each lost in their own thoughts. Cooper's mind shifted from his confrontation with Ava—because, really, it could hardly be called romantic—to Ty Brannon. The man was hiding something other than his allegiance to the IRA and his cousin. Something big, something crucial. And until he found out what it was, he had a feeling they would be doing circles around this case without ever cracking it wide open.

Feeling the need to talk it out, he faced his partner. "Ty played ignorant on that email, but I think we can agree he's lying."

Marco nodded. "Yep. It's safe to say that email was from Ned."

"But what does it mean? Or rather, what does 'she' mean?" Cooper wondered, the wheels of his mind turning over what Ty had said. "Is that just code for the FBI like we assumed or are we missing something else entirely?"

"I don't know." Marco pulled onto Main Street, the sidewalks just beginning to fill with tourists on their way to breakfast. "He doesn't think we'll find enough to convict him, though, which makes me want to work harder just to prove him wrong."

"I agree. But we didn't come all the way down here just to fail. We know he's guilty. What we need to find is proof that Ty gave Ned the ability to access the Swiss account and withdraw funds. Once we have that, we can nail him to the wall."

"Well, like Ty mentioned, he didn't open the account until a few years after his trip to Ireland and the withdrawals have only been occurring for the last fifteen or so from that particular branch. Without a record of a phone call or email between them—neither of which we've been able to find so far—I don't know how else we can prove it."

"And he's not going to confess," Cooper grumbled, feeling frustrated. "We've scoured his office, his files, and all we have is that damn email and the plane ticket which only proves he met with Ned."

"Might be time to call up Horvath, see what he thinks we should do," Marco suggested, parking the car outside the Lucky Fox office.

Cooper reached for his cell phone. "Good idea."

They went into the office as Cooper dialed his boss's number. As it rang, he put it on speaker and took a seat at Ty's desk.

When Horvath picked up, sounding grumpy at being awoken on a Saturday morning, Cooper smiled. "What do you mean you don't work weekends? You just leave that to us minions, huh?"

"When you're on top of the heap like I am, you can have some days off," Horvath replied, erupting in a throaty cough. When he had alleviated it with what Cooper suspected was coffee, he continued. *"What'd Brannon have to say about the plane ticket?"*

"Very little. In fact, that's why I'm calling..." Cooper sat back in the chair and rubbed his face. "We've gone through practically everything. All his computer files, the boxes of paperwork here in the office, phone records, emails...I can't find any record of Ty giving Ned the account number or the security code for the Swiss account."

"It's possible he provided both in a letter that was mailed," Horvath said. *"If so, we won't find record of it."*

"Right. He keeps claiming he had no idea the money was being withdrawn from the branch in Dublin, but I find that hard to believe. How does a million dollars go missing without a business man like Ty Brannon noticing?"

Horvath grunted in agreement.

Cooper sighed. "I'm starting to think we're not going to find anything useful here. It may be time to pack it in and keep an eye on Ty to see if he contacts Ned in the future."

"I need you to stay in Fox Hills a bit longer, kid. I won't authorize your return just yet."

Cooper's brow furrowed. "But we've been here a couple of weeks now. If there's nothing else to find—"

"*There is.*" Horvath's voice took on the deep, authoritative tone he got when he was putting his foot down. "*Ned is a very real threat. We have to maintain our presence in Fox Hills.*"

"But he's on the SDU watchlist. It's not like he can fly on over here. And even if he could, why the hell would he? He probably knows Ty's being investigated. He wouldn't even make it out of the airport."

Horvath released a long, unsteady breath. For a moment he was silent, as though he were deciding what to say. "*Look, kid, Ned doesn't give a damn about the FBI investigating Ty. He only has one motive, and it's an angle we're hoping to take advantage of. In order for everything to go to plan, you have to stay on top of the Brannons.*"

"What's his motive? I don't understand." Cooper sat up as Marco came into the room, having heard Horvath's words on speaker. He shrugged at the confused look his partner gave him.

"*Just do what I said. Keep searching through Brannon's files and keep a low profile until you hear otherwise from me. Capisce?*"

Cooper frowned. "All right."

After he hung up the phone, he stared at Marco in bewilderment. "I was right. There is something we're missing. And if what Horvath said is any indication, whatever it is, it's a big fucking deal."

"So what are we gonna do about it?" Marco asked, sitting down across from him.

"Stay put. Keep our heads down. Await further instruction." Cooper tapped his hands on the desk, feeling restless. "Something tells me this is bigger than you and I. This goes higher up."

"Well, I guess we'll find out, won't we?"

AVA COULDN'T sleep. She'd done her best to force it, but all she had been able to do was toss and turn and curse the memory of Cooper's mouth on hers. The thrill of it still lingered, aching deep within her no matter how hard she tried to ignore it.

Despite the unanimous decision to maintain their distance from each other, she knew it wasn't going to happen. Until he returned to DC—hopefully not having destroyed Lucky Fox in the process—they were going to be involved. Maybe not romantically, but professionally. And though her emotions were already at the forefront, he seemed to be keeping his meticulously in check. How he could go from kissing her senseless to coolly indifferent in one fell swoop was beyond her comprehension. As much as she wanted to rule her life with reason, she was too honest with herself to deny what felt natural. What felt right. And kissing him, as big of a mistake as it was, was something she desperately wanted to do again.

The fact that she knew she couldn't—and shouldn't—give in to the temptation made it all the more appealing.

Irritated with her own weakness, she got out of bed and padded into the kitchen. Remy eyed her sleepily from his place by the hearth, but didn't move to greet her. Even she wasn't worth getting up at midnight for.

She grabbed a bottle of Lucky Fox 101 and collapsed into a chair at the dining table. Pouring herself a glass, she knocked back the liquid and welcomed the heat.

When she heard the front door open, she turned to see Adam walk in. He paused when he saw her, his eyes narrowing.

"What are you doin' up?" he asked, hanging his coat before stepping into the kitchen.

Ava shrugged. "Couldn't sleep."

He tucked his hands into his pockets. "I see. Well, since I know you won't tell me what's going on, I hope you don't mind if I just go to bed."

"Adam. Wait."

He paused, one eyebrow arched. "Yeah?"

"Come sit with me." She got up to get him a glass and set it down on the table. Pouring a healthy dose of whiskey into it, she nudged it toward the chair across from her.

Adam sat and reached for the drink. He stared at it for a moment, then lifted his eyes to hers. "Feeling charitable tonight?"

"Lonely is a better word for it." Lifting her glass in a toast, she offered him a weary smile. "It's time I told you what's been going on."

He tensed, an awareness sharpening his features. "Is that right?"

She drank, then set down her glass with a dull thud. "Yep. I can't carry this burden anymore. It's killing me."

A strange burst of sympathy filled him as he studied her, sensing her unhappiness. He tried to hold onto his anger with her for holding out on him as long as she had, but found he couldn't. "What is it, darlin'?"

She raised her eyes to his. "The FBI believes Daddy has been sending money to our family in Ireland to fund the IRA."

His brows knit together. "The what?"

"The Irish Republican Army." She took another sip of whiskey to chase away the bitterness the word gave her tongue. "They're a terrorist organization. They recently set off a bomb in Dublin that killed a bunch of people. Our second-cousin, Ned, is the one they believe to be responsible."

"Shit," Adam said dully, his eyes glazing over as he processed the news. "So that's why they're here, then? Not the taxes?"

She nodded. "The unpaid taxes were what caught the attention of the IRS and led them to the account they think Ned's been withdrawing money from, but yes. This isn't about the taxes."

Adam knocked back the rest of his whiskey before pouring himself another, shaking his head. "They're wrong. Dad wouldn't do this. He's never even mentioned the IRA before. Why would he send money to them?"

"That's what I said," Ava said. "Until I found out more."

"What?"

"Daddy told me he's never met Ned or any of our family in Ireland. But the FBI found an old plane ticket to Belfast in his office. Cooper confirmed to me today that he admitted going to Ireland and meeting with Ned."

Adam's face fell. "Christ, Ava."

"I know." She reached for his hand, giving him a moment to digest what she had just told him. "Now you know why he's been so distant lately. The FBI is closing in on him. Soon they'll have proof of what he's done, and we may lose him."

"No." Adam ripped his hand from hers, rising to his feet. He glared down at her. "I don't believe it. I won't. They probably planted that plane ticket or something. They've had it out for him from the beginning. And you've been helping them, haven't you?"

"They didn't plant the ticket, boyo," a voice said from the living room. They both turned and saw their grandfather walking toward them, bundled up tight in his favorite blue robe. "And Ava's been cooperatin', just as she should to keep up appearances."

Adam sank back into his chair, dread filling him. "You're sure about the ticket?"

"I'm sure he went to Ireland," Joe confirmed, settling into the chair beside Ava. He grabbed her glass of whiskey and sipped it. "But I refuse to believe he's been willingly handing money over to Ned to fund his violent exploits."

Ava pursed her lips. "I don't want to believe it either, but he won't talk to us. Other than the warning he gave me to stay away from Ned and the others in Ireland, he hasn't said a word."

"*What?*" Adam demanded, stunned.

Her eyes became heavy as tears threatened to fall, spurred by the memory of that day on the shooting range. "First he said that I should take care of you if anything happened to him or to Mama. Then he made me promise never to contact our relatives in Ireland. He wouldn't tell me why, but when I asked Cooper about it, he said it's possible Daddy fears retaliation from the IRA."

Joe went red in the face, while Adam simply looked flabbergasted. When he found the ability to speak, he let his temper boil over. "*This* is what you've been keeping from me all this time? We could be in danger and you didn't see fit to clue me in?"

"We're not in danger—"

"Why the hell isn't the FBI doing something about this?"

Ava's own anger flared. "What do you think they're here for, Adam? They're trying to figure this all out."

"No, they're trying to put Dad in prison. What they should be doin' is going after the guy who's bombing innocent people."

"They can't." Ava shook her head, gritting her teeth. "Unless Ned's on U.S. soil, they can't go after him. Don't you understand? That could cause an international incident if they just hopped on over there and arrested him."

"So what, then?" Adam grunted, crossing his arms. "We're just supposed to sit here and let the FBI play politics with our lives?"

"Quiet, the both of you," Joe snapped, clearly having had enough. His eyes burned as he stared back and forth between them. "Don't speak on things ye don't understand. Nobody's in danger. Ned won't be comin' after any of us."

"How do you know?" Ava asked, feeling her own temper waning in the shadow of his mightier one.

Joe's mouth quivered in a scowl. "Because he's on the list. Unless he finds a way to sneak into the country, he can't leave Ireland."

Ava exhaled, feeling some measure of relief at the idea. "Well, that's good, then."

"It still doesn't change anything," Adam argued. "If anyone in town finds out about this, or if they find enough to convict Dad, then we're fucked. We'll lose everything."

"They won't convict him because he's not guilty," Joe fired back, unwilling to let go of his faith in his son. "The fact that they've found so little thus far only proves he's done nothin' wrong."

"Or it proves he's really good at covering his tracks," Ava countered.

Adam's hands clenched into fists on the table as he glared at his sister. "Whose side are you on, Ava? Ours or the FBI's?"

Her lips parted in surprise. "What the hell is that supposed to mean?"

"Just what I said." The look he gave her was so full of derision that it hit her squarely in the chest like a poisoned dart. "You think none of us have noticed how close you've gotten to that agent? People are talkin', and it ain't good. Makes me wonder what kind of back room, or *bedroom*, deals you've been makin' with him."

Her vision went red. She jumped to her feet, only to have her grandfather stop her from pouncing on her brother.

Joe squeezed her arm tightly, his eyes on Adam. "That's goin' too far, boyo. I won't hear talk like that in me own home. Now apologize."

Adam grimaced, guilt swimming low in his gut. He did his best to ignore it as he met his sister's eyes. "I'm sorry I said it, but I won't take it back. Not until you prove me wrong." He got to his feet, downing the last of the whiskey in his glass. "Goodnight."

As he stalked off, Ava let her grandfather lower her back into the chair. The red in her vision blurred as mortified tears began to fall. Joe wrapped an arm over her shoulders and pulled her in close, pressing a kiss to the top of her head.

"It's all right, dearie. He didn't mean it."

"Yes, he did," she mumbled, wiping away the tears. This time, she *was* ashamed of them. Mostly because in some ways, Adam was correct. She hadn't made any deals with the FBI to sell out her own father, but she was entirely too close to going to bed with one of them. What did that say about her?

Nothing, she decided. Cooper wasn't the one who'd put her family in this position—her father was. For now she needed to decide how to juggle the two and still maintain her sanity. If she didn't, then she would lose not only her father, but her heart as well.

Fifteen

Ava spent the next few days consumed with work at the distillery. She put in overtime in addition to her scheduled tours, doing everything she could to put both her father and the FBI out of her mind. Her grandfather joined her, just as eager to forget the troubles their family was facing.

He refused to speak about any of it, preferring to maintain the happy-go-lucky persona everyone expected from him. Though this habit of his usually bothered her, she appreciated it now when she wanted nothing more than to deny any of it existed.

To her surprise, the FBI was laying low. The team from Louisville had gone home, leaving Cooper and Marco alone to continue the investigation. But even they seemed to have slowed their progress. The owner of the Fox Hills Inn, an old friend of hers, confided that the agents rarely left the hotel anymore. They seemed to be hanging around waiting for something, but nobody knew what.

Orders, maybe. A slip up from her father. Information from an outside source. All of it was possible. And since they hadn't seen fit to speak to her since the day they'd come by the house, she was left in the dark.

She just wanted her old life back—her family at peace with itself, her company's reputation intact, her future far less uncertain. What she had lost since the FBI had come to town amounted to more than she'd realized. And all she had gained were tricky emotions and a heaping mess of doubt.

Pausing beside one of the towering racks inside the barrel house, she leaned against the nearest barrel and shut her eyes. Releasing a long, steadying breath, she tried to center herself and not give in to the temptation to dwell on it all. She said a silent prayer for clarity and peace, helpless to do anything more. Surely the end to this madness had to be in sight. If not, then she didn't know what she'd do.

Her eyes opened, her attempts to beat back the wave of anxiety failing. What she needed was a distraction away from home where she could clear her mind, regain her focus.

It had been nearly a year since she'd been to the city; seen the races, walked the streets. How refreshing it would be to mingle with people who didn't know her face, who had no clue what storm clouds raged over her family. People she had no reason to pretend in front of.

She checked her watch, saw it was nearly one o'clock. If she got her grandfather to cover her late afternoon tours, she could make it to the three o'clock race at Churchill Downs. Just in time to order a mint julep and place a few bets.

Rushing to the house to change, she considered if she wanted company or not. Brandy was likely stuck working at the bar, and Adam was still not speaking with her. Her mother didn't care for horses and her father was holed up in his office.

As she touched up her makeup and changed into a scarlet red blazer and dressy jeans, the one face she'd been trying to forget popped into her mind.

Well, hell. She slapped her forehead, even as a glitter of hope shot through her. It was worth a try, she decided. The worst he could say was no. Though she was never one to take no for an answer. Not when she wanted something badly enough.

Within fifteen minutes, she was pulling up to the Fox Hills Inn. She spotted the black sedan parked out back and wondered how he would react to seeing her. It was brash and impulsive, but then again, so was she.

She had planned to coax his room number from her old friend at the front desk, but luck was on her side. She spotted him seated inside the tiny sandwich shop the hotel offered, reading an old tattered copy of *Fahrenheit 451*.

"Hey," she greeted as she plopped down into the chair across from him.

Cooper blinked in surprise, lowering his book. His smile was quick, instinctive, and warmed her heart. "Hey, you. What's up?"

"Wanna get out of town with me?" she asked, nodding with her head for the door.

He dog-eared the page he was on and set the book aside. "Out of town?"

"Yeah. I need to get out of here for a while. I figured you could use a break, too."

Amusement softened his face. "I really shouldn't."

"Why not? You don't look busy."

He shrugged. "I'm doing stuff. And besides, I thought we were working on keeping a safe distance from each other. Or did you already give up on that? I know I can be pretty irresistible."

She arched a brow. "Get over yourself. You weren't my first choice."

"Ouch." He chuckled, running a hand through his hair. "Still, though. It's probably a bad idea."

She got to her feet. "Suit yourself. But you're missing out."

"Where are you going, anyway?"

A slow grin spread over her face. "The races. Churchill Downs."

That got his attention. In one swift movement, he rose from his chair, pocketed the book and downed the last of his coffee. "Count me in."

"Why the sudden change of heart?"

He followed her out of the sandwich shop. "I can't allow a lady to go unaccompanied to the horse track. That would be downright ungentlemanly of me. Also, I think horses are really cool. Just ask Marco."

She snorted and hopped into her Chevy pickup truck. When he slid in beside her, she patted his hand companionably. "What a swell guy you are, Slick. You're gonna make some girl very happy someday."

"I'll settle for making you happy today, Ava," he replied, offering her a sincere smile that had her insides melting.

"Well. Lucky me, then."

HE'D BEEN prepared for the sights, the sounds, even the smells. But what he hadn't anticipated was the rush he got watching those horses take flight across the dusty track. From his seat under the open patio, he had chills running over his arms that had nothing to do with the brisk fall air and everything to do with the thrill of the race.

Cooper's mouth fell open as he took in the sheer power exploding out of each horse as they thundered in unison around the track. Clad in a range of colors—blue and red and green and gold—they were mere blurs as they tore past him in a deafening drumbeat of hooves. His heart sprinted nearly as fast as they did, his eyes unblinking so he wouldn't miss a single moment.

When the horses vaulted over the finish line at last, he fell back against his seat and let out a rush of breath.

"Wow. That was awesome." He laughed, turning to Ava with a huge grin. "Now I get why people come to these things."

Ava held up the ticket stub for the bet she'd placed. "They also come for the money, Slick. I just won fifty bucks."

"No shit?" His gaze drifted back to the track, where the horses were busy being walked around and the winners congratulated. "I was going to offer to buy you another drink, but I'd say this round's on you."

"Actually, I'm starving. Why don't we get something to eat?"

He looked back at her, eyebrows raised. "This is starting to feel like a date, which we both agreed was a bad idea."

She leaned in conspiratorially, the suggestion in her eyes nearly stopping his heart. "Nobody has to know. Why d'you think we came all the way out here? I wanna have some fun before I return you."

He tore his eyes off of her and cleared his throat, his imagination running wild. "Right. Fun. Okay, let's go."

A playful smile brightened her face as she stood and pulled him to his feet. "There's this amazing little street café my father used to take me to. We can sit outside and people watch. You'll love it."

Though she didn't say anything more about it, he could tell that just the mention of her father put a damper on her mood. He intended to see she forget all her worries, at least for one night.

An hour later they sat at a quaint metal table lit with candles and sweet-smelling coral dahlias, right on the sidewalk of one of Louisville's biggest downtown streets. People passed by, bundled into coats and scarves and sharing laughter as the sun gave way to twilight and coaxed life out of the streetlamps.

Ava rested her elbow on the table, her chin in her palm. Her eyes were warm as she regarded Cooper. "I think it's time you shared some of those secrets of yours. You know all of mine."

He sipped his glass of bourbon on ice, amused by her. "What do you want to know?"

"Where'd you grow up?"

"Queens." He thought back to the old neighborhood with its towering brick buildings and tree-lined streets cluttered with cars and trash cans and people. "But we moved to Connecticut when I was sixteen."

"What's New York like?" The soft glow of candlelight teased the gold out of her hair as she twirled a strand of it around her finger.

"Nothing like here," he mused. "I guess it's what you'd expect—busy, exciting. Everyone's in a rush to get somewhere and avoiding eye contact is a way of life. My mom always hated the city anyway. She was relieved to get of there."

"And your dad?"

He averted his eyes, taking another drink. "He was a cop. He died before we moved."

Ava's face fell, picking up on the grief in his voice. She reached for his hand. "I'm sorry."

"It's okay." He squeezed her hand in return, a half-smile chasing away the strain around his eyes. "It was a long time ago."

Sensing he didn't want to talk about it, she avoided asking more. As curious as she was, she'd been raised with more manners than to pry. "So how did the son of a cop from Queens get into the FBI?"

"I wanted to make a difference."

She snorted. When she saw he was serious, she stifled her laughter. "Oh. Sorry. That's very noble of you."

"The world's a dangerous place," he continued, turning his hand over so he could run his thumb along her skin. His eyes followed the movement, entranced by the smooth slopes of her knuckles. "Nobody should have to live in fear for their lives. Much less in America."

"That's why I keep a shotgun by the door and know how to use it."

"Sometimes that's not enough." He let that old familiar ache fill him as he thought of his father and the monsters who had taken his life. His eyes lifted to hers. "But it's better than nothing."

Her lips curved. "Yes, it is."

The sight of her smile had the darkness receding from his mood. He basked in the light of it, comforted despite everything. When he was with her this way, just the two of them, all the complications of the case didn't seem to matter. Her father's undoubtable connection to the IRA and his own orders to bring the man down were simply background noise in a song he'd heard the instant he saw her for the first time in the distillery.

She was unlike anyone he'd ever known—all hardwired passion yet smooth as the whiskey her family created, while he was a city-hardened seeker of justice. They'd found something in each other that neither was even looking for, something impossible to resist.

And when she looked at him that way, hazel eyes afire with homegrown compassion and that smile tinged with a hint of spice, she was more beautiful than any other creature in the world.

"God, you're gorgeous." The words were out of his mouth before he'd even realized he had said them aloud.

That dimple flashed in her cheek as her smile grew. One of her brows rose, slow and deliberate. "Why, thank you kindly."

"Did I just say that?" He let out a laugh and brushed his free hand through his hair. "I swear, something about you makes me want to break all the rules. That's never happened before."

She drew closer, delighted at how flustered he was. It was adorable on him. "It ain't against the law to call a woman beautiful, Slick. In fact, it's a surefire way to grab her attention."

"And here I thought I had that already." He angled his head, taking a moment to consider her. "You're one hell of a conflict of interest, Ava. But I can't bring myself to say no to you. No to this." He motioned with his hand. "Whatever it is."

Her heart fluttered, warming her with its beat. "Then don't. It'll be our secret."

"And when the case is over and I go back to D.C.? What happens then?"

"Then this little affair of ours will be done and we'll go our separate ways," she decided, offering him another smile. "I'd rather experience something spectacular for a short while than miss out on it entirely because I'm afraid of what's to come. Wouldn't you?"

"Yeah. I would." He lifted her hand to his lips, pressing a kiss to her knuckles. It sent her pulse jumping in quick, wild bursts. "I'm going to enjoy knowing you. Short lived as it may be."

"Me too, Slick." She released a steadying breath, undone by the open honesty in his eyes. "Me too."

LATER THAT evening, she pulled into the parking lot of the Fox Hills Inn and cut the engine. Cooper shifted in the seat beside her, his hands clenched tightly over his knees. He cast a curious look in her direction, as though gauging what she wanted to do.

Funny, she thought. She'd never had a guy care so much about what she thought was best before. It was incredibly refreshing.

Her lips curved as she unbuckled her seatbelt and leaned over, pressing a smooth kiss to his cheek. She felt him slowly breathe out, then back in as he cupped her face and brought her mouth to his. Her heart raced as she swiftly climbed into his lap.

She took advantage of the moonless night and the late hour to savor the moment. Her hands drew back into his dusted gold hair as her body shivered beneath his touch. When he caressed the arch of her back, soft and slow, she deepened the kiss and gave it all she had.

Cooper held her close, vaguely concerned over who may wander by and catch them and at the same time recklessly indifferent about it. At that moment, he couldn't have given a rat's ass if his boss of all people stumbled upon him engaged in a heated kiss with the daughter of a suspect. All that mattered was that she was there with him, this fireball of heat and light and boundless passion.

He realized then that he had never wanted anything—or anyone—more than he wanted Ava Brannon. Even if it was a fool's errand, destined to leave him burdened with regret and heartache, at least it was real. The most real thing he had ever experienced.

"Come up with me," he murmured, not even realizing he was saying it. He was too caught up in the taste of bourbon on her tongue and the scent of spiced apples in her hair.

She let out a laugh, low and deep and delightfully husky, letting her head fall back so he could sample the skin along her throat. "A Southern lady doesn't sleep with a man on the first date, Slick. We require courtship."

"Okay, I can do that," he panted, pulling her face back to his for another kiss. "Just don't leave yet."

She nodded, her body molded around his as he took what she offered without hesitation. Her breath quickened and shook as his hands tightened over her hips, fingers digging into her skin. Marveling at the display of power blended with the tender, slow-burning way he kissed had her lost and found all at the same time. He had this ability to tear down every last thought in her brain while filling her with a vibrant, impossible desire.

Overtaken by it, she nearly gave in then and there. The thought of what it would be like to slide over him, skin-to-skin and nothing but heat, stole her breath with its intensity. Propriety, and an ounce of panic over her own emotions, had her retreating from the urge.

Peeling away from him, she noticed that steam clouded the windows, encasing them in a misty cocoon. Her lips curved as her eyes met his. "Good Lord, the boy can kiss."

Cooper grinned. "Tell me you'll be back for more, then."

"I couldn't stay away even if I tried." She brushed back strands of hair from his forehead, admiring the smooth planes of his face and the rich blue of his eyes. "They grow 'em good up North. I can't believe I've been missing out all these years."

"I could say the same thing about you." He reached for her hand, brought her palm to his lips. He pressed a tender kiss to her skin, eyes closing as he breathed in her scent one last time. "When can I see you again?"

She pulled her hand away, though it pained her to do so. In that moment she wanted nothing more than to follow him upstairs, away from the prying eyes of the world, and explore every last inch of him. Because she knew she shouldn't, she eased back into the driver's seat and released a long sigh.

"I don't know. I'll come by. Or call you. I still have that business card."

"Okay." He saw she was struggling inwardly with something and had a pretty good idea what it was. Taking her hand in his, he offered her a smile. "If at any time this stops feeling right for you, you can tell me. I'll back off the second you no longer want this."

Her throat clenched, moved by how caring he could be. How considerate. Instead of responding, she simply leaned over to kiss him one last time.

"Goodnight, Slick."

"Night, Ava." He slipped from the truck and closed the door. She watched him wander around to the front of the hotel, hands tucked into his pockets, until he disappeared from view.

With her heart soaring, she started the truck and headed on home.

CHAPTER

Sixteen

Fresh from her morning run, Ava danced into the kitchen singing Miranda Lambert's "Heart Like Mine." Her voice clashed with the sound of her mother's music, some old country tune Ava hadn't heard in ages.

She turned it down and gave her mother a cheek kiss and a big smile. "Morning, Mama. How'd you sleep?"

"Just fine. You're in a good mood," Sandra observed. The morning sunlight angled in from the window and lit up her auburn hair and the smooth lines of her youthful face. Her linen apron was lightly dusted with flour from the dough she'd made minutes before.

"It's a beautiful day." Ava moved to sniff happily at the bacon crackling on the stove. "I'm thinking of seeing if Daddy wants to go shooting with me later. After work, of course." She grabbed the orange juice from the fridge. As she poured some into a glass and started singing again, she caught her mother staring at her. "What?"

"Nothing." Her mother returned to whisking a bowl of eggs, a knowing smile on her face. "Do you need anything at the market? I'm heading down there today."

Ava dumped the last of the orange juice into her glass and raised the carton. "More juice."

Adam sauntered into the kitchen, already showered and dressed for the day. Ava shot him a look as she closed the fridge, her mood dampened at the sight of him. Guilt and resentment swirled within her. "You're up early."

He ignored her, like he'd done for the last few days since their argument, and prepared himself a cup of coffee. He took a quick sip and faced their mother, a polite smile on his face. "Morning."

Sandra let him kiss her cheek and continued to whisk the eggs, clearly trying to ignore the tension in the air. "Adam, honey, would you like some breakfast?"

"No, thanks. I need to run."

"You know, the bar's not open this early," Ava reminded him, leaning against the kitchen island and folding her arms.

He couldn't resist correcting her. "I ain't goin' to the bar."

"That's a surprise." She cocked her chin with a sneer. "Don't tell me you're heading into the city looking for trouble. Last time I nearly had to bail you out of jail."

Sandra let out a sigh and rested her hands on her hips, her eyes darting between her two children. "Will you both just quit it? There's too much fightin' going on in this house. I'm sick of it."

Ava rolled her eyes. "He's the one who's been ignoring me all week."

Adam's jaw clenched as he lifted his coffee mug to his lips. Ava knew he wouldn't be stupid enough to bring up the details of their argument in front of their mother. They were both too committed to preserving her cheerful ignorance on the issue to let it slip.

"Hard to talk to you when you're not around. Where'd you go yesterday?" he asked, his statement challenging her to lie. He would know if she did, anyway, which she knew made lying pointless.

"To the races." She pushed away from the counter, deciding to shower before breakfast in an attempt to avoid further questioning.

He stepped in front of her as she tried to pass. "With that FBI agent? I heard you picked him up at the Inn."

Ava silently cursed the wagging tongues of a small town. "Who said that?"

"Josie over at the pharmacy. She was walking to work and saw him get into your truck. Naturally, she told old man Thornton and he told Miss Joy who spread the word around the bakery, which then trickled into the bar. I only found out because Brandy asked me about it, wonderin' if I knew where the two of you were headed."

"I invited him to the races with me, that's all it was. You can reassure everyone that nothing immoral is going on."

"You sure about that?" Adam's lips spread in a sick smile. He knew her too well. "I still stand by what I said the other night. I'll take it back when you prove me wrong. So far, you're doing a shit job."

"Go to hell," she growled, pushing past him. When he started to follow her down the hall toward her room, she whirled around, hands in fists at her sides. "How would you like it if I went around town spreading gossip about you and Brandy, huh? I know something happened between the two of you. Not sure what exactly, but she's God awful at hiding things from me and Lord knows you're not much better. Maybe I should start a rumor that you slept with her and then dumped her like all the other poor women you come into contact with. How d'you think that'd go over with the folks in town?"

Adam's eyes blazed with fury. "You wouldn't."

Ava let out a huff of breath. "No, I wouldn't. But only because I love Brandy too much. If it wouldn't hurt her then I'd seriously consider it just to teach you a lesson."

"I ain't ever laid a hand on her that she didn't want placed there," he defended, his face flushing. "Just leave her the hell out of this. She doesn't deserve to be dragged into our family's shit."

Her brows furrowed at the passion in his tone, the righteousness. She'd never heard him defend anybody so ardently before. "For once, you and I agree. Christ, Adam, you love her, don't you?"

His breath came out in shallow huffs as he averted his eyes. "No. I slipped up and we kissed, but no. She doesn't feel that way about me."

Ava blinked. "Um, we are talking about Brandy here, right? The same Brandy who I've watched fawn over you forever?"

His gaze shot back to hers. "She said no."

"Well, she's obviously just tryin' to save face." Ava softened, weary from the fight and the notable unhappiness in her brother's eyes. "Whatever. Why should I care if you want to ruin your life? Not like I can offer you advice, anyway. My love life's always been just as big a train wreck as yours."

He angled his head. "So you are seeing this agent, then?"

She shifted her weight. "It's complicated, okay? But it has nothing to do with Daddy or the case or anything at all."

"Have you ever thought that he might be using you?"

She started laughing. "He's not that clever. He's got too honest of a face to pull off a lie like that."

"What do you really know about him, Ava? Seriously?" Adam asked, lowering his voice so their mother wouldn't hear. "He wants to pin this IRA shit on Dad. That makes him enemy number one as far as I'm concerned. How do you know that he's not just hanging around trying to get you to slip up on something that could put Dad behind bars?"

"What the hell could I possibly say that would incriminate him?" Ava charged, fighting to keep her temper in check. "I don't know anything and Cooper knows that. He's been nothing but honest with me."

"Has he?" Adam distanced himself, eyeing her doubtfully. "Be careful, darlin'. I'll be watching you."

After he'd walked away, she drifted into her bedroom and quietly shut the door, her heart not wanting to give credence to his words.

AS HE drove the short distance to the distillery, Adam mulled over his sister's lunacy. He had never considered her stupid, but flirting with the FBI agent was bad news. How she couldn't see that—or if she did, how she could rationalize it to herself—was beyond him. It seemed clear cut and obvious that the FBI wanted only one thing—their father behind bars for funding terrorism. And from the looks of it, they weren't going to leave until they got their man.

He didn't want to believe his father was guilty, but he wasn't a fool, either. He'd known from the start that the FBI was after more than just fines and penalties for tax fraud. If his sister had only trusted him sooner with the truth, maybe he could have saved her from her own pitiful yearnings for this agent.

Special Agent Cooper Lawson. Adam's lip curled in disgust as he pictured the man, all slick and charming with an ice cold intellect hidden beneath a friendly façade. He'd never met a man quite like that before. People in the South tended to be of a more honest, what-you-see-is-what-you-get nature. He held no such trust for this man in the crisp black suit.

Ava was free to make her own mistakes, but not when those mistakes impacted the family and most important-ly himself. He had never been the over-protective brother ordering her to keep her legs closed as he had always been too preoccupied with his own trysts. Now he wondered if his lack of guidance in some way led to her ridiculous choices in men.

First Beau, who from a mile away was clearly a cruel, arrogant son-of-a-bitch, and now for some unknown rea-son the very FBI agent trying to tear apart their family. It seemed like a page out of a psychology book on hostage behavior. Fall in love with the captor or whatever. It was downright pathetic.

If Ava was going to go down this self-destructive path, then he needed to take matters into his own hands. His grandfather had never once looked to him or trusted him to take his place and run the company, but there was no reason he couldn't. He was just as capable as Ava, if not more so giv-en her actions of late. And unlike his sister, he was loyal to family and would fight *for* them, not against them.

It was time to put the vices of his past behind him, and finally take control of his life. Starting with securing the po-sition he should have had from the start.

He walked into the distillery, head high and a sense of business about him. The large, warehouse-type build-ing was bustling with moving machines, churning vats of mash, and employees going about their daily duties. The smell of sweet corn filled his nostrils and brought on a sense of pride.

The distillery foreman, Ed Barrow, approached him with a questioning smile.

"Mornin', Adam. What brings you here?"

Adam regarded the man with a heated stare. "I have something to discuss with you, Ed. It's about my sister."

"Is Ava all right?" Ed asked, shoving his clip board under his arm so he could adjust his ball cap. The white dress shirt he wore was already dampened with sweat from his busy morning.

"Physically, she's fine." Adam patted Ed's shoulder, angling him toward the offices. "However, I'm afraid she may be in a position to compromise the stability of Lucky Fox. I felt you should know what's goin' on before everything goes down."

"What in God's name are you talkin' about?" Ed shuffled into his office ahead of Adam, who closed the door behind them. He took a seat before Ed's desk and sat back comfortably.

"I know you've seen the FBI sniffin' around here," Adam began, inspecting his fingernails. He turned his attention back to Ed. "Haven't you?"

"Well, of course. Everybody has," Ed confirmed. He settled into the chair behind his desk, looking uneasy. "Joe said that was just about taxes or some such thing."

Adam tilted his head. "It was and it wasn't. I only just learned of the true meaning behind the FBI's visit, and unfortunately it isn't good."

Ed's face blanched. "What is it?"

"I can't give you details, but in essence it involves a lot of money being transferred overseas that's unaccounted for. Ava's been working with the FBI agents to pin this on my father. She wants him out of the picture."

"Ty? Ty ain't ever done nothin' illegal. The man's a saint." Ed shifted in his seat, shaking his head. "And Ava, she loves your daddy. I don't see her selling him out like this."

"Well, she is." Beginning to lose his patience, Adam leaned forward, linking his hands together in front of him. "She and that one agent have become...romantically involved."

Ed blinked, as though not understanding the statement. When he put two and two together, his eyes widened and his mouth opened to form a silent 'O'.

Adam nodded. "Now you see the predicament we're in. She's been working with him *against* this company's best interests. If she has her way, Lucky Fox may be forced to close its doors."

"That girl loves this place. She'd never want it closed," Ed defended, his loyalty to Ava seeping into his voice.

Adam realized he was losing the battle. "I'm not sayin' she wants it to close. All I'm sayin' is her actions will inevitably *lead* to us having to shut down if this scandal with the money goes public."

Ed rubbed his chin, looking doubtful. "So what is it exactly that you want me to do?"

"Nothin', Ed, I'm just filling you in on what's goin' on," Adam replied, rising to his feet. His hands slipped into his pockets. "I know we've never been very close and I've been more of an embarrassment to Lucky Fox than an asset, but I care about this company and the Lucky Fox family. I don't want to see my sister's blind desires jeopardize all you and my grandfather have worked to build."

"So these agents are bad news then, huh?"

"They want to throw my father in prison. For the life of me I can't figure out why my sister is helping them, but it's become obvious to me that she is."

Ed's face fell as he numbly accepted Adam's words. He shuffled through some of the paperwork on his desk, his gaze falling upon a framed portrait of his wife and kids. Adam saw him tear up a bit and felt a stab of guilt hit him in the gut.

"Look, Ed. This isn't a reason to panic, okay?" Adam ran a hand through his hair and sighed. "I'll take care of everything. I'll save this company and I won't let the FBI take my father."

Before Ed could respond, Ava threw open the office door and leaned inside. She started to speak only to catch eyes with Adam and frown.

"What're you doing here?"

Adam shrugged, his chin jutting out in a defensive gesture. "Just catchin' up with Ed."

Ava glanced between her brother and her foreman, noting the latter was damp with sweat and teary-eyed.

"Something tells me it's more than that." Ava stepped into the room and went to Ed. "Everything okay?"

Ed tried to nod, but his face flushed instead and he climbed to his feet. "You lied to me, Ava. Right to my face. To all our faces. You said it was only about taxes, but it's more, ain't it?"

"Excuse me?" she stammered, taken aback by the angry heat that colored his face. She looked at Adam, who only met her stare with equal obstinacy.

Before Ed could answer, her cell phone rang. She lifted a finger for Ed to hold on as she dug it out of her back pocket and answered it.

"*It's Beau.*"

"Now's not a good time, Sheriff." She glared at her brother, needing to take long, slow breaths just to quell the urge to pummel him.

"*It's about your mama. She's been taken to the hospital. You need to get down there immediately.*"

Her heart did one quick, violent lurch. "What happened? Is she okay?"

His voice took on a softer, more somber tone, as if even he couldn't believe the words he was about to say. "*She was*

robbed downtown while getting out of her car. She's been shot.
I'm gonna be honest, sweetheart, it's not lookin' good."

Ava swayed on her feet, her mind flashing with images of her mother taking on an armed attacker. She didn't even register that Adam had come to her side, his hand on her shoulder and fearful concern in his eyes. "Where is she?"

"They had to airlift her to Louisville."

She didn't wait to hear more and hung up the phone. In an instant, she was barreling out of the office with Adam on her heels.

"What happened?" he demanded, his voice clipped with terror.

"Mama's at the hospital." Ava wiped away the tears that fell down her face as she swept past curious employees and out into the daylight. She didn't bother to speak again until she was buckled into her truck with Adam in the passenger seat.

"Wh—"

She cut him off before he could repeat his question. "Beau says she was mugged downtown and the guy shot her." Her voice cracked as she pulled onto the dusty gravel road. "He said it's bad."

Adam fell into silence and her earlier disgust with him vanished under anxiety for their mother. Keeping her eyes straight ahead, she roared down to the highway and then kicked it up to near one hundred miles-per-hour, her hands locked tight on the steering wheel.

A DUEL vision of auburn hair and panicked faces, Ava and Adam skidded to a stop before the reception desk at the hospital. They both spoke at once and the receptionist had to motion for them to slow down and repeat their request.

Ava took the lead. "Sandra Brannon. What room?"

The middle-aged brunette tapped into the computer, lips pursed as she looked up the name. "Here we go. Ms. Brannon has just come out of surgery and is recovering upstairs. Are you family?"

"Yes," Adam cut in, unable to stand still. "Just tell us what goddamn room. Please."

The woman rattled off directions and handed them visitor stickers and Ava and Adam were gone, vaulting toward the elevator. In three minutes flat they were halfway across the hospital and careening for their mother's room.

A tall woman of Indian descent wearing a white doctor's coat stepped between them and the door, eyeing the visitor badges on their chests. "You're here to see Ms. Brannon? She's still unconscious. It's best if you wait."

"No." Ava shook her head, tears brimming hotly in her eyes. "Just let us see that she's okay."

The doctor nodded, sympathy lining her face. "The bullet just barely missed her heart. We were able to remove it, but unfortunately she's lost a lot of blood."

"But she'll live, right?" Adam demanded, his hand instinctually finding Ava's. They held on to each other, united.

"She's not out of the woods just yet." The doctor's lips pressed together in a firm line, as though she was trying to find the best way to deliver the news. "We've done all we can for now. I'm sorry."

A single sob escaped Ava's throat. She curled into her brother, resting her forehead on his shoulder. He held her close, unable to breathe.

"We want to see her," he said, his gaze firm and unwavering. The doctor considered his request for a moment. She then nodded and backed out of the way, motioning for the door.

"You have five minutes."

Adam led Ava toward their mother's room, his mind numb as if in a dream as he opened the door. The first thing he saw was their mother lying on a hospital bed, hooked up to machines that were beeping and dripping fluids into her body. The heartbeat on the monitor was slow and steady, and seeing it broke something inside of him. She was alive. No matter how bad she looked with shadows under her eyes and her face waxy and pale, her heartbeat meant hope.

Ava parted from him and walked slowly forward. She reached out tentatively to touch her mother's hand, finding it hard to look at her face. If she just focused on the hand, she didn't have to acknowledge the deathly stillness of her mother's features.

Lowering herself into a chair beside the bed, Ava kept her hand on her mother's and bent her head to cry.

Adam was at her side immediately, kneeling down to cradle her head to his chest and provide comfort, both for her and for himself.

"How could this happen?" Ava moaned, sniffling and struggling for air. "She keeps that .38 in the glove compartment. Why didn't she use it?"

"Maybe she didn't have the chance," Adam guessed, attempting a look at their mother. He gritted his teeth. "I hope they caught the bastard. I'm gonna gut him alive."

Ava gently pushed him away so she could stand, needing to see if her mother would wake up. "Mama? Can you hear me?"

She ran her hand over her mother's dampened forehead, brushing aside strands of hair. Sandra's eyelids fluttered as her lips parted, and Ava nearly burst into tears again.

"Oh, please wake up. You're okay now. We're here." Ava squeezed her hand once more, a bolt of hope shooting through her as her mother's eyes opened. They stared unseeing for a moment, then slowly blinked and shifted to meet Ava's.

"My babies," she whispered, so weak Ava could barely hear it.

"Yes, Mama. We're both here."

Adam crammed up beside Ava, stroking his mother's face. "How're you feelin'?"

Sandra's eyes closed as she fought for breath, shaking her head. Her mouth opened and closed soundlessly for a moment before she spoke again. "Da warned me not to marry him. But love him I did. Lord, forgive me."

Ava faltered, taken aback by the foreign lilt of Ireland in her mother's voice. She caught Adam's eyes and he looked equally as confused.

Turning back to their mother, Ava frowned. "What was that, Mama?"

Sandra's eyes flew open, her hand reaching into the air, searching for something to grab onto. It latched onto Ava's wrist and held on weakly. "He's evil. Got the Devil in him, he does."

The monitors sounded an alarm as her heart rate skyrocketed, her blood pressure mounting to dangerous levels. Panic rose in Ava's throat like a geyser. "Get the nurse!"

Adam tore out of the room. Ava held her mother's hand tightly in hers and struggled to calm her down. "Just rest now. You're safe."

"No. No." Sandra groaned, looking feverish. Her eyes were manic and wet with tears as she stared at Ava. "Your father. Stay away from him. He's coming for you."

"What?" Ava asked, dumbfounded. Then her mother's eyes rolled back and her head fell against the pillows. Her body began to tremble and jolt and seconds later a nurse was rushing into the room, nudging Ava aside. Adam was with her, pulling her out of the way as the monitors shrilled and other nurses raced in to answer the call.

It took only a minute for the heartbeat to flat line, and another two minutes to attempt CPR. Ava watched in numb horror as moments later they pronounced her mother dead.

She thought she remembered screaming. Or maybe it was simply the roaring rage of grief thundering in her head, blinding her to reason. She couldn't possibly be dead. Images of mother just that morning cooking breakfast with flour on her apron and the sun in her hair shuddered through her, surreal and stunningly painful.

Clinging to her brother as the nurses gave them space to grieve, Ava felt her legs give out and collapsed with him onto the cold linoleum floor. She sobbed into his shoulder, her fingers digging at the fabric of his shirt.

A voice broke through the haze, a shout that brought a sick feeling to her gut. Her father rushed past them and into the room that held his wife, his hands in his hair and his face wrought with pain.

"No." Ty gasped, falling before Sandra's bedside and staring at her in disbelief.

Ava tilted her head to stare at her father, fresh tears slipping down her cheeks. In that moment, her mother's delirious words of warning fled her mind. As she watched her father mourn their loss, the sight of it ground her shattered heart to dust.

CHAPTER
Seventeen

Cooper stared at the computer screen, reading the words over and over again.

I know she's with you.

He played with a metal slinky he'd found in Ty's desk, letting the metal rings fall from left to right as he moved his hands. His eyes narrowed as he thought over everything he knew about Ned and Ty Brannon, and what the meaning of the mysterious email could be.

Though it was entirely possible that it meant nothing or was unrelated to their case, he couldn't let it go. Something told him it was much more important than he realized. And since he had literally nothing else to go on at the moment to move the case forward, he was stuck analyzing the few bits of evidence they'd already found.

"Hey, crack the code yet?" Marco asked, leaning into the room. He sipped noisily on a soda, his lips puckered around the straw.

"Nope. It's important, though, I can feel it," Cooper replied. He stretched his arms over his head and yawned, wanting nothing more than a hot shower and a beer. "You hear from Horvath yet?"

"Not yet. Looks like were stuck twiddling our thumbs for now."

Cooper frowned. "All this inaction is killing me."

"I look at it like an extended vacation," Marco decided with a grin. He motioned around the office. "Granted, this isn't exactly the place I'd vacation to, but hey, it beats desk work back in D.C."

Setting the slinky aside, Cooper shut the laptop and rose to his feet. "Do you miss it? The city?"

"Hell yeah. These small towns close in on you after a while." Marco led the way out into the main office, where the late afternoon sunlight was filtering in through the windows. "I swear, if I have to run into that asshole sheriff again, I'll—"

A brisk knock at the door interrupted his sentence. Cooper looked out the window and spotted Beau standing outside.

He snorted and glanced back to Marco. "Here's your chance to tell him exactly what you'll do."

Opening the door, he offered Beau a grin. "Hey, Sheriff. What can I do for you?"

Beau's face was solemn and unamused, setting off instant alarm bells in Cooper's brain.

"It's Sandra Brannon. She's been taken to the hospital. I just thought you should know."

"Christ, is she all right?" Cooper asked, stepping back to invite Beau in.

Beau raised a hand to decline, preferring to stay outside. His face tightened with anger and grief. "I just got word from Ava that she didn't make it."

Cooper's heart sank, stunned by the news. Marco hovered beside him, just as shocked.

"What happened to her?" Marco asked.

Beau adjusted his belt. "She was gunned down by the market. Looks like a robbery attempt. Her purse is missin' and witnesses reported seeing a man in black assaultin' her as she got out of her car. He got away on foot before anybody could catch up with him. I have a team out searchin' right now."

Cooper's brow creased. "A robbery? That's unusual, isn't it?"

"First armed robbery since I've been Sheriff," Beau confirmed. "Don't think there were too many under my father, either. Fox Hills is a safe town."

"So that's why you're here, isn't it?" Cooper continued, leaning against the doorframe. "You suspect it isn't just your typical robbery."

"Given the high profile nature of the Brannons and your current investigation, I'd reckon there's somethin' more at work here," Beau replied. His eyes darted between the two agents. "Do y'all want to tell me what's really goin' on? If the Brannons are in danger, I need to know about it. I can't protect my town if I'm in the dark."

Cooper shared a look of dread with Marco, a lump forming in his throat. "The email."

"I know *she's* with you," Marco recalled, stunned. "Shit, how did we miss that?"

"I don't know." Cooper rubbed his face with his hands. They'd never once assumed Ned could be talking about Sandra Brannon in his email. Now it seemed so pathetically obvious. He turned back to Beau. "I'll let Agent D'Amico fill you in, Sheriff. I've got to go check on the Brannons."

He got the name of the hospital from Beau and took off for Louisville. He hated thinking about Ava suffering under the weight of this monstrous tragedy, especially since he knew it had to be the work of Ned Brannon.

Worst of all, this meant that Ava herself could be in grave danger.

ADAM NEVER once left her side. Despite everything that had come between them, he didn't abandon her when she needed him most. That had to count for something, Ava knew. Something that, no matter what he'd done, was worth all the forgiveness in the world.

Their father had left shortly after seeing their mother's body. He hadn't even bothered to speak to them. Instead he had run, clearly desperate to be alone. Ava couldn't understand the urge. The last thing she wanted was to sit in silence with her own tormented thoughts, not when they were filled with images of her mother right before her last breath. She needed to keep moving, keep busy, attend to what needed to be handled and take back as much control of the situation as she could. Thankfully, Adam seemed to understand that, and together they would deal with their father later.

As she signed paperwork and spoke numbly with doctors and nurses and receptionists, she did her best not to break into a rage again. It bubbled just beneath the surface, a single word or thought away from exploding out of her. She couldn't let it, wouldn't allow herself to dissolve into helplessness. She had to be strong, if not for Adam, then for herself.

While awaiting one last round of paperwork, Ava fell back into a chair in the waiting room. Adam sat beside her, wrapping an arm protectively over her shoulders.

He kissed the top of her head. "I don't want to be your enemy, darlin'."

Ava exhaled, her eyes closing as she curled into him. Fresh tears sprang into her eyes. "I don't either. Mama didn't want us to fight."

His breath hitched on a sob. When he spoke, she could hear the raging grief that mirrored her own in his voice. "I should've told her I loved her every damn day. She was so special. Why didn't I ever say it?"

"I know." Ava faced him, cupping his cheek in her hand. "I may not be able to tell her, but I still have you. I love you, Adam. I love you so damn much."

"I love you too." He pulled her in for a hug, then slowly released her. "I'll always stick by you. We came into this world together. Odds are we'll leave it together, too."

She nodded, wiping under her nose with the back of her hand. A weary laugh escaped her throat. "You better not die before me. I can't handle going through this again."

"I ain't goin' nowhere." His eyes fell to the floor as he sank back into his chair. "I'm surprised Grandpa's not here."

"I'm sure he's dealing with Daddy. There's nothing more to see here, anyway."

As if her grandfather could be walking in at any second, she looked toward the entrance of the waiting area. Instead she watched Cooper come through the doors. Her heart lurched and tumbled and without hesitating she jumped from her seat and ran to him.

He caught her midstride and held her close. She buried her face in his neck, releasing a shuddering breath. "Thank God you're here."

He pulled away and gripped her shoulders. Determination blended with the sympathy in his eyes. "I'm so sorry, Ava."

She nodded, glancing over her shoulder at Adam. He was busy talking on his cell phone, likely to Brandy. Turning back to Cooper, she led him to a secluded area of the waiting room.

"I didn't want to think about it before, but now might be the time to start," she began, brushing away a stray tear. She met his eyes and let the easier emotion of anger take over. "This kinda thing might be commonplace where you come from, but not in Fox Hills. People don't just get robbed and gunned down on Main Street this way."

A darkness crept into his eyes. "My thoughts exactly. And the sheriff's too, for that matter. Marco's filling him in on the IRA situation as we speak."

Ava paled, but stood firm. "This has to be Ned's doing. He wants to punish my father."

He thought of the email, and it only steeled his resolve. "I believe so, yes."

"So what's the FBI gonna do about it? What's to stop Ned from going after my brother or my grandfather?"

Or you, Cooper thought, but knew she would never worry about her own safety. "Your mother's cell phone was stolen with her purse. We'll start by tracking it with GPS and see if we can find out where it's been taken. If we're lucky, it'll lead us straight to the killer."

"If he's stupid and doesn't trash the phone," Ava retorted, wrapping her arms over her torso. "Look, I don't know if it means anything or not as she was pretty delirious, but Mama warned me to stay away from my father right before she died. I think she had an idea of what he was involved in. His dealings with Ned could be what got her killed, and she knew it."

Cooper sighed. "I need to speak to your dad, see if he'll admit to being involved with Ned."

"And if he doesn't?" Her voice broke as a shiver raced over her skin. "He's lied before, what's to stop him from lying now?"

"Someone close to him wasn't dead before," he countered. He hated himself when he saw those tears come back into her eyes. "Christ, I'm sorry. Come here."

As he wrapped her in his arms, he pledged a silent vow to get retribution. The case had already become a personal one for him, but now it was tenfold. He knew Ava's pain better than she could understand, and nothing was going to stop him from hunting down the man behind her mother's murder.

"**WAIT A** minute. Let me make sure I got this." Cooper stared down at Beau, seriously losing his patience. "We gave you Intel on Ty's connection to the IRA—including that email—to help aid your investigation into Sandra Brannon's murder and now you're telling us it actually *was* just a robbery?"

Beau's neck flushed as his eyes shifted back and forth between Cooper and Marco. They stood inside the Sheriff's station, a humble brick building in the heart of town. Inside the station was just as modest, with gray linoleum floors and cluttered metal desks.

"I don't know what to tell you," Beau told him flatly. "We apprehended a man just outside of town matching the description of the assailant. His driver's license lists his address as a place on the outskirts of Louisville and he has a rap sheet a mile long full of robbery and assault charges. It's likely he was traveling through and needed some quick cash and things got out of hand. He's being questioned as we speak."

"What about the weapon?" Cooper demanded, certain they had the wrong man.

"He probably tossed it somewhere along the way."

Marco's eyes narrowed. "Well, we need to speak to him before you jump to any conclusions."

Beau shook his head. "He's my suspect, and this is my case. I'll handle it."

Cooper threw up his hands, frustrated. "So why the hell did you come to us, then? If that man in there is the one who shot Mrs. Brannon, then he must be connected to the IRA somehow which makes it my case, not yours. So either you let me in there to speak to him, or I make trouble for you and trust me, you're not gonna like it."

It surprised Cooper to see a flicker of doubt and hesitation darken Beau's face. His eyes darted around the room for a second before he spoke, his voice lowered. "Do what you want, fellas, but my hands are tied. What I personally believe happened doesn't matter anymore."

"What are you talking about?" Cooper asked.

Beau only stepped back, holding up his hands in a show of peace. "I'm sorry. I got an investigation to wrap up."

Cooper stared daggers into his back as he walked away. Marco nudged him with an elbow before leading the way out of the station.

Once back inside their sedan, Cooper immediately grabbed his phone and dialed Horvath. He needed the full weight of the FBI for this one. Come hell or high water, he was going to talk to that suspect.

Horvath answered on the third ring, sounding agitated. "*What is it?*"

"Sandra Brannon is dead," Cooper informed him, his gut churning uncomfortably.

"*I know.*" Horvath sighed. "*It's a real shame.*"

"They're claiming it was a robbery, but my gut tells me otherwise. Remember that email Ty got? It must've been referring to his wife. We just didn't realize it until it was too late."

"It looks like a pretty clear cut robbery to me. And there's no proof that email even came from Ned, kid. Don't jump the shark here."

"Wait, what?" Cooper shot Marco a stunned look. "You can't be serious."

"This is all just an unfortunate tragedy. I don't want you getting involved—let the local boys handle this one. Keep your focus on the rest of the Brannon family. Especially Ty."

Cooper rubbed his temple, not believing what he was hearing. "You want me to believe that this is all just a coincidence? That Brannon's wife being murdered has nothing to do with Ned?"

"That's exactly what I'm saying. Now let it go. Stay put and wait for further instruction."

Horvath hung up before Cooper could respond. He set aside the phone, then slammed his hands against the steering wheel.

Marco shook his head. "We both had a feeling this thing goes higher up. I think we just got our answer."

Cooper scowled. "They got to the goddamn sheriff, who came to us because he *knew* something was off, and now we're being given orders to stand down. What the hell is going on here?"

"Something bigger than us, buddy." Marco patted him on the shoulder, mustering up a sad smile. "Look, I hate the injustice of it as much as you do, but we gotta trust Horvath. If they're manipulating this thing to look like something it isn't, then there must be a good reason for it. Who are we to stand in the way of that?"

"The least they could do is fill us in." Cooper let out a rush of breath and brushed back his hair. "Then I wouldn't feel so helpless. What am I going to tell Ava?"

"Sometimes these things are on a need-to-know basis, and unfortunately we're pretty low on the totem pole." Marco stared out the windshield, looking pensive. "And as far as Ava's concerned...tread lightly there, Coop. Ask yourself if she's worth losing your career over."

Cooper eyed his partner angrily. "That's not what you said a week ago."

"Her mother wasn't assassinated by the IRA a week ago," Marco reminded him. "All I'm saying is she's going to expect you to work a miracle, and unfortunately your hands are just as tied as the sheriff's in there."

"Her mother warned her that Ty was dangerous," Cooper told him, recalling what Ava had said to him earlier that day. "She must have known the IRA was coming for them."

"Maybe she did." Marco rubbed the dark stubble on his chin and sighed. "Either way, there's nothing more we can do at this point but wait."

Cooper's head fell back against the seat, frustration eating away at him. "I know you're right, but that doesn't mean I accept it."

"We've always just been pawns in a greater game, my friend."

Cooper rolled his head to meet Marco's eyes. "I don't want to play anymore."

Marco offered him a knowing grin. "But you will, because you have to know how it ends."

PART 04

LUCKY FOX
DISTILLER'S CHOICE

Too much of anything is bad, but too much
good whiskey is barely enough.
~ Mark Twain ~

CHAPTER

Eighteen

As night fell, Ava finally walked up the front steps of her home with her brother at her side. Adam held her hand tightly, not willing to let go even as they stepped inside and closed the door.

For a long moment, they stood in the quiet stillness that would never again fill with the aroma of their mother's cooking or the sound of her laughter. Ava breathed in deeply, wanting to savor the last lingering scent of their mother's perfume. Soon it would fade completely, just like the warm, inviting presence she had always given the home. They would do their best to keep her memory alive, but in time even that would be gone.

Squeezing Adam's hand, she walked into the kitchen. Her grandfather was sitting at the dining table, a half-empty bottle of Lucky Fox 101 at his side. He looked up as they entered, his eyes bloodshot and wet with unshed tears. His mouth stiffened as he got to his feet and met Ava halfway into the room, wrapping her in his arms.

When he released her, he immediately went to Adam and offered him the same embrace. "This has been a tragic day for us all."

Ava sniffled, though her eyes were dry. "I can't believe she's gone."

"None of us can," Joe said, shaking his head sadly. "But we must go on."

She looked down the hall toward her father's office. "How's Daddy?"

Joe sighed. "Shut up tight in that room of his since he came home. Won't speak to me."

"Has he eaten anything? We can't just let him wither away in there."

"Give him time, dearie. He'll come around."

Adam shifted his weight, looking restless. "Have you heard anything from Beau?"

Joe nodded, a violence coming into his eyes. "Said they caught the bastard, thank the Lord. What I wouldn't give to get my hands on him."

Ava's eyes widened. "They caught him? Is he connected to the IRA?"

"Beau says the lad's from the city, an ex-con likely traveling through town looking for a quick buck." He paused, eyeing his grandchildren with concern. "I told ye both, Ned cannot hurt ye here. Yer letting yer imaginations get carried away. Our girl was simply in the wrong place at the wrong time. It can happen to anyone."

"But it didn't happen to anyone," Ava snapped, feeling her defenses rise. "It happened to *her*. Daddy warned me to stay away from Ned, and before Mama died she told me to stay away from Daddy. None of that is coincidence and don't you *dare* tell me I'm overreacting."

"She's right." Adam folded his arms, coming to stand beside his sister. "We don't buy that it was just a robbery. This was planned. Probably some kind of retaliation."

Joe's mouth fell open. "I can't believe what I'm hearin' from the both of ye. Ye actually believe the IRA had a reason to want yer mother dead?"

Ava hesitated. She recognized what a long shot it was when he said it, but pride wouldn't let her back down. "All I know is people in Fox Hills don't just get gunned down in the street like this. Until I know otherwise, I won't stop believing Ned's involved."

"Fools, the both of ye," Joe grumbled, waving them off angrily. "I need a drink."

He stumbled back to the dining table. Ava met Adam's eyes and pursed her lips, her temper still on fire. Needing to release it on the target of her anger, she headed for her father's office and slammed her fist against the door.

"Let me in!" she shouted, hitting the door a second time so hard it reverberated through the walls. Tears began to stream down her face, hot with rage. She pictured her father inside, sitting at his desk, calmly sipping a glass of bourbon while their mother rotted in the morgue. The image filled her with a hatred so strong she seriously considered breaking the door to pieces just to get at him.

When he didn't so much as answer her request, she rested her forehead against the wood and gritted her teeth. "So help me God, if this was because of you I will make you pay."

Shoving away from the door, she turned and disappeared into her own bedroom.

Adam watched her go in silence, his hands clenched into white-knuckled fists at his sides. He would have joined her in attempting to reach their father, but then that door would have been ripped in half and he would be forced to face the old man. He wasn't sure he was ready for that yet.

If his father *was* responsible, would he even be sorry? Not that an apology would ever make up for it. No, only revenge would do.

Riding on the thought, he missed the soft knocking sound on the front door. He heard it the second time, and had to release a heavy breath and relax his hands before having the ability to answer it.

Brandy stood on the other side, huddled into a soft gray pea coat and white scarf, her blonde hair tossed up by the wind. The pure emotion on her face, all sorrow and sympathy and understanding, stopped his rage like a tree stops a speeding car.

Without a word he stumbled to her, letting her hold him tight against the onslaught of pain. Proud as he was, he didn't even care that she would see him cry. She was the last person who would ever judge him.

"Adam. God, Adam, I'm so sorry," she murmured, pressing her face into his hair as he clung to her. She rubbed his back, wishing the movement could take away all his pain. Her heart yearned to absorb all of it, just so he wouldn't suffer one more minute. Her eyes closed and she breathed deeply, her throat constricting with emotion.

Adam eased away from her. "Shouldn't you be working?"

"The bar's closed tonight. Most places are, actually. The entire town's grieving right along with you." She cupped his face, tears welling at the corners of her beautiful eyes. "She touched so many lives. We all loved her."

He nodded, knowing his own life would never be the same. "She didn't deserve to go that way. I should've been there to protect her."

"You couldn't have known," Brandy assured him. Her hands fell as she glanced through the open front door, a sad smile crossing her face. "I'll miss her so much. In many ways, she took my mama's place all those years ago when she ran off. And again when my grandma passed a few years back."

Adam averted his eyes, having forgotten that Brandy had known a grief just a strong. He tended to forget that there was much more to her behind that sunny smile.

"Come inside, darlin'." He ushered her into the house and out of the cold, sealing her inside the warmth. When they came into the kitchen, he saw that his grandfather had gone to bed. Just as well, he didn't think he could stand the sight of the old man anymore.

Brandy wrung her hands together as she stared around the kitchen, reeling at the knowledge that Sandra would never again cook there. "It doesn't get easier," she remarked, her heart aching. "Losing someone you love. Especially to such a senseless tragedy."

"My mother was murdered, Brandy," Adam told her, his mouth set in a grim line. "It wasn't a robbery."

Brandy's brows pinched together as they locked eyes. "I don't understand."

His face flushed as his anger over it all returned. "I don't have proof and the cops are denying it, but Ava and I know the truth. She was killed because of my father's connection to the IRA. They're a terrorist group in Ireland. My family over there is in bed with them."

She blinked, the suggestion completely out of the blue. Her head shook back and forth. "This is crazy, Adam. It makes no sense."

"It makes complete sense." He shoved his hands into his hair and stepped back from her, jaw tightening as he combated his own fury. "Why the hell do you think the FBI has been in town all this time? They don't give a shit about taxes. They know my father gave money to these assholes in Ireland and now my mother's been killed for it."

Her hands flew up to cover her mouth. "Good Lord."

He scowled, feeling mean and self-righteous. "And if it wasn't for the goddamn FBI sniffing around, this probably would've never happened."

The realization of it overwhelmed him with a new kind of rage. His hands began to shake as he squeezed them into tight fists. Before he could stop himself, he whirled around to ram one directly into the wall. Plaster and wallpaper shredded beneath the force of the blow, scraping his skin and giving him a blessed release for his anger. He yanked his hand free and stared down at the blood smeared across his knuckles. A morbid pleasure coursed through him at the sight of it. In his mind it was a punishment to soothe his guilt.

Brandy was at his side in an instant, inspecting his hand. He ripped it away from her and retreated, too full of ire to trust himself not to take it out on her accidentally. "Leave me alone, Brandy. I appreciate you comin' by, but I just gotta go for a drive or somethin' and clear my head."

"Please don't get behind the wheel," she begged, inching toward him with her hands out. "I'll drive you anywhere you want to go. I don't want you to hurt yourself."

"I'm just pissed, not suicidal," he snapped. "I can take care of myself. Now get out."

Her eyes filled as her face crumpled with despair, and the sight of it killed him. He turned away from it, unable to look any longer. "Never mind. I'll go."

He tore out of the room, not bothering to grab his jacket, and headed for his truck.

Brandy raced out onto the front porch only to watch him drive away, his taillights fading into the dark.

AVA CAME out of her room when she heard Brandy leave. She inspected the gaping hole in the wall her brother had created, her fingers trailing over the broken plaster. She knew that although they had both done their best to be strong for each other hours earlier, that façade had shattered. Her outburst at her father and Adam's destruction of the family home left a static charge in the air, one that prickled her skin and chilled her to the bone.

She had heard his words about the FBI being in some way responsible for this. Part of her agreed, as much as she didn't want to. Though it wasn't right, she had to believe that if the FBI hadn't come to Fox Hills and begun investigating her father, Ned may not have retaliated this way. Then again, maybe it had only been a matter of time before the entire IRA scandal erupted in their faces. Ned clearly had no qualms against murder, be it his own family or innocent people.

The entire business of it made her sick to her stomach. She didn't blame Cooper. How could she? He certainly hadn't wanted this. But she couldn't ignore the fact that before he'd come to town, her life had been a hell of a lot simpler.

Her cell phone buzzed in her pocket. When she saw Cooper's name on the caller-ID, she debated ignoring it. Realizing he could possibly have more information on her mother's killer, she answered.

"Hi, Slick."

"*Hey, you.*"

She closed her eyes at the sound of his voice, comforted by it despite everything. She moved over to sit at the dining table, where her grandfather had left the nearly empty bottle of whiskey and his glass. Pouring herself a shot, she downed it and let out a slow exhale. "Got any news for me?"

He was quiet for a moment, making her wonder if he was still on the line. When he finally spoke, there was a hint of bitterness in his tone. "*I'm still working on it. The local PD is calling it a robbery and refuses to budge on that. They won't let me talk to the suspect.*"

"So flash that shiny badge of yours and force your way in," she replied heatedly, not willing to accept that. "If you need me to hold Beau back while you have a word with the suspect, I can do it."

"*That's not how this works, Ava. I think you know that.*"

"I don't care. I deserve the truth."

"*I know. Which is why I'm not going to give up. But it may take some time to cut through all the red tape. As much as it kills you, you'll have to be patient.*"

"Patient," she repeated, refilling her glass with the last of the whiskey and tossing it back with relish. She slammed the glass down on the table and swallowed. "I ain't ever been a patient woman, Slick. I don't see me startin' now."

"*I know. Trust me, I understand what you're going through. I know it's hard. But there's something bigger at work here. Until I get to the bottom of it, you'll need to hang tight. Okay?*"

"How the hell could you understand?" she fired back, letting the hot kick of whiskey fuel her anger. "I have to put my mother in the ground because a madman wanted her dead. And now I'm being told he may get off scot free because of God knows what. So yeah, I'm frustrated and hurting and pissed off."

"*I understand better than you think,*" he replied, his tone callous and devoid of its usual warmth. He had never once spoken to her like that, and hearing it made her realize she'd let her temper run amok.

"All right. I'm sorry, okay?" she said, leaning forward to pillow her head in her arms. Her eyes closed as she exhaled, releasing her anger as best as she could. "Tell me what happened to you. Please. I need to think about something else."

"*I can't.*"

She pictured his face, creased with misery and regret, and began to cry. "Please."

"*I'll be in touch.*" With that, he hung up. She held the phone to her ear a while longer, conceding to the wretched depths of sorrow at last.

CHAPTER

Nineteen

S he's dead."
    Ned fixed his gaze on his most trusted confidant, a dark
intensity coming over his eyes. "Are ye sure?"

    Ronan nodded, stepping into the office and closing
the door behind him. He stood before his boss's desk, a ma-
nila folder in his hand. "Our man in the States managed to
evade capture. He says the police have arrested another in
connection with the shooting."

    A pleased smile lifted Ned's lips. "Fools." He eased back
in his chair, clasping his hands behind his head as his grin
grew larger. "A fine day it is, then. Dare I ask how me cousin
is takin' the news?"

    "I imagine yer payback has crippled him, Boss. Howev-
er..." Ronan's stern features twisted slightly, signaling what
Ned knew to be a bad sign.

    "Out with it, then," Ned grumbled, letting his hands
fall back to the desk. "I take it something went wrong?"

"Not quite." Ronan shook his head. "I had our man forward the contents of her cell phone to me. I thought perhaps ye'd like the pictures as a memento, of sorts."

Ned's brow creased with suspicion. "What did ye find?"

Ronan lowered his long frame into the chair across from Ned and handed him the file folder. "See for yerself."

Without hesitating, Ned opened the folder and inspected the photographs inside. There were dozens of them, mostly of her with his cousin and his traitorous uncle. He paused when he uncovered a close-up image of her flanked on either side by a smiling young man and woman in their late-twenties.

The likeness was startling. From the shade of their auburn hair to the curve of their cheekbones to the fullness of their mouths, they were her spitting image. Save for the eyes and the strength of their chins—those he knew they hadn't inherited through her bloodline. Those had come from somewhere else entirely.

Somewhere far more disconcerting.

"These are Ty's children?" he asked, a fluttering tick in his right cheek the first sign of his outrage. He struggled to keep his breathing level as he continued to stare purposefully into the eyes of the twins, haunted by the familiarity he saw there.

Ronan bowed his head. "Aye. It appears he raised them in Fox Hills. He's done a good job keeping them off the radar, until recently. I discovered this image on the company's website as well."

He dug a piece of paper out of his coat pocket, unfolded it, and placed it on the desk. It was the family portrait of the Brannons, with Joe at the heart and Ava and Adam at his sides. Ty stood in the back. Ned glared at his cousin's face, envisioning tearing the man apart for what he'd done. For what he'd kept hidden all these years.

All of his earlier delight was gone. In its place was a rage more violent than any he had ever felt. Even worse than the discovery that she was alive, having evaded him for all these years, was this latest blow. This was an unquestionably worse betrayal.

"Bring me my sons," he ordered. He took a long drink of whiskey to help cool his temper, infuriated to see his hand tremble.

Ronan quickly left the room and returned moments later with Rhys and Killian. Both approached their father's desk in silent reverence.

Ned finally tore his eyes from the photograph to face his sons. "We have business to attend to in the States. I need ye to make the arrangements for us to travel."

Rhys and Killian exchanged a curious look. Rhys spoke first. "May I ask what for?"

Ned tossed the photograph onto the desk, a sneer tightening his features as his sons inspected it. "There's a couple of long lost sheep that have strayed from the flock. It's time we brought them home."

THE FUNERAL was held on a calm, peaceful Sunday morning. As if by grand design, the sunlight warmed the faces of those present and songbirds flitted about the elm trees, their voices soothing and filled with magic.

It was a day her mother would have adored, Ava thought. A day as sunny and lovely as the woman being laid to rest.

Adam stood to her left, Brandy a permanent fixture at his side. Ava took notice of the way her brother held on to her old friend, and as unhappy as the day was, the sight of it pleased her. Her mother would have loved to see the two of them come together. She liked to imagine her mother looking down on them, delighting in it all the same.

To her left was her grandfather. He stood upright and proud, a quiet smile on his face as the preacher recalled tales of Sandra's generous nature and open heart. Everyone, including Joe, had fallen in love with her from the moment she'd come to Fox Hills nearly thirty years earlier. The proof was in the hundreds of people who came to pay their respects, all touched in some way by the woman she had been lucky enough to call her mother.

Tears swam in Ava's eyes as she looked across the mahogany casket covered in pink and white lilies to her father. Though he was surrounded by people he had known all his life, Ava got the impression he felt so very alone. His gaze stayed glued on the box that held his wife, unwavering and hard as stone. Whatever he was feeling, be it grief or guilt or bitterness, he was keeping it to himself. Since the day she had died, he'd done nothing but that. He hadn't even attempted to defend himself against Ava's accusations or questions. Instead he had retreated into a comatose silence, beyond reaching. Until he came up for air again, she knew she'd be unable to get through to him.

As the casket was lowered into the ground, the preacher read off scriptures and Ava closed her eyes. She focused on his comforting voice, letting a sense of peace wash over her. For now, in this moment, she was content to lay her mother to rest and know Heaven had gained the brightest of angels.

When it was through and the crowd dispersed for the reception at the church, Ava held tight to her grandfather and Adam as they walked up the grassy slope to the parking lot. Her father followed close behind, but made no move to join them.

She spotted Cooper leaning casually against his sedan, dressed in his suit and tie with his golden hair catching the sun. With his hands tucked in his pockets and sunglasses hiding his eyes, he looked so official and intimidating. The subtle curve of his lips at the sight of her said otherwise.

Adam tensed, but she ignored his disapproval and went to Cooper anyway.

"Hey." She began to hug him, thought against it and held out her hand instead. "I'm glad you came by."

He removed his sunglasses and accepted her handshake, his eyes glued to hers. A quiet compassion softened his face. "I'm sorry to bother you. I just need a second of your time."

"It's okay." She didn't even realize her hand was still in his until he squeezed it and let go. His eyes drifted over her shoulder and when she turned, she saw he was staring intently at her father as he climbed into Joe's truck.

"Has he said anything?" Cooper asked, referring to Ty.

Ava shook her head. "We've barely spoken at all. I've never seen him like this."

"He may have a guilty conscience."

Her heart ached at the thought, wishing beyond all hope that this was just some insane nightmare. "He knows I blame him. Until he comes around, I don't expect I'll get anything out of him."

She tilted her face up to Cooper's, wanting nothing more than to seek comfort in the safety of his arms. If it wasn't for the lingering funeral guests curiously watching her on the way to their cars, she would have.

"So is there any news?" she asked.

"Not really." He slipped his sunglasses into his coat pocket, avoiding her gaze. "The investigation into your mother's death has been put on hold. I think they're waiting for something, and it's my belief it has to do with Ned."

"But they won't tell you?" She urged him to look at her, needing to see the truth of it in his eyes.

"The local PD is still maintaining that it was just a robbery, but they're having trouble building their case. The man they caught isn't as solid a suspect as it appeared at first."

"How so?"

He slipped his hands into his pockets. "I pestered the Sheriff this morning and got him to admit that they were pressured into making a quick arrest and to work out the details later. He's worried they don't have enough evidence to hold him. They may have to let him go."

Ava let out a rush of breath, her mind turning over this new information. "But he's probably not our guy, right? So if he's innocent he should be set free. Then they can find the real shooter."

"In theory, yes." Cooper angled his head, his face lined with stress. "With the investigation being put on hold, the only conclusion I can come to is that they're waiting for Ned to make another move. I'm under strict orders to keep an eye on your entire family. I think they're waiting for Ned to come to the States."

She crossed her arms against a chill that swept over her. "Why won't they just tell you the truth? Why all the secrecy? What are they hiding?"

"If I knew, I'd tell you." A ghost of a smile lifted the corners of his mouth. "I know one thing for sure—Ned Brannon is behind this, and though I'm being kept in the dark on some of the details, the FBI is working something behind the scenes. They don't want your mother's death to be tied to Ned. I think they want him to believe he got away with it to encourage him to come back for the rest of you. Most likely they're hoping he'll smuggle himself into the States to take care of Ty personally."

224 | KATIE JENNINGS

"They're using us as bait," she murmured, feeling sick and furious all at once. "I can't believe this."

He caught her by the arms before she could walk away, forcing her to look at him. "If it's true, then you could be in danger."

Her lip curled as hate filled her. "So let him come try and take me out. I won't go down without a fight."

"Of course you won't." Affection and regret softened his voice as he stared into her eyes. "Until this blows over we'll be keeping watch over you and your family, but I can't be there every second of the day. You need to arm yourself."

She pulled back her coat, revealing the holstered pistol at her waist. One of her eyebrows raised at the impressed look he gave her. "I know how to shoot it, too. In case you were wondering."

"I don't doubt that." He attempted another smile and brushed strands of hair from her forehead.

She grabbed his hand and cradled it against her cheek. "I'm sorry about what I said the other night. About you not understanding. It wasn't fair. But I do hope that when you're ready, you'll tell me what happened to you."

He swallowed the lump that formed in his throat, humbled by her words. "I'll be sticking around for a while it seems. I hope you don't get sick of me."

She shook her head, a dozen emotions crossing her face. "In spite of everything, Slick, I like having you around."

"In spite of everything, I like being around." He twisted a piece of her hair around his fingers, admiring the way the auburn turned scarlet in the sun. "You should go. Your family will be expecting you."

Ava looked around and noticed that everyone had left the cemetery. On impulse, she stood on her toes and gave him a tender, lingering kiss, then turned and walked away.

CHAPTER

Twenty

In the week following her mother's funeral, Ava discovered a lot of things about grief. One was that if she managed to distract herself long enough, the pain subsided. It didn't fade completely—that she knew would never happen. But it did give her the chance to continue on with her life.

The other thing she had learned was that everyone dealt with grief differently. Her grandfather, being of a similar temperament, dove back into work and busied himself as often as he could. He fixed on a smile and did his best to bring everything back to the way it was, and only occasionally did she stumble across him during a time of haunted reflection. In those moments, his bright mood was dampened by a storm cloud, darkened by an anger she understood only too well. So she'd sit down, wrap her arm around him and let silence say all the words she knew needn't be said.

Adam was a different story. Having no work to occupy him, he spent his days with a bottle of whiskey and a vile temper. He snapped at anyone who dared speak to him and did his best to pick every imaginable fight he could. He was begging for trouble, itching for a release of his pain in the only way he knew how. It destroyed her to see it, especially when nothing she said or did seemed to shake him out of it. What they all needed was time.

But waiting out the thunderstorm only made her more anxious. Every day she felt like a child expecting a monster to jump out at her. Ned—or one of his cronies—could be around every corner, lying in wait. She wanted to believe her grandfather when he said that Ned couldn't get to the States, but if Cooper was correct and that was exactly what the FBI wanted, then what would stop him? And what would she do when he inevitably arrived in Fox Hills, eager to pick them off one by one?

A violent rage filled her at the thought. She rested her elbows on the desk in her office, burying her face in her hands. Her fingers dove into her hair as she tried to breathe, overcome with emotion at the thought of him laying a single finger on anyone she cared about. He had no right, no matter what her father had promised him. Whatever business they'd had together had been decimated the second the FBI found out about it, which meant no more money from Lucky Fox whiskey would find its way into the hands of the IRA. If it was the last thing she did, she'd see to it that Ned paid for the torment and destruction he'd caused within her family, even if it meant facing him herself.

A dull ache formed behind her eyes, a side effect of her stress. She rubbed her temples and desperately wished for a glass of whiskey to chase the pain away. Knowing that would make her just as bad as her brother, she pushed the thought aside and got to her feet. Better to jump back into work than succumb to an emotional crutch.

She walked out into the distillery, catching the notice of a few employees. They offered her hesitant smiles and nervous looks, as if she were a ticking time bomb set to explode into a rage of grief and torment at any moment. Seeing the concern in their eyes only reminded her of what she'd lost, so she did her best to ignore them.

Her grandfather appeared through the distillery doors, waving excitedly at her with a bottle of whiskey tucked under one arm.

"Today's the day, dearie!"

Seeing the bright grin on his face as he raced over cheered her up considerably. "For what?"

He skidded to a stop and held up the bottle for her to see. "For Lucky Joe's Single Barrel Bourbon."

Her lips parted in surprise as she accepted the bottle, inspecting the label their best graphic artist had designed. It had an old, black and white photo of her grandfather with one foot resting on an overturned barrel and a bottle of whiskey in his hand, with bold text across the bottom declaring it as "Lucky Joe's." The picture had been taken the day he'd opened the Lucky Fox distillery, and the endless ambition and pleasure showed on his youthful face. She swore his eyes twinkled with mischief even in the photograph.

"It's beautiful." She turned the bottle over, admired the backside with its brief history of the feud along with a picture of the distillery. Her eyes met his. "How does it feel to have your own single barrel bourbon?"

"Like a dream," Joe replied, beaming at her with pride. "Come on now, let's have ourselves a toast."

She led the way back into her office and dug out two glasses from her desk drawer. Pouring them each a healthy drink, she took a seat and lifted her glass.

He raised his as well, his smile both filled with joy and marked by sorrow. "To Sandra, the loveliest lady I ever had the pleasure of knowing."

Ava clicked her glass to his, then lifted her eyes to the ceiling and toasted the air. "To you, Mama."

They both drank. Ava let the whiskey mingle on her tongue, thrilling in the brilliant combination of flavors and sensations and smells. When she swallowed, a warmth spread over her that tingled all the way down her spine.

"Lord, that's good," she murmured, taking another sip.

Joe nodded. "Aye. Of all the troubles lately, at least we have this to show for it."

She reached for his old, weathered hand and held it tightly in her own. "And we still have each other. We'll get through this."

"I know, dearie. I have faith."

COOPER STOOD at the window of his hotel room, his eyes on the street below. Being a typical Sunday night, most of the local businesses were closed and people were tucked safely inside their homes. The charming town of Fox Hills slept all around him, as serene and beautiful as an oil painting.

How long would the peace last? he wondered. How long before Ned made his next move?

A day? Another week, another month? Or would he not bother, content with having taken the life of one Brannon for the time being?

Without any real idea on what his superiors were planning, he was left bitterly in the dark. He was no closer to learning the truth than he'd been when Ava's mother had been laid to rest. The suspect the Sheriff had arrested had been set free, the evidence against him not enough to press charges. Since then, the investigation remained on hold and Cooper was left with no more instructions than to stay put and keep an eye on Ty.

The wait was killing him, and he knew it was taking a toll on Ava. She had been doing her best to stay strong and resume her life like normal, but he could see the restless energy in her eyes. She craved action and resolution just as badly as he did.

If only the idea of what that action would mean didn't terrify him so much. Would he be able to protect her if Ned came knocking? Hell, he wanted to believe she could take care of herself. But what if she needed him and he wasn't there?

Shaking off the sick feeling, he turned away from the window and collapsed into the armchair by his bed. He flipped on the television and mindlessly skipped through the channels until his cell phone rang.

He saw Ava's name and hurriedly answered. "Everything all right?"

"*I'm fine, Slick,*" she replied, a hint of humor in her voice.

He relaxed. "Good. What's up?"

"*I have a surprise for you. Come meet me at the tasting room in twenty minutes.*"

He couldn't help himself. "What's the surprise?"

"*Don't make me scold you for trying to spoil it. You'll find out soon enough.*"

She hung up before he could respond. He chuckled, intrigued by the mystery.

Several minutes later he was pulling up in front of the distillery. He parked in the empty lot and walked to the glass entrance doors. A soft, golden light emanated from within, where he could see Ava behind the tasting counter. She glanced up when he knocked, her teeth flashing in a grin.

She wandered over and welcomed him inside. "Hey."

"Hi." He turned after she shut the door and locked it, giving her a curious look. "So what's the surprise?"

"First things first." She grabbed his collar and dragged him in for a heated kiss, her mouth cruising over his. When she pulled away, she bit her lower lip and smiled. "Right this way."

He forgot to breathe for a second before he trailed after her, his eyes following the sway of her hips. She wore her usual faded jeans and plaid shirt, which she rolled up to the elbows as she rounded the bar and placed a couple of glasses on the counter. She set a bottle of whiskey in front of him and showed off the label. Her smile was electric.

"This is my grandpa's signature bourbon. It's not for sale just yet, but I wanted to give you a taste and see what you think."

He recognized the pride in her voice, the passion, and adored her for it. "I'm honored."

"You should be," she mused, uncorking the bottle and pouring a generous amount into each glass. "You're only the third person to try it—after me and Lucky Joe himself. It's a single barrel bourbon, which means all of the bottles for this batch come from one very special barrel. After they're gone, there won't be any more."

"Wow." Cooper accepted the glass from her and eyed the amber liquid inside. "You sure you want to waste it on a novice like me?"

"Consider it a show of good faith." Her smile softened as she held her glass up to his. "I trust you, Cooper. I hope in our time together you've come to trust me, too."

It was the first time she'd used his real name. The sound of it falling from her lips, gilded with Southern glory, moved him in ways he couldn't explain. "I do."

"Good. Then let's drink to that." Her glass met his in a cheerful clink before she drank.

He followed her lead, catching the woodsy aroma as he sipped. The toasted spice hit him first, the burn and the heat of it catching him off guard. But what followed was a medley of flavors so complex he couldn't put a finger on them all. Instead, he took more into his mouth just to try pinpointing them, impressed by how beautifully they came together.

Ava watched him silently, enjoying the range of emotions passing over his face. He sniffed and sipped and contemplated the bourbon as though it were some great mystery to solve. She supposed in a way it was, though there was never a wrong answer when it came to what a person could taste in a whiskey.

"I'm gonna take a wild guess here and say this is your favorite," she said at last.

He set down the glass, bemused. "It's incredible. I mean, wow."

"Isn't it?" She leaned onto the counter, resting her arms on the wooden surface with the glass held in her hands. "It's funny as hell to watch you dissect whiskey like it's a science experiment."

"I do not."

She laughed. "Yeah, you do. But that's okay. I think it's my favorite thing about you."

"Not my wit or dashing good looks?"

"Those are nice, too." She covered his hand with hers, more at ease than she'd been in days. Just being in his presence had that effect on her. "Can I tell you a secret, Slick?"

"Of course."

Her heart skipped at the sight of those blue eyes holding her own. "When all of this is over and you have to leave, I'm really gonna miss you." She lifted her free hand before he could speak. "I know we said from the start that this was just for fun, but I've gotten used to having you around. And with Mama gone and Adam on a bender and so many things in my life turned upside down, you've kind of become my rock. Crazy as it sounds."

"It sounds less crazy than you think," he told her, bringing her hand to his lips. He kissed her skin and breathed in the scent of vanilla and bourbon and knew his heart was lost to her. "When I came here I never expected to find someone like you. Someone who understands loss the way I do."

Her breath caught in her throat. Unable to speak, she simply nodded.

He offered her a kind smile. "You asked me before what my motivation is for my job. I didn't tell you because it's not something I share with strangers. I don't feel like you're a stranger anymore."

His eyes fell to their joined hands as he lazily caressed her thumb. "I used to want to be a cop, just like my dad. Like most young boys, he was my hero. I would watch him put on his blue uniform and badge and see the pride in my mother's eyes when she looked at him. He put his life on the line every day to protect perfect strangers. There's nothing nobler than that.

"Everything changed when I was sixteen years old. The day started like any other. I woke up, went to school, slept through Spanish class. Then around mid-morning someone came into the classroom to let us know that two planes had flown into the World Trade Center towers. One had collapsed, and the other was still burning."

Ava winced. She remembered the day well. While she had been hundreds of miles away, safe from the carnage, Cooper had been front and center.

He continued. "They told us to stay put, but that they'd be contacting our parents to come pick us up. A few kids in my class had parents who worked in the towers, and so many of us had family in the city. I remember being so confused. We were all wondering how a plane could hit a building, much less two at the same time. What were the odds? None of us even thought about *why* it had happened.

"The teacher turned on the television so we could see the news report. Minutes later we watched the North Tower collapse. They were filming people running in the street, covered in ash with scraps of paper flying in the air. Then they showed a clip of a policeman carrying a businesswoman in his arms, both of them coated head-to-toe in dust. It hit me then that my dad was probably down there, helping save people from the wreckage. It didn't even occur to me that he could've been *inside* one of the buildings when it crumbled. Turns out, he was in the North Tower. Without realizing it, I'd witnessed the moment the building came down around him and took his life."

Ava let go of the breath she'd been holding, her heart breaking. With tears sliding down her cheeks, she squeezed his hand and grieved for him. "That's awful. I can't even imagine...God, Cooper, I'm so sorry."

He nodded, aching from a wound that had never fully healed. "He died a hero. My mom never let me forget that. But after that day, I knew I couldn't be a cop. I had to aim higher if I wanted to destroy the monsters responsible for his death. So I joined the FBI, and I've been moving up the ranks and waiting for my chance to get justice ever since."

Silence fell as Ava absorbed the weight of what he had just told her. Despite how painful it must have been to relive the experience, she was grateful he had opened up about his past. Now she felt she finally understood him.

Without a word, she rounded the bar and embraced him, holding him tight against her as she released a heavy sigh. "Thank you for telling me."

He framed her face in his hands, brushing aside a tear that fell with his thumb. "I told you I understood how you felt."

"That you did. And I, being a stubborn fool, refused to believe you. Forgive me."

The last dredges of his pain faded in the light of her smile, and for the first time in forever he felt like he could breathe.

"I think your stubbornness is my favorite thing about you," he teased.

Her lips pursed into a playful pout. "Not my sexy laugh or Southern charm?"

"What can I say? I like rebellious women. It keeps things interesting."

"Nice guy like you should settle down with a pretty little blonde in a white picket fence house," she mused. "Most men can't take the heat."

"I think you already know I'm not most men."

Her pulse jumped at the look in his eyes. "No. I don't reckon you are."

He captured her mouth with his, impatient and with something to prove. She curved into him, her hands roaming over his back as her heart thundered in her ears. It wasn't just about wanting him anymore, she knew. They were connected now, bonded by tragedy and joined together by circumstances that should have made them enemies. Her heart had other plans, and when it filled close to bursting with love for him she realized it was about damn time.

Cooper broke free of her, out of breath and dazed. He didn't even know what was happening to him, or why just being near her made him feel like he was having a heart attack. She was a jumpstart to his system that defied everything he had ever known. And when their eyes met, he swore the whole world stood still.

Her lips curved in a sultry smile. "What are you waiting for?"

"Hell if I know." He dragged her against him, his hands in her hair and his mouth on hers. She wrapped herself around him like a vine and before he realized what was happening, they were on the floor.

She rolled him onto his back and unbuttoned his shirt, pressing her mouth greedily to the slope of his collarbone. Freeing him of his shirt, she sat up and pulled off her own, revealing the tanned skin and practical white bra underneath. Her hair tumbled over her shoulders and he couldn't resist diving into that sea of auburn red.

She gasped when his tongue trailed over her neck, sending a smooth shiver through her body. Urgency hit her like a rushing wave and had her tugging at the waistband of his slacks, exposing him. He flipped her over so she was beneath him, and within seconds he'd peeled off her boots and jeans and brought his mouth back to hers.

Her breath came quick and labored as she arched up to meet him, thrilled when his hands ran down the length of her body, landing on her hips as he positioned himself over her. She looked into his eyes the moment he slipped inside of her, and watched the blue in them go opaque with desire.

He hovered for a moment, drunk on her like she was one of her family's whiskies. Then he drove into her again, and the sound of his name on her lips echoed in his mind like a siren's call, addictive and surreal. He marveled in her beauty as he dove in head first, letting go of everything else. All that mattered was Ava.

They moved together as one, fast and breathless and desperate. Her head fell back as the first wave swept over her, a hot shock that blasted through her system. Her eyes flew open in stunned surprise.

"Sweet Jesus, Slick," she managed, her body shuddering against his.

He urged her to look at him and picked up the pace. His cobalt eyes darkened with an intense hunger that refused to let her go.

"Again, Ava," he ordered, needing to feel the power of her release once more. The heat of her consumed him, drove him to a kind of madness he'd never before experienced. It roared within him, and all he could think about was watching her succumb to the pleasure he gave her, over and over again until there was nothing left.

Her mouth found his, lost in the heat and the pounding of her own heart. Soon she was cresting over the peak again, and this time when she cried out, she dragged him with her into the fire.

CHAPTER
Twenty-one

He awoke to the sound of birds chirping. It was such an unusual noise that at first he thought he was still dreaming, but after opening one eye he saw the source and it all came rushing back to him.

Ava.

There were trees outside her bedroom window. Darting among the branches he spotted a few russet sparrows, chasing each other in a dance as old as time.

Cooper closed his eyes again, releasing a long breath. He could feel her curled up beside him, her body warm and soft against his own. He glanced down and saw she was fast asleep, her lips parted and strands of hair falling over her face. On impulse he brushed them away, losing himself in memories of the night before.

If there was anything he could have done to make it harder to leave Fox Hills, this was it. It wasn't the sex or the sharing of secrets, it was the falling flat on his face in love with her. He knew it had been brewing in his system ever since the moment they first met, but now there was no denying it. He cared about her in a way he had never cared for anyone in his entire life. And accepting that fact brought a bittersweet ache to his heart.

Eyeing the clock on her nightstand, he saw it was just after six in the morning. If he was lucky, he could leave without her family noticing. It hadn't seemed to matter the night before when they had stumbled into the house, drunk on whiskey and each other. Now he realized just how bad it would be if anyone knew what they had done.

One look back at her had him wanting nothing more than to rouse her awake and lose himself in her all over again. But she was so peaceful while she slept, all the sharp edges of her foxy face smooth and relaxed. It was best for both of them if he left.

He eased out of bed and dressed as quickly as he could, then knelt down to press a kiss to her forehead. She stirred beneath him, her eyes fluttering open.

"Hi," she murmured, her lips spreading in a slow smile.

"Hey, you." He caressed her face, aching for just one more moment. "I need to run. But I'll call you later, okay?"

She nodded, then snuggled back into the blankets. "Bye, Slick."

By the time he stood, she had already fallen back asleep. Amused, he grabbed his coat and slowly opened her bedroom door. The house was silent as a tomb. Feeling confident that he could make his escape, he stepped into the hallway and closed her door behind him.

Just then Ty emerged from his office down the hall.

The two men stared at each other, and Cooper's heart slammed into his throat.

Ty's brows drew together. "What are you—" His eyes shot to Ava's bedroom, then widened with understanding. "Oh."

Cooper finally found his voice. "I'm not gonna lie to you. This is exactly what it looks like."

Disapproval hardened the lines of Ty's face, but he looked too tired to argue. "So it is."

Since he couldn't get out of the situation, Cooper decided to take advantage of it. "How are you doing, anyway? You've been avoiding us all week."

"I just had to bury my wife, Agent Lawson. I'm sorry if I haven't felt up to entertaining the FBI," Ty grumbled, pushing past to head into the kitchen.

Cooper followed him. "Actually, that's exactly why I wanted to speak to you. The local PD is insisting it was a robbery gone bad, but I think you and I both know otherwise."

Ty ignored his statement and put on a pot of coffee. When it was brewing, he faced Cooper. "What are you still doing here, son? I have nothing to say to you."

"Ned Brannon had your wife killed to punish you. We both know that's the truth. Help me prove it."

A scowl darkened Ty's face. His hand shook as he swiped it through his hair, looking sick to his stomach. "I'm done helping the FBI. I never wanted any of this. It was all her idea, and now she's dead. I have nothing left."

Cooper frowned, confused by his statement. "What was her idea?"

Cold laughter bubbled out of Ty. "Don't you get how *pointless* you are? How pointless all of this is? It's just been for show. You've been investigating a crime that wasn't even committed."

"What are you talking about?" Cooper's heart began to race as he fought for understanding. "You've been sending money to your cousin for the purpose of funding the IRA."

Ty crossed his arms and leaned against the kitchen counter. "Yes, I have. And the FBI helped me do it. In fact, they *asked* me to."

Cooper shook his head, a thousand denials racing through his mind. Then it hit him, and he could have kicked himself for not having thought of it before. "You're an informant."

Ty nodded. "And have been for twenty seven years. They tell me it's highly classified information, for my protection. Not that any of it matters now." He turned away to pour himself a cup of coffee, giving Cooper time to process all of it.

"If you're an informant, why did they let us open the investigation on you? Why not just tell us?"

Ty moved to the kitchen island, taking a long sip of coffee. He placed a second cup in front of Cooper out of habit and ingrained Southern manners. "They needed a reason to cut off the money to Ned, and the less people who knew the truth the better. You'd be surprised how easily information like that can get to the wrong ears."

Cooper accepted the coffee, but didn't drink. "So why cut off the money supply now? And what's the goal?"

"It took those two Americans getting killed in Dublin for us to get permission to finally make a move on him. But I told your boys it wouldn't be enough to convince him to leave Ireland for the States. He needed one more push."

Ty's expression creased with pain, and he lowered his head. Cooper waited patiently for him to continue. When he spoke again, his voice cracked with a deeply rooted misery. "I knew if he saw Sandra, he'd want to take her away from me."

"He wasn't aware you've been married this whole time?" Cooper asked, unsure he followed what Ty was saying. "Ty, who was she to Ned? Was she important somehow?"

Ty gripped his coffee mug in his hands so hard his knuckles turned white. He shook his head, tears spilling from his eyes. "She was everything. *Everything*."

He released the mug before it could be thrown and stormed out of the room, slamming himself shut inside his office. Cooper stared after him, stunned by what he'd just learned. And even more confused than ever before.

I know she's with you.

Christ, the FBI had used her as bait, and now she was dead. It was all their fault.

The realization struck him like a blow to the head. He reeled from it, unable to believe the role he had to play in this perverse game of cat and mouse. Ava's mother was killed in cold blood because the FBI put her in the sights of a madman. A madman who they knew would be triggered to murder if he knew of her existence.

No wonder Ty was ruined. He'd gambled with the lives of his family to try and bring down his cousin, and it backfired. Cooper couldn't even imagine how that must feel.

Anger and guilt snuck under his skin and festered, blinding him to anything else. He reached for his cell phone and stalked out of the house to where his car was parked a ways down the road. He dialed Horvath's number and grew angrier with each ring.

"*Don't you know what time it is?*" Horvath grunted sleepily.

"Why the hell didn't you tell me that Ty Brannon is an informant?"

There was silence on the line for a good thirty seconds. Cooper hopped into his car and rested his head back against the seat, trying without success to calm down.

Horvath finally spoke. "*Who told you that?*"

"He did. He said the FBI used his wife as bait to lure Ned Brannon to the States. Please tell me you knew nothing about this. Please tell me it's a goddamn lie."

Another moment of silence. "*It's not a lie, kid.*"

Cooper closed his eyes, horrified. "I can't believe this."

Horvath sighed. "*I know how it sounds, but you have to trust me when I say we never intended for Mrs. Brannon to get hurt. We expected Ned to come if he knew she was here.*"

"Why does he care so much about her?"

"*I can't tell you that, kid. I'm sorry. I really shouldn't be telling you any of this. It's above your security clearance.*"

Cooper's jaw clenched as fury washed over him. "I want off the case. I'm done. I won't be a part of this bullshit anymore."

"*The Brannons need you right now. Our intelligence confirms Ned has plans to leave Ireland very soon. I need you to keep a low profile and watch over the kids.*"

"The kids?"

"*Ava and Adam Brannon. He's coming for them next.*"

Cooper's blood froze. "Why?"

"*If I told you that, it would compromise everything else I can't tell you. Just know they're the target, but you can't say anything to them. If any of you start acting differently it'll throw up red flags and Ned won't come. We have to get him on U.S. soil if we want to arrest him.*"

Cooper felt sick. "You're using her as bait, just like her mother."

"*We've run out of options. This time we know he's coming. I need you to keep them safe.*"

He knew he had no choice. Not because of his allegiance to the FBI, but because of his love for the woman who had already suffered so much at the hands of Ned Brannon. "All right. I'll stay."

"*Good. Since I know you'll feel the need to fill in D'Amico, make sure he keeps his goddamn mouth shut.*"

He didn't have the energy to be amused. "I will."

After he hung up, he tossed the phone aside and rubbed his face. He didn't want to lie to Ava, but he also knew exactly how she would react to hearing that Ned was coming for her and Adam. She'd take the fight to him without hesitation and demand answers, not caring that she might die. To her it would be worth it just to have the chance at getting revenge for what happened to her mother.

What if she found out that her own father wasn't a criminal after all, but an informant for the FBI? How would she take the news that her mother's death was the result of a botched operation? That she'd been nothing more than bait and her father had let it happen?

It would kill her, Cooper realized. Even more so than thinking he was involved with the IRA. And whatever role her mother played in all this, he was certain that would come as a blow to her as well.

For now he'd keep those secrets to himself. She'd hate him for it later, but if it would keep her safe then it was worth the risk of losing her heart.

AVA SPENT the entire day checking her phone, waiting on his call.

It bugged her to be *that* girl, but she couldn't help it. She missed him, even though it had been less than eight hours since they had spoken. And really, that hadn't counted. She'd been half-asleep and not nearly appreciative enough of the fact that he had been naked in her bed. All that meant was she would need to make it up to him later, a thought that put her in an incredibly good mood.

She went through the motions with her daily tours, eager for the day to end. She toyed with the idea of inviting Cooper dancing again, thinking how fun it would be to show him off. Not that they should be flaunting their affair, but he would look good in a tight pair of jeans and cowboy boots. Plus, dancing for her was always a fun sort of foreplay and the thought of teasing him senseless on the dance floor was too juicy to resist.

Humming to herself, she cleaned up the bar after the last tasting of the day, waving goodbye to the final guests. As she rinsed off glencairns and set them out to dry, her phone rang.

Butterflies exploded to life in her stomach as she fumbled to answer. "Hey! I was just thinking about you."

"*Liar.*"

"No, really," she replied, resting her hip against the counter. "I was imagining how good you'd look in cowboy boots. I should get you a pair."

"*Only if I get to put you in a Yankees ball cap.*"

She cringed. "Oh, hell no. That's not gonna happen."

He chuckled. "*Too bad. If you're not too busy, I thought I'd stop by the distillery.*"

"I'd like that, but I don't know if it's a good idea for you to be seen hanging around here too much."

"*I'm going to be whether you like it or not. So get used to it.*"

She blinked, startled by the change in his voice. Beneath the carefree humor was a dark concern she couldn't miss. She glanced around to be sure none of the employees were listening, then lowered her voice and spoke again. "Is Ned coming? Did you find out for sure?"

At first he didn't say anything, but his silence told her all she needed to know.

"*While we wrap up on the investigation on your father, I'm tasked with keeping an eye on your family. That's all I can tell you.*"

An ice cold chill raced over her skin. She shook it off, choosing rage over fear. "I can't promise to leave him alive if I see him first, Slick. I hope you can respect that."

He sighed. "*I knew you'd say that. Look, I won't be leaving your side for a while. Marco's gonna keep watch on Adam and your dad, and I'll be undercover at the distillery with you and Joe."*

"What am I going to tell my employees? They're bound to notice you hanging around."

"You'll figure something out."

She could already hear the firestorm of gossip this would stir up. But if her family was in danger, then it was better to have more help rather than none.

"All right. C'mon on over." A smile tugged at the corners of her mouth as she grabbed a bottle of whiskey from behind her. "I'll have a glass of Irish waiting for you."

CHAPTER

Twenty-two

Adam didn't think anything could make his mood worse, but being followed around by an FBI agent for an entire week was sure doing the trick. At first he shrugged it off as a mild annoyance, but the minute the guy started showing up at Whiskey Bent everything changed.

Brandy was at the bar. And he didn't like the way she and that jackass smiled at each other.

He shot Marco a snide look, his glass of whiskey halfway to his lips. "You know, it's so typical of you government types. Y'all slack off until something bad happens and then you're so far up our asses we can't even see straight."

Marco stopped scanning the bar crowd and faced Adam with a grin. "And here I thought we were becoming friends. We have a lot in common, you know."

Adam snorted. "How d'you figure?"

"Well, we both love bourbon." Marco tapped his index finger to his lip thoughtfully, then shook his head. "I guess that's about it. But hey, it's something, right?"

"I don't want to be your friend." Adam turned away, irritated. "And you'd best keep your city boy hands off my girl."

Marco rested his forearm on the bar. "You know, you keep saying that like it's going to somehow make her yours. But from what I can see, you two are lost somewhere in the friend zone and can't seem to find your way out of it. It's a shame, really. She's hopelessly in love with your sorry ass and you're over here drinking yourself to death."

Adam gritted his teeth. "What the hell do you know, anyway?"

"I know she's looking over here right now, wondering what I'm saying to piss you off so badly." Marco laughed, glancing around the room again. "Plus you can learn a lot about a guy if you hang around him for a week."

Unable to resist, Adam shifted his gaze and met Brandy's eyes down the bar. Her cheeks flushed and she quickly looked away, but it lifted his spirits all the same.

Marco nudged him in the shoulder. "Maybe it's time to drop the bottle, pal. A girl like that won't wait around forever."

She'd already waited too long, Adam thought bitterly. He just wasn't ready to be the man she needed. Hell, he didn't know if it was possible. And even if it was, she'd made it clear she didn't want to be with him. So that was that.

He threw back the last of his whiskey and slammed the glass down on the bar. "Save your judgment, asshole. I got enough problems without you in my ear givin' me a pep talk."

"Hey, you think I like this gig?" Marco asked with a derisive sniff. "This has been the most boring week of my life. Coop gets to hang with your sister—who is way cooler than you, by the way—and I'm stuck hanging out with a miserable drunk."

"It's been two goddamn weeks. Don't you think if the guy who murdered my mother was gonna come back for more, he would've done it by now? Maybe you should be out there hunting him down instead of babysitting." Adam growled, losing his patience. "Besides, I can take care of myself."

Marco's eyebrows shot up. "Sure you can. What're you gonna do? Drink him under the table?"

In half a second Adam was on his feet, dragging Marco from the barstool with his hands wrapped tight around his shirtfront. Adam bared his teeth, their faces mere inches apart. "Just leave me the hell alone."

He released Marco and backed away, trying to reign in his temper. He knew he'd taken the agent by surprise, and also that he was tiptoeing a dangerous line. One wrong move and he'd be thrown in jail.

Most of the patrons were staring at him, including Brandy who was making her way over. There was worry in her eyes when she reached him.

"Everything all right?" she asked, looking back and forth between him and Marco.

Marco adjusted his shirt, his dark eyes honed in on Adam. A clear warning flashed in them before he faced Brandy. "Yep. We're cool. Nothing to worry about, sweetheart."

Adam grimaced at the loose term of endearment, but let it go. His eyes met Brandy's. "Sorry, darlin'. I'll get out of your hair."

He shrugged into his coat and started for the door, only to have her race around the bar and stop him. She forced him to look at her.

"Are you all right to drive? I can take you home if you just wait a few minutes till my shift is over."

Adam stared into her eyes, sick with regret and bitterness. He shook his head. "No. I could use the walk."

"You sure?" Her hands twisted together in front of her, a sign she was stressed. He added that to the long list of other things he blamed himself for.

"Yeah. Don't worry about me." Because it felt right, he cupped his hand around the back of her neck and pulled her in for a quick, tender kiss. He felt her stiffen against him, then give in until he released her.

He stepped away and left the bar without looking back, not wanting her to see just how weak he was for her.

Marco paid the tab and silently followed him, keeping a safe distance behind.

"DOES IT ever get old doing the same tour day after day?" Cooper asked, walking with Ava through the barrel house. It was late and the staff had gone home, giving them the entire steel building to themselves.

Ava eyed him playfully. "When you love your job, it never gets old."

"I love my job, but there's still boring days." He spun her against him, his mouth teasing hers. "Like being here with you, for example. So boring. I can't believe they stuck me with this shitty job."

She laughed, nipping at his lower lip. "I'd say as far as jobs go you've got it pretty damn good."

He shrugged, considering her point. "Well, there are those afterhours moments when I get to do this."

He pushed her up against the nearest wall of barrels, his face a breath from hers. He exhaled slowly, aching for her even though she was only inches away. She angled her mouth to meet his, kissing him in that way she had that stole the air right out of his lungs.

They had spent the better part of the week this way, tangled up and lost in each other. He'd almost forgotten his reason for being there, though it was always at the back of his mind. Each day that passed it became less and less relevant and surrendering to her became everything.

Stolen kisses in the barrel house, midnight walks to nowhere, more whiskey than he'd ever consumed in his whole life. The days with her were dipped in gold and the nights more brilliant than starlight. She was his every waking thought, his every breath, and though he'd never been one to suffer from addiction, he suffered from her. That smoky smile, her full-bodied laugh, the flecks of green in her eyes that came out only when they made love by firelight. He was consumed by her, fully and absolutely.

And knowing he was keeping a terrible secret from her was killing him.

"I should get you home," he murmured, his mouth trailing over hers. "It's getting late."

Ava's eyes fluttered open, her smile wicked. "I can think of something better we could do."

He groaned when her hand drifted downward, teasing him. "Christ, Ava. Someone's gotta be responsible here. They'll come looking for you."

"Let them," she decided, drawing back from him. "You think I care what anyone thinks at this point?"

He met her eyes and knew she didn't. "I guess your dad already knows. It doesn't get much worse after that."

She frowned. "What are you talking about? When did he find out?"

Cooper could have kicked himself for that slip up. He wracked his brain for some excuse, knowing he couldn't admit to having spoken to Ty that first morning. "He heard me leave your house the other day. He watched me drive away."

Relief erased the worry lines from her face. "Oh. Well, not like it matters. We've barely said a word to each other since…"

She didn't have to finish her sentence. He knew exactly what she was thinking. "Hey, look at me." She did, and he offered her a warm smile. "Everything's gonna be okay."

"I hope you're right." She lifted her hand to his cheek, tracing the light stubble he'd let grow over the last week. "You're looking more and more like a country boy every day, Slick."

He grinned. "Is that a good thing?"

She brought her lips to his. "Everything about you is a good thing."

AFTER COOPER pointed out that they could get caught, Ava started noticing all the questioning looks and hushed conversations of those around her. The distillery employees were the worst, but she couldn't help that. They saw Cooper lurking around and many hadn't accepted her excuse that it was simply a formality related to the tax investigation. It didn't help that whenever Cooper was nearby she lit up, making eyes at him from across the room every chance she got. Everyone had expected a longer mourning period from someone who had so recently lost their mother.

The truth was that not a day, or even an hour, went by that she didn't think of her mother and the unjust way she'd been ripped from their lives. But keeping her focus on the launch of Lucky Joe's single barrel bourbon, loading her guns in preparation for war with Ned, and savoring every moment alone with Cooper was distraction enough to help her move on. She'd get her revenge, she was sure of it. She just needed to practice patience, like Cooper had advised.

Her mood soured at the thought while she waited for her next tour to matriculate in the tasting room. She was getting tired of waiting around like a sitting duck. If something didn't happen soon, she was going to explode.

As her group gathered around, she fixed on a smile. At the back, her eyes landed on an attractive man with russet hair and piercing blue eyes. He was staring at her intently, and when they made eye contact the edge of his mouth curved in a knowing grin. The sight of it caught her off guard, but she was used enough to the occasional suggestive look from a man to not let it get to her.

"Welcome to Lucky Fox Whiskey!" she began, placing her hands on her hips as she eyed the rest of the group. Several people stood before her, mostly middle-aged couples and retirees with a few outlying younger city folk. It looked to be a good crowd, minus Mr. Calvin Klein in the back who was standing with his arms crossed and that smug smile still on his face. "My name is Ava Brannon, and I'm the granddaughter of Lucky Joe, the founder and master distiller here at Lucky Fox." She turned around to lead them further into the distillery showroom with the giant copper stills. "As you can see, unlike most other bourbon distilleries, we triple distill our bourbon to guarantee optimum flavor and clarity."

"You mean you do it the Irish way."

She spun on her heel to see who had spoken, saw the man in the back give her a curt nod. There was a lilt to his voice, similar to her grandfather's but smoother, like cream over ice. She guessed him to be British, and offered him a smile. "Triple distillation is not unique to Ireland, but yes. We do things with an Irish flair to reflect Lucky Joe's heritage."

One of the man's eyebrows slid up at her words. "I thought he had a feud with the Irish Brannons? Why do things their way then?"

Heat shimmered over her skin as her temper sparked. It wasn't the question that bothered her so much, it was the way he asked it. Like he wanted to rattle her nerves and pick a fight.

"Because he's not too proud to admit they had a good way of doing some things," she replied, trying not to let her irritation show. She could feel the rest of the group growing uneasy at the exchange, and knew she needed to stamp it out. "It was the recipe he didn't agree with. He knew the flavor would be better if blended with grain whiskey and his family disagreed. So he packed up and came to Kentucky, and the rest, folks," she held out her arms and offered the crowd a brilliant grin. "Is history. Now, let's talk about how bourbon's made and what makes it different than Irish whiskey..."

For the remainder of the tour, the Brit was quiet. She kept an eye on him regardless, noting how he stared around the distillery looking completely unimpressed with the entire operation. It made her wonder if he was some kind of competitor, but they did little to compete with the British market. So who was he, if not that?

By the time the tour came to an end and the patrons gathered around the tasting bar to test their newfound knowledge of whiskey, Ava had nearly forgotten all about him. She was having such a good time answering questions and sharing jokes with the other guests that when a few of them cleared out and he swept in to take their place at the bar, it gave her a jolt.

He smiled, nicer this time, and she tried to relax.

"Let me guess. You'd like to try the Irish first?" she asked, setting a fresh glencairn in front of him.

He nodded. "I would. I'm sorry if I came off as rude earlier. I hope I didn't offend."

She studied his face, all fine lines and roguish good looks, and decided he was relatively charming when he wasn't wearing a scowl. "Not at all, honey." She turned to grab the bottle of Irish whiskey from the shelf, then poured a sample into his glass. "Now, you've seen how we make the whiskey. That's just science. But what you taste will be unique to each individual palate. I could tell you what to expect, but I think it's best to leave it a surprise."

His eyes lowered to the glass as he studied the liquid inside. He gave it a quick swirl, then brought it to his nose. She watched his brows crease as he deciphered the aromas, and when he at last gave it a taste shock registered over his face.

Ava angled her head. "Not what you expected?"

He set the glass down, looking unsure of himself. He pursed his lips and met her eyes. "It tastes like flowers. It's quite different from what I'm used to."

"And what's that?"

A hardness came over his expression, his eyes blazing. He seemed to consider how to respond, only to decide not to answer her at all. "I'll try the Distiller's Choice next, please."

She obliged him, though warning bells went off in her head. She quickly scanned the room for Cooper, but he was nowhere to be found. Most likely he had stepped out to make a phone call to check in on Marco.

"You'll notice a difference between the Irish and the bourbon," she said conversationally, ignoring the flutters of panic in her belly as she fell into her routine. "Bourbon has a more robust flavor and is a bit heavier on the tongue."

He lifted his glass to the light, then breathed in the aroma before taking a sip. He appeared less affected by it than the Irish whiskey. "It's a fine drink, to be sure. Though not as sophisticated as I'd like." His eyes met hers, and she felt her stomach clench in knots. "You know your stuff, Miss

Brannon. And clearly you love what you do. That kind of passion is a rare find."

"I was raised on it," she told him, wondering why he felt the need to compliment her. "It's in my blood."

An odd little smile crossed his face. "Mine too. Take care, Miss Brannon."

He got up to leave, not bothering to taste anything else. She stared after him, grateful he was gone but curious about him all the same. Maybe he *was* a competitor, she decided. Who else out there would claim to have whiskey in their blood?

CHAPTER

Twenty-three

Though she had never mastered cooking the way her mother had, Ava figured she wasn't half bad. She had managed to bake the chicken without burning it and her mashed potatoes were a little lumpy, but altogether tasty. The gravy was giving her trouble, but once spread over everything else it wouldn't matter.

Cooper rested a hip against the counter beside her, a beer in his hand and a playful grin on his face.

She shot him an annoyed look while she viciously stirred the gravy. "I got this. Stop looking so concerned."

He held his free hand up in a show of peace. "I know you do. But you might want to pull those biscuits out."

"Shit." She threw open the oven door and saw the biscuits turning more brown than golden. She nearly grabbed the baking sheet without oven mitts but caught herself just in time. When she pulled them out of the oven, she let out a relieved breath and tossed the pan on the stove. "There, see. Not burned."

"Check the underside."

She did, and saw that while the tops were merely brown, the bottoms were black as night. "Oh, hell."

Cooper burst out laughing. She smacked him with the oven mitt for good measure. "Shut up, Slick. It's not funny."

He caught her wrist and pulled her in, kissing the tip of her nose. "It's okay. We'll just break off the burnt parts. No harm, no foul."

Her eyes narrowed. "This is all your fault, you know."

"If it'll make you feel better, I'll take the blame."

She cocked her chin, a subtle smile forming on her lips. "What a gentleman."

He started to reply, only to be cut off by the sound of someone clearing their throat. They both turned and saw Joe standing behind them. He was eyeing Cooper strangely, like he couldn't decide just how he felt about the situation.

Ava recovered first. "Hey. Dinner's almost ready. You hungry?"

Joe crossed his arms. "Aye. I see we're having company."

Cooper faced Joe, knowing he was treading on rocky ground. "She took pity on me. It's been a while since I've had a home cooked meal."

A ghost of a smile flitted over Joe's features. "Well, our girl isn't so talented as her mama, but she does all right."

Ava pointed at Cooper. "He's the reason the biscuits are burned. Everything else, everything *I* did, is great. I promise."

She turned away to get dishes out of the cupboards, and Joe gave Cooper a conspirator's wink before wandering over to the dining table.

Cooper breathed out in relief, pleased her grandfather wasn't going to push the subject of his infatuation with Ava. The old man had seen enough to know the truth.

"I invited Marco to join us," Ava said, bringing the casserole dish over to the table. "Told him to bring Adam with him. If I can't coax my brother out of the bar, maybe he can."

Cooper chuckled as he helped her bring the rest of the food to the table. The doorbell rang.

"I'll get it," Cooper offered, heading for the front door. He opened it to find Marco standing on the porch, alone. "Hey. I thought you were bringing Adam with you?"

Marco shrugged, entering when Cooper stepped aside. "He didn't want to come. Now me, I don't turn down a home cooked meal. He'll be okay by himself for an hour."

Cooper patted his partner on the back. "Well, you're in for a treat. We've got burned biscuits and lumpy mashed potatoes."

Marco faced him, humor in his eyes. "Good job, Coop. Sounds like you found the only Southern woman who doesn't know how to cook."

"To be fair I was a bit of a distraction," Cooper mused, leading the way into the kitchen.

"Lucky you."

Ava's smile faded when she saw Marco was alone. "Where's Adam?"

"He wasn't hungry." Marco sniffed the air and admired the food laid out on the table. "Oh, man. Cooper's a liar. This looks amazing."

He settled in at the dining table while Ava shot Cooper a questioning look. "Were you seriously talkin' crap about my food before you've even tasted it?"

Joe was already seated and piling his plate high with chicken and potatoes. "Careful, boyo. A smart man never insults a lady's cookin'."

Cooper's brows rose. "I didn't say anything."

"Just sit down and eat." Ava scolded him before taking a seat herself. She spooned food onto her plate while Marco gave a groan of approval.

"Oh, yeah. This chicken's awesome."

"Thank you." Ava smiled, cutting into a piece. "It was one of Mama's recipes."

Marco met Cooper's gaze, a knowing look passing between them. Cooper cleared his throat before speaking. "Your father won't be joining us?"

Ava pursed her lips. "I can't make him eat," she said simply, a hint of regret masked by the anger in her voice. "Just like I can't make my brother eat, either. Seems I'm pretty damn useless these days. I can't fill my mama's shoes, no matter how hard I try."

She threw up her hands, tears suddenly brimming in her eyes. Joe placed a hand on her forearm to comfort her.

"There now, dearie. No one expects ye to be anythin' but yerself. Those two will come around, ye'll see."

She sniffed, embarrassed by her own rampant emotions. "I know. I'm just sick of worrying about them."

"If it makes you feel better, your friend Brandy has been keeping an eye on Adam," Marco chimed in, giving her a sympathetic smile. "He's spending a lot of time over there, but she's monitoring his drinking. I think he just needed time away from the house."

"He's not as strong as you are," Cooper added, his eyes shifting to Joe. "Both of you."

Ava nodded. "I think we'll all feel better once we have closure."

"Speaking of that, are ye any closer to catchin' the bastard that done this to our girl?" Joe asked.

"The local PD has a lead. They're keeping us posted," Cooper told him, knowing it was partly a lie. He couldn't say more than that without giving too much away.

Joe scowled and picked at the potatoes on his plate. "It's a damn shame the first one they caught wasn't our guy. I thought for sure this nightmare would be over by now."

Ava reached for her grandfather's hand. "It will be soon. I can feel it."

ADAM WATCHED Brandy explain the different flavors of Lucky Fox whiskey to a tourist at the bar, content to simply observe. Strands of her honey blonde hair kept falling over her face. Every time she tucked them back behind her ear, the charm bracelet she'd gotten from her grandparents one Christmas would slide down her arm, little metal trinkets clicking together in a soft rain of sound. Her blue eyes would occasionally venture to his and brighten in a way that warmed him from the inside out.

At some point she'd swapped his glass of bourbon for a cup of ice water, and he sipped it absently as he thought up ways to talk to her. Things he'd say, promises he'd make. She deserved the world, and he wanted nothing more than to give it to her.

The drink he had indulged in for most of the day gave him a slight boost in confidence. And, though he hated to admit it, the pesky FBI agent's remark the day before about Brandy being hopelessly in love with him didn't hurt, either. Not that he completely trusted that the agent knew what he was talking about. But once he looked for it, really looked for it, he thought he could see her love for him all over her face.

He'd screwed up the last time, he understood that now. Kissing her senseless in a drunken stupor and then pretending it meant nothing had hurt them both. Even if she had played along and claimed it didn't matter, he knew better than to believe her excuses now.

The only thing holding him back was himself. He was a mess. A tornado of grief and rage and regret, and no matter how many days passed he wasn't getting better.

What he wanted was something to hope for. Something to chase away the pain.

What he needed was Brandy.

He started to motion for her attention as she broke free of the tourist, but a man lowered onto the stool beside him and got to her first.

"I'll take a Guinness, love."

Brandy nodded and fetched his beer, popping the top off for him. "Here you are." She glanced at Adam. "Doin' okay, baby?"

Adam lifted his water cup with a half-smile. "Yeah. Thanks for the water, darlin'."

"Don't mention it." She smiled and turned away.

The stranger beside Adam took a long pull on his beer, then set it down and began to peel off the label. Adam tried to nonchalantly study the man, having caught his Irish accent. It wasn't often foreigners came around Fox Hills, and with the news of his father's connection to the IRA, an Irishman in town was cause for alarm.

The man was a couple of years older than himself and though lanky, was lined with solid muscle and clothed in a black button up shirt and tailored jeans. His chestnut hair was cropped at the jawline and loosely slicked back from his face. From a quick study of his profile, Adam noticed a distinct crescent-shaped scar along the stranger's cleft chin.

When the man turned and caught his eye, Adam looked away.

"Where I come from, men drink beer and whiskey in a bar. Not water," the stranger said, a hint of humor easing the edge off his voice.

Adam shrugged. "Gotta sober up. If I go home drunk, I'll be in trouble."

The man faced him with a knowing grin. "Ah. The wife'll have yer head, is it?"

"I'm not married," Adam replied, though his eyes went briefly to Brandy before landing on the stranger. "My sister. She likes to run my life."

"Sounds like ye got yerself a problem, mate." The man lifted his beer in a sign of comradery, and Adam got his first real good look at his face. He didn't look like a tourist. He had the edgy features of a conman, and the trickster's grin to match it.

"You from Ireland?" Adam asked, suspicion churning low in his gut. He cast another look at Brandy, but noticed she was busy counting change back at the register. If all hell broke loose, he hoped she'd grab the shotgun he knew lay beneath the counter.

"Aye. Belfast." The man stretched out his free hand, an eagerness flashing in his green eyes. "Name's Killian."

Adam accepted the handshake warily. "Adam."

"Ye one of the Brannons, Adam?" Killian asked, releasing his hand.

Adam felt a chill race over his skin. "Yeah. Why do you ask?"

Killian smiled again and sipped his beer. "Nice distillery ye got here. Decent whiskey."

"Thanks." Adam jostled the ice in his cup, his eyes narrowing. Down the bar, he noticed Brandy pull out her cell phone and slip into the back. He didn't have time to wonder what she was up to when the Irishman spoke again.

"Name like Brannon, there must be some Irish in that blood of yers. Have ye ever been?"

"No," Adam said flatly, though he caught himself before he told the man to take a hike. If this was, as he suspected, somehow tied to Ned and the IRA, then he needed to play it out until he got the truth. Since his FBI stalker had chosen to take the night off, he was on his own for this one. "But I hear good things. Green hills, good whiskey. Pots of gold and rainbows."

Killian laughed. "Aye. It is that."

"So what brings you to Kentucky?" Adam asked, trying to play it casual.

"Whiskey, of course." Killian tossed back the last of his beer, set the bottle down. "And family business. But no time for that nonsense now. I'll see ye around, mate."

He tossed a twenty dollar bill on the bar and left. Adam frowned, wondering if he'd read the man all wrong. Just then Brandy came back behind the bar and went straight to him.

"I just called Ava to come get you," she said, twisting a piece of blonde hair around her fingertip. "Don't be mad. It's just that guy was giving off some bad vibes and without Agent D'Amico here…"

Adam's brows rose, even as his heart thumped at her words. So she'd been suspicious of the Irishman, too. "I can take care of myself. I don't need my sister coming to my rescue."

Brandy sighed, exasperation creasing her face. "I know, but that guy…there was something off about him."

"I picked up on that, too," Adam told her. He rubbed his chin. "Oh well. Odds are he's just a tourist. If he wanted to kill me, he would've done it."

"Oh, Adam." Brandy's hand flew to her heart, looking sick to her stomach. "Please don't talk like that."

He brushed off her comment, but his insides warmed all the same. "Goes to show you how useless the Feds are. He wasn't even here when that guy showed up. I had to do his work for him."

"Yeah, well, you don't need to be puttin' your life at risk to catch him. That's what the agents get paid to do," Brandy reasoned, refilling his water. She met his eyes as she handed him back his cup. "Please promise me you won't do anythin' stupid."

Adam's mouth quirked in a grin, unable to help himself. She was so cute with that worry line between her brows. "Would you miss me if I died, darlin'?"

She stiffened, not appreciating his humor. "You know I would."

Ava came through the doors then, Cooper and Marco on her heels. Brandy offered up a smile before tending to other patrons at the bar.

Adam turned in his seat, held up his water. "See? Not drinking. No need to panic."

Ava glared around the bar, looking like a livewire ready to crack. "Where is he?"

"Who?"

Her hands fell to her hips as she regarded him with a heated stare. "The Irishman."

Adam shrugged. "Left a few minutes ago."

"Okay. You need to tell me everything he said to you." Ava sat down beside him while Cooper and Marco closed in to listen.

Adam recalled the conversation as best he could, then met eyes with Cooper. "He said his name was Killian. Probably a fake name."

Marco's mouth fell open. "You've got to be shitting me."

Cooper looked incredibly uneasy. "Killian Brannon is the younger of Ned's two sons. Most likely that was him. Which means if he's here, his brother Rhys and Ned himself probably are too."

Ava paled, her breath hitching in her throat. "Oh God. There was another one. He came by the distillery today.

Sounded British to me, but he could've been faking it. It didn't even occur to me that he could related to Ned. Related to *me*."

Cooper pulled out his cell phone and brought up a picture of a man with russet hair. "This him?"

She nodded, in a daze. "Yeah. Shit. He was right there. I didn't think—"

"It's okay, you didn't know," Cooper said. "It's my fault. I should've shown you their pictures earlier. I just honestly didn't expect them to make the trip. It's risky enough smuggling Ned into the country. His sons are even more high profile. Killian almost went to prison for that bombing in Dublin, but Ned managed to secure his release. They're being watched very closely by the Irish government. I can't imagine how they made it through."

Ava's hands tightened into fists. "If he shows his face again, I'll kill him."

Cooper urged her to look at him, shaking his head. "These are very dangerous men, Ava."

She got to her feet, one brow arched as if to challenge his statement. "That's why I carry a gun. C'mon, Adam. Let's go home."

She pulled Adam to his feet and led him out of the bar. Once safely inside her truck, she faced her brother and felt the first flicker of panic trace across her skin. "Ned's sons had the chance to kill us both today and didn't take it. That tells me they want something else from us. We need to find out what it is."

Adam nodded, feeling sick. "I think the younger one will be back. I can try and get answers from him. Play right into his hand."

Real fear formed a lump in Ava's throat. "It's risky, but it may be the only way."

"We have to do this for Mama."

"You're right," Ava replied, a steadfast determination filling her. "They have to pay for what they've done."

CHAPTER

Twenty-four

W ell, we sure weren't expecting this to happen," Marco said as he drove through the night, Cooper beside him. He slammed his hand against the steering wheel. "The guy was probably hanging around just waiting for me to leave Adam alone so he could swoop in."

Cooper scanned the quiet streets of Fox Hills out the window, searching for any sign of Ned and his sons. "What I can't understand is why make conversation? Why not just kill Ava and Adam if that's the goal?"

"It must not be."

The words hung in the air, a heavy reality they had no choice but to accept. If Ned had no intention of murdering Ty's children, then what did he plan to do? It reminded Cooper of something he'd thought up weeks ago, something that seemed ridiculous in the light of everything that had happened since. Yet it made more sense than anything else.

"He's gauging their weaknesses to find out which of them he can manipulate to take their father's place. Just because Ty goes down doesn't mean one of them can't pick up the slack. They need Lucky Fox money."

Marco stared at him. "Yeah, but he had their mother murdered and they know that. Why the hell would either of them buy into what he's selling?"

"He doesn't know what they know yet," Cooper reminded him, running with the thought. "For all he knows, they bought into the botched robbery attempt story. Which is why he sent his sons in to see what would happen. And since neither of them recognized Rhys or Killian nor seemed overly suspicious, I'm willing to bet they make another pass at it. They came a long way to just give up now."

Marco pulled onto Main Street and passed the bar. A few gruff-looking locals were standing out front, laughing with each other. "So even *if* Ned were to get Ava or Adam to agree to help him, what is he going to offer in return? Ty went into it willingly, but how would Ava and Adam benefit from this?"

"First off, we're kidding ourselves if we think Ava is the one they'll pick," Cooper pointed out. "Adam is the weaker link. He's less involved in the company and is looking for a purpose. Killian will have picked up on that, guaranteed. Secondly, all Ned has to do is offer Adam the very thing he's always wanted—a place at the table. Respect from family. Honestly, if Ned hadn't made the mistake of killing Sandra when he did, I bet he could've persuaded Adam pretty easily to join his side."

"But he couldn't resist taking Sandra out first."

"For reasons we're being kept in the dark on." Cooper sighed, frustrated to be so close to the truth and yet so far from it at the same time. "Our best hope of catching Ned is to have Adam lead us right to him."

Marco's hands tightened on the steering wheel. "You're asking the guy to walk straight into the lion's den, Coop. You really think he can handle it?"

Cooper nodded. "Yes. As big of a screw-up as he is, he'd do anything to avenge his mother. He and Ava both."

"Yeah, but can he handle it?" Marco asked again, looking uncertain.

Cooper looked out the window again as a light rain began to fall, wishing he didn't feel so doubtful himself. "At this point, he's all we got."

AFTER WORK, Brandy slipped into pajamas and her favorite fuzzy blue robe. She prepared herself a cup of chamomile tea, lost in thoughts of Adam and the strange Irishman.

She had known from the second the man opened his mouth that he was trouble. His rough and tumble appearance hadn't helped either, and she was used to tough, blue-collar Kentucky boys. There was just something about him that screamed danger in the most violent sense of the word.

Ever since Adam had told her of his family's connection to the IRA, she had thought about little else. She had done some research into the organization, found the roots of their cause to be noble and perhaps justifiable. But the violence—while far less common than it used to be—was something she could never condone.

How could a man she had considered to be a kind of second father align himself with murderers? And not just that, but help fund their operation behind everyone's backs? He had taken money from the company his father had built and sent it back to the same people Joe had run from, to be used with deadly intent.

It was obvious that Ty Brannon was not the man everyone had thought him to be. In the end, she supposed he had paid for that deception with the death of his wife. It broke her heart to think that Sandra had been caught in the crossfire, and that Ava and Adam were suffering for it. She wished more than anything for the ability to help them, for a way to ease their burden. But she was just a girl from small town Kentucky. She wasn't the FBI, the CIA. She couldn't turn back time or bring back their mother. The most she could do was try and be there for them, a shoulder to cry on when the pain was too great to bear.

Tears sprang into her eyes at the thought. It killed her to know Adam was hurting. No matter what there was between them, she would always care about him. She had loved him her entire life, even if he never knew how to love her in return.

A quiet knock at the front door startled her out of her thoughts. She stared at it for a moment, wondering who could be coming to see her so late. When she went to the door and looked through the peep hole, relief shimmered over her.

She opened it and smiled. "What brings you here?"

Adam had his hands tucked into the pockets of his jeans and a troubled look on his face. "Can I come in?"

"Of course." She tightened her robe around her and stepped aside, welcoming him in. He turned to face her as she shut the door.

"I'm sorry to bother you. If it's a bad time, I can go," he offered.

"Not at all. Can I fix you some tea?"

"No, thanks." He rocked back on his heels and glanced around her living room as though wondering where to begin. "I found out that Irish guy at the bar tonight is my cousin. He's a known member of the IRA."

Brandy paled. "Good Lord. What does he want?"

"I don't know." Adam met her eyes, and she watched his cool façade crumble to pieces. "I thought he wanted me dead. Now I'm not so sure. I need to see him again, try and play into his hand and see if I can get the truth. I'm—" His voice cracked and he averted his eyes. "I'm scared, Brandy. These bastards want to hurt my family and I don't know if I'm strong enough to stop it."

She could tell he hated himself for it. That he felt weak and helpless. She realized then exactly how she could help— by reminding him that he was good enough.

"Come here, baby." She wrapped her arms around him, pleased when he tightened his hold on her and buried his face in her hair. Her heart shuddered as she rubbed his back. "You've spent too much of your life selling yourself short. Your family needs you. And as much as I don't want you to, I know you can do this."

His hands twisted into the material of her robe, then released as he eased back and looked into her eyes. "Thank you." He started to touch her cheek, then hesitated and stepped away from her, feeling like he was crossing some imaginary boundary. "I don't know why I came over here and bothered you with this. I've taken up enough of your time. Excuse me."

He pushed past her toward the door, but she caught his hand and spun him back to her. Without reservation she brought her mouth to his and kissed him, her arms winding around his neck. He fell into it like a river does to the sea, a natural blending of one water into another.

She released his lips to trail kisses over his jawline and cheekbones, seeking to soothe, to comfort. When his body relaxed against hers and he whispered her name, she knew it was working. And when he brought her back for another kiss, her knees went weak and her heart wept.

Gripping his shoulders, she rested her forehead against his and fought to breathe. It took everything she had to reel herself back in, to give him the most she could offer without sacrificing her own bruised feelings. His hands slid into her hair and coaxed her eyes open.

His own were afire with emotion. "Tell me right now, darlin'. Is this what you want? Because if it isn't, I'll leave you alone."

She chewed on her lip and backed away, uncertain how to answer him. Of course it was what she wanted. But how could she ever trust him not to walk away?

Understanding there was no reward without some risk, she blew out a breath and asked the question she should have asked him ages ago. "Do you want to be with me? Not just for one night and not just because you're hurting, but because you want me more than anybody else?"

Adam nodded, knowing he had been a fool for far too long. "I've done nothing to deserve it, Brandy, and very little to prove myself worthy. But here's the thing—it's always been you. Maybe I was too stupid to realize it or too drunk to notice how I hurt you, but my eyes are open now. And all I can see is you."

For a moment she said nothing, and he wondered if she even believed him. He could have kicked himself for ruining his last chance, but then a single tear fell down her cheek and her lips curved into that beautiful smile.

"What took you so long?" she asked. She cut off his reply with a kiss, joy and relief surging through her all at once.

He melted into her, certain of what he wanted for the first time in his life. A feeling of hope filled him, blending with the desire for her that had always been there, burning beneath the surface.

Brandy slipped out of his arms and unbelted her robe, hoping he couldn't see her hands tremble. It wasn't out of anxiety or fear, but out of an anticipation as old as time. Her eyes held his as the robe tumbled down her back and to the floor, leaving only the sky blue cotton camisole beneath.

She took his hand and brought him into her bedroom. He took in the lacy, snow white bedspread, blue floral wallpaper, and charming pastoral paintings. It was all so very Brandy that he felt a smile tug at the corners of his lips. Then she turned to face him and shakily lifted up his T-shirt.

He let her help him out of it, then watched curiously as her eyes traced over the planes of his bare chest. She bit back a shy smile and moved to unbutton his jeans, only to have him stop her.

"Easy, darlin'. One thing at a time." He leaned in to run his mouth over her neck, sending a shiver down to her very toes. Her hands skimmed along his chest, then dove into his hair as her head fell back.

"Can I tell you something?" she asked, thinking her heart might beat out of her chest. She curved into him, lost in the sensation of his tongue tracing along her skin.

"Of course."

"I've never done this before."

He paused, then eased back to look into her eyes. "You haven't?"

She blushed, though she knew it was nothing to be ashamed of. "There was never anyone...I just never felt comfortable enough with a guy to...to do it."

A slow smile crept over his face. "You were waiting for me."

One of her eyebrows rose. "Not exactly."

"What about that asshole Jeremy?"

She smiled at the memory of how jealous Adam had been when she went on a few dates with the star quarterback from their high school. He was a nice enough guy, but they hadn't clicked. The breakup had been mutual and a relief to them both.

"Nope. Not even him." She angled her face up to his, humor in her eyes. "And he was an awful kisser. You're much better."

Adam's gaze lowered to her mouth, his pulse quickening. "Damn right."

As if to prove it, he pulled her in for a kiss that stole her breath away. His hands dove under her nightgown and roamed over her back, drawing her in close. She shivered against him, her fingers fumbling for the clasp on his jeans. He slipped out of them and drew her camisole over her head, taking in the sight of her soft curves and ivory skin before lifting her onto the bed.

She spread out as he covered her body with his, kissing every inch of her as he went. Her fingers tightened in his hair as a low moan escaped her lips, overcome by the heat. Need coursed through her, steady and rich like velvet. When his hand dipped between her legs she cried out for him, her hips bucking as new and incredible sensations rolled over her, stealing the very breath from her lungs.

The heat built from low within, then swelled until she thought her heart might explode from the pressure. "Adam. Adam, wait, I—"

He watched the first rising wave overtake her, bringing a flush to her cheeks and a stunned awareness to her eyes as they locked on his. At the edges of his control, he captured her mouth again and ranged over her, aching to take her. He trembled with it, fighting back the beast knowing she deserved the gentleman. He broke the kiss and caressed her face, a love like he had never felt before washing over him.

"Are you sure?" he asked.

She nodded, breathless. He slid inside of her, holding back as best as he could. He saw the brief flicker of discomfort and pain cross her face, then marveled at the desire that replaced it. She held his gaze, her lips curving in a warm, contented smile.

The words tumbled out of him before he could even think, as if they had always longed to break free. "I love you, Brandy."

Relief and joy danced in her eyes the second before she kissed him. She brought her mouth to his ear and whispered, "Just let go."

The dam broke inside of him and he thrust into her again, taking care to be as gentle as he could. She moved with him, pressing soft kisses along his neck and the slope of his shoulder as her hands trailed over his back.

He buried his face in her hair, lost in her. Lost to her. He sank into the warmth she offered, the love he had always resisted setting his heart brilliantly aflame.

PART 05

LUCKY FOX

IRISH ☘ WHISKEY

Whiskey, like a beautiful woman, demands appreciation.
You gaze first, then it's time to drink.
~ Haruki Murakami ~

CHAPTER

Twenty-five

Ava curled up with a wool blanket on the front porch swing, listening to the crickets with a glass of bourbon in one hand and a Remington 1911 pistol in the other. The moon peeked through the cloud cover, casting a hazy white glow across her family's land. A cold breeze blew past her face and rustled the remaining leaves clinging to a nearby maple tree, shaking a few to the ground.

In the peaceful quiet of night, she almost forgot the turmoil she faced. The men who lay in wait somewhere in Fox Hills might as well of been part of a nightmare she had just awoken from. But she knew they weren't, and that this was no dream. It was real, and the danger she faced wasn't going away. Until Ned and his sons were in custody, this sur- real horror would remain her reality.

Headlights cut through the darkness as a car ap- proached the house, tires crunching over the gravel road. She held her breath until she could make out the outline of Cooper's black sedan, then released it on a relieved sigh.

Tucking the pistol away, she sipped her drink and waited for him to park.

He climbed out of his car and walked up the steps, then leaned back against the railing. "Well, we didn't see anything. My guess is Ned's not staying in Fox Hills, but somewhere nearby."

"Probably. Where's our little Italian friend?"

"We saw Adam's truck parked outside Brandy's place, so Marco headed back to the hotel to get some sleep," he told her, attempting a smile. "He's been running on empty."

Ava nodded and rose to her feet. She hugged him, resting her cheek against his chest. "We all have. I'm so glad you're here."

He pressed a kiss to the top of her head. "I wouldn't be anywhere else."

She held him tighter, at that moment content to never let go. They fell into a comfortable silence, joined only by the sounds of the night.

When she spoke again, dread settled into the pit of her stomach. "We need to use Adam to get to Ned."

Cooper shifted as she looked up at him, regret coming into his eyes. "Are you okay with that?"

"He can do it," she said confidently. "It was his idea. He knows what's at stake."

"I'm surprised you didn't volunteer." He stroked her face, curious to hear her reasons.

Her mouth twisted in a sneer. "I can't guarantee I could sit there long enough without beating the guy's face in. The Brannons aren't known for bein' patient people, but Adam has a bit more of it than I do."

A subtle smile softened his expression. "I'm going to fit Adam with a wire so we can record the conversation and hopefully Killian will tell us Ned's whereabouts. Then we'll come in and arrest him. As long as Adam stays put, he won't be in any danger. I promise you."

"God, I hope you're right." She drew back and hugged herself, sick with worry. "I wish I could do this. Maybe I should. I can hang around the distillery tomorrow and see if Rhys turns up again—"

"He won't."

Ava frowned. "How do you know?"

"Because they're looking for the weak link, and it isn't you." He avoided her eyes, wondering if the time had come to tell her the truth about her father being an informant. "I believe Ned wants a replacement for your father. He still needs Lucky Fox money."

"You think *that's* what he's after? That he'd risk getting picked up by the Feds just to talk Adam and I into giving him more money? After he *killed* our mother?"

"As far as he knows, her death has been attributed to a robbery," Cooper explained. "That was done on purpose so he would think he'd gotten away with it and come to Fox Hills."

She straightened, a line forming between her brows. "Well, it worked. He's here. Now if I could just get my father to stop avoiding me, maybe I could get him to help."

Cooper tensed. "He is helping, Ava. More than you think."

"What do you mean?"

His eyes held hers, dark and somber. "He's an FBI informant. He always has been. I didn't even find out myself until a week ago."

Disbelief hit her like a slap to the face. "You're lying."

"Would I lie?"

She stood there in shock for a moment, unsure what to make of it. Finally she shook her head, fury taking over. "I don't think so, but then again you kept this from me for an entire week. What the hell else do you know that you're not telling me?"

Despite wanting to console her, he knew better than to touch her and kept his hands at his sides. "You know there are things I can't tell you. Classified information. I shouldn't even be telling you this."

"Then why are you?"

"Because you deserve to know who the real villains are. Your father wants to take Ned down just as badly as you do." He eyed her in that serious, honest way he had and it only fueled her temper further.

"I can't believe this." She turned away, her hands diving into her hair. Knowing the truth suddenly gave everything a different perspective. She faced him again, disgust in her eyes. "So all of this has been one giant ruse, then, huh? They sent you down here to investigate my father for show, damaging our reputation and wreaking havoc on our lives in the process. All for what? To fool Ned?"

"I didn't know any of this until a week ago, I promise you," he defended, hating to see her look at him like that. He edged closer to her, needing to make his case. "Hate me all you want, but this is the truth."

She backed away, her body shaking with rage. "Any hate I feel for you is nothing compared to what I feel for my father right now."

Before he could respond, she stormed into the house and went straight to her father's office. She beat her fist against the door, shouting for him, then gave up all propriety and shoved her way inside.

Nothing but an empty room greeted her.

She exhaled and stalked toward his bedroom, only to find it empty as well. A quick look throughout the rest of the house confirmed it. He was gone.

"Where—"

"His car's not here," Cooper said as he rushed into the living room, his cell phone already out and half-dialed.

A bolt of fear shot through her. "I didn't even notice. When did he leave?"

"Probably while we were at the bar with Adam," Cooper guessed, lifting his phone to his ear. He waited for three rings before Horvath picked up. "Ty Brannon's missing."

Ava did one more sweep of the house, checking his bedroom to see if any of his belongings were gone. Everything looked as it should, bringing on a worse feeling of dread. Had he been taken while they were away? How much time had they wasted by assuming he was still locked up in his office?

She came back into the living room to find Cooper pacing by the fireplace, his voice cold as ice as he spoke into the phone. Joe came out of his bedroom then, looking confused by the tension in the air.

"What's the matter, dearie?"

She pounced on him. "Have you seen Daddy?"

Joe shook his head. "Not since this morning when I took him his breakfast. Why?"

"His car's gone and he's not here. He could be in danger."

"Now why would ye say a thing like that?" Joe asked, offering her an easy grin. "He's probably just out gettin' a drink. Lord knows he could use one."

Ava grabbed him by the shoulders, needing him to understand the gravity of the situation. "Ned's here in Fox Hills. So are his sons."

Joe blinked. "Impossible."

"Apparently not." She turned as Cooper hung up the phone, eager for information. "Well? What'd they say?"

"He left his cell phone behind so the Bureau can't track him. They don't know where he is, but I'm willing to bet Ned made contact and he went straight to him."

"Why the hell would he do that?" she demanded, though he didn't need to say it. She knew the answer. A fear darker than anything she had ever felt before simmered low in her gut.

Joe glared at Cooper. "Is all of this true? Is Ned here in the States?"

Cooper nodded. "Yes. And your son is out for revenge."

NED CIRCLED the chair lying dead center in the empty warehouse, his footsteps echoing over the concrete floor. In the light of the rows of florescent bulbs hanging from the ceiling, the lines of his face were harsh and unforgiving. His eyes held those of his captive as he paced, his hands clasped behind his back.

"I've come a long way, cousin. Taken a huge risk. I only did so because I wanted to look ye in the eye when ye confess to what ye've done."

Ty held perfectly still in the metal chair they'd roped him to, unwilling to show any fear. His mouth twisted in disgust as his gaze followed Ned. "I don't deny any of it. You might as well kill me. Because if I get free, I'm comin' after you."

Ned feigned a look of surprise. "Come after me? I'm untouchable. I've evaded capture and lived openly for years. The Gardaí, yer foolish Feds. None of them can get me."

Ty let out a dark laugh. "You're wrong. I know your greatest weakness. Hell, she was mine too. Killin' her was the stupidest thing you've ever done."

Ned's right eye twitched as his temper crested. "Ye both betrayed me. The two people I loved most in this world stabbed me in the bloody back."

"There was never any love between us, Ned," Ty corrected coldly. "Only necessity."

In a lightning fast movement, Ned grabbed Ty's shirt collar and dragged their faces together. They glared into each other's eyes, violence and a deep-seated hatred sparking in the air.

"I welcomed ye in despite yer da the traitor," Ned spat. "I could've shut ye out. Had every right to."

Ty sneered. "You wanted my money. For years I sent it to you without question, but that's all done now. The Feds have got you right where they want you and it's only a matter of time until you're locked away for good."

Ned released him and straightened. His voice was low and deadly as he spoke. "What did ye tell them?"

"More like, what *haven't* I told them," Ty replied recklessly. "I've been feeding them your dirty secrets for over twenty years. All those late night calls from payphones and throwaway cell phones. Every time you asked for more money, they were watchin'. Waitin' for you to give them a reason to take you out. The Dublin bombing was the last straw." When Ned flushed red in the face and his hands began to shake, Ty gave a fierce grin. "It was her idea, you know. She wanted to take you down and knew exactly how to exploit your weaknesses to do it."

Ned ripped the 9mm pistol out of his belt holster and shoved the tip of the barrel into Ty's forehead. He breathed furiously through his nose, his lips pressed into a tight line.

Ty closed his eyes, his smile spreading. "Lord, do it."

Ned's finger rested on the trigger, a pull away from murder. He stared at the welcoming acceptance on his cousin's face and knew instantly death wasn't punishment enough. Drawing back his hand, he slammed the butt of the pistol against Ty's temple, slicing a gash into his skin. Blood pooled and trickled down his face, and Ned rejoiced in his cousin's cry of pain.

"I took more pity on her than I will you," he said viciously, re-holstering the gun. He bent down and grabbed Ty's chin, forcing their eyes to meet. "I think drawing this out and making ye watch me destroy everything ye love is payback enough."

"You already took what I love." Ty gritted his teeth, tears in his eyes from the pain. His hands balled into fists as he strained against the bonds. "You'd be better off killin' me."

A knowing look flashed over Ned's face, joined by a cruel smile. "Why, Tyler. What about yer dear children?"

Sweat dripped down Ty's forehead, joining the wash of blood. "Given the look on your face I trust you know the truth by now."

"Aye." Ned eased back, releasing Ty's chin. "Why should that comfort ye?"

"Because now I know you won't kill them."

"An interestin' theory," Ned mused.

"Sandra loved Ava and Adam." Remorse shadowed Ty's expression, chasing away his anger. He closed his eyes and bowed his head, grief consuming him. "She gave her life to protect them. That has to mean something to you."

"Sandra…" Ned drew out the name on a long breath that turned into a dark laugh. "I preferred her real name."

When Ty said nothing, Ned decided they had talked long enough. His hand clenched into a fist and he hit his cousin hard enough to knock the chair over and spill his blood onto the concrete.

CHAPTER

Twenty – six

W e found his car," Beau announced as he came into the living room, though by the look on his face it wasn't good news. "No sign of Ty, though."

Ava shot up from her seat on the sofa and went straight to him. "Where was it?"

"Parked on the side of a county road halfway between here and Louisville," he explained, looking past her to Joe. "There was no sign of a struggle, no indication he'd been taken against his will. Based on the tire tracks it looks like someone met him out there and picked him up."

Ava frowned. "How'd he know to meet them all the way out there? If there was a call or something can't we trace it?"

Cooper came into the room then from Ty's office, holding up his cell phone. "I just talked with Marco. I asked him to check if there'd been any emails on Ty's account. He found one from the same address that sent the original threat. It listed coordinates that probably lead right to that road."

"So he did go willingly, then," Ava realized, her heart sinking. "He wanted to confront Ned."

Cooper approached her, his hands falling on her shoulders. "We'll get him back."

Tears welled in her eyes. "He could already be dead."

He nodded, not willing to sugarcoat anything for her. "He could. Or he might not be. Our best option is to wire Adam immediately and have him wait at the bar for Killian to show up again. The rest of us need to act as if nothing is wrong. Ned won't leave until he gets what he came here for."

Ava let out a rush of breath. "Then let's give it to him."

ADAM SAT in his usual seat at the bar, feeling like a worm on a hook. He tried to act casual, to not give any indication of the firestorm raging within. Containing his temper was the only way for the plan to work.

The equipment the FBI agents had taped to his chest grew warm from his body heat. The tape itched his skin, but he knew better than to scratch it. He'd been coached on how to act, what to say, and when to bail out if the conversation got too heated. He ran over those instructions in his head a dozen times, knowing he was a dead man if he screwed it up. His father was at risk now, which meant there was more riding on this than ever before.

Down the street at the Lucky Fox office, Ava and the Feds were listening in. They were counting on him to find out where his father was being held. They had to give off the impression that they weren't worried about Ty's whereabouts and that they had no reason to think foul play was involved. Blissful ignorance was going to be his saving grace.

Brandy kept watch on him from down the bar, the FBI on her cell phone's speed dial if things got out of hand. He offered her a half-hearted smile, trying to focus on her instead of the fear turning his gut inside out. She smiled in return, but kept her distance as instructed so as not to deter Killian from joining him.

Adam didn't know how long he sat there. An hour, two maybe. Time, as usual when he found himself inside the bar, was irrelevant. He would sit there all evening if that's what it took, nursing his glass of whiskey till the sun came up.

When he saw Brandy's eyes shoot to the front door and widen slightly, he knew the moment had come. Though his body wanted to tense up, he took a deep breath and sipped his drink instead. A man settled onto the stool beside him and patted him on the back.

"I thought ye'd be here," Killian said, his teeth flashing in a shark's grin. He nodded to Brandy for a beer, then folded his hands together on the bar.

Adam met his eyes, making sure to appear downtrodden and pissed off. "According to my sister, this is all I do." He lifted his glass in a solitary toast and sneered. "Guess I can't deny it."

"We all got our vices." Killian's smile widened. "And our wardens. Me brother is mine. Me da says he got all the civilized blood while I got all the savagery, so it's usually me gettin' into trouble and him bailin' me out."

Adam snorted, bowing his head. "Yep. Us too."

Brandy brought over Killian's beer and left to tend other customers, though Adam noticed her attention remained discreetly on him and Killian. Upping the ante, he faced the man and put as much derision into his voice as he could muster.

"I'm just a big joke to my dad. To my whole family, really. I'm sick of it."

Killian eyed him thoughtfully. "Then why don't ye leave?"

Adam grimaced. "And go where? I don't have many options."

"Sure ye do. It's a big country." Killian tossed back his beer, then set it down and began tearing at the label. "Speaking of family, there's something for the two of us to discuss. That's why I'm here."

A bolt of anxiety raced through Adam. He drank his whiskey to hide the tremor of his own hand. "Oh yeah?"

"It's that family matter I mentioned yesterday."

Adam fought to keep the eagerness from his expression. "What, you got a controlling bitch for a sister, too?" He pictured Ava's irritation at hearing him say that and had to keep himself from snickering.

Killian ignored the statement and stared at him pointedly. "Will ye take a walk with me, Adam? It's best if we don't have this conversation here."

Warning bells went off in Adam's head. "A walk? To where?"

A slow smile crept over Killian's face. "Well, it's really more of a drive. I think ye'll find what I have to say quite… life changing."

Adam swallowed the lump that formed in his throat, but maintained his cool. He shrugged. "I don't know, buddy. I just met you. How do I know you're not just tryin' to rob me?"

Killian chuckled. "I suppose ye don't, but I promise I'm a good Catholic boy and don't steal from strangers. The point is, ye seem unsatisfied here. Unfulfilled. I can offer ye somethin' better."

Adam made sure to still appear distrustful, knowing it was expected. No one in their right mind would hop into a stranger's car on a whim. Unless, of course, that person was desperate and a little intoxicated.

He tossed back the last of his whiskey and slammed the glass down on the bar. "All right. Let's go. I'm sick of this shithole, anyway."

"Good man." Killian grinned and tossed some cash onto the bar before Adam could dig out his wallet. "I got this round. Consider it a show of good faith and may it be only the first of many drinks we'll share."

Adam attempted a smile. "Thanks." His eyes went to Brandy as he slipped into his coat, hoping she understood from his curt nod that he had things under control. If he was lucky, he would be taken to where his father was being held captive. With the tracking device attached to the wire under his shirt, the Feds would have no trouble zeroing in on the location once he was there. All he had to do was play along, not act suspicious, and pray he wasn't walking into a death trap.

Killian placed a hand on his shoulder and directed him out of the bar. A few of the patrons eyed them curiously as they left, but Adam ignored them. For once, he didn't have time to worry about wagging tongues and gossip.

They pushed through the doors and out into the night. Rain had begun to fall, and Adam pulled his coat tighter around his body to keep the equipment dry. The last thing he needed was for it to short out right before he got what he came for.

Killian didn't seem to mind the rain at all. He shot off a text from his phone, then looked at Adam with a sharp grin. "Me brother'll be here any second."

"So what is this offer?" Adam asked, water dripping down his face. He tucked his hands into his coat pockets. "If it's slinging drugs, I ain't into that."

"Let's just say the life ye've been leadin' is a lie," Killian replied easily, his eyes scanning the street. "I'm here to show ye the right way, the only way. And once ye know, I suspect ye'll never want to come back to this life ever again."

Adam's blood chilled. He knew Killian must be talking about the IRA, but his understanding ended there. What about his life was a lie? And why would whatever Killian had to tell him make him want to up and leave Fox Hills? Leave his family?

"Ah, there he is." Killian pointed to a black SUV that appeared through the rain. When it came to a stop in front of them, he opened the back door and motioned with his head. "Get in."

Adam hesitated, certain this was a huge mistake. Then again, he had come this far. He couldn't let fear get the best of him now. Besides, Ava would go. And since she was secretly listening in, he couldn't let her hear him chicken out. He would never hear the end of it if he got this close and then failed.

He hopped into the backseat but didn't touch the seatbelt, just in case he had to bail out at some point. The driver turned and stared at him, his gaunt face and electric green eyes shadowed with distrust. Once Killian was safely inside, the man turned his attention back to the road and gunned the engine, wasting no time.

Adam wondered what the hurry was.

"So where are we goin'?" he asked, praying his voice didn't crack from nerves.

Killian twisted in his seat. "A warehouse in Louisville."

"Seriously?" Adam grimaced, hoping to look more irritated than alarmed. "Can't you tell me whatever is you want to tell me here in town? Why do we gotta go all the way to the city?"

"Because what we have to show ye is in the city," Killian told him, the passing streetlights highlighting the excitement in his eyes. He turned his attention to his brother. "What do ye think, Rhys? Should we tell him now?"

At first Rhys didn't respond, leading Adam to wonder if he had even heard the question. When he did speak, his voice was softer, graver than his brother's. Adam got the sense that while Killian may have been the wild, reckless one, Rhys was the more threatening of the two. "Da found out from the traitor that the Feds are still in town. Did ye check him for a wire?"

Killian's face fell. His eyes darted back to Adam. "Well, fuck. Did the Feds get to ye first?"

Adam shook his head, though he had a feeling his expression gave it away. Panic ripped through him as he struggled to come up with a good lie. "They're investigating the company, not me. Hell, they've barely spoken two words to me since they came to town. It's my sister and dad they've been dealin' with." He fixed an angry look on his face, hoping to distract them. "Why does it matter, anyway? Are you boys fugitives or somethin'?"

Killian started laughing, a dark, demented sound that sent a chill down Adam's spine. "Oh, yer a right fool if ye think we're that stupid."

He reached out then and lifted up Adam's shirt, revealing the recording device beneath. He bared his teeth and tore the device from Adam's skin. Fury lit up his face as he stared it, then at Adam. "If you weren't me brother, I'd kill ye for this."

Adam started to open the door to jump out, but hesitated at Killian's words. "Wait, *brother?*"

Killian shook his head as Rhys set the child locks on the doors. "Aye. And if ye hadn't been cooperatin' with the

Feds, this could've gone smoothly. Instead it looks like we'll have to do this the hard way."

Adam sank back in his seat, eyes wide. "You're my brothers? How is that possible?"

Killian turned back around, showing Rhys the recording device. Adam realized then that Killian had missed the GPS tracker on his waistband. He slipped it off and tossed it on the floor, hoping Killian wouldn't notice it if he checked him again.

As Rhys pulled onto the highway and kicked up their speed, Killian opened the window and tossed out the recorder. He then pulled a pistol out of the glove compartment and aimed it straight at Adam's chest. "Hand me yer cell phone."

Adam stared at the gun, a new fear settling over him. Based on what Killian had said before, he didn't think they'd kill him. But he wasn't positive they wouldn't wound him.

He handed over his cell, which Killian also chucked out the window. He settled back in his seat, the gun resting in his lap as he spoke in hurried whispers to Rhys.

Adam shut his eyes and bowed his head, fighting to breathe. He thought of Brandy in that instant, realizing he may never see her again. He could still feel the warmth of her kiss, the smooth touch of her fingertips. In his mind he saw her beautiful smile, always so full of life and honesty and grace. What would she do when she found out he had been taken?

She'd cry, he thought, and his heart panged horribly. He'd always hated to see her cry.

He lifted his head, filled with a rush of fearless determination. Not willing to give up now, not when he'd just started to turn his life around, he lunged forward and wrapped his arm into a chokehold around Killian's neck. The SUV swerved as Rhys reacted to the threat on his brother, bringing them directly into the path of oncoming traffic.

AVA FOLLOWED Cooper and Marco in her truck as they tracked the device attached to Adam. She didn't know how Killian hadn't noticed it, but considered it nothing short of a miracle. If they were lucky, Ned's sons would be leading them straight to the warehouse in Louisville where, hopefully, her father was being held. Then they'd go in guns blazing and take back what was stolen from her and arrest Ned in the process.

At least, that's how she hoped it would go down. In reality, she knew Cooper would likely call for backup and they would want to scope out the place and determine the risks before taking action. She had no patience for that at this point. She just wanted her father and brother home safe. If that meant she had to go in and get them herself, then so be it. She wasn't above breaking the rules to get her way, not when it meant the safety of her family.

Cooper hadn't even wanted her to follow them, but he knew better than to think he could stop her. Anything short of handcuffing her to a light pole wouldn't be enough to keep her away.

Her mind raced as she drove, a million different questions competing for her attention. She had heard, loud and clear, the proclamation Killian had made upon discovering the wire.

If you weren't me brother, I'd kill ye for this.

There hadn't been time to dwell on it before as they had been rushing out to follow the SUV, but she thought of it now while she sat in silence. If what Killian said was true, then that meant she and Adam shared at least one parent with these monsters. Surely it wasn't her mother, who they had played a role in murdering. So that left only her father, in which case why had they been raised by Ned and why were they holding Ty captive now?

None of it made any logical sense, which meant he must have been lying. But then why lie about a thing like that? To convince Adam to help them? To establish a close family tie that didn't exist?

Cooper's brake lights suddenly flashed as he slowed his speed. Ava saw several other cars up ahead, all at a dead stop with a few at odd angles, some stuck in the dirt median. Metal and glass were scattered over the concrete and blue and red police lights lit up the night.

She cursed under her breath as Cooper hopped out and ran to inspect the cars involved in the accident. It looked like three or four in total, nothing too serious. She watched him and Marco speak with the police on the scene and rolled her eyes. They were wasting valuable time.

Then Cooper turned and raced toward her truck. She rolled down the window for him.

"What is it?"

Cooper rested his hands on the door frame and bent his head to meet her gaze. "Looks like a hit and run. Witnesses said a black SUV swerved into oncoming traffic and took out a few cars, then drove off. It was probably our guys."

Ava's heart stopped. "Adam. Do you think he's hurt?"

"The damage to the SUV must not have been too serious if they drove away, but in all likelihood they'll ditch it the first chance they get."

"We have to keep tracking them," she snapped, impatience getting the better of her. "We've wasted enough time."

He nodded. "Right."

She watched him jog back to the car and climb inside. He drove around the collision and sped off, her tailing just a breath behind. All she could think about was what could have caused the crash. The only explanation she had was that Adam, God bless him, had tried to fight back.

CHAPTER

Twenty – seven

Rhys pulled the SUV up to the curb beside a vacant warehouse in Louisville. The driver's side door was barely hanging on and the windshield was cracked, but other than that the vehicle was intact.

Immediately following the crash, Killian had hopped into the backseat and wrestled Adam into submission. The guy was tough, tougher than Adam had anticipated. It hadn't taken long before he'd been punched so hard in the face that he saw stars, too dazed to fight back. His hands had been bound with twine behind his back so tight he thought it might have cut off the blood flow.

By the time he'd gotten his senses back, they were already in the city. He had stared out the window helplessly, furious with himself for failing yet again. So he gathered his strength and waited for the next opportune moment to strike, refusing to let the bastards have their way.

The warehouse loomed like a concrete mountain above them. The rain had stopped, though a dense fog remained that, in the light of the street lamps, gave everything an ominous glow. He felt a sick feeling wash over him the second before Killian threw open the car door and yanked him out.

"No time to waste, boyo. Gotta keep movin'.'"

Adam sneered at him, though the movement caused pain to shoot through his injured face. "Untie me, asshole. I ain't done with you yet. Fight fair like a man."

Killian let out a bark of a laugh and smacked Adam hard on the back to usher him along. "Who do ye think yer talkin' to? I could mop the floor with ye. In fact, maybe I should untie ye just to teach ye a lesson…"

"Shut up, brother. We do nothin' till we get instructions from Da," Rhys cut in, casting a disapproving glance at his brother.

Killian shrugged. "We still need the girl. I expect he won't want to do anythin' more 'til we have her."

"We have to leave this place. It'll be crawlin' with the Feds before long," Rhys said, staring around the street before making his way to a small metal door cut into the side of the building. He knocked twice, then a third time in a distinct pattern. Seconds later the door opened and they walked inside.

The building was lit with rows of fluorescent lights. Thousands of square feet of empty concrete floor spread out before them, with one thing resting in the middle of it. A chair, with a man tied to it with rope.

Adam's heart slammed into his throat when he saw his father. Ty was staring at him with such sadness in his eyes, looking worse for the wear with blood and dirt on his face and business suit. Beside the chair was a smearing of dried blood, the coppery smell of it meshing with the industrial scent of concrete.

"Dad," Adam muttered, trying to scramble out of Killian's grasp to get to his father. Killian only held him back, chuckling to himself.

Adam then noticed another man, a bit older than his father, walking alongside them. He was tall and strongly built, dressed in camo pants and a tightly fitted T-shirt. Waves of light brown hair threaded with gray feathered back from his face. His stride was purposeful, strict, and from the scars and dark tattoos marring his skin, Adam had the feeling the man had known war of some kind.

He led the way to where Ty was sitting, then turned to face Adam.

A smile cracked the lines of the man's harsh face as he eyed Adam with relish. "I don't know how ye pulled it off, Tyler. He looks nothin' like ye."

Ty looked into Adam's eyes as though silently pleading for forgiveness. When he said nothing, the man walked over to Adam and cupped his chin, tilting his face side to side. Adam stared into a set of hazel eyes that matched his own, and found he couldn't breathe. It wasn't only out of fear, but out of recognition.

Suddenly Killian's words took on a whole other meaning.

"I'm Ned Brannon," the man said, examining Adam like he were a fly pinned to a board. "By now ye will have heard of me. But much of what's been said is nothin' but lies. Ye deserve to know the truth about who ye are. Where ye come from. And where ye belong."

Adam stared unblinking into Ned's eyes, unwilling to be shaken by him. "You killed my mother. And now you have my father tied to a chair. What part of that is a lie?"

Ned eased back and released Adam's face. He was about to speak before Rhys interrupted him.

"Sir, the Feds will be here any minute. We need to move."

Ned's eyes narrowed, but he nodded and Rhys set about unstrapping Ty from the chair while Killian held fast onto Adam. Ned gave Adam one more indulgent look.

"Have patience, my son. Soon ye will have the truth."

WHEN THEY drove up to the warehouse and parked behind the damaged SUV, Ava leapt from her truck. She would have stormed her way in if Cooper hadn't held her back, instructing her to keep behind him. She started to resist, but didn't want to waste time arguing. The sooner they got inside, the better.

Cooper and Marco, guns raised and at the ready, approached the single steel door in the side of the building and attempted to open it. Finding it unlocked, Marco nodded to Cooper to go ahead. He slowly stepped inside, Marco watching his back with Ava a few steps behind.

When Cooper lowered his weapon and let out a sigh, Ava shoved past Marco and stared around the empty warehouse.

She cursed under her breath, realizing they were too late. All that remained was a single metal chair, alone in the middle of the high-ceilinged room. She would have ignored it, but then she saw the blood.

"Sweet Jesus," she gasped, stumbling toward the chair with wide eyes and a horrified heart. She fell to her knees, knowing the blood was her father's. Her throat clenched as she stared around at it, her hands curling into her hair. The bastard had tortured him. Spilled his blood. Vengeance soared through her like a phoenix and burst into flames. "I'll kill him for this. I'll fucking kill him if it's the last thing I do."

Cooper helped her to her feet an instant before she broke. He said nothing and simply held her while she raged, her screams muffled by his chest. Her hands clenched into fists around his shirt, then weakened as her spirit grieved. She had already lost one parent. She couldn't lose the other.

She pulled away from him, wiping at the tears that spilled down her face. "I don't understand. The tracking device led us here. Where are they?"

Marco stepped back into the warehouse, holding up the device. "It was on the floor of the backseat in the SUV. Adam must have removed it."

Ava felt the last of her hope shatter to pieces. "So what now? How do we find them?"

She met eyes with Cooper, needing an answer.

He only bowed his head. "The best we can do now is contact rental car companies in the area, see if Ned or his sons rented the car they're using. But I'm betting they got it from an IRA contact. They wouldn't be stupid enough to rent or steal something."

Disbelief shot through her. "There has to be something else. Anything."

"Well, there is one thing," Marco said, lifting an index finger in the air.

Cooper glared at him. "No."

Marco frowned. "You didn't even hear what I had to say."

"I know what it is, and the answer is no," Cooper asserted, his hands tensing over Ava's shoulders.

She stepped back from him, her eyes on Marco. "Tell me. What is it?"

Marco ignored Cooper's disapproval and faced Ava. "We were talking on the way over here, and we think we know what Ned is after."

Ava's eyes narrowed. "You mean other than Lucky Fox money?"

"I mean *instead* of the money. In fact, I don't think he gives a shit about the money at all. What he cares about are his kids. As in, you and Adam."

One of her eyebrows rose. "Excuse me?"

Cooper crossed his arms, a reluctant sigh escaping his lips. "You heard what Killian said. He called Adam his brother. Which means, obviously, that makes you Killian and Rhys's sister. Seeing as the two of them are a few years older than you that makes your mother far too young to be their mother, so the connection isn't shared there. That leaves only the father, and though theoretically possible, I find it hard to believe that Ned's first wife got impregnated by Ty. Therefore, that leaves only one possibility."

"Ned is my father," Ava said numbly, another tear falling down her cheek. She made no move to brush it away.

Sympathy clouded Cooper's eyes. "Yes."

"But, but then that means Mama *knew* him," Ava managed, revulsion washing over her.

"Up until a few weeks ago, you were sure your father didn't know Ned, either," Cooper replied. "This clearly goes much deeper than any of us anticipated."

She rubbed her face, needing to stay focused. "So then what is your plan to find Ned?"

Cooper exchanged a knowing look with Marco, then turned back to her. "Ned has one twin. He's not going to leave until he gets the second to take home to Ireland."

"He plans to force me and Adam onto a plane to Ireland with him?" Ava nearly laughed it was so absurd. "I'd like to see him try."

"He got into this country, he can get back out again if we don't find him in time."

She saw the anger contort his expression. "From the look on your face, I guess you'd prefer I just go hide in a hole somewhere until the storm blows over."

Cooper motioned toward the chair and the blood. "You've seen what Ned is capable of, Ava."

Her hands fell to her hips. "I also know that he probably won't kill me. At least not at first. I have to try. If he really wants me, then it won't be long before he makes contact and then I'm gone." She straightened, a sense of pride and duty bolstering her resolve. "I'll go get my family myself if y'all don't want to help."

Marco's brows shot up and Cooper edged closer to her, jabbing a finger into her chest. He looked angrier than she had ever seen him before. "This is still my investigation. I have just as much a right to be here as you do, if not more so. I'm here to protect your life, not risk it."

"Oh, but Adam was worth risking? And my mother?" she growled, furious tears in her eyes. "Why was it okay to sacrifice them but not me?"

"Because we were in control back then. At least we thought we were," Cooper retorted, his hands diving into his hair as he turned away. He let out a frustrated breath and closed his eyes. "This is why we should've never gotten involved, Ava. My feelings for you are getting in the way of my ability to do my job."

She tossed up her hands. "There's no time for that now, Slick. I'm sorry. We can worry about whatever the hell is going on between us later, once my dad and brother are home safe."

He faced her again, his expression impossible to read. "Fine. Get in your truck. We'll follow you home. You can wait there for Ned to make contact."

She hesitated, not ready yet to be done with the argument. The cold detachment in his tone doused her temper and left her feeling hollow. When Cooper turned away and headed for the door, she realized it was over whether she was ready for it or not.

THERE WAS no sleeping that night. Ava sat on the front porch with her grandfather as the clouds gave way to an explosion of stars, a half-empty bottle of bourbon between them. They each took occasional swigs of it to ease the burden on their minds.

Her cell phone lay in her right hand, silent and dark. She stared at it, praying for it to ring. The sooner Ned contacted her, the sooner she could confront him. She itched for it the way a boxer longs to enter the ring, gloves up and poised for battle against his opponent. Until she had her chance to fight, she was left feeling helpless.

Cooper and Marco were back at their hotel, waiting on word from her while they did their best to gather reinforcements and plan things on their end. She wished Cooper hadn't been so distant with her, but in the end it was probably for the best. From the very beginning their relationship had been headed for a dead end. Maybe this was the very thing to bring them back to reality. They couldn't be together and it had been foolish to even humor the idea. Now they both were suffering, on top of everything else that was happening around them.

It was nothing but a distraction, she thought bitterly. Then she remembered the look he often gave her right before they kissed, that kind of quiet, intense sort of wonder that came into his eyes, and her heart ached with longing and regret.

Joe absently patted the long rifle laying across his lap while Remy sprawled out at their feet, emitting quiet doggie snores. Ava rubbed his belly with her foot as she took another drink of bourbon straight from the bottle.

Off somewhere in the distance, a mournful train blew its whistle.

"There's no sense in it," Joe said suddenly, pursing his lips in an angry pout. "No sense at all."

Ava laid her hand upon his, knowing he was referring to the bombshell she had delivered to him earlier that night. "I don't know what to make of it either."

"Yer ma was raised outside Dallas. Ty met her at the university. She's never been to Ireland." Joe's face creased with doubt and a vile hatred. "Ned's a goddamn liar. I won't believe a word of it."

"Trust me, I don't want to believe it either," Ava replied, eyeing her phone again. "If it is true and I'm Ned's daughter, then my entire life has been a lie."

"No." Joe grunted, turning to face her angrily. "Ye mustn't say that. I won't have it."

Her brows rose as she stared out into the darkness. Silent tears welled in her eyes. "God, I miss Daddy and Adam. Without them here I feel so empty."

Joe squeezed her hand, his voice softening. "I know, dearie. I know it hurts."

She laid her head upon his shoulder and breathed in the familiar scent of earthy oak and whiskey. It smoothed the sharp edges of her anxiety, giving her some measure of comfort. At least she still had her grandfather. Even if, by Ned's account, Joe Brannon may actually not be her grandfather after all.

CHAPTER

Twenty-eight

Ava didn't remember falling asleep, but woke up tucked into her own bed. Immediately her hand went to the cell phone on her night stand, panicked she may have slept through a phone call. Seeing nothing on the screen, she let out a long breath and fell back against the pillows.

The events of the previous night rolled over her like a toxic fog. Bit by bit it filled her mind with fear and anxiety until she thought of nothing else. What was going to happen to her family? What if they were wrong and Ned didn't want her and was already on his way back to Ireland with her father and brother held captive? How would she ever forgive herself for not trying harder to save them?

She didn't want to feel so hopeless, but it was hard not to. She felt like she was losing. Every decision seemed to take her even further away from getting justice for her mother. And being at odds with Cooper and Marco only made it worse. She knew all they wanted to do was help. But it was her life to risk as she chose, and in the end if it meant certain death she would still pursue Ned.

She may not be winning, but she wasn't a quitter. Until the game was over, she would make sure she remained an active player in it.

Sitting up, she noticed a steady rain falling outside. A heavy mist hung in the air, casting everything in an ominous gray haze. What she wouldn't give for just an ounce of happy sunlight. Something to brighten her spirits, even if only for a moment.

After taking a quick shower and slipping into jeans and a comfortable knit sweater, Ava left her room in search of coffee. In the kitchen, she found her grandfather seated at the island with Brandy at his side.

They both turned as she entered, and Ava's heart broke at the sight of her good friend.

"Oh, Brandy," she managed, seeing the strain in her friend's eyes.

Brandy rose to her feet and met her halfway through the living room, pulling her into a tight hug. "Adam. Oh God, Ava. Adam."

"I know." Ava released her, both their eyes filled with tears. "I'll get him back. I promise."

Brandy nodded, her lower lip trembling. "I didn't want him to do this at all. But he was so brave. He wouldn't listen to me."

Regret crept in on Ava and she wished she had gone in her brother's place. "He knew the risk. We all did. Now we have to fix it."

"What are we going to do?" Brandy asked, leading Ava over to the island and ushering her into the seat beside Joe. She then set about preparing a cup of coffee for her.

"I'm waiting for Ned to contact me," Ava told her. She pulled her cell phone out of her pocket and laid it on the tile counter. "When he does, I'll know what to do."

Brandy brought over the steaming mug, filled to the brim with black coffee, and set it in front of Ava. "How do you know he will?"

Ava gave her a brief rundown about the possibility of Ned being her father, finally sipping her coffee after she finished.

Brandy was stunned. "Are you sure he's your father? What about Ty?"

"I'm not positive, no." Ava stared at her coffee, feeling sick again. "And no matter what the truth is, I only have one father. And it's not Ned."

Joe rubbed her back in an attempt to comfort her. "Damn straight, dearie. We won't let this bastard do more damage than he has already done."

Ava offered him a grateful smile, then turned to Brandy. "How're you holding up, honey?"

Brandy chewed on her lower lip, her hands toying with her own cup of coffee. "I didn't sleep. But then y'all probably didn't either. I can't stop thinkin' about them hurtin' Adam." A sob escaped her throat and her hand flew up to cover her mouth. She shook her head when Ava started to get up to comfort her. She let out an embarrassed laugh. "I'm sorry, that ain't helpin' none. I'm fine."

Pity washed over Ava. "Adam will be okay. He's tougher than he looks. And besides, he's got you to live for now."

Brandy burst into tears and this time didn't stop Ava from soothing her. Ava wrapped her in a warm embrace, needing comfort just as badly as she wanted to give it.

"It'll be okay, honey. I promise. I'll make this right."

Brandy pulled away and wiped at her tears. "I know. Oh, y'all are so strong. I'm just a mess."

Ava smiled fondly. "I'd say. But falling in love with my idiot brother will do that to you."

"More like him finally fallin' in love with me," Brandy corrected, her lips curving. "I've always loved him."

"Thank God he saw the light at last," Ava mused, though the happy thought was brief. She glanced over at her phone, wishing desperately that it would ring.

Seconds later it exploded to life, and she nearly jumped out of her skin.

Joe and Brandy stared at her anxiously as she grabbed it off the counter. A cold shock hit her as she read the caller-ID.

"It's from Mama's phone," she managed, fear and grief lodged inside her throat. She swallowed it back and answered, letting her anger take over. "Hello?"

"*Is this Ava Brannon?*" the voice asked, rough and rich with the lilt of Ireland.

"Yes. Is this Ned?"

"*Aye. I believe I have somethin' of some importance to ye.*"

"Just tell me where to meet you, asshole. Let's not waste any time on niceties." Her jaw clenched around the words and it took all she had to not rip into him.

Ned chuckled. "*I suspect ye know everythin', then?*"

"I know you want to see me. So tell me where to go."

"*Actually, I believe this'll work best if I come to ye instead. Just stay where ye are, love. I'll be there shortly.*" He paused, and when he spoke again his voice had taken on a firmer, more serious tone. "*Me men are watchin' yer home and the Feds in their hotel. If ye raise the alarm or send for them, I will not come and Ty Brannon dies. Do we have an agreement?*"

Ava pursed her lips. "Yes. I'll be waiting."

She hung up the phone and tossed it aside. Releasing a heavy, drawn out breath, she faced Brandy and her grandfather. "Ned's coming here. Right now. He's watching the house, so I want both of you to go into one of the back bedrooms and keep out of this. This is between me and Ned."

Joe looked offended and Brandy frightened.

"We face this together, dearie, or we don't face it at all," Joe insisted, getting to his feet with a fierce look in his eyes.

Ava knew she wouldn't be able to convince him. "All right. Fine. But don't expect me to save your sorry ass if you get into trouble. I already got two men I gotta rescue. I don't need to worry about a third."

Brandy wrung her hands together. "Shouldn't you call Cooper and Marco?"

Ava shook her head. "Ned says he's got men watching them. If they make a move to head on over here, he won't come. Besides, I don't need to. They already heard all of it."

"How?" Brandy asked, her brows drawing together in confusion.

A sharp smile lifted the corners of Ava's mouth. "They tapped my cell phone. Not sure what their plan is, but at least they know what's goin' down. As for me, I'm gonna go wait out on the porch. I got a date with a madman."

COOPER ROSE from his chair in Marco's hotel room, working over the situation in his mind. He paced the floor, rubbing the stubble on his chin.

Marco glanced up at him from his seat at the desk. His laptop lay open in front of him where they'd just listened to Ava's conversation with Ned. "We have reinforcements on standby. Should I call them in?"

Cooper frowned, continuing to pace. "Not yet. Ned's expecting that."

"Well, so what, then? We just leave Ava out there to defend herself against this psychopath?"

Cooper shot him a testy look. "Don't forget this was your idea. I was against this plan from the beginning."

Marco waved off the comment. "It was the only way to get Ned and you know it. We just gotta figure out how to get in there undetected and nab him before he escapes. Maybe set up a road block on the highway out of town?"

"Maybe. I need to call Horvath. Give him the update," Cooper decided, reaching for his phone. He dialed the number and waited impatiently for his boss to answer.

"*You get word from Ned?*" Horvath asked in lieu of a greeting.

"Yep." Cooper put him on speaker phone so Marco could hear. "Ava just got the call. Ned is heading to her house to meet with her as we speak. He told her he's got men, likely one of his sons, keeping watch on us here at the hotel to make sure we don't go help her."

"*He's a ballsy sonofabitch, isn't he?*" Horvath replied. "*Broad daylight. Obvious location. He's just asking to get caught. I'm gonna be honest, something about this doesn't feel right.*"

"My thoughts exactly." Cooper stopped moving and lowered onto the edge of the bed. "I would call for backup and have the troops storm the house but if we scare him off and he gets away, we miss our chance."

"We can send in units on foot, have them keep out of sight until Ned is within reach," Marco suggested.

"*Hmm...*" Horvath fell silent, clearly thinking it over.

Cooper buried his face in his hands. "We have to act fast. He could be there any minute, and Ava's by herself—"

"*I know this case and the people involved in it are important to you, kid, but we can't be brash,*" Horvath replied. "*Years of meticulous man-hours have gone into this investigation. I won't have that compromised when we're this close to the goal.*"

"So what's the plan then? What should we do?" Cooper asked.

"*I want you to stay put. If Ned's got someone watching the building, then any movement from you two will indicate that we know what's going on. I'm going to send one of the team over dressed as a civilian and see if he can spot the watchdog. I'll have the others keep a discreet eye on the Brannons' property for confirmation of when Ned arrives. Just hold tight for now."*

Cooper scratched his head, a thought occurring to him. "You know, he may not *drive* there. Ned's not stupid and he's resourceful enough to do better than that."

Marco perked up. "What are you thinking?"

A loud, rumbling noise came from above, growing louder by the second. They both stared up at the ceiling.

"Helicopter," Cooper muttered. He met eyes with Marco in stunned discovery. "He's going to her by helicopter."

AVA HEARD the sound long before she spotted its source cresting over the trees of her property. A sleek black helicopter swooped in and hovered over the field nearby, then slowly lowered to the ground, the wind of its blades whipping up the branches of nearby trees.

Joe burst out of the house, his eyes on the helicopter and his favorite long rifle clutched in his hands. "Sweet Mary Mother of Jesus."

Ava jumped to her feet and ushered him back inside, gritting her teeth. "You have to wait. I know it's hard, but please. If he sees you with a gun he may just shoot Daddy and I will *never* forgive you."

Joe's face crumpled with hurt pride and guilt. "Fine. Have it yer way. But he lays a hand on ye and I'll shoot the bastard."

"Love you." She kissed his cheek and raced outside, watching from the porch as the doors of the helicopter opened and a man stepped out.

Though he was a ways off, she knew just by the arrogance of his stride that he was Ned. In his military-style clothing and combat boots, he navigated the rain-slicked terrain with his eyes locked on hers. A bolt of fear shot through her as he walked purposefully toward her, as though nothing in world could stop him.

Her gaze went back to the helicopter, where she saw the man she now recognized as Rhys unloading two men with their hands bound behind their backs. One was her father, bloodied and bruised in his dusty suit, and the other was Adam. Thankfully, he seemed to be unharmed. Rhys held an AK-47 rifle that he shoved into their backs, forcing them to walk a few paces forward.

Relief fluttered through her stomach at seeing them alive, but she knew better than to count her blessings too soon. She turned her focus back to Ned as he came to a stop halfway between her and the helicopter. He stood still and proud, his hands clasped behind him.

She got the impression he intended for her to join him in the field. A compromise, she figured, to ease her away from the safety of her home and onto neutral ground. One glance behind her and she saw Joe peeking through the drapes. She frowned at him and gave a curt shake of her head, then marched out to meet Ned.

All she needed to do was buy time. She had faith in Cooper that the FBI wouldn't be far behind. If she could just keep Ned grounded and talking, they may stand a chance at catching him off guard.

Her feet crunched over the gravel driveway, then sunk into the marshy grassland beyond. A light mist was falling, cooling her already freezing skin. She resisted the urge to rub her arms and shiver, not wanting to appear weak in the presence of the man who held her family hostage. Instead she stood as tall and proud as he was, determined to match him.

As she got closer, she noticed the way he seemed to drink her in with his eyes, hazel ones that matched her own. If she needed any proof of his relation to her, it was in those eyes.

"All right. I'm here," she declared, coming to a stop about five feet away from him. She rested both hands on her hips and cocked her chin.

Ned's face split in an odd little smile. "So ye are. How unfortunate it is that it's taken this long for us to meet. She stole ye from me, ye see. Without me even knowin' ye existed. But I'm going to remedy that right now."

Ava's eyes shot over his shoulder to where her father and Adam were waiting by the helicopter. They were staring at her in silence, bitterness and rage etched into their faces.

She looked back to Ned. "Just tell me what you want. I don't need your sob story or your life history. All I care about is everybody gettin' out of this alive."

Ned shifted his weight, angling his chin as he continued to stare at her. "A trade. I'll let the traitor go, and ye will be comin' with me."

She took a deep breath, released it. "What about Adam?"

"He's not part of the deal," Ned said coldly, his smug smile fading. "I could just take ye right now and kill me cousin, but because yer me daughter I'm willin' to make a compromise with ye. I will let him live, if ye come with me."

"Back to Ireland."

"Aye." He bowed his head in a gallant gesture. "It's where ye belong, love."

"You really are crazy," Ava murmured, shaking her head. Her lip curled with disgust. "You killed my mother. Why the hell would I ever want to live with you?"

A bright hatred flashed in his eyes, chilling her to the bone. "That woman was a traitor. She knew the consequences of her actions and that if I ever found her alive I would kill her. That was a choice she made."

Ava nearly found his accusation amusing. Were they even speaking about the same woman? "None of this makes any goddamn sense. How did the two of you even know each other?"

Ned let out a derisive sniff, a dark smile crossing his face. "She was me wife. And the youngest woman to ever join the ranks of the IRA."

CHAPTER

Twenty-nine

Ava did laugh this time. "You've got to be kidding me? You expect me to believe that my mother, sweet, never-hurt-a-fly Sandra Brannon, was a member of the IRA and your *wife*?"

The humor disappeared from Ned's expression. "Whatever lies she told ye don't change the truth. To me she was Colleen McVey, a vibrant young thing with fire in her heart for the liberation of Ireland. She was only sixteen when we married, against her da's wishes. I'd never met anyone like her in me whole life." He paused, regarding her curiously. "Ye have her spark, Ava. I only wish I'd been the one to raise ye."

His words stunned her. Reality hit like a sledgehammer to her chest, relentlessly painful. Her mother's final words at the hospital. Her strange accent. The pure fear in her eyes.

Da warned me not to marry him. But love him I did. Lord, forgive me. He's evil. Got the Devil in him, he does.

Ava felt nauseas. Her hand came up to cover her mouth as her mind raced.

Your father. Stay away from him. He's coming for you.

Her gaze lifted to Ned, and her entire world came crumbling down.

"It's true," she managed. "She told me you were coming. That I should stay away from you. I thought she meant Ty…"

Ned grimaced. "Colleen left one day without a word. I thought she'd been captured, or worse, killed. Then the Gardaí showed up and arrested me. Someone had given them information on the bombing we'd planned for later that week. There were only three people who knew the details, meself, me right hand Ronan Campbell, and Colleen. It was easy enough to figure out what had happened."

"So then how did she wind up over here?"

"After some convincin', me cousin informed me that she made a deal with the SDU and your Feds in exchange for information on all me dealings, enough to almost land me behind bars. She went to Ty, convinced him to turn on me as well. For years I searched for her, never realizin' she was hidin' in plain sight, pretendin' to be married to me own cousin. Pretendin' *my* children were his."

"She didn't tell you she was pregnant when she left." Ava imagined her mother's heartache, her choice to save her children from a life of murder and destruction. "She gave up everything for us. To raise us here, with Joe and Ty."

Ned sneered. "It wasn't right, takin' ye from me like that. I had me sons from me first marriage, but the two of ye were me and *Colleen's* children. She was the love of me life. Despite her betrayal, I would do anythin' to have ye back. And have. I've risked everythin' to come here."

Ava saw the honesty in his eyes, and for the briefest of moments felt pity for him. His intentions didn't relieve him of his sins, but at least she understood his motives and could sympathize with his desire to raise his own children. In a way it was noble, but his methods tarnished any semblance of pride she could have in him.

She owed her mother everything for saving her and Adam from that hell of a life. There was no way she was going to let Ned force her into it now, not after everything her mother had sacrificed.

But time was running out. The Feds were nowhere to be seen, which meant she had to keep Ned busy somehow. Though the idea sickened her, she knew she had to play to his weaknesses. It was her only option.

She offered him a sad smile, bringing tears of sympathy into her eyes. "You really care that much about us, huh?"

Ned nodded, taking a step forward. "Aye. Ye should've never been brought to this place. Raised by traitors to the cause. Raised knowin' nothin' of where ye come from."

Ava avoided his intense gaze, hoping she looked remorseful while she only really felt rage. It took all she had to conceal it beneath a false façade of compassion.

"If I'd known, I might have come to you myself," she said, nearly choking on the words.

Ned got even closer, reaching out now to touch her. "It wasn't yer fault. That's why I don't blame ye or yer brother. We can make this right, startin' today."

She lifted her eyes to his, feeling a tear fall down her cheek. It was born out of disgust, but she let him believe it was love. "Maybe we could."

He smiled the instant his hands touched her shoulders. He squeezed them gently, much like her other father used to always do, and she had to bite her tongue until it bled to keep from striking out at him for having the nerve.

A gunshot rang out, echoing through the mist. A split second later Ned jolted and cursed in pain. He dragged her to the ground and covered her protectively with his body, releasing a pistol from his belt. He aimed it at the house, and Ava raised her head to see her grandfather standing on the porch, long rifle at the ready.

When Ned fired, she screamed.

"WE HAVE *Killian in custody. Time to go, boys."*

Cooper leapt out of his seat, pulling Marco with him. "Thanks, Boss. We're on our way over there right now."

"The team is ahead of you. Hang back and move in only if needed until Ned's been apprehended."

"Got it." Cooper hung up the phone and was out the door of the hotel room at breakneck speed. Marco was a breath behind him, stuffing half a bagel into his mouth. They all but flew down the stairs and were outside the main entrance within seconds.

Across the street, Cooper spotted an unmarked cruiser with lights flashing in the windshield and an agent placing Killian under arrest. Another agent stood by, talking on the phone.

Cooper waved to them before hopping into his own car. Marco slid in beside him and they hit the road, headed to Lucky Fox and Ava.

Cooper didn't take a breath until they reached the distillery. A group of unmarked FBI cruisers out of Louisville were blocking the road, preventing them from getting closer. When Cooper parked and got out, one of the agents jogged to meet him. He was a few years older than Cooper and already bald, his lean, pale face strained and serious.

"We have shots fired," the agent said breathlessly, pointing in the direction of the house. It was somewhere beyond the trees, out of sight and lost in the mist.

Cooper's insides twisted. "Any idea who did the shooting?"

"Seems the old man shot first," the agent explained, wiping his brow with the back of his hand. "Our men are moving in. From what we can tell, Ned was hit, but not fatally."

Marco cursed under his breath. "Where are Adam and Ty Brannon?"

"They're inside the helicopter. The older son is armed with an assault rifle and is holding them hostage."

"And Ava?" Cooper asked, unsure he even wanted to know.

The agent nodded. "She's with Ned halfway between the copter and the house."

"Christ." Cooper looked toward the house, an uneasy feeling washing over him. "She's right in the line of fire."

Another agent trotted over to them, holding a radio in his hand. "We have a ceasefire. Suspect is now speaking with the old man, who no longer has his weapon. Not sure what's happening, but this could get ugly, fast."

Cooper knew exactly what Joe was up to. "He's having a long overdue conversation with his enemy."

"How do you think that's gonna end?" Marco asked dryly, shaking his head.

"They're Irish. The only way to end a conversation like that is a fight."

AVA COULDN'T take her eyes off the bloodied mess her grandfather had made of Ned's shoulder. A couple inches to her left and the bullet would have hit her instead. Despite the close call, there was no one else in the world she would've trusted to make that shot.

Ned kept pressure on the wound, blood leaking between his fingers. His other hand held his pistol, aimed temporarily at the ground. He stood tall and faced Joe man-to-man as her grandfather came, unarmed, to speak to him. Ned held Ava back, keeping her out of Joe's reach.

"'Tis mighty brave of ye to come face me like this, traitor," Ned snarled, his breath coming out in tight, strained gasps between his teeth.

Ava noted how pale he looked, and had the stark realization that he might simply bleed to death.

Joe's eyes narrowed, his hands clenched into fists at his sides. Though he was nearly a foot shorter than Ned, he stared at the man fearlessly.

"Don't speak on matters ye don't understand, boyo," Joe growled. "That was between yer grandfather, father, and meself. And it wasn't about violence and hate. It was business."

"Ye spit in the face of the entire family. I'd call that personal."

"I set out to make me own way in this world. Never harmed nobody. But look at ye. Yer nothin' but an evil, murderin' sonofabitch yer ma would be deathly ashamed of. Lord, if she could see ye now. Takin' yer own blood as hostages, tryin' to kidnap yer own kids."

Ned's free hand tightened over his pistol, but he didn't raise it. "So ye admit they're mine."

Joe waved off the statement. "They're as much yers as a colt to a stallion. I can see the resemblance, to be sure, but it wasn't ye who raised them. Me son did that, and a fine job he did. Ye won't be takin' em, not if I have anythin' to do with it."

"Ye can't stop me, Joe. No one can," Ned replied, a mad smile twisting his lips. "What ye fail to understand is I always get what I want. Call it the luck of the Irish." At last he lifted his pistol, pointed it between Joe's eyes. Despite his injured arm, his hand barely trembled. "Yer luck ran out the day ye left Ireland."

To Ava, everything seemed to move in slow motion. Ned raising the gun, her grandfather's eyes growing wide with awareness of his own peril, the breeze sending a cold shiver down her spine. Out of the corner of her eye, she spotted men in black descending upon the helicopter. A second later, a strangled shout cut through the air.

Ned hesitated but one brief flickering moment, and that was all the agents needed.

A shot came from out of nowhere and struck Ned in the chest. He doubled over, falling to the ground and crying out in rage and agony. Within moments two agents were on top of him. He cursed violently as they pinned him to the ground, cuffing his wrists and ignoring his screams of pain as they pushed his wounded shoulder into the mud.

Ava stumbled backward, finding herself in her grandfather's arms. She hugged him, delirious with relief.

"Did that just happen?" she asked, a shaky laugh escaping her throat.

Joe nodded, pressing a kiss to her forehead. "Ye did good, dearie."

"Lord, you were brave." She clung to him, unwilling to let go just yet. She needed to reassure herself that he was unharmed, that this wasn't a daydream. It was really over.

She heard someone shouting her name. Cooper raced toward her across the field, fear and relief lining his face.

Her grandfather let go seconds before Cooper reached her, scanning her body for any injury. He grabbed her shoulders, then let his hands rise up into her hair, then around to cup her face.

"How are you not shot?" he asked, shaking his head even as his mouth twitched into a grateful smile. "I mean,

I'm glad. But Christ, Ava, you were right in the middle of all this."

She shrugged, then turned to watch the Feds haul Ned away. He tried to wrestle his way free, but the pain and loss of blood seemed to get the best of him. His eyes met hers, and she couldn't resist slipping on a sly smile and waving to him.

Ned scowled but said nothing. Ava stared after him, then faced Cooper again. "Took y'all long enough to show up. I was startin' to lose hope. Thought I might end up goin' to Ireland after all."

"You know I wasn't going to let that happen," Cooper told her.

"I know." She smiled, then looked back at the helicopter. "Thank God they're okay."

Cooper followed her gaze, saw Adam and Ty being helped out of the helicopter by one of the agents and freed of their bonds. He gave Ava a gentle nudge, sensing her urgency. "Go. Be with them."

Ava started off at a run toward her brother and father, her eyes blurring with tears. When she reached them, she threw her arms around her father first.

"Daddy." She let out a shuddering breath, a sob caught in her throat.

Ty squeezed her tight, nearly breaking down himself. "Hi, baby."

She felt him tense up from the pain, and eased back to examine him. His face was bruised and bloodied, one of his eyes swollen shut. She reached up to gently touch it, horrified. "I'm so sorry this happened to you."

Adam placed a hand on her shoulder, his eyes on their father. "You took one hell of a beatin', Dad."

Ty's lips pressed together in a firm line as he regarded them both. "If y'all don't want to call me that anymore, I'll understand. There's been far too many secrets I've been keepin' from you. Secrets you deserved to know the truth about."

Ava and Adam glanced at each other, then back at him.

"You did what you felt you had to do," Ava said. "We don't blame you for that."

"If anything, we're sorry we doubted you," Adam added. "We didn't realize you were working with the Feds all along."

Ty nodded, then attempted a tired smile. "I'd like to clean up and rest a bit, then I promise I'll tell y'all everything. Deal?"

With the two of them at his sides, they held each other and made their way to the house, Joe joining them along the way. The Feds were swarming the property, and Ava spotted Cooper with Marco, speaking with a few of the other agents. An ambulance drove up to the house, ready to take Ned to the hospital. His son Rhys was being loaded into the back of one of the cruisers alongside his brother.

Cooper caught her eye and when he smiled, an ache blossomed within her chest. Once things settled down they would talk, she thought. First she had to see to the comfort of her family.

As they approached the house, Brandy flew out the front door and straight into Adam's arms. He went weak in the knees, both exhausted and sick with relief. Simply holding her, breathing in the vanilla scent of her perfume, made everything right again.

"Are you hurt?" she asked, her hands fluttering over his shoulders and chest and arms. Her fingertips traced over the cut on his lip. "What did they do to you?"

Adam managed a smile. "I'm just fine, darlin'."

Brandy cupped his face, then stood on her toes to gently kiss him. He pulled her in close, deepening the kiss, ignoring the pain and welcoming the warmth she gave.

He closed his eyes and nuzzled her cheek, feeling like he could finally breathe. His father was home, his sister and grandfather were safe, Ned and his sons were in custody. They could move on with their lives and leave the nightmare behind.

He eased back and admired the soft beauty of Brandy's face. A slow, rich burn spread throughout his body, a sensation he welcomed with ravenous delight. "There was a time there when I didn't know if I'd ever see you again. It tore me up inside."

She smiled, warm and sweet, even as tears pooled in her eyes. "You probably say that to all the girls."

He shook his head, needing her to understand. "No. I told you I loved you that night before they took me. I've never said that before. Never felt strongly enough about anybody to say it."

"And I felt too vulnerable to say it back to you," Brandy replied sadly. "I hated myself for that. Especially when I realized I may never have the chance to."

"Well, now you do." He angled his head with a teasing smile.

She laughed. "You're right. I do." She took a deep breath, then released it. Her eyes raised to his. "I'm in love with you. Always have been. It hasn't been easy, but the heart wants what the heart wants. And I've only ever wanted you."

He caught her mouth with his, his hands winding back into her hair. "I'm gonna spend the rest of my life making that up to you," he murmured, his lips cruising over hers, drinking her in. "I promise you. I will never be that fool again."

CHAPTER

Thirty

While her father showered and her grandfather went down to the distillery, Ava sat at the dining table with a cup of hot tea. She stared straight ahead at nothing in particular, drowning in her own tormented thoughts.

Happy as she was for the entire mess to be over with, she didn't feel as relieved as she had hoped. Instead she felt hollow, fractured in a way she wondered would ever be repaired. What Ned had revealed to her about both her father and her mother had been earth-shattering. How could she ever think of them the same after that?

She refused to ever stop thinking of Ty as her father, no matter how torn she was inside. He was the man who had raised her, who had given her mother sanctuary and accepted her children as his own despite the risk to his life. Surely above all the people involved, he was a hero. A saint among men. She was proud to call him her father.

Her mother, on the other hand, was a more shocking revelation. The woman she had known all her life had been living a lie. She had changed her identity and pretended to be someone she wasn't. For Ava, the thought of spending years beholden to a secret so damning was mind-boggling. Her honest, straightforward nature wouldn't permit her to understand how anyone could make it work.

But Sandra had. Or, Colleen, as Ned had called her. Colleen McVey had stolen away to America and turned from a radical revolutionary of the IRA into a well-mannered, Southern housewife, accent and all. What an actress she had been, Ava thought sadly. To have pulled off this grand disguise and evade Ned and any scrutiny from others for nearly three decades.

She wondered if Colleen herself had eventually forgotten her real identity. Had she ever become so consumed in playing the role of Ty Brannon's cheerful, well-to-do wife that she forgot all about her previous husband, her old loyalties, friendships, and goals? Did she ever have moments of doubt where she missed Ireland and all she had forsaken to give her children a better life?

Ava supposed she would never know the truth. Somehow she would have to learn to live with that.

A polite knock on the front door preceded Cooper entering the house. He stepped into the kitchen, smiling at her.

"Hey, you."

Ava looked up at him, mentally shaking off her troubled thoughts. "I bet your boss is one happy camper. Not only did you get Ned, you got his sons, too."

"Score three for the good guys." He walked toward her with his hands inside his pockets, looking as out of place in her home as ever. A city-slicked FBI agent inside her mother's quaint country kitchen was as strange as a shiny Mercedes Benz in an old barn.

She warmed her hands over her cup of tea, her heart pounding. "So, you'll probably be gettin' out of here soon. Now that it's all over."

Cooper nodded, avoiding her gaze. "Yeah. It'll be nice to get home. I didn't even realize how long I've been gone."

Ava snorted, darkly amused. "It's been one hell of a ride, Slick."

"It definitely has."

She took a sip of her tea and released a long breath. "Look, I'm sorry we fought before. I think we both had valid points. But I really don't want to leave things on a bad note."

"I don't either." He regarded her curiously, regret softening his eyes. "You were just afraid for your family, and I wasn't being fair. I'm sorry for that."

Her chin jutted out, pride getting the best of her. "They needed me. I couldn't just let them die because you didn't want me to take a risk."

"I know. And as an agent, I should've put the advantages of that risk above everything else. But I struggled with that." He paused, feeling his own heart constrict at the memory of letting her go straight into the arms of a killer. "It was unprofessional. I hope you'll forgive me."

Ava raised her cup to her lips again, hoping to hide the emotions roaring through her at that moment. Shame at putting him in that position in the first place, and disappointment that he couldn't admit the real reason for his refusal to let her go. Not that it would make things any easier if he were to say he loved her as much as she loved him, but at least then there would be honesty between them. Instead they had only erected a wall of duty and pride.

"I forgive you," she said finally, forcing a smile onto her face. "I hope you'll come down and visit us once in a while. When you're not too busy catching the terrorists of the world."

He chuckled, though inside he ached to hold her. To gather her close and tell her everything he didn't know how to say. It was easier, in his eyes, for the break to be clean. "I'm sure Marco will probably drag me down here for a proper tour of the distillery."

"He'd love it," she replied, amused by the thought. Then she remembered the first time she'd seen Cooper when he'd joined her tour group, a cool drink of water in his pressed suit with that boyish grin. He wore that smile now, though it was noticeably less cheerful. Seeing it flat out broke her heart and had her feelings erupting out of her mouth without thought. "This sucks, Slick. I didn't realize it would hurt so badly."

His face fell and he shifted his feet, almost like he didn't want to have the conversation. She could see his reluctance, and couldn't help but feel angry at him for it.

She jumped to her feet and went to him, saying nothing as she dragged him against her for a fiery kiss. After a moment's hesitation he buckled and caved, his hands roaming over her back and his breath hot over her lips. She broke the kiss and looked into his eyes as her hands twisted around the lapels of his suit jacket.

"Do you want this to be over?" she asked, eyes afire with resentment, doubt, and pride. "We could try and make it work. This doesn't have to be the end."

She had practically yanked her own heart out and handed it to him, and the only thing he offered her was a single, cold shake of his head.

"Yes it does, Ava," he said, backing away from her. He held her at arm's length and watched the insult and pain ravage her face.

"Damn you." She shoved him as hard as she could, reeling as she turned away and covered her face in her hands. She knew there were tears in her eyes, felt them spill in hot streams down her cheeks. She hated him for it. Hated herself for feeling so much, for letting it go this far. "Just go. I never want to see you again."

Cooper braced himself, stunned by her outburst and tormented by the sound of her agony. Knowing he had caused it made it even worse.

"Ava…"

"No." She whirled around, her face blotchy but her eyes clear and mean. She pointed at the door. "You know the way out. If the FBI needs anythin' more from me, send someone else. We're done here."

He struggled to breathe, but said nothing as he turned away. He wouldn't subject himself to one of her wild rages, not when he was in the right. She had known from the start how this would end. Her inability to accept it now wasn't his problem. If anything, she was the one being ridiculous.

Wasn't she?

He had his own life to live, his own goals. He had a career back in Washington D.C., a mission to take down the men who had been responsible for killing his father. There was no room in his life for a relationship, much less a long distance one with someone who had her own hectic schedule and plans.

He continued to rationalize it in his head as he left, shutting the door with a quiet click behind him. He didn't even look back at the house, already knowing he would spend the rest of his life trying to forget the woman who called it home.

ADAM SAT comfortably on the sofa, Brandy curled up beside him. Ava was on his other side, nursing a glass of whiskey and looking worse for the wear. Across from them, their father and grandfather were seated in opposing arm-chairs, ready to at last talk about the past.

Ty leaned forward to rest his elbows on his knees, his own glass of whiskey held tightly in his hands. His face was clean and shaved, his dark hair brushed and the bruising around his right eye beginning to fade. He stared into the amber liquid as he spoke. "I was eighteen when I first visited Ireland. I don't know what made me go. I suppose it was a kind of teenage rebellion." He looked to his father, amusement softening his expression. "My entire life I'd heard of nothing but the feud. It'd been made clear to me that I was to never meet my extended family, that they were, as my father put it so eloquently, nothing but liars, cheats, and scoundrels."

"I was right, wasn't I?" Joe said, eyebrows raised.

Ty nodded. "I didn't think so at the time, but in hindsight, yes, you were." He turned back to his children. "During my trip, I became close with Ned. He was a few years older than me and I looked up to him. He commanded attention in a way I'd never been able to do, and seeing how others admired him so much made me admire him too. He introduced me to the entire family, to his sons, to all his friends, and to his new wife, Colleen."

Ava tensed, finding it hard to hear her father say her mother's real name. She wondered if she would ever get used to it.

Ty continued. "His first wife had passed away a year earlier and he'd wasted no time replacing her. But I got the impression that he and Colleen shared something special. Eventually I found out it was the *cause*. The fight for the liberation of Ireland from British control.

"Being raised in America, I knew very little about what was goin' on or what side to take. Apparently the Irish side of the Brannon family had been deeply imbedded in the

IRA since right after my father left in 1961. Ned and my Uncle Jack were running the whiskey business as a front for the organization, pouring nearly all their profits into the cause. To this day I don't know how they did it without landing in prison, but I imagine they had connections deep within the system to keep them safe."

"What about Mama?" Ava asked, caring less about Ned's business and more about who her mother had been. "What was she like back then?"

A smile teased the corners of Ty's mouth. "She was a spitfire. She walked into a room and quite literally lit it up. I swore everybody was in love with her, but she only had eyes for Ned. They fed off each other in a dangerous, all-consuming way. It was obvious they'd have to burn out sometime, but that might've been my jealousy talkin'." He took a slow sip of whiskey, closing his eyes briefly. "It didn't take long during my stay for me to witness the true reality of what Ned and his associates were up to. They weren't simply supporting a cause monetarily and politically. They were at war. When I saw his underground bunker filled with automatic weapons and pipe bombs, I couldn't believe my eyes. He wanted to *kill* people. And so did Colleen."

Ava's eyes shot to Adam, the two of them speechless.

"They believed the best way to get what they wanted was to relentlessly attack the British troops and police. For years they'd been at it, and even though the worst of it seemed to be in the past, Ned was determined to keep the fight alive. That was why, when the time came for me to return to Kentucky, he cornered me and made me swear my allegiance to him. To be honest, I was too afraid to say no. He said that if I wanted to belong in the Brannon family, to be at his side as a warrior and a cousin, I needed to help him by sending as much money as I could. But I had to be discreet about it, or else I'd get myself thrown in prison."

He shook his head. "I told him I'd do my best, but I was only eighteen. My father was still very much in charge. I said I'd be in touch, and that as soon as I was able, I'd help him. He seemed satisfied with that, patted me on the back, and let me go. But when I got home, I had no intention of ever contacting him again. And for two years, I didn't."

Ty let out a long breath. "Then one day, out of the blue, Colleen showed up at my college dorm in Louisville. I barely recognized her. She was too thin and the fire had gone out in her eyes. Instead she just looked scared. She told me that she'd cut a deal with the SDU and the Feds to supply them with inside information into Ned's dealings, and in exchange they'd let her come to the States for protection. But it was only on one condition—that she convince me to help her by going undercover and exposing my cousin's plans and secrets. I almost didn't believe her, but then an agent showed up and confirmed everything she'd told me. I was her only hope to not only escape the violence, but to bring down a murderer.

"I wanted to say no," Ty admitted. "It would've been easier to have just brushed her off. It wasn't my problem and I'd already decided I wanted nothing to do with Ned. But then she told me her reason for leaving him and the cause she'd dedicated so much of her life to. She was pregnant."

Tears welled in his eyes, and Ava's heart broke. She reached over to hold his hand in a show of unity and gratitude.

He looked at her with a smile. "She said when she found out she was pregnant, she'd been workin' on a plan to place a car bomb under the vehicle of a well-known diplomat. She took the test on a hunch, and realized she was correct. It apparently shook some sense into her, and she realized all the violence Ned thrived on was no environment to raise a child in. So she took the plan to the police and offered information in exchange for immunity and escape. They gave her one better. They gave her over to the FBI, and they brought her here and gave her a whole new identity.

"She asked me to be her husband and the father of her baby. I didn't have the heart to say no. How could I? I still loved her, and now she'd come to *me*. Chosen *me* instead of Ned. So I did as she asked, and after about a year of preparation I was contacting Ned offering him money while the FBI monitored every conversation and every money transfer. Oh, and I suddenly had two babies to raise instead of just one. You can imagine how upside down my life was. And how blessed all at the same time."

Ava squeezed his hand. "I never once doubted your love for her or for us. You were the best father we could have asked for. We're the ones who are blessed."

"I'm grateful to hear you say that. When the Feds came to me and said that, after years of gathering Intel and tracking money to the IRA, they were going to open an investigation and lure Ned to the States to arrest him, I was afraid the life Colleen—Sandra—and I had carefully constructed for you would fall apart. Unfortunately, my fears were correct. After losing her I gave up my will to live. I didn't care if Ned found out what I'd done, in fact I wanted him to. I wanted to confront him and make him pay for takin' her away from me. Though, I suppose it was ironic that he also wanted to make *me* pay for takin' her away from *him* in the first place."

"She came to you," Ava corrected. "She did the right thing. You both did."

"Yes. And I hope I gave her the best life possible, given the circumstances." He knocked back the last of his whiskey, then rose to his feet. Ava stood and let him pull her into a tight hug.

He kissed her forehead and stepped back, facing the others. "If y'all are satisfied, I'm gonna go to bed. I believe I've had enough excitement for one day."

Ava sat back down as he left, facing her grandfather. "Did you have any idea she was from Ireland?"

Joe shook his head. "Not at all. Our girl was quite the actress. But one thing can't be denied, dearie."

"What's that?"

"She loved ye both so much she gave up everythin'. Let that be a lesson to ye to not waste her sacrifice."

His words hit Ava hard. All she could think about was Cooper's face when she had told him she never wanted to see him again.

CHAPTER

Thirty-one

Coming home to his apartment was like waking up from a long dream. Everything was exactly as he had left it a month and a half earlier. The stacks of paperwork on his desk, thriller novels and books on American history scattered on end tables and every available shelf space, *Schindler's List* still inside his DVD player.

Cooper set down his suitcase and stared around the cluttered mess and all he could think about was how much he missed Ava.

He sighed, not wanting to dwell on their parting words anymore. He had done enough of that on the plane ride home. It hadn't helped that Marco kept asking him about her, as if the simple explanation of, "It wasn't going to work out anyway," wasn't good enough.

He realized now what a mistake it had been to get involved with her in the first place. He had let himself get caught up in all that heat and for the first time in his life, had taken a risk on something despite knowing it would end badly. In a sense, he had guaranteed his own broken heart. There was only one thing to do in a situation like that, he knew. Toughen up, reestablish priorities, and move on.

Walking into his bedroom, his eyes caught the framed photograph resting on his nightstand of him and his father. He had been eleven years old, and his father had just taken him to the Yankees game. They both sported blue ball caps and matching grins.

He lifted the picture, missing his father so damn much it killed him inside. Somehow though, the pain seemed old and worn out compared to the fresher ache in his heart. Ava had lost one of her parents, too. It was a connection they shared, something that had brought them together. Since when did thinking of his father make him automatically think of her?

When his phone began to ring, he set aside the picture frame and saw Horvath's name on the caller-ID. He rubbed his temple as he answered.

"Yeah."

"*I take it you made it home safe?*" Horvath asked, the sound of him slurping coffee immediately following his question.

"Got in an hour or so ago. Had to get food and drop Marco off first," Cooper replied, lowering down onto the side of the bed. "It's cold as hell up here, Boss."

Horvath chuckled. "*You did good work in Fox Hills, kid. I'm proud of you.*"

"Thanks." Cooper looked out the window, seeing the first snowflakes begin to fall. "It was a hell of a ride."

He didn't know what made him say it, but repeating Ava's phrase regarding their relationship only ripped open the wound and made it bleed.

"*Listen, I took the liberty of forwarding your dossier over to the Operations Branch in charge of investigating Al-Qaeda. They like what they see. Nothing's for sure yet, but there may be a spot for you over there. I know it's something you've wanted for some time now."*

Cooper blew out a breath, stunned. "Oh, wow. That's incredible. Thank you, sir."

"I'll be sad to lose you, but you've earned it."

A million thoughts flooded Cooper's brain, all of them competing for his attention. At the forefront was the overwhelming feeling of doubt that he couldn't seem to shake. While he wanted to celebrate finally getting one step closer to his goal, the motivation just wasn't there. He stared at the image of him and his father once more, anticipating the feelings of purpose and vengeance to pour over him. In its place rose a quieter sense of acceptance, of peace.

Maybe, for the first time, he could finally lay the past to rest.

"Cooper?"

He jolted back to reality, realizing his hands were shaking. He swallowed, overwhelmed by his own thoughts. "Yeah, I'm here."

"You don't sound too thrilled. Do you not want the job?"

"No, no of course I want the job," Cooper replied, rising to his feet to pace. "It's just that…"

While he tried to find the right words to say, Horvath began to laugh again. *"I had a feeling this would happen."*

"What? You thought what would happen?" Cooper demanded, his shoulders tensing up.

"I forwarded your dossier to one other department. Needless to say, they immediately accepted and were shocked you would even consider it. They were very impressed with your work. It would feel like a demotion, but I think you'd appreciate the change of scenery."

"What is it?"

"You'd be part of the Joint Terrorism Task Force down in Louisville. They've got a spot for you right away, if you're interested."

Cooper had to sit down again. "You contacted Louisville about me? Why?"

"*Well, it came to my attention that you were bending the rules a bit down there. Being a nice guy, I didn't hound you on it, but I did come very close to yanking you off the case. Fraternizing with anyone related to a suspect is a punishable offense. Then again, Ty Brannon was never really a suspect, was he?*"

"No," Cooper murmured. He closed his eyes, tormented with indecision. How had it happened that he was being presented with his dream job and the job that would let him be with Ava all on the same day?

"*If you want some time to think on it, so be it. I just thought I'd give you the option.*"

"You want me to choose between the job of a lifetime and the woman I love," Cooper replied bitterly. "I wish you'd only given me one choice and kept the other to yourself."

"*Why? Life's too short, kid. Either you make a career or you make a home, it's tough to have both. Now's the time to decide which one suits you best.*"

Cooper lowered the phone after Horvath hung up, his head spinning. What did he want, exactly? To spend the rest of his life chasing after a ghost? Or to live in the here and now and take a chance on happiness and love?

Before he could process it all, he heard a knock on his front door. He let out a breath and went to answer it.

His lips parted as he opened the door and saw Ava standing there, dressed in her blue jeans, plaid shirt, and leather boots. She smiled, slow and bright, and he knew in that moment he was being given a second chance.

"Hi, Slick," she greeted, angling her chin in that sassy way she had. "Can I come in?"

"How—what—sure, sure. Come in." He backed up to invite her inside, watching as she stared around his apartment curiously. He shut the door and faced her, unsure what to do with his hands. "What are you doing here?"

"Marco gave me your address and since I missed your flight, I hopped on the next one. But I'll just get straight to the point." She wandered around his living room, inspecting a few of his books and his towering collection of DVDs. "You have to understand somethin' about me, honey. I ain't the kind of girl who begs for things. God has always blessed me with what I need, so I was content." She turned and met his eyes, one of her brows arched in an arrogant curve. "Then you came along. And at first I kind of liked you, then I hated you, then I liked you again. But then I fell in love with you. And so you can see what kind of position this puts me in when you decide to leave me."

He shook his head. "I didn't—"

"Quiet now, Agent Lawson." She smiled again, though it was sharp around the edges. "You wanted to leave, and my pride wouldn't allow me to beg for you to stay. Besides, I get it. You had a whole life to get back to." She motioned around his apartment, amusement in her voice. "Though it's a bit less glamorous than I expected."

He shrugged, then crossed his arms. "Where are you going with this?"

She planted her hands on her hips and stared him in the eye, and he could all but see the sparks flying off of her. "The point is, I never beg. But here I am, laying my heart on the line to tell you I love you and I wanna find a way to make this work. If you still don't want to be with me, then that's fine. I'll go. But understand that once I'm gone, it's for good. I won't be doin' this again."

He blinked, taken aback by her statement. He had never been so humbled by someone in all his life. Seeing her there, open and honest and so very much the Ava he'd fallen in love with, repaired every last bit of his damaged heart. "This is pretty crazy timing, you know. I just got off the phone with Horvath. He offered to get me a job with the team working to take down Al-Qaeda."

"Oh. Well, wow, that's great. Congratulations."

He stepped closer to her, needing to erase the disappointment from her expression. "He also said the field office in Louisville has a position for me."

Her eyes widened as a hopeful grin spread over her mouth. "Yeah?"

"Yeah." He ran his hands up her arms, caressing her skin. "I was just deliberating over what to do seconds before you came knocking on my door."

"I see," she drawled, her head falling back so her eyes could meet his. Her hands slowly drifted up his chest to toy with his tie. "So what're you gonna do?"

He framed her face, his thumbs tracing over her cheekbones. "What do you think?"

He leaned in to kiss her and she backed away, shaking her head. "No. I can't let you do that. I won't come between you and justice for your father's death. I wouldn't be able to live with myself knowing you'd given that up just to be with me."

Cooper nodded. "You're right. And I probably would have resented you for it at some point. But things are different now."

"How so?"

He placed a hand over his heart, hoping he could put how he felt into words. "I've spent the last thirteen years chasing a ghost, Ava. I'm ready to stop now. I've finally found something I care about more than getting revenge. Besides, my dad wouldn't want me to miss out on happiness just because of what happened to him. He'd want me to live."

She stared at him, unsure what to say. "Are you sure?"

"I've never been more certain about anything in my entire life." He went to her again, his hand cupping around the back of her neck as his mouth found hers. He kissed her slowly, tenderly, and felt his world shift perfectly back into alignment. "Do you really love me?"

"You stupid fool, of course I do." She laughed. "Even with all your city-boy quirks."

He snorted. "Please. I just had to spend the last several weeks learning your ways. The least you could do is embrace mine."

"Okay, it's a deal. Now tell me you love me so I can call this trip a success."

"I love you." He kissed her again, needing to prove it. "God, I love you."

"Good." She wrapped her arms around his neck and let him spin her around, her heart soaring. "If you had rejected me I would've had to torch your apartment."

He set her down, his eyebrows raised. "You're joking, right?"

"Maybe, maybe not," she teased, tapping his chin playfully. "Guess you'll never know."

He grinned. "Sounds like I made the right decision, then."

"Yes, you did. I know exactly how I want to celebrate."

She dug into her purse and unearthed a bottle of Lucky Joe's Single Barrel Bourbon.

"How—"

"Don't worry about the hows, Slick. Just find me a couple of glasses."

"What would you have done if I'd turned you down?" he asked, unable to help himself.

She eyed the bottle, testing the weight of it in her hand. "Hit you over the head with it, most likely."

"Ouch." He chuckled, then went to grab a couple of red plastic cups from the kitchen. When he walked back into the living room, she gave him an incredulous look.

"What?" He held the cups out so she could pour the whiskey. "It's all I got."

"Well, it'll have to do, then," she mused, filling each cup. "Just know my ancestors are rolling over in their graves right now."

"Please. I know you're too Southern to deny the practicality and versatility of a red solo cup."

"True enough." She set the bottle aside, raised her cup, and offered him a brilliant smile. "To a new job, new beginnings, and damn good bourbon."

He tapped his cup to hers, took a sip, then kissed her again. He loved how the whiskey tasted even better on her lips.

Their eyes met, and he drank in the sight of her. "That really is some damn good bourbon."

I want a trouble maker for a lover,
Blood spiller, blood drinker, a heart of flame,
Who quarrels with the sky, and fights with fate,
Who burns like fire on the rushing sea.

~ Rumi ~

ABOUT THE AUTHOR

Katie Jennings is the author of the popular fantasy series The Dryad Quartet as well as the award-winning romantic family drama series The Vasser Legacy. Her paranormal romance, *So Fell The Sparrow*, won an Honorable Mention in the 2014 Readers' Favorite International Book Awards. Her bestselling contemporary romance, *Things Lost In The Fire*, is a semi-finalist in romance in the Kindle Book Awards.

A Los Angeles native, she now lives in beautiful North Idaho with her husband, who thinks she's the biggest nerd ever. She's a firm believer in happy endings and loves nothing more than a great romance novel.

She was the daughter of rock legends...

He needed to solve the mystery of her past...

also available
from bestselling author
KATIE JENNINGS

in paperback & eBook

www.ingramcontent.com/pod-product-compliance
Lightning Source LLC
Chambersburg PA
CBHW020224180626
46810CB00006B/2042